A COMPANY OF SWANS

By the same author:

A COUNTESS BELOW STAIRS
MAGIC FLUTES

A COMPANY
OF SWANS

Eva Ibbotson

St. Martin's Press
New York

A-1

Library of Congress Cataloging in Publication Data

Ibbotson, Eva.
  A company of swans.

  I. Title.
PR6059.B3C6   1985   823'.914   85-1710
ISBN 0-312-15323-6

First published in Great Britain by Century Publishing Co. Ltd.

First U.S. Edition

10 9 8 7 6 5 4 3 2 1

For Patricia Veryan

A COMPANY OF SWANS

CHAPTER ONE

THERE WAS no lovelier view in England, Harriet knew this. To her right, the soaring towers of King's College Chapel and the immaculate lawns sloping down to the river's edge; to her left, the blue and gold of the scillas and daffodils splashed in rich abundance between the trees of the Fellows' Gardens. Yet as she leaned over the stone parapet of the bridge on which she stood, her face was pensive and her feet – and this was unusual in the daughter of a professor of classics in the year 1912 – were folded in the fifth position.

She was a thin girl, brown-haired and brown-eyed, whose gravity and gentleness could not always conceal her questing spirit and eagerness for life. Sensibly dressed in a blue caped coat and tam o'shanter bought to last, a leather music case propped against the wall beside her, she was a familiar figure to the passers-by: to ancient Dr Ferguson, tottering across the willow-fringed bridge in inner pursuit of an errant Indo-Germanic verb; to a gardener trimming the edges of the grass, who raised his cap to her. Professor Morton's clever daughter; Miss Morton's biddable niece.

To grow up in Cambridge was to be fortunate indeed. To be able to look at this marvellous city each day was a blessing of which one should never tire. Harriet, crumbling bread into the water for the world's most blasé ducks, had told herself this again and again. But it is not cities which make the destinies of eighteen-year-old girls, it is people – and as she gazed at the lazy, muddy river and thought of her future and her home, her eyes held an expression which would have better become a little gutter starveling – a bleak and shipwrecked look devoid of happiness and hope.

Professor Morton was already in his forties when, at a reading party in Switzerland, he met an English girl working as a governess to

1

the children of a Swiss industrialist living in an ochre-coloured castle across the lake.

Sophie Brent was enchanting, with big brown eyes, soft dark-gold hair and a beguiling chuckle. She was an orphan, poor and unprotected as only a governess can be and deeply impressed by the attentions of the serious, stern Professor with his firm opinions and cultured voice.

They married and returned to the tall, grey house in Cambridge where the Professor's elder sister Louisa – a gaunt and iron-haired spinster who kept house for him – welcomed with outer resignation and inner chagrin the foolish, useless girl who had ensnared her brother.

Number 37 Scroope Terrace, off the Trumpington Road, was a house where 'Waste Not Want Not' was the motto. Louisa Morton counted the fish-knives on Thursdays and the silver plate on Saturdays and kept in her bedroom a box labelled 'String too short to tie'. Though the Professor had a substantial private income in addition to his salary, she had been heard to upbraid the cook for the unbridled expenditure of three-farthings on an ounce of parsley. Invitations to dine with the Mortons were among the most dreaded events in the University calendar.

In this cold, dark house filled with the smell of boiled fish and the sniffs of depressed housemaids, the Professor's pretty young wife wilted and drooped. Sophie saw little of her husband for the Professor wined, dined and had his being in the comfort of his College, returning to Scroope Terrace only to sleep. Though presumably acquainted with bright-eyed Nausicaa laughing with her maidens on an Aegean shore, with marvellous Sappho and her 'love-loosened limbs' – and indeed with all those gallant girls who had welcomed Jupiter in the guise of Swan or Bull or Shower of Gold – the Merlin Professor of Classical Studies was a dry and narrow-minded pedant. His published work consisted mainly of splenetic articles in which he vilified those who dared to disagree with his view that Odes VI and VII in the *epinikia* of Bacchylides had been incorrectly separated, and his lectures (from which all women were rigorously excluded) were confidently regarded as being not only the most boring in the University, but the most boring in the world.

The Professor's passion for his young wife soon cooled. It was clear that Sophie would be no use to him in his career. Though constantly instructed by himself and Louisa, she seemed quite unable to learn

2

the most basic rules of academic protocol. Again and again her patient husband caught her out in the most appalling lapses: attempting to seat the wife of the Professor of Divinity below the wife of the Professor of Mathematics and once, in a tea-shop, smiling at a young lecturer who was wearing *shorts*. When he was passed over for the Mastership of his College it was Sophie he blamed and Louisa – who had never really relinquished the reins of the household – now gathered them even more firmly into her bony and frugal hands.

It was into this house that Harriet was born.

Babies, as everyone who cares for them knows, come trailing their own particular essence. There are grave, contemplative babies still patently solving some equation of Euclidean geometry begun in another world, scrawny high-powered babies apparently shot into life without the slightest need to eat or sleep, and placid agricultural babies whose only concern is to thrive.

But sometimes . . . just sometimes, there are babies who appear to have swallowed some small private sun, rosy and endlessly obliging babies who explode into laughter long before one's hand has actually touched their stomachs – laughter which has less to do with being tickled than with sharing and being together – and love.

Such a baby was Harriet Jane Morton in the first two years of her life: a baby who offered you her starfish of a foot, her slobbered rusk . . . a cornucopial life-affirmer from the start.

Then Sophie Morton, whose passion the child had been, caught a chill which turned to pneumonia and died. Two weeks later, Louisa dismissed the country girl who had been Harriet's nurse.

Within months the plump, rosy baby became a serious, bird-thin and almost silent little girl. As though reflecting a scarcely comprehended grief, her hair darkened, her hazel eyes lost their green and golden lights and settled to a solemn brown. It seemed as if the very skin and bone and muscle of this bewildered little being had changed into a minor key.

Soon, too soon, she taught herself to read and vanished for long hours into her attic with a book, to be discovered by one of the servants shivering with a cold she had been too absorbed to notice. If she spoke now, it was to her invisible playmate – a twin brother, fleet-footed and strong – or to the small creatures she befriended in that loveless house: the sparrows which settled on her window-sill; a squirrel she had called down from the one tree in the raked gravel rectangle which was the Mortons' garden.

Yet it would be wrong to say that Harriet was neglected. If Louisa found it impossible to love this child of the frivolous usurper who had ensnared her brother, she was determined to do her duty. Harriet was conveyed to music lessons and to dancing classes which the family doctor, disconcerted by her pallor and thinness, recommended. She was regularly aired and exercised, sent on long walks with whatever ancient and grim-faced maid survived Louisa's regime. If her father grew crustier and more bigoted as the years passed, he could still recognise academic excellence and himself taught her Latin and Greek.

And presently she was sent to an excellent day school most highly recommended by the ladies of the Trumpington Tea Circle who ruled Louisa Morton's life.

No child ever loved school as much as Harriet. She was ready to leave with her satchel an hour before it was time to go; she begged for any job, however menial, which would keep her there in the afternoon. Arithmetic lessons, sago pudding, deportment . . . she enjoyed everything because it was shared by others and accompanied by laughter – because there was warmth.

Then a new headmistress came, detected in the vulnerable dark-eyed child a potential scholar, and herself coached her in English and History: lessons that Harriet was to remember all her life. After two terms she sent for Professor Morton in order to discuss Harriet's university career. Did he favour Newnham or Girton, she enquired, pouring tea for him in her charming sitting-room – or would it be sensible to choose an Oxford college so as to give Harriet a fresh environment? Though it was always foolish to prophesy, she would be extremely surprised if Harriet failed to get a scholarship . . .

From the interview which followed both parties were invalided out in a state of fulminating rage. To the Professor it was genuinely incomprehensible that anybody could have lived in Cambridge for one week and not known his views on 'women in the university'. And, unable to trust his daughter to this suffragette upstart, he took Harriet away from school.

That had been a year ago and Harriet could still not pass the familiar red brick building without a lump in her throat.

*

Now she threw her last crust of bread, narrowly missing the head of the Provost of St Anne's who appeared suddenly in a punt beneath

4

her, poling his blonde wife and pretty daughters down-river. To have hit the Provost would have been a particular disaster for he was her father's enemy, having criticised Professor Morton's entry on Ammanius Marcellinus in the Classical Dictionary, and his wife – whose friendly wave Harriet could not help returning – was even worse, for she had been found (while still secretary of the Association of University Wives) unashamedly reading a book by someone dirty called Sigmund Freud while in a hansom parked outside Peterhouse.

'Poor child!' said the Provost when they were out of earshot.

'Yes, indeed,' agreed his wife grimly, looking back at the forlorn little figure on the bridge. 'How such a charming, sensitive child came to be born into that household of bigoted prigs, I shall never understand. It was a crime to take her away from school. I suppose they regard it as a perfectly fitting life for her – arranging flowers in a house where there are no flowers, taking the dog out when there isn't any dog.'

'There is a young man, one hears,' murmured the Provost, expertly shooting beneath Clare Bridge, and raised his eyebrows at his wife's most unladylike snort.

The Provost was correct: there *was* a young man. His name was Edward Finch-Dutton; he was a Fellow of the Professor's own College, St Philip's, and though his subject was Zoology – a new and upstart discipline of which it was impossible to approve – the Mortons had permitted him to come to the house. For there had been 'unpleasantness' about the decision to keep Harriet at home. Even the Master of Trinity, who ranked slightly below God, had taken the Professor aside after the University sermon to express surprise.

'After all, you have made quite a little scholar of her yourself,' he said. 'I had a most enjoyable chat with her the other day. She has some highly original views on Heliodoras – and a delightful accent.'

'If I taught Harriet the classics, it was so that she could make herself useful to me at home, not so that she could become an unfeminine hoyden and a disgrace to her sex,' the Professor had replied.

Still, the encounter had rankled. Fortunately, in her dealings with her niece, Louisa had one unfailing source of guidance: the ladies of the Trumpington Tea Circle who had seceded from the Association of University Wives when it became clear that the parent body could no longer be relied upon to uphold etiquette and protocol. It was these ladies – headed by Mrs Belper, Louisa's special friend – who had suggested that the best solution for Harriet might be an early marriage. Seeing the sense of this the Mortons, rejecting various men who had shown an interest in Harriet (for unaccountably the child seemed to have the gift of pleasing) had selected Edward Finch-Dutton. He had a First, was sensible and ambitious and was related – albeit distantly – to the Master of St Swithin's, Oxford. Not only that, but his mother – a Featherstonehaugh – had been accustomed to visit Stavely, the district's most beautiful and prestigious home.

It was the long, serious face of this excellent young man that Harriet saw now as she looked into the water; and as always, his image brought a stab of fear.

'Don't let me give in, God,' she begged, tilting back her head, sending the long soft hair cascading down her back as she searched the quiet, dove-grey sky of Cambridge for some portent – Halley's comet; the pointing finger of Isfrael – to indicate deliverance. 'Don't let me marry Edward just to get away from home. Don't let me, God, I beg of you! Show me some other way to live.'

A church clock struck four, and another . . . and suddenly she smiled, the grave little face utterly transformed as she picked up her case. Somehow her dancing lessons had survived; those most precious times were left to her. And abandoning the resolutely silent firmament, she quickly made her way beside the verdant lawns towards King's Parade.

Ten minutes later she entered the tall, shabby building in Fitzwilliam Street which housed the Sonia Lavarre Academy of Dance.

At once she was in a different world. The streets of Cambridge with their bicycles and dons might never have existed and she could be in St Petersburg in the Tsar's Imperial Ballet School in Theatre Street, where Madame Lavarre – then Sonia Zugorsky – had spent eight years of her childhood. A tiled stove, incorrectly installed by a baffled Cambridge plumber, roared in the hallway; the sad Byzantine face of St Demetrius of Rostov stared at her from the icon corner . . .

And everywhere, covering the panelled walls, climbing up the stairway, were daguerrotypes and paintings and photographs . . . of Kchessinskaya, erstwhile mistress of the Tsar, *en pointe* in *Esmerelda* . . . of the graduation class of 1882 with Madame in a white dress and fichu, demure and doe-eyed in the front row . . . of rose-wreathed Taglioni, the first Sylphide of them all, whose ballet slippers had been cooked and eaten by her besotted Russian admirers when she retired.

For it was not genteel ballroom dancing which was taught by Madame – beached-up in Cambridge after a brief marriage to a French lecturer who died – but the painful and manically disciplined art of the ballet.

Harriet hurried upstairs, smiling as she passed the open door of Room 3 from which came the sounds of a Schubert *impromptu*, its rhythm relentlessly stressed to serve the wobbly *pliés* of the beginners with their gap-teeth and perilously slithering chignons. 'My Pavlova class,' Madame called it, blessing the great ballerina whom she knew and cordially disliked. For these were the children of mothers who on some shopping trip to London had seen Pavlova in *Giselle* or *The Dying Swan* and had come to believe that perhaps ballet was not just something done by girls who were no better than they should be.

There were only four pupils in the advanced class with Harriet and all of them were there before her in the changing-room. At first they had been aloof and unfriendly, rejecting Harriet with her snobbish university background. Phyllis – the pretty one, with her blonde curls – was the daughter of a shopkeeper; she had added ballet to 'stage' and already danced in pantomime. Mabel, conscientious and hard-working and inexorably fat, was the daughter of a railway clerk. Red-haired Lily's mother worked in the Blue Boar. Harriet, with her 'posh' voice, arriving at the beginning with a maid to help her change and skewer up her hair, had been an object of derision and mockery.

But now, survivors of nine years under the whip of Madame's tongue, they were all good friends.

'She's got someone with her,' said Phyllis, tying her shoes. 'A foreigner. Russian, I think. Funny-looking bloke!'

Harriet changed hurriedly. In her white practice dress, her long brown hair scraped back from her face and coiled high under a bandeau, she was transformed in a way which would have disconcerted the ladies of Trumpington. The neat and elegant head; the long, almost unnaturally slender throat; the delicate arms all signalled an unmistakable message – that here in this place Professor Morton's quiet daughter was where she belonged.

The girls entered, curtseyed to Madame – formidable as always in her black pleated dress, a chiffon bandeau tied round her dyed orange hair – and took their places at the *barre*.

'This is Monsieur Dubrov,' Madame announced. 'He will watch the class.'

She stabbed with her dreaded cane at the cowed accompanist, who

7

began to play a phrase from Delibes. The girls straightened, lifted their heads . . .

'*Demi-plié . . . grand plié . . . tendu devant* . . . pull up, everybody . . . *dégagé . . . demi-plié in fourth* . . . close.'

The relentless, repetitive work began and Harriet, emptying her mind of everything except the need to place her feet perfectly, to stretch her back to its limit, did not even realise that while she worked she was for once completely happy.

Beside the petite and formidable figure of Madame stood Dubrov, his wild grey curls circling a central dome of pinkly shining scalp, his blue eyes alert. He had seen what he wanted to see in the first three minutes; but this portly, slightly absurd man – who had never danced a step – could not resist, even here in this provincial room, tracing one perfect gesture which had its origin in Cecchetti's class of perfection in St Petersburg or – even in the fat girl – the *épaulement* that was the glory of the Maryinsky. How Sonia had done it with these English amateurs he did not know, but she *had* done it.

'You will work alone now,' ordered Madame after a while. 'The *enchaînement* we practised on Thursday . . .' and led her old friend downstairs. Five minutes later they were installed in her cluttered sitting-room, stirring raspberry jam into glasses of tea.

'Well, you are quite right,' said Dubrov. 'It is the little brown one I want. A lyrical *port de bras*, nice straight knees and, as you say, the *ballon* . . . an intelligent dancer and God knows it's rarely enough one sees a body intelligently used.' But it was more than that, he thought, remembering the way each phrase of the music has seemed literally to pass across the child's rapt, utterly responsive face. 'Of course her technique is still—'

'I've told you, you cannot have her,' interrupted Madame. 'So don't waste my time. Her father is the Merlin Professor of Classical Studies; her aunt comes here as if there was a bad smell in the place. Harriet was not even allowed to take part in a charity performance for the police orphans. Imagine it, the orphans of policemen, is there anything more respectable than that?' She inserted a Balkan Sobranie into a long jet holder and leaned back in her chair. 'The child was so disappointed that I swallowed my pride and went to plead with the aunt. *Mon Dieu*, that house – it was like a grave! After an hour she offered me a glass of water and a biscuit – one biscuit, completely naked, with little holes in it for drainage.'

Madame had changed into French in order to do justice to the horrors of the Mortons' hospitality. Now she shook her head, seeing through the clouds of smoke she was blowing out of her imperious nose the twelve-year-old Harriet standing in the wings of the draughty, improvised stage of the drill hall, watching the other girls dance. All day Harriet had helped: pinning up Phyllis's butterfly costume, ironing the infants' tarlatans, fixing Lily's headdress for her solo as Princess of Araby . . . And then just stood quietly in the wings and watched. Madame had repeatedly heard Harriet described as 'clever'. In her own view, the girl was something rarer and more interesting: *good*.

'No,' she said now, 'you must absolutely forget my poor Harriet.'

'Surely to travel is part of every young girl's education?' murmured Dubrov.

'They do not seem unduly concerned about Harriet's education,' commented Madame drily. 'She is to marry a young man with an Adam's apple – a cutter-up of dead animals, one understands. But I must say, I myself would hesitate to let a daughter of mine travel up the Amazon in your disreputable *corps de ballet* and endure Simonova's tantrums. What are you after, Sasha; it's a mad idea!'

'No, it isn't.' The blue eyes were dreamy. He passed a pudgy but beautifully manicured hand over his forehead and sighed. Born of a wealthy land-owning family which had dominion over two thousand serfs somewhere on the Upper Volga, Dubrov might well have led the contented life of his forebears, riding round his estates with his borzois at his heel and seasonally despatching the bears and boars and wolves with which his forests were plentifully stocked. Instead, at the age of fifteen he visited his godmother in St Petersburg and had the misfortune to see the sapphire curtains of the Maryinsky part on the première of Tchaikovsky's *Sleeping Beauty*. Carlotta Brianzi had danced Aurora, Maria Petipa was the Lilac Fairy – and that was that. For the last twenty years, first in his homeland and latterly in Europe, Dubrov had served the art that he adored.

That this romantic little man should become obsessed with one of the truly legendary names on the map of the world was inevitable. A thousand miles up the River Amazon, in the midst of impenetrable forest, the wealth of the 'rubber barons' had brought forth a city which was the very stuff of dreams. A Kubla Khan city of spacious squares and rococo mansions, of imposing fountains and mosaic pavements . . . A city with electric light and tramways, and shops whose clothes matched those of Paris and New York. And the crown

9

of this city, which they called Manaus, was its Opera House: the Teatro Amazonas, said to be the most opulent and lovely theatre in the world.

It was to this theatre that Dubrov proposed to bring a visiting ballet company led by the veteran ballerina he had the misfortune to love; it was to recruit young dancers for the *corps de ballet* that he had visited his old friend Sonia Lavarre.

'Manaus,' murmured Madame. 'Caruso sang there, didn't he?'

'Yes. In ninety-six. And Sarah Bernhardt acted there . . . So what more fitting than that the Dubrov Ballet Company should dance!'

'Hmm. The fee must be good, if Simonova has agreed to go.' But her face belied her words. She had worked with Simonova in Russia and knew her to be an incomparable artist.

He shrugged. 'There is more money in those few hundred miles of the Amazon than in all of Europe put together. They paid Adelina Patti a thousand dollars to appear for *one night*! Everybody who has gone out there and managed to acquire a piece of land has made a killing with the rubber trees; Spaniards, Portuguese, Frenchmen, Germans. The English too. The richest man of all out there is English, so they say.'

'So why do you come to me for dancers? Why are all the young girls not queueing up to go out there with you?'

Dubrov sighed into his glass of tea. 'Diaghilev has all the best dancers. The rest are with Pavlova.' He glanced at her sideways from beneath his Santa Claus eyebrows. 'And of course there are a few who don't like the idea of the insects and the diseases and so on,' he admitted. He threw out a dismissive hand and returned to his present preoccupation. 'I could take the blonde with the curls, I suppose, but I can get girls like that from an agency. It's the little brown one I want. Let me talk to her myself; perhaps I can persuade her.'

'How obstinate you are, my poor Sasha! Still, it will be interesting for all the girls to hear of your plans. I shall stop the class early and Harriet can listen with the others. It is always instructive to watch Harriet listen.'

So the advanced class was stopped early and the girls came down. Phyllis had removed her bandeau to let her curls tumble round her face, but Harriet came as she was and as she sank onto a footstool, Dubrov nodded, for she had that unteachable thing that nevertheless comes only after years of teaching: that harmonious placing of the limbs and head that they call *line*. And obstinately, unreasonably – for

10

she would be only one of twenty or more girls – he wanted her.

Like all men of his class, Dubrov had had an English governess and spoke the language fluently. Yet beneath his words, as he began to describe the journey he would make, there beat the grave exotic rhythm that enables the Slavs to make poetry even of a laundry list.

'We shall embark at Liverpool,' he said, addressing all the girls yet speaking only to one, 'on a white ship of great comfort and luxury; a ship with salons and recreation rooms and even a library . . . a veritable hotel on which we shall steam westwards across the Atlantic with its white birds and great green waves.'

Here he paused for a moment, recalling that Maximov, his *premier danseur*, had managed to be seasick on a five-minute ferry crossing of the Neva, but rallied to describe the beneficial effects on the Company of the ozone, the excellent food, the long rest as they lay back on deck-chairs sipping beef-tea . . . 'But when at last we reach the port of Belem in Brazil, our real adventure will only just be beginning. For the ship will enter the mouth of the greatest river in the world – the Amazon – and for a thousand miles we shall steam up this waterway which is so mighty that they call it the *Rio Mare* . . . the River Sea.'

He spoke on, untroubled by considerations of accuracy, for the flora and fauna of Brazil were quite unknown to him, and as he spoke Harriet closed her eyes – and saw . . .

She saw a white ship steaming in silence along the mazed waterways of the River Sea . . . She saw a shimmering world in which trees grew from the dusky water only to find themselves embraced by ferns and fronds and brilliantly coloured orchids. She saw an alligator slide from a gleaming sand-bar into the leaf-stained shallows . . . and the grey skeleton of a deodar, its roots asphyxiated by the water, aflame with scarlet ibis . . .

Standing in the bows of the ship as it steamed through this enchanted world, Harriet saw a raven-haired woman, pensive and beautiful: La Simonova, the Maryinsky's brightest jewel and beside her, manly and protective, the leonine *premier danseur*, Maximov . . . She saw, streaming away from them on either side like a formation of wild geese in flight, the white-clad dancers who would be Simonova's snowflakes and cygnets and sylphides . . . and saw a golden-eyed jaguar peer from the trellis of green in wonder at the sight.

Dubrov had reached the 'wedding of the waters', the place where the leaf-brown waters of the Amazon flowed distinct and separate beside the black waters of the Negro. It was up this Stygian river that he now took them and there – shining, dazzling, its wonder reflected in Harriet's suddenly opened eyes – was the green and gold dome of the Opera House soaring over the roofs of the city.

'We shall be giving *Swan Lake*, *Fille Mal Gardée* and *Casse Noisette*,' said Dubrov. 'Also *Giselle* – and *The Dying Swan* if Pavlova does not sue.' He paused to wipe his forehead and Harriet saw the homesick Europeans, the famous 'rubber barons', leaving their riverside palaces clad in their opera cloaks, their richly attired wives beside them, saw them converge in boats from the river's tributaries, in carriages, in litters carried through the jungle, on to the Opera House ablaze with light . . . heard their gasps of wonder as the curtain rose on Tchaikovsky's coolly sumptuous woodland glade – while outside the howler monkeys howled and the brilliantly plumaged parakeets flew past.

Dubrov paused to light a cigar and threw a quick glance at Harriet. Even with her eyelashes she listens, he thought – and went on to speak of the 'Arabian Nights' lifestyle of the audience for whom they would dance. 'There is a woman who has her carriage horses washed down in champagne,' he said, 'and a man who sends back his shirts to London to be laundered,' – and here Madame smiled, for as she had expected a small frown mark had appeared between Harriet's eyebrows. Harriet did not think it necessary to wash carriage horses in champagne or to send one's laundry five thousand miles to be washed.

Dubrov now was nearing the end of his discourse. Lightly, almost dismissively, he touched on the triumph, the innumerable curtain calls which would follow their performances of the old *ballets blancs*, chosen particularly to appeal to those exiled from their own culture; then with a last flourish he brought the Company back to England, laden with jewels and silverware, with ocelot and jaguar skins – to loud acclaim and an almost certain engagement at the Alhambra, Leicester Square.

'You may go now,' said Madame when Dubrov had been thanked, and as the girls slipped out Phyllis could be heard saying, 'I wouldn't fancy going out there, would you? Not with all those creepy-crawlies!'

'And the Indians having a gobble at you, I shouldn't wonder,' added Lily.

But when Harriet prepared to follow her companions, Madame barred her way. 'You will remain behind, Harriet,' she commanded. And as Harriet turned and waited by the door, her hands respectfully folded, she went on, 'Monsieur Dubrov came here to recruit dancers for the tour he has just described to you. He has seen your work and would be willing to offer you a contract.'

'Your lack of experience would of course be a disadvantage,' interposed Dubrov quickly. 'Your salary would naturally be less than that of a fully-trained dancer.'

It was this haggling, this evidence that she was not simply dreaming, that effected the extraordinary change they now saw in the girl.

'You are offering me a *job?*' she said slowly. 'You would take *me?*'

'There is no need to sound so surprised,' snapped Madame. 'Any pupil in my advanced class has reached a professional standard entirely adequate for the *corps de ballet* of a South American touring company.'

Harriet continued to stand perfectly still by the door of the room. She had brought up her folded hands to her face as women do in prayer, and her eyes had widened, lightened – shot now with those flecks of amber and gold which had seemed to vanish after her mother's death.

'I shall not be allowed to go,' she said, addressing Dubrov in her soft, carefully modulated voice. 'There is no possible way that I can get permission; and I am only eighteen so that if I run away, I shall be pursued and retrieved and that will make trouble for others. But I shall never forget that you wanted me. Never, as long as I live, shall I forget that.'

And then this primly reared girl with her stiff academic background came forward and took Dubrov's hand and kissed it.

Then she gave Madame her *révérence* and would have left the room, but Dubrov seized her arm and said, 'Wait! Take this . . . there may after all be a miracle.' And as she took the card with his address, he added, 'You will find me there or at the Century Theatre until April the 25th. If you can reach me before then, I will take you.'

'Thank you,' said Harriet; then she curtseyed once more and was gone.

*

Edward Finch-Dutton was dissecting the efferent nervous system of a large and somewhat pickled dogfish. The deeply dead elasmobranch lay in a large dish with a waxed bottom, pins spearing the flaps of its rough and spotted skin. The familiar smell of formalin which permeated the laboratory beat its way not unpleasantly into Edward's capacious and somewhat equine nostrils. He had already sliced away the roof of the cranium and now, firmly and competently – his large freckled hands doing his bidding perfectly – he snipped away at the irrelevant flotsam of muscle, skin and connective tissue to reveal, with calm assurance, the creature's brain.

'The prosencephalon,' he pronounced, pointing with his seeker at the smooth globular mass, and the first-year students surrounding him in the Cambridge zoology laboratory nodded intelligently.

'The olfactory lobes,' continued Edward, 'the thalamencephalon. And note, please, the pineal gland.'

The students noted it, for with Dr Finch-Dutton's dissections the pineal gland *could* be noted, which was not always so with lesser demonstrators. Eagerly they peered and scribbled in their notebooks, for their own specimens awaited them, set out on the long benches of the lab.

So assured was Edward, so predictable the state of things in the cartilaginous fishes, that as he proceeded downwards towards the medulla oblongata, squirting away intrusive blood clots with his water bottle, he was free to pursue his own thoughts. And his thoughts, on this day when he was to dine at her house, were all of Harriet.

Edward had not intended to marry for a considerable period of time. Having obtained his Fellowship it was obviously sensible to wait, for he agreed with the Master of St Philip's that eight or even ten years of celibacy was not too great a price to pay for the security of an academic life.

Yet he intended to lead Harriet to the altar a great deal sooner than that. True, he would see very little of her: St Philip's rules about women in the College were particularly strict, but it would be good to know that she was waiting for him somewhere in a suitable house on the edge of the town. Her quiet and gentle presence, the intelligent way she listened would be deeply comforting to a man who had set himself, as he had done, the onerous task of definitively classifying the Aphaniptera. In five years – no, perhaps that was rash – in eight years, when he had published at least a dozen papers and his ascent of the promotional ladder was secure, he would let her have a baby. Not just because women never seemed to know what to do without little babies, but because he himself, coming from an old and distinguished family, would like to have an heir.

14

He laid down his scissors, picked up his forceps, began to prise up the left eyeball – and paused to look at Jenkins, a sixteen-stone rugger Blue from Pontypridd. Jenkins was much given to fainting and eyeballs, so Edward had found, were always difficult.

'Go and sit at the other end of the lab, Jenkins,' he ordered now, and the huge muscular Welshman ambled off obediently to sit beside Dr Henderson, a refugee from the crowded botany lab who was bubbling carbon dioxide through a tank in which an elderly parsnip silently respired.

Edward demonstrated the recti muscles of the eye and began on the tricky dissection of the cranial nerves. The best time to propose to Harriet, he had decided – and for them to become officially engaged – was at the St Philip's May Ball. The Mortons' permission for him to take Harriet (in a suitably chaperoned party of course) was tantamount to an expectation of this sort. He had set aside an adequate sum of money for a ring and after the engagement would be able to work for at least two years without further interruptions before it was necessary to make preparations for their wedding. The thought of waltzing with Harriet brought a faint smile to his long and studious face. He had seen her first at a performance of the B minor Mass in King's College Chapel and been much taken by her stillness and concentration – been much taken too, it had to be admitted, by her delicate profile and the way one pointed ear peeped out between the strands of her loose hair. Of course it had been gratifying to find that she was the daughter of the Merlin Professor – it would be hypocritical to pretend otherwise – but the knowledge that his feelings for her were basically disinterested gave him an enduring and justifiable satisfaction.

Half an hour later the students had dispersed and were bent over their own dissections while Edward, his hands behind his back, walked slowly between the benches, putting in a word here, an admonition there. Even Jenkins had recovered and was working busily.

'Please, Dr Finch-Dutton, I don't know what this is?'

Edward flinched. It was a girl who had spoken – an unsuitably pretty brunette who worked with two other Girtonians on a separate bench. The girls were the plague of his life. He was almost certain that they taunted him deliberately, for his detestation of women students was as well-known and as strong as that of his future father-in-law. Last week's practical, when the class had dissected the reproductive system, had been a nightmare. Though he had particularly instructed Price to give the girls a female fish, the technician had failed in his duty as so often before and they had called him incessantly to demonstrate organs whose names it was quite atrociously embarrassing to pronounce in the presence of ladies.

But today there was no danger and having explained to the brunette, on whose slender neck a cluster of escaping curls most disconcertingly danced as she bent over her work, that she was in the presence of the trigeminal nerve, he retreated to the shelter of Henderson's parsnip.

At five, the practical concluded, he made his way along the corridor to his corner of the research lab where a neat row of black boxes – each containing a hundred perfectly mounted microscope slides of flattened fleas – awaited him. He had classified (mainly by means of the bristles edging the head capsule) some eighteen species, but this work would take a lifetime. Not that he regretted taking on the Aphaniptera . . . his supervisor had been perfectly right when he said that fleas were virgin territory . . . but before he placed the next slide under his binocular, Edward allowed himself a long and lusting look at the serried rows of butterflies pinned in cases on the wall above him. Fleas were Edward's bread and butter, but the Lepidoptera were his passion.

Punctually at six-thirty, he tidied up and bicycled back to his rooms. But before he prepared to shave and change into his dinner-jacket, he sent one of the college servants to the buttery for a pork pie. Edward had not yet dined at the Mortons', but he had twice taken luncheon there and knew that it was best to be prepared.

*

It was to be a rather special dinner-party – the first time that Edward had been to dinner and the first chance for Marchmont (the new Classics lecturer) and his young wife to meet the Professor in the relaxed informality of his home.

So Louisa was taking trouble. In the dining-room grate, behind the iron grille of the fireguard, at least half-a-dozen coals were actually alight, constituting by the standards of Scroope Terrace a blazing fire. Moreover she had permitted the maids to replace the electric light bulbs which she had removed, for reasons of economy, from the central chandelier. The carpet, with its squares of brown and mustard, had been freshly brushed with tea-leaves, the Professor's

16

portrait in cap and gown hung straight above the sideboard and though she had baulked at the purchase of flowers so early in the year, the cup that her brother had won as an undergraduate in the Horatian oratory contest made, she thought now, an excellent epergne.

Descending to the basement, she found in the kitchen a similar air of festive abandonment. To her everyday soup of turnips and bacon bones Cook had added chopped carrots, giving the broth a pleasant yellowish tint. A cold codling waited in liquid for its *sauce tartare* and the leg of mutton (a real bargain from an enterprising butcher who specialised in cheap meat from injured but perfectly healthy animals which had to be despatched *in situ*) was already sizzling in the range.

'That seems to be all right, Cook. What about the dessert?'

Cook motioned her head towards a large plate on which a coffee blancmange, just turned out of its mould, still shivered faintly.

'I'm going to stick glacé cherries round it,' offered Cook.

'I must say that seems a little excessive,' said Louisa. She frowned, thinking. Still, it was a dinner-party. 'All right, then – but halve them first.'

She made her way upstairs again and was just in time to encounter her niece coming in from her dancing class.

It was always difficult for Harriet to leave the friendly, interesting streets and re-enter the dark house where the temperature generally seemed to be several degrees lower than that outside. Today, with Dubrov's words still sounding in her ears, she stood more forlornly than usual in the hallway, lost in her unattainable dreams – and justifiably annoyed her aunt.

'For goodness' sake, Harriet, don't dawdle! Have you forgotten we have dinner guests? I want you changed and in the drawing-room by seven o'clock.'

'Yes, Aunt Louisa.'

'You are to wear the pink crêpe de chine. And you can put up your hair.'

In her attic Harriet slowly washed, changed into the hideous dress her aunt had bought in the January sales and embarked on the battle to put up the long, soft hair which only curved slightly at the tips and needed a battery of pins to keep it in the coronet of plaits which the Trumpington Ladies had deemed suitable. She would have given anything for a quiet evening in which to re-live what had happened . . . anything not to face Edward with his pompous and proprietary

17

manner and the underlying kindness which made it impossible to dislike him as one longed to do.

When she had finished she went over to the bookcase and took down a volume of poetry, turning the pages until she found what she was looking for: a poem simply called 'Life':

> I asked no other thing,
> No other was denied.
> I offered Being for it;
> The mighty merchant smiled.
>
> Brazil? He twirled a button
> Without a glance my way
> 'But Madam, is there nothing else,
> That we can show today?'

She stood for a long time looking at the verses in which Emily Dickinson had chronicled her heartbreak. Loneliness had taught Harriet that there was always *someone* who understood – it was just that so very often they were dead, and in a book.

*

Two hours later the dinner-party was in full swing, though this was perhaps not the phrase which would have occurred to pretty Mrs Marchmont, supping her soup with a slight air of disbelief. She had been warned about the Mortons' dinner-parties, but she had not been warned *enough*.

At the head of the table, the Professor was explaining to Mr Marchmont the iniquity of the latest Senate ruling on the allocation of marks in the Classical Tripos. Edward was valiantly discussing the 'dreadful price of everything' with Aunt Louisa, while in the grate the handful of smouldering coals – kicked too hard by the underpaid parlourmaid – blackened and expired.

The soup was cleared. The cod, whose *sauce tartare* surprisingly had come out slightly blue, arrived.

'Well, Harriet, and how did you fare today?' asked the Professor, addressing his daughter for the first time.

'All right, thank you, Father. I went to my dancing lesson.'

'Ah, yes.' The Professor, his duty done, would have turned back to his neighbour but Harriet, usually so silent, spoke to him once more.

'A man came to see Madame Lavarre. A Russian. He's going to take a ballet company up the Amazon to Manaus. To perform there.'

Edward, assessing his piece of fish which did not, after all, appear to be a fillet, said, 'A most interesting part of the world, one understands. With a quite extraordinary flora and fauna.'

Harriet looked at him gratefully. And possessed by what madness she did not know, she continued, 'He offered me a job . . . as a dancer – for the length of the tour.'

Her remark affected those present profoundly, but in different ways. Her father laid down his fork as a flush spread over his sharp-featured face, Louisa opened her mouth and sat gaping at her niece, while Edward's shirt-front – responding to his sudden exhalation of breath – gave off a sharp and sudden 'pop'.

'He offered *you* a job?' said the Professor slowly. 'You? *My* daughter!' He stared incredulously at Harriet. 'I have never in all my life heard of such an impertinence!'

'No!' Harriet, knowing how useless it was, could not resist at least trying to make him see. 'It's an honour. A real one. To be chosen – to be considered of professional standard. And it's a good thing to do – to take art to people who are hungry for it. Properly, objectively *good* like in Marcus Aurelius.'

'How dare you, Harriet? How dare you argue with me!' His daughter's invocation of the great Roman Stoic, clearly his own property, had dangerously fanned the flames of the Professor's wrath. He glared at Louisa; she should have been firmer with the girl, taken her away from that unsuitable Academy years ago. Though actually Louisa had said often enough that she saw no point in wasting money on dancing lessons, and it was he who had said that Harriet could continue. Was it because he could still remember Sophie waltzing so gracefully beneath the lamplit trees in that Swiss hotel? If so, he had been suitably punished for his sentimentality.

'Please, Father. Please, let me go!' Harriet, whom one could usually silence with a look, seemed suddenly to have taken leave of her senses. 'You didn't let me stay on at school, you didn't allow me to go to France with the Fergusons because they were agnostics . . . well, I understood that – yes, really, I understood. But this . . . they take a ballet mistress, it's absolutely respectable and I would be back in the autumn.' She had pushed away her plate and was gripping the edge of the table, the intensity of her longing turning the usually clear, grave face into an image from a *pietà*: a wild-eyed and beseeching Magdalene. 'Please, Father,' said Harriet, 'I *implore* you to let me go.'

A scene! A scene at the dinner-table. Overwhelmed by this ultimate in disasters, Louisa bowed her head over her plate.

'You will drop this subject immediately, Harriet,' barked the Professor. 'You are embarrassing our guests.'

'No. I won't drop it.' Harriet had become very pale, but her voice was steady. 'You have always thought dancing was frivolous and silly, but it isn't – it's the most marvellous thing in the world. You can say things when you dance that you can't say any other way. People have danced for the glory of God since the beginning of time. David danced before the Ark of the Covenant . . . And this journey . . . this adventure . . .' She turned imploringly to Edward. '*You* must know what a wonder it would be?'

'Oh, *no*, Harriet! No, the Amazon is a most unsuitable place for a woman. For *anyone!*' From the plethora of dangerous diseases and potentially lethal animals, poor Edward – meaning only to scotch this dreadful topic once and for all – now had the misfortune to select the *candiru*. 'There is a fish there,' he said earnestly, 'which swims into people's orifices when they are bathing and by means of backwards pointing spines becomes impossible to dislodge . . .'

A moan from Louisa brought him to a halt. Orifices had been mentioned at dinner, and before ladies. Orifices and a scene in one evening! Casting about in her mind, she could not see that she had done anything to deserve such a disgrace. And as poor Edward flushed a deep crimson and Mrs Marchmont suppressed a nervous giggle, the Professor rose and faced his daughter.

'You will leave the table immediately, Harriet, and go to your room.' And when she did not rise instantly: 'I think you heard me!'

'Yes.' But she remained perfectly still, looking at her father, and in a moment of aberration he had the mad idea that *she* was pitying *him*.

Then she gave a little nod as though some transaction was now completed, and with the fluid grace that was her legacy from that damnable dancing place, she rose, walked to the door and was gone.

Everyone now made Herculean efforts, but it had to be admitted that even by Morton standards the dinner-party was not proving a conspicuous success. Edward, torn between fear lest Harriet after all should turn out to have 'ideas', and regret that she had been punished like a naughty child, was not his usual self. Mrs Marchmont in her thin dress was so busy trying not to shiver that she contributed little. It was left to valiant Mr Marchmont to sustain the conversation, which he did heroically until, biting into his mutton, he inexplicably encountered a lead pellet and broke a tooth.

*

Alone in her attic, Harriet threw herself down on the bed. Growing up in this gloomy house, she had taught herself a discipline for survival in which the weakness of tears played no part.

Yet now she cried as she had not cried since her mother's death. Cried for her lovely, lost adventure, for the unattainable forests and magical rivers she would never see; cried for the camaraderie of fellow artists and a job well-done.

But her real grief lay deeper. She was honest enough to admit that few girls in her position would have been allowed to travel to the Amazon. It was not her father's refusal that so devastated her now; it was his bigotry, his hatred, his determination not to understand. And lying there, her hair in damp strands across her crumpled face, Harriet gave up the long, long struggle to love her father and her aunt.

It was for this loss above all that she wept. She had learned, during the long years of her childhood, to live without receiving love. To live without giving it seemed more than she could bear.

CHAPTER TWO

HARRIET HAD always loved words: tasted them on her tongue, thought of them as friends. The word *serendipity* was one she valued especially, its meaning rooted in the world of fairy tales: 'The faculty of making fortunate discoveries by accident.'

It was this word she thought of later when she remembered her encounter with a small boy called Henry in the maze at Stavely Hall. All her subsequent adventures stemmed from this one meeting and from the trust she saw in the child's eyes; nothing she experienced afterwards was more unlikely or more strange.

The visit to Stavely, which occurred a week after the ill-fated dinner-party, was the climax of the year for the ladies of the Trumpington Tea Circle. Weeks of preparation had gone into the expedition, for Stavely was forty miles to the west in the rolling Suffolk countryside and had awaited the benison of motor transport to make it a comfortable day's outing. Letters had been sent, the substantial fee mentioned by Mrs Brandon for a tour of the house and permission to picnic in her gardens had been agreed. Now as they waited outside the house of their president, Mrs Belper, for the arrival of the charabanc, the ladies found it necessary to remind Harriet again and again of her good fortune in being included in the party.

These ladies of the Tea Circle had presided over Harriet's young life like a flock of black birds in a Greek play. There were some thirty of them who had met originally in the home of Hermione Belper, the full-bosomed wife of St Philip's meek and undersized bursar, in protest against the carryings-on of the Association of University Wives which not only admitted coloureds, foreigners and Jews, but had raised money – in a series of coffee mornings – for the purpose of enabling the Fitzwilliam Museum to buy a painting which had turned

22

out to be of a lady not only nude, but crudely and specifically naked.

Mrs Belper had proposed the formation of a new Tea Circle to uphold the values of old-fashioned womanhood and of the Empire, and since her house – only a stone's throw from Louisa's – was named Trumpington Villa, the unsuspecting suburb of Trumpington found itself lending its name to the new association.

It was the Tea Circle ladies who, through Louisa, decided what Harriet should wear, which families were suitable for her to visit and where she could go unchaperoned; it was they – scattered like an army of secret agents through the town – who reported to Louisa when her niece removed her gloves in public or had been seen talking in far too friendly a manner to a shop assistant.

In the eyes of these ladies, Harriet's good fortune was all the greater because Edward Finch-Dutton, too, was to come to Stavely Hall.

The decision to include a man in the party was one which Mrs Belper and Aunt Louisa had debated for hours. The advantages of inviting Edward were clear: his mother had been on visiting terms with old General Brandon (the owner of Stavely) when he was alive and this fact, if mentioned in advance, would greatly increase their chances of being welcomed in person by his daughter-in-law, who in the continuing absence of her husband was Stavely's reigning mistress. Both Mrs Belper and Louisa were passionate visitors of stately homes and lived in constant hope of converting a mere 'sighting' – that of a distant marquis crouched over his herbaceous border or a viscountess entering her carriage, for example – into an actual meeting during which sentences were exchanged. And Isobel Brandon, a grand-daughter of the Earl of Lexbury, was rumoured to be red-haired, beautiful and elegant beyond belief.

As against this, there were the obvious dangers of allowing the 'young people' to get out of hand. Stavely was reputed to be the most magnificent and romantic of East Anglia's great houses and the thought of Edward and Harriet disappearing into some impenetrable yew arbour or lingering behind a carved oak screen was too horrible to contemplate.

'But we shall be able to prevent that, Louisa,' Mrs Belper had decided, coming down in favour of Edward. 'After all, there are more than thirty of us. I shall talk to the girls.'

So Mrs Belper had talked to them – not to eighty-seven-year-old Mrs Transom, the widow of the Emeritus Professor of Architecture, a 'girl' of whom little could be expected, but to Millicent Braithwaite who single-handed had pulled three drunken undergraduates from a high spiked wall as they tried to climb into Trinity, and to Eugenia Crowley who was amazingly fleet-footed from cross-country running with her pack of Guides – and they had promised that the young couple would never be out of sight.

Edward accordingly had been invited and now, sensibly deciding to mix business with pleasure, he stood beside Harriet, dressed for the country and holding his butterfly-net, a strong canvas sweep-net for those insects which preferred to hop or crawl along the ground, and a khaki haversack containing his pooter, his killing bottle and his tins.

The omnibus arrived; rugs, parasols and hampers of food were loaded on. Miss Transom climbed aboard and began to heave her aged, cantankerous mother on to the step. Eugenia Crowley, twitching with responsibility, and Millicent Braithwaite – a deeply muscular figure in a magenta two-piece and kid boots – performed a neat pincer movement, placing themselves one in front of and one behind the seat which contained Edward and Harriet – and the bus set off.

Harriet had not wanted to come; she could imagine nothing less enjoyable than trailing round a great house in the company of the Tea Circle ladies, and Edward's presence was an added burden for present always in her mind was the dread that one day she would be driven to yield – to accept, if it came, his offer of marriage. If she married Edward, she could have a garden in which flowers actually grew; a dog; a pond with goldfish. She could sit in the sun and read and have her friends. But at this point always she stopped her thoughts, for somewhere in this imagined garden there was a pram with a gurgling baby: *her* baby, soft and warm.

But not *only* hers. And as so often before Harriet gave thanks for Maisie, the melancholy and eccentric housemaid who had given her, when she was six years old, such a comprehensive and unadorned account of what people did to bring babies into the world. Harriet had lain awake in her attic for many nights trying to comprehend the complicated unpleasantness of what she had heard, but now she was glad of Maisie's detailed crudity. Too easy otherwise, when she read of Dante's sublime passion for his Beatrice or (in melting and mellifluous Greek) of the innocent Daphnis' pursuit of Chloe, to imagine love as some glorious upsurge of the human spirit. It was of course, but not *only*, and now as she gently drew away her arm from Edward's – which was growing warm in the crowded bus – she knew

24

that that way out was barred.

But what way was open? Her father, the night after the dinner-party, had himself gone to Madame Lavarre and stopped her dancing lessons once and for all. There was nothing left now: nothing.

Only I must not despair, thought Harriet. Despair was a sin, she knew that: turning one's face away from the created world. And resolutely she forced herself not just to look at, but really to *see* the greening hedges, the glistening buttercups, the absurd new lambs – setting herself, as unhappy people do, a kind of pastoral litany.

And presently she succeeded, for the gentle peaceful countryside under the light wide sky was truly lovely and it was spring and there had to be a future somewhere, even for her. So that when Edward said, 'This is very pleasant, Harriet, is it not?' she was able to turn to him, pushing back her loose hair behind her ears, and smile and agree.

But when at last the bus turned in between the stone lions on the gate-posts and they drove down Stavely's famous double avenue of beeches towards the house, Harriet's soft 'Oh!' of pleasure owed nothing to the deliberate exercise of will. She had expected grandeur, ostentation, pomp . . . and found instead an unequivocal and awe-inspiring beauty.

Stavely was long and low, built of a warm and rosy brick: a house which had no truck with fortifications and moats and battlements, but proclaimed itself joyously as a place for living in – for music and banquets and the raising of fine children. Sheltered by a low wooded hill, the Hall faced serenely south into the sun and with its stone quoins, mullioned windows and graceful chimneys most gloriously avowed the principles of the Tudor Renaissance; '*Commoditie*, *Fitnesse* and *Delight*'.

'Out we get, girls!' cried Mrs Belper. 'We have just ten minutes to stretch our legs and then we meet at the front door at twelve o'clock sharp for a tour of the house.'

The 'girls' got out. Mrs Transom was lowered down and tottered away on the arm of her daughter, while – followed at a discreet distance by their conscientious chaperones – Edward and Harriet made their way through the gatehouse arch towards the formal gardens.

If Harriet's first impression of Stavely had been of overwhelming beauty, her second was of neglect. The fine trees of the beech avenue were indestructible, as was the parkland where clumps of cattle moved slowly over a sea of grass. But here, close to the house, where

25

everything depended on a careful husbandry, it was clear that something was wrong. Weeds straggled over the gravel paths; the yews in the topiary, the formal lines of the knot-garden were blurred for want of trimming. This was a sleeping house, its decline masked by the tenderness of the green creeper hiding a garden door, by the young leaves of an unpruned rose laying its tendrils across a window. A house awaiting the kiss of a prince – a *rich* prince, Harriet corrected herself, guessing at the multitude of gardeners and groundsmen that would be needed to succour Stavely's loveliness.

'Was it like this when you used to come here, Edward?' asked Harriet. 'So overgrown and neglected?'

'No, I don't think so. But remember I was very small and after Colonel Brandon died we never came again. His son – the present owner – was not at all friendly to Mama.'

By the main door where all the ladies were now assembled, a disappointment awaited them. Although Aunt Louisa, who acted as the Circle's secretary, had specifically mentioned Edward Finch-Dutton's presence in the party in her confirmatory letter, there was no sign of Mrs Brandon. Instead a gloomy, ancient and cadaverous-looking individual with a bald and liver-spotted pate introduced himself as Mr Grunthorpe, the family butler, and leading them into a huge, panelled room he immediately began his patter.

'The room we now find ourselves in is known as the Great Hall. You will please observe the outstanding examples of Elizabethan plasterwork and panelling. Above the archway we see a carving of the twelve apostles . . .'

'Very fine,' said Mrs Belper.

'Note also the chimney-piece surmounted by the Brandon arms impaling those of Henrietta Verney, who was united to the family by marriage in the year 1633,' droned the patently uninterested Mr Grunthorpe.

Harriet noted them . . . but noted too the dust that lay on the backs of the carved chairs, noted the dull streakiness of the long refectory table . . . the cold creeping through the room as though it was years since a fire had burned in that splendid grate.

They moved on down a corridor and into the Drawing-Room – a delightful room filled with Hepplewhite furniture – but here too was the same neglect. One yellow damask curtain was half-drawn across the window as though the effort of pulling it back had been too much for some indifferent housemaid. The fender was unpolished, the crystal chandelier lacklustre and dull.

In the Dining-Room, with its walls of dark Cordoba leather, there was an unfortunate diversion.

'I want to go to the lavatory,' announced the ancient Mrs Transom in a surprisingly loud, firm voice.

'No, you don't, Mother,' hissed her daughter. 'Not now, you don't – you've been.'

'What do you mean, no, I don't?' said the old woman angrily. 'I may be old, I may be useless, I may be someone whom everyone would like to see dead and laid out on a slab, but I still know when I want to go to the lavatory and I want to go to the lavatory *now*.'

A hurried consultation followed. The butler, more bored than pained, issued instructions, holding out his mottled hand in case the information rendered might produce a tip. Mrs Transom was led away on the arm of her unfortunate daughter – and the party trooped into the Library.

Oh, the poor books, thought Harriet, running her handkerchief surreptitiously along the dusty, calf-bound volumes on an open shelf. Here was Horace who had so loved the foolish Lesbia and Sappho who had turned loneliness into the most moving verses of the ancient world – and here Harriet's own special friend, the emperor Marcus Aurelius whose *Meditations* she now pulled out and opened at random, to read:

Live not as though a thousand years are ahead of you. Fate is at your elbow; make yourself good while life and power are still yours.

Only, what *is* good? wondered Harriet. She had thought of it as submission, virtue, not setting up her will against others. But might it mean something else? Might it mean making yourself strong and creative? Might it mean following your star?

The butler glared at her and she replaced the book. However poor I was, reflected Harriet, I would always dust the books. And I would always find flowers, she thought, remembering the drifts of wild narcissi she had seen as they came up the drive. And once again she wondered what ailed this marvellous house.

They trooped up the grand staircase, admiring the carved newel posts, while from below came the anguished baying of Mrs Transom's daughter who had taken a wrong turning and lay becalmed in a distant hallway. Here were the private apartments of the family – the upper Drawing-Room, the bedrooms – past which the cadaverous Mr Grunthorpe, enjoining silence, now led them bound for the Long

Gallery on the top floor.

Harriet had fallen a little behind the others, weary of the absurd antics of her 'bodyguard' and planning, if a side staircase could be found, the rescue of the Transoms.

She was thus alone when a door was suddenly thrown open and a woman's voice, high and imperious, cried out, 'No! I don't believe it! It *cannot* be as bad as that!'

Involuntarily, Harriet stopped. The luxurious room thus revealed, framed in the lintel of the door, might have come from a painting by Titian. There was a four-poster hung in blue silk, a dressing-table with a silver-trimmed mirror, a richly embroidered chair . . . The covers of the bed were thrown back and beside it stood a woman in a white negligée with a river of dark red hair rippling down her back. She had brought up one of her arms against the carved bedpost as though for support, and a little silken-haired papillon lay curled on the pillow looking at her with anxious eyes.

'Even my idiot of a husband could not have gone as far as that,' she continued. 'You are trying to frighten me.'

A maid moved about the back of the room, laying out clothes, but it was to someone unseen that the woman spoke – a man whose low-voiced answer Harriet could not make out.

'*Oh!*' The rapt exclamation came from Louisa who had returned to admonish her loitering niece. Her long face was transfigured; her mouth hung slightly open with awe.

A sighting! Here without a doubt was the lady of the house, Isobel Brandon, in whose veins flowed some of the bluest blood in England. For while Harriet saw a beautiful and imperious woman driven to the edge of endurance by some calamity, Aunt Louisa saw only the grand-daughter of the Earl of Lexbury whose wedding some ten years earlier at St Margaret's, Westminster, had required a double page of the *Tatler* to do it justice.

But Mrs Brandon now had seen them.

'For God's sake, Alistair, shut the door! You can't go anywhere until those wretched women have stopped trooping through the house. And anyway, I sent all the documents to—'

The door closed. Harriet and her aunt joined the others. Mrs Transom's daughter had discovered another stairway and pushed her mother up it – and the party entered the Long Gallery.

A long, light room with a beautiful parquet floor . . . The walls nearest the door were taken up by family portraits of the Brandons.

28

Among the dull paintings, varnished into uniformity, only two caught Harriet's attention: a likeness of the old General, almost comical in the obvious boredom and irritation shown by the sitter at being compelled to sit thus captive for the artist; and one of Henrietta Verney who had linked the Brandons to her illustrious house – a vivid intelligent face defying the centuries.

'Is there no portrait of the present owner?' enquired Mrs Belper.

'No, ma'am. The present owner is abroad a great deal and has not yet sat for his portrait.'

And is not likely to either, thought Mr Grunthorpe with gloomy satisfaction as he pointed out a view of Stavely's west front by Richard Wilson.

Harriet wandered for a while, not greatly interested in the conventional landscapes and battle scenes. Then right at the end of the gallery she came across an entirely different group of pictures – chosen, surely, by someone outside the family. Light, sun-filled modern paintings: a Monet of poppies and cornflowers; a Renoir of two girls in splendidly floral hats sitting on a terrace . . . and one at which she stood and looked, forgetting where she was, forgetting everything except what she had lost.

No one has understood the world of dance like Degas. The painting was of two ballet girls in the wings of the Paris Opéra: one bending down to tie her shoe; the other limbering up, one leg lifted on to the *barre*, her head bent over it to touch her ankles. This painter who all his life was obsessed by the beauty of women at work had caught perfectly the weariness on the girls' faces, the pull of their muscles, the fierce, unending discipline that underlies the tawdry glitter of the stage.

And even Edward, coming up to Harriet with his usual proprietary air, saw her face and left her alone.

Ten minutes later the tour was completed and the ladies back in the entrance hall. It was here that Mr Grunthorpe met his Waterloo. Aunt Louisa, the Circle's secretary, advanced towards him and thanked him on behalf of her group for showing them round. Mr Grunthorpe, his rapacious hand curved in expectation, murmured that it had been a pleasure. He was still staring at his empty hand in total disbelief as Louisa, following the other ladies, disappeared through the front door.

There now followed the selection of a suitable site for the picnic. This was not a simple matter, but at last they were settled in a sheltered spot in the sunken garden, the hampers brought from the charabanc, rugs spread and parasols arranged, and the ladies fell to.

Edward was at first pleased to sit beside Harriet enjoying the excellent food they had prepared. Though exceptionally quiet even for her, she looked very pleasing in her blue skirt and white blouse and he particularly liked the way she was wearing her hair: taken back under a velvet band and loose on her shoulders. But after a while he grew restive; he was, after all, an entomologist and here not only for pleasure.

'Come, Harriet,' he said presently. 'I want to replenish the laboratory teaching specimens. Will you help me?'

She nodded and rose and they moved off in the direction of the croquet lawn, while at a discreet distance the stalwart Millie Braithwaite, eschewing her after-luncheon nap, pursued them.

For nearly half an hour Edward, bent almost double, moved absorbedly across the grass, flicking the heavy sweep-net to and fro over the ground.

'Pooter, please, Harriet!' he would say from time to time, straightening up, and she would hand him the little glass tube with its rubber pipe into which he would suck the hopping, wriggling, jumping little creatures; then, 'killing bottle!', and that too Harriet would put into his hand so that the miniature flies and bright bugs and stripy beetles could find, among the fumes of potassium cyanide, their final resting place.

As they moved slowly towards the terrace Edward suddenly perceived, on a blossoming viburnum bush, a large and golden Brimstone butterfly. At once he became transformed and the heavy cumbersome sweep-net, the crouching position were abandoned. Plucking the gossamer butterfly-net from Harriet, he almost danced up the steps. This was a new Edward: a lithe and entomological Ariel. For a few moments he hovered, measuring his prey – then, with a magnificent sideways sweep of the net, he struck!

'Got it!' he announced with satisfaction and as Harriet approached, he pinched the fluttering creature's thorax between his forefinger and thumb.

A neat and expert movement: an instant and humane death. But it made a noise which Harriet had not expected – a small but distinct 'crack' – and it was now that she told Edward he must excuse her for a while and left him.

Walking unthinkingly, she found herself in a small copse through which there ran a stream, its banks carpeted with more primroses than she had ever seen.

If the first butterfly you see is a yellow butterfly, then it will be a good summer, Harriet knew that. But if the first butterfly you see is a dead butterfly, what then?

She had come to an orchard. The lichened pear trees were in blossom, the apples still in pink-tipped bud. What a heavenly place, thought Harriet, for here Stavely's neglect only added to its loveliness, and as if in echo to her thoughts she found herself on a wide track which must have branched off from the main avenue, in front of a sign saying: 'To Paradise Farm'.

She hesitated, not uninterested in the idea of Paradise, but the glimpse of tall chimneys and tiled roofs half-hidden in the trees suggested a house far more important than an ordinary agricultural dwelling and, not wishing to trespass, she retraced her steps. Finding a door in an ivy-covered wall, she entered a walled garden and here for the first time encountered a gardener – a bent old man pottering among the broken frames who acknowledged her greeting so ill-temperedly that she went out again, walked through the stable yard, passed an overgrown tennis court – and saw behind it a curiously shaped clump of yew hedges, irregular and dark.

Of course. A maze . . . She had heard the maze at Stavely mentioned: a famous one, as intriguing and clever as that at Hampton Court. Jokes had been made about it on the bus and Mrs Brandon, in her letter, had forbidden the ladies to enter it.

'Harriet! Harriet, where are you?'

Aunt Louisa's high petulant voice in the distance sent Harriet quickly foward and unhesitatingly she entered the maze.

It was very silent between the yew hedges, which almost closed over her head; on the mossy paths her light feet made not the slightest sound. The idea of a labyrinth had always alarmed Harriet and the story of Theseus and the Minotaur had been one of her favourite ways of terrifying herself as a child, but now she wandered unhurried and in peace for it seemed to her that there were worse things than to be abandoned in this green and secret place.

Which didn't mean that she was not lost. All the theories that people had about turning always to the right or always to the left did not seem to be very *good* theories. She wandered on, twisting this way and that, disturbed by nothing except a nesting blackbird which flew up from the hedge. And then, quite without warning, she took a last

31

sharp turn and found herself in the circular sweep of grass which constituted the core, the very heart of the labyrinth.

'Oh!' exclaimed Harriet, startled.

For sitting on a stone bench beside the mildewed statue of a faun was a hunched figure so small, so self-contained that it might have been the spirit of the maze itself. Then it looked up, as startled as she was, and Harriet saw a small boy with dark red hair and a pale, rather pinched little face almost covered by a large pair of spectacles. A child of about seven years of age trying to shield, with hands woefully too small for the task, a large black book.

'I'm so sorry,' said Harriet in her low, soft voice. 'I didn't mean to disturb you, I expect you wanted to be alone.'

'Well, yes, I did,' said the boy, now pressing the book against his diminutive sailor-suited chest. He looked at the girl standing in front of him. She was a grown-up – he could tell that because her blue skirt touched the ground – and grown-ups could make trouble; but as he stared at her anxiously, she smiled – a terribly friendly, crunched-up sort of smile – and he knew that it would be all right, that she would not betray him. 'But I don't mind as long as you don't tell anyone. I'm not supposed to read this book, you see. It's forbidden.'

'I promise not to tell anyone,' said Harriet. She came over and sat down on the bench beside him, noting with a pang the fragile, elderly-looking legs, the feet in their black strap-shoes hanging so high above the ground. 'I was always reading books I wasn't supposed to when I was little. I used to tie a piece of cotton to my toe and to the door-handle, so that when someone came in my toe twitched and I had time to put the book under my pillow before they saw it.'

'Did you?' The boy was impressed, lifting his spectacles a moment to look at Harriet. His eyes were unexpectedly beautiful: large grey eyes with a golden rim round the iris. 'My name is Henry,' he now offered. 'Henry St John Verney Brandon.'

'Mine is Harriet Jane Morton,' said Harriet, realising without undue surprise that she was in the presence of Stavely's heir. And solemnly, for they were both people of great politeness, they shook hands.

It was then, their credentials exchanged, that the child lowered the book and laid it carefully in Harriet's lap, open at the title page.

'Would you like to see it?' he asked.

For a moment she could not speak. The coincidence was too

uncanny, here in this dreamlike place.

'Is anything the matter, Harriet?' Henry's russet head was tilted anxiously up at her, for she had given a little gasp and put one hand to her mouth.

'No . . . it's all right.' She forced herself to speak calmly and sensibly. She did not know what she had expected Henry to have carried off into the secrecy of the maze – perhaps some pathetic explanation of the so-called 'facts of life'. Instead, now she read:

AMAZON ADVENTURE
Being the account of a journey with rod and gun
along the Rivers Orinoco, Negro and Amazon
by
Colonel Frederick Bush, D.S.O., M.C.

'It's just so extraordinary, Henry. You see, I have been thinking and thinking about this place. For a whole week I've thought of nowhere else. And then I find you . . .' she shook her head. 'It's a beautiful book,' she said. 'Absolutely beautiful.'

'Yes, it is, isn't it?'

Fellow bibliophiles, they looked with satisfaction at the thick pages with their wavy edges, the sepia illustrations protected by wafer-thin paper; drank in the smell of old leather and dust, while Henry – an impeccable host – led her into his promised land.

'That's an anaconda – it was twenty feet long before Colonel Bush killed it – and here's a canoe full of Indians: friendly ones, not the kind that shoot you full of arrows. Those are terribly dangerous rapids in the background; the Colonel had to drag his boat out of the water and carry it over the hill when he got to them. And somewhere there's a *lovely* one of a whole lot of capy . . . capy-somethings, like huge guinea-pigs. Look!'

They pored together over the herd of large, somewhat absurd rodents basking on a sand-bank. Not all the pictures were very clear, for the intrepid Colonel had wielded his Kodak under conditions of quite spectacular hardship, but to Harriet and Henry each and every one was of absorbing interest. There was one of a steamer of the Amazon Navigation Company going down the river; one of a rubber gatherer, a *seringueiro*, crossing a creek on a felled tree . . . And several of the author: a splendid man in a topee, lying in his hammock at a bivouac, standing with his gun astride a dead jaguar . . . arm-in-arm with an Indian chief in a lip-disc who came scarcely to his waist.

'It doesn't hurt them, having their mouths like that,' explained Henry reassuringly. 'They like it – they sort of stretch their lips gradually. It's an honour.'

Harriet nodded, as entranced as the little boy. 'Is there a picture of Manaus, Henry?'

'Yes, there is.' Enormously pleased to be able to oblige her, he turned the pages carefully, his square-tipped fingers uncannily like those of old General Brandon in the portrait the gloomy Mr Grunthorpe had shown them in the Long Gallery. 'Look, here it is! It's called "the Golden City". Why is it called that, do you know?'

'I think it's because everyone there is so rich,' answered Harriet thoughtfully. 'But I'm not sure. People have always thought about gold in South America and searched for it. Golden cities with golden roofs; golden palaces where there's hidden treasure. "Eldorado", they call it.'

She gazed at the picture – an elegant cathedral, a flight of steps, a park with palm trees. In the distance, blurred, some other buildings. Was that faint criss-crossing in front of one of them a line of scaffolding? The book was dated 1890 – just about the time that the Opera House was begun . . . Avidly she began to read the text, only to be recalled by a small sigh from Henry. Glad as he was to have found for her the city she had requested, he yearned inevitably for the tree sloth and giant electric eel which awaited them.

'What I don't understand, Henry, is why you are not supposed to read this book,' said Harriet when they had studied all the pictures. 'Surely it's a good book for someone young to read? A book about adventures?'

There was a pause while Henry pondered, evidently putting her through some final test.

'It's because it belonged to "the Boy".' He spoke with a curious awe, looking up at her to gauge the effect of his words. 'He's a secret, you see. No one's allowed to talk about him and if I ask anyone, Mama gets cross. I took it from old Nannie in the Lodge, when she was asleep. It was his absolutely favourite book and he left it for her when he went away.'

'He lived here, then?'

'Oh, yes. But he did something bad, I think, and they sent him away. Before I was born, this was – about when Grandfather died. He had the book for his ninth birthday, Nannie said. Sometimes she tells me a bit about him when she's had her medicine.'

34

'Her medicine?'

Henry nodded. 'It's called Gordon's Gin and it's in a big bottle by her bed; when she's had some, she tells me about him. She just calls him "the Boy", as though there weren't any other boys in the world. He was very wild and very brave. He climbed the oak tree by the gatehouse roof and swung over to the parapet – and he had a huge black dog that followed him everywhere and when he went away the dog stopped eating and died.' The child's eyes shone with hero-worship. 'He had a cross-bow too and he could shoot for miles and he didn't wear spectacles and he wasn't afraid of the dark. At least, I don't think he was – Nannie didn't say.'

'I expect he was older than you, Henry,' said Harriet gently. 'I expect when you're his age you will be just like him.'

'No.' Henry shook a resigned head. 'Cook says I'm as clever as a cartload of monkeys, but he was clever *and* brave. He could ride anything.' He sighed. 'I can't ride anything. I fell off Porridge, who's only a Shetland pony; the girths slipped. He made a tree-house in the Wellingtonia; that's about a hundred feet high – you can still see some of the planks at the top – and he built a dug-out canoe like Colonel Bush's and launched it on the river and got as far as Appleby Meadows before it sank.'

Harriet turned back the pages to glance at the flyleaf. 'July 5th 1891', she read. If "the Boy" had been nine years old then, he would be a man approaching thirty now, but she said nothing, realising that to Henry it was necessary that this magical being should exist outside the rules of time.

'Grunthorpe knew him. That's our butler. He didn't like him; he said he was a changeling.'

'A *changeling*? Why, Henry?'

The child sighed. 'Because he could talk to animals. It wasn't natural, Grunthorpe said.' There was a pause before Henry added in a carefully expressionless voice, 'I told Grunthorpe I was going to be an explorer when I grew up and join an expedition, but he said I couldn't because explorers don't wear spectacles.'

Needing a few moments to control her anger, Harriet fixed her gaze on the mildewed statue of the faun. 'I find that a most extraordinary remark, Henry,' she said presently in a detached, calm voice. 'Consider, for example, the insects. For you must admit that the insects are a trouble. The mosquitoes, the blackfly and this one here' – she searched for the page in which Colonel Bush had devoted a

35

paragraph to the ravages of the tabanid fly. 'It would seem to me perfectly obvious that insects like that could get into a person's eyes, and that would be very awkward if he was paddling a canoe. Now if I was in charge of an expedition, the man I would put in front – in the very front of any boat – would be the man with glasses.'

Henry said nothing, but after a moment – while not exactly coming to lean against her – he moved along the stone bench so that even the small space which had been between them was there no longer, and when Harriet turned to look at him she found herself staring at the riot of impending incisors and cavernous gaps which betokened Henry's peculiarly ravishing smile.

For a while they sat together in companionable silence. Then: 'Sometimes I think he'll come back. "The Boy", I mean,' said Henry shyly. 'And then everything will be all right again.'

'Isn't it all right now?'

'No. Because Papa has deserted us and Mama gets angry and the servants keep leaving and we have to have "Tea Ladies" going through the rooms.'

'Yes, I see. That isn't very nice.'

'I don't *think* it's my fault?' said Henry, his small face pinched and anxious once again.

'How *could* it be your fault, Henry,' she answered passionately. 'How could it be?'

So far they had felt themselves quite alone, but now the voices of the agitated ladies calling her name seemed to be getting closer and, conscious of limited time, Harriet said, 'Henry, you may think this quite incredible, but only a week ago I was offered a job to go out to the Amazon, as a dancer. To Manaus. To this very place.' She pointed to the book, open once more at the picture of 'the Golden City'. 'Only they won't let me go.'

Somehow it seemed perfectly natural to talk to this diminutive child as though he was a fully-fledged adult.

Henry turned towards her, a puzzled look on his face.

'But Harriet,' he said, pronouncing her name with professorial clarity and a certain reproach, 'you're grown-up, aren't you? You can do what you like?'

She looked down at his russet head, tilted up at her trustfully as he proclaimed her adult status. And suddenly she was flooded with a feeling of the most extraordinary power and elation. So strong was this feeling that she rose to her feet and in a voice entirely different

36

from the one she had used hitherto, she said, 'Yes. You are perfectly right, Henry. I *am* grown-up.'

The change in her momentarily deflected Henry from his purpose. She looked so pretty all at once that he wondered if it might be possible, by achieving a sudden spurt in growth, to marry her. But more urgent than his matrimonial plans was the request he was about to make, and slipping down from the bench he came up to her and lifted his small hand to pluck gently at her sleeve.

'Harriet, I think he's there. "The Boy" . . . in the Amazon. I'm *sure* he is. Nannie says he was always talking about it. Will you find him and tell him to come back? Will you, Harriet? *Please?*'

And Harriet, now, did not say one of the things that came into her head. She did not say, 'Henry, the Amazon basin is a million square miles – how can I find someone whose name I do not even know? And even if I found him, he would probably be a pompous empire-builder with a big moustache and refuse even to talk to me.'

She said none of these things; she said only, 'I will try, Henry. I promise you that if I get there, I will really and truly try.'

But now the ladies, searching the grounds, had received some dreadful news. Questioning the surly gardener, they had elicited the information that Harriet was secreted in the maze with a young man. 'Young Mr Henry,' the gardener had admitted.

Here was disaster! After all their care and chaperonage, the salacious girl had eluded them!

'Millicent! Eugenia! Go and deflect Edward,' ordered Hermione Belper. 'We don't want a fight. The rest of us will get her out. Come, Louisa!'

And to a woman the ladies of Trumpington, with ancient Mrs Transom by no means in the rear, plunged into the maze.

Chapter Three

WHAT MARCUS AURELIUS had begun by causing Harriet to question the meaning of the word 'good', Henry with his trust and optimism completed. She determined to escape and to do so competently, and casting about for ways and means she remembered a girl called Betsy Fairfield who had been briefly at school with her in Cambridge, but now lived in London.

Betsy was pretty and a little silly and exceedingly good-natured. Harriet had written some essays for her and lent her some history notes and a friendship had developed. Now Betsy, who was a few months older than Harriet, was 'doing the season'; she was already going to balls and was to be presented at court. Her mother was an easygoing, kindly society lady who had been kind to Harriet.

The afternoon after the visit to Stavely, accordingly, Harriet – finding herself alone – unhooked what Aunt Louisa still referred to as 'the instrument' from the dark brown wall of the hallway, asked for Betsy's number and was eventually put through to her friend.

'Betsy, this is Harriet.'

'Harriet? How lovely!' Shrieks of perfectly genuine if transient enthusiasm emitted from the cheerful Betsy. 'How are you?'

'I'm all right. Listen, Betsy, I want you to do me a very great favour. Will you?'

'Yes, of course I will. Goodness, I always remember that essay you wrote for me about the Corn Laws. And the one about the "bedchamber question". I got an "A" in both – the only time ever!'

'Well, listen; I want you to get your mother to write a note to my Aunt Louisa, asking me to stay. I'd like her to write it straight away and I want her to ask me for three weeks. Do you think she would?'

'*Of course* she would! Will you really come? That would be

38

absolutely marvellous! You can help me with my court curtsey; you were always so good at dancing. Poor Hetty's got water on the knee and we don't know whether—'

It was a while before Harriet could interrupt the spate of words in order to say, 'And Betsy, when your mother's written the note could you telephone me yourself to arrange the journey? Ask for me personally? Would you do that? I promise not to be a nuisance.'

'Goodness, you won't be a nuisance. Mother really likes you; she's often said—' But at this point Betsy recollected what her mother had said about Professor Morton's treatment of his daughter and the conversation was terminated.

Betsy was as good as her word and her mother wrote a charming note to Louisa requesting Harriet's presence in London. That Mrs Fairfield's uncle was a viscount helped to determine the issue; that and the fact that since the night of the unfortunate dinner-party, Harriet had not really been herself. Betsy rang up the day after the note arrived and when they had spoken, Harriet informed Aunt Louisa that the Fairfields would meet the 10.37 from Cambridge on Thursday morning. She packed her own suitcase and her aunt, reflecting on the fact that they would be saving on Harriet's food for three weeks, actually suggested to the Professor that he might care to give his daughter a guinea, so that she would not be entirely dependent on her friend – and this he did. And so, at a quarter-past ten on Thursday morning, Harriet was assisted into a 'Ladies Only' carriage at Cambridge Station and put in charge of the guard.

That there was no one to meet her at King's Cross was not surprising, since she had told Betsy that she would be arriving on the following day. Harriet gave up her ticket and posted two letters she had written in the privacy of her bedroom. One was to her aunt announcing her safe arrival at the Fairfields'; the other was to the Fairfields and was full of apologies and regrets. Her father's cousin had been taken seriously ill in Harrogate and they were all leaving immediately for the north . . . She hoped so much to be able to join them later but at the moment, as they would understand, her aunt did not feel that she could spare her . . . She would post this letter on her way through London and remained their disappointed but affectionate Harriet.

This done, she stood bravely in line for a cab and when her turn came, gave the driver the address of the Century Theatre in Bloomsbury.

*

There were seventeen swans, an uneven number and a pity, but the mother of a girl Dubrov had engaged from the Lumley School of Dance in Regent Street had gone to Dr Mudie's Library and looked up the Amazon in *Chambers' Encyclopaedia* – and that had been that.

Now, in the dirty, draughty and near-derelict theatre in Bloomsbury he had hired for the last week prior to the Company's departure, Dubrov was watching his *maître de ballet* rehearsing the *corps* in Act Two of *Swan Lake*. The moonlit act . . . the white act . . . the act in which the ravishing Swan Queen, Odette, is discovered by Prince Siegfried among her protecting and encircling swans . . .

The Swan Queen, however, was at the dentist and the *premier danseur*, Maximov, who played the Prince, was not on call until four o'clock. It was the swans that were at issue and here all was far from well. For from the swans in *Swan Lake* the choreographer demands not individuality or self-expression but a relentless and perfect unison. Above all, these doomed and feathered creatures are supposed to move as one.

'Again!' said Grisha wearily, turning his white Picasso clown's face up to the heavens. 'From the second entry. Remember heads *down* on the *échappés* and when you take hands it is to the front that you must face.' He hummed, demonstrated, became – this comical wizened little man – for an instant a graceful swan. 'Can you give me five bars before section 12?' He nodded to Irina Petrova and the ancient accompanist stubbed out her cigarette in the discarded *pointe* shoe she had been using as an ashtray and lowered her mottled hands on to the piano keys.

And there's still Act Three of *Fille*, thought Dubrov, watching out front – and *Giselle* and we've scarcely touched *The Nutcracker*, with five days to go. I must be mad, taking out four full-length ballets. But he hated the chopping and dismemberment that was so fashionable – plucking out an act here, a *divertissement* there . . . And his principals were good: not just Simonova and Maximov, but Lobotsky, his character dancer, and the young Polish girl whom Simonova feared but to whom she had ceded the Sugar Plum Fairy . . .

'Cross over!' yelled Grisha. 'Both lines! And the legs are *croisé* behind you – all the legs!' His voice rose to a shriek. 'You there at the end! What is your name – Kirstin . . . *Where are you going?*'

Where the slender sad-faced Swede was going, just as in earlier

40

rehearsals, was upstage right, performing rather beautiful and mournful *ports de bras* as was invariably done at this point in the version of the ballet she had learned in Copenhagen. The petite and exquisite French girl, Marie-Claude, on the other hand, still carried a torch for the Paris Opéra version (which cut five minutes out of the Act Two running time to give the citizens time to refresh themselves) and had *bourréed* off altogether during a previous run-through to be discovered alone and puzzled in a corridor.

Even with the Russian girls who made up the bulk of the *corps* – marvellously drilled and strong-backed creatures who rightly knew that only in their country was the art of ballet seriously understood – all was not well. For the hallowed steps which Petipa and Ivanov had devised for Tchaikovsky's masterpiece in St Petersburg had been wickedly tampered with by a rogue ballet master in Moscow and little Olga Narukov, finding herself *en arabesque* opposite a swan giving her all to her *ronds de jambe*, had stamped her foot and declared her intention of returning to Ashkhabad.

The disconsolate Kirstin was comforted by the girl next to her and the rehearsal was resumed. An hour later – exhausted, hungry and dripping with perspiration – they were still practising the fiendishly difficult pattern at the end of the act where the diagonal lines of swans cross over and dissolve to form three groups: unequal groups, since the number seventeen is notoriously difficult to divide by three.

It was at this point that a stage-hand came up to Dubrov and said, 'There's a young lady asking to see you. Said you said she could come.'

'Oh?' Dubrov was puzzled. 'Well, bring her along.'

The man vanished and reappeared with a young girl in a blue coat and tam o'shanter, carrying a small suitcase. A schoolgirl, it seemed to him, with worried eyes.

'I'm Harriet Morton,' she said in her low, incorrigibly educated voice, 'from Cambridge. You saw me at Madame Lavarre's. You said . . .' Her voice tailed away. She had made a mistake; of course he had not wanted her.

'Yes.' Dubrov had recognised her now and smilingly put a hand on her arm. 'Grisha!' he called. 'Come here!'

The swans came to rest, the music stopped and Grisha, frowning at the interruption, came over to Dubrov.

'This is Harriet Morton,' said the impresario. 'Your eighteenth swan.'

The ballet master stared at her. What was he supposed to do now, at the eleventh hour, with this English child?

'I have just rearranged everything for seventeen,' he said sourly.

'Well then, rearrange it back again,' answered Dubrov.

Grisha raked her with his coal-black eyes. The height was right – she would fit in with the smaller girls and she didn't look stupid like some of the others. All the same . . .

'Which version of *Lac* is it that you have danced?' he enquired cautiously. 'Of *Swan Lake*? The Petipa-Ivanov? The Sermontoff?' and as she remained silent, 'Not that abomination that Orloffsky has made in Krakov?'

Harriet swallowed. 'I have not danced in any of them, Monsieur.'

'Not in *any* of them?' The ballet master mopped his brow. 'You are joking me?'

She shook her head.

'And *Casse-Noisette*? The last act – which production?'

'No production. I have never danced in *Casse-Noisette*.'

Grisha sighed and became placatory. Obviously the girl was so nervous she had lost her wits. 'In English it is called *The Nutcracker*. In this ballet you have been a snowflake?'

'No.'

'Or an attendant to the Sugar Plum Fairy?' Grisha continued imploringly. He broke into the 'Valse des Fleurs', revolved, swayed, became an icing-sugar rose.

Harriet shook her head once more and looked beseechingly at Dubrov. But the impresario, who seemed to be enjoying himself, was staring at the ceiling.

'But a Wili?' persisted Grisha desperately. 'A Wili in *Giselle*?' And making a final bid, 'A chicken, then? In *Fille Mal Gardée*, a little chicken?' A broken man, he executed a few rapid and chicken-like *échappés*.

Harriet lifted her head and in a voice she just managed to hold steady said, 'I have never danced on any stage before.'

A strangled sound came from Grisha. 'Impossible,' he managed to say. 'It is impossible! In five days we leave.'

She made no attempt to entreat or argue, but he saw her bring her small white teeth down on to her lower lip to stop it trembling, and then she bent down to pick up her case.

Grisha swore lustily in Russian. 'You have your *pointe* shoes with you?'

'Yes.'

'Then put them on. And hurry!'

*

'On the programme you will appear as Natasha Alexandrovna,' said Dubrov to Harriet as she sat opposite him in his office, a shawl over her practice dress. 'Dancers cannot have English names.'

'Natasha! Oh . . .' She leaned forward, her eyes alight and on her face the memory still of that terrifying, gruelling, awful and marvellous hour she had just spent on stage.

'Why? Because of *War and Peace*?'

'Yes. I used . . . oh, to *be* Natasha, for years and years. It made me so angry with Prince Andrei.'

'Angry!' Dubrov glared at her. 'What are you saying? Prince Andrei is the finest portrayal of goodness in our entire literature.'

'Goodness? How can it be good to get someone so ready for love and for life . . . so absolutely ready – and then just go away and leave them? Like setting them some kind of good conduct exam!'

'An exam which, however, she failed.'

'How could she *help* failing!' Harriet leaned forward, flushed. 'When you are so ready and longing, and the person you love just goes. He didn't have to go – it wasn't the war.' She broke off, suddenly aghast at her impertinence; she had never spoken like this in Scroope Terrace. 'I'm sorry.'

Dubrov waved away her apology. 'Not at all – Smetlikov, one of our critics, takes a very similar view. However, we must get down to business. You will attend class every morning at ten. The rest of the time you will work to learn the *corps de ballet* roles. There are five days to do this and of course the voyage. It is impossible. You will do it.'

'Yes.'

He looked up, to see again that extraordinary illumination of her face from within which had followed Grisha's order to put on her dancing shoes. To be told to do the impossible seemed to be all that she desired.

'The tour is extended. We shall go on to Lima and Caracas, so we will be away all summer.' And as she nodded, 'Have you somewhere to stay?'

She flushed. 'Well, no, not actually. I was wondering if I could sleep in the dressing-room just until we sail?'

'Impossible.' He sighed. 'I will speak to one of the girls – perhaps

43

Marie-Claude or Kirstin will find room for you in their lodgings. You have money?'

'A little.'

'Good.' He put the tips of his plump fingers together and said reflectively, 'Of course, if someone should come here and ask me if I am employing a girl called Natasha Alexandrovna in my *corps de ballet*, I shall have to say "Yes". But if they ask me if I am employing a girl called Harriet Morton, that is a different matter. Of such a girl I naturally know nothing!'

'Oh . . . *Thank you!*' She paused. 'You see, my father . . . didn't exactly give me permission.'

'Yes,' said Dubrov heavily, 'I gathered this. Perhaps you should tell me . . .'

Later, meeting Grisha in the corridor, he said, 'Well, how is she, my little protégée?'

Grisha shrugged. 'It is a pity. But there; it is only their horses that the British train properly. And now it's too late . . . I think?' He pondered and added. '*Elle est sérieuse.*'

Serious. Not lacking in humour; not pompous or self-important, but serious – giving the job the full weight of her being.

Dubrov nodded and passed on.

*

The principal dancers, unlike the rest of the Company who were in lodgings or hostels, were accommodated in the Queen's Hotel in Bloomsbury until their date of departure: a draughty place with dingy lace curtains and terrible food, but handy for the theatre and where the proprietors were friendly and accustomed to the vagaries of their foreign guests.

In this hotel, as in all the others where the dancers had stayed, Dubrov's room adjoined that of the ballerina, Galina Simonova. Since Simonova's views on 'passion as an aid to the dance' were well-known, it might be concluded that Dubrov enjoyed what were technically known as conjugal rights, and this was so. Dubrov's rights, however, were granted to him on such uncertain terms – were so dependent on the state of Simonova's back, her Achilles tendon and her reviews – that he had learned to temper the wind to the shorn lamb in a way which was not unremarkable in a man who had once written a ninety-stanza poem in the style of Pushkin entitled *Eros Proclaimed*.

44

The evening of Harriet's arrival at the theatre, he found Simonova lying on the sofa – an ominous sign – staring with black and tormented eyes at her left knee.

'It's going again, Sashka; I can feel it! Dimitri has given me a massage, but it's no use – it's going. We must cancel the tour!'

He came over to sit beside her and felt her knee, considerably more familiar to him than his own. 'Let me see.'

Her knee, her cervical vertebrae, the bursa on her Achilles tendon . . . he knew them like men know their children and now, as his stubby fingers moved gently over the joint, he wondered for the thousandth time why fate had linked him indissolubly with this temperamental, autocratic woman.

Sitting with balletomane friends in his box in the *bel étage* at the Maryinsky in St Petersburg, he had picked her out of the *corps*. 'That one,' he had said, pointing at the row of water sprites in *Ondine*, and he was right. She became a *coryphée*, a soloist . . .

It was not difficult in those days to enjoy her favours; he was young and rich and could present her own image to her in the way that women have always found irresistible. 'If you give me half an hour to explain away my face, I could seduce the Queen of France,' said Voltaire – and Dubrov, though uninterested in royalty, could have said the same.

He bought her an apartment on the Fontanka Canal and she was moderately faithful for she was obsessed by dancing – by her career. Outside revolutions rumbled, Grand Dukes were assassinated and picked off the cobbled streets in splinters, but to Simonova it mattered only that she ended badly after her *pique* turns in *Paquita* or started her solo a bar too soon. And because it was this that he loved in her – this crazy obsession with the art that he too adored – he put up with it all, became manager, masseur, choreographer, nurse . . .

She rose steadily in the ranks of the Maryinsky. They gave her the Lilac Fairy, then Swanhilda in *Coppelia* and at last *Giselle*. After her first night in that immortal ballet, he watched one of the great clichés of the theatre brought to life – the students unharnessing the horses from her carriage in order to pull her through the streets – but later she had cried in his arms because she had not got her fall right in the Mad Scene: it was clumsy, she said, and the timing was wrong.

A year later she threw it all away in a stupid, unnecessary row with the management, refusing to wear the costume they had designed for her in *Aurora's Wedding* and appearing instead in a costume she preferred. She was fined and told to change it. She refused. No one believed it would come to anything for the hierarchical, bureaucratic theatre was full of such scenes, but Simonova with childish obstinacy forced the director to a confrontation and when she was overruled, she resigned. Resigned from the theatre she adored, from the great tradition which had nourished her, and went to Europe. And Dubrov, too, exiled himself from his homeland, sold his interests in Russia and created a company in which she could dance.

Since then they had toured Paris and Rome, Berlin and Stockholm, and it was understood between them that she hated Russia, that she would not return even if they asked her to do so on bended knees. For eight years now they had been exiles and it was hard – finding theatres, getting together a *corps*, luring soloists from other companies. Of late, too, there had been competition from other and younger dancers – from Pavlova, who had also come to Europe; from the divine Karsavina, Diaghilev's darling, who with Nijinsky had taken the West by storm. Simonova owned to thirty-six, but she was almost forty and looked it: a stark woman with hooded eyes and deep lines etched between her autocratically arched brows.

'We should never have attempted this tour,' she said now. 'It's madness.'

Fear again. It was fear, of course, that ailed her knee . . . fear of failure, of old age . . . of the new Polish dancer, Masha Repin, who had joined them three days earlier and was covering her Giselle . . .

'You have told them it is my farewell performance?' she demanded. 'Positively my last one? You have put it on the posters?'

Dubrov sighed and abandoned her knee. This was the latest fantasy – that each of her performances was the last, that she would not have to submit her ageing body to the endless torture of trying to achieve perfection any more. He knew what was coming next and now, as he moved his hand firmly to her fifth vertebra, it came.

'Soon we shall give it all up, won't we, Sashka, and go and live in Cremorra? Soon . . .'

'Yes, *dousha*, yes.'

'It will be so peaceful,' she murmured, arching her back to give him better access. 'We shall listen to the birds and have a goat and grow the best vegetables in Trentino. Won't it be wonderful?'

'Wonderful,' agreed Dubrov dully.

Three years earlier, returning from a tour of the northern cities of Italy – in one of which a critic had dared to compare Simonova unfavourably with the great Legnani – the train that had been carrying them towards the Alps had come to a sudden stop. The day was exquisite; the air, as they lowered the window, like wine. Gentle-eyed cows with bells grazed in flower-filled fields, geraniums and petunias tumbled from the window-boxes of the little houses, a blue lake shimmered in the valley.

All of which would not have mattered except that across a meadow, beside a sparkling stream, one of the toy houses proclaimed itself 'For Sale'.

To this oldest of fantasies, that of finding from a passing train the house of one's dreams, Simonova instantly responded. She seized two hat-boxes and her dressing-case, issued a torrent of instructions to her dresser and pulled Dubrov down on to the platform.

Two days later the little house in Cremorra – complete with vegetable garden, grazing for a substantial number of goats, three fretwork balconies and a chicken-house – was his.

Fortunately, in Vienna the critics were kind and it was not too often that Simonova remembered the little wooden house which a kind peasant lady was looking after. They had spent a week there the year after he bought it and Dubrov had been rather ill, for there was a glut of apricots in their delightful orchard and Simonova had made a great deal of jam which did not set. Of late, however, Cremorra was getting closer and Dubrov, to whom the idea of living permanently in the country among inimical animals and loosening fruit was horrifying, now searched his mind for a diversion.

'I employed a new girl today,' he said. 'The one I told you about in Cambridge. Sonia's pupil. She ran away to come to us, so no doubt I shall be arrested soon for luring away a minor.'

'Is she good?'

The fear again . . . but behind the panic of being overtaken, something else – the curiosity, the eagerness about the thing itself: the dance and its future.

'How could she be good? She is an amateur.'

'But Sonia taught her, you say?' They had been friends of a sort, she and Sonia who, a few years older, was already in the *corps* when Simonova joined the company. Together, infuriated by the antics of a visiting 'star', they had unloosed an ancient, wheezing pug-dog on to the stage during a ballet called *Trees* . . .

'Yes, but three times a week. Oh, you know how the British are about the arts – the gentility, the snobbery. It's a pity, for if they chose

47

they could make marvellous dancers of their girls. Perhaps one day . . .'

'Why did you want her then?'

Dubrov, about to embark on the quality he had detected in Harriet – a totality and absorption – changed his mind. Simonova had started on a routine that was all too familiar – the lavish application of cold cream, the knee bandage, the wax ear-plugs to eliminate the noises of the traffic – which in about three minutes from now would result in his being chastely kissed on the forehead and dismissed.

'She has ears like Natasha's,' he said.

The ballerina spun round. 'Like *Natasha*'s? In *War and Peace*? But Tolstoy doesn't describe her ears.'

Dubrov shrugged. 'I don't need Tolstoy to tell me what her ears were like.'

It worked. The jealousy on her face was instantaneous and owed nothing to her profession. 'You are an idiot.' She put the ear-plugs back in the drawer, wiped off the cream with a piece of gauze.

'*Chort!*' she said. 'I'm tired. Let's go to bed.'

*

Harriet had always longed to be allowed to work. Now her wish was granted a hundredfold. There were constant disasters as this most unfledged of swans, this newest of snowflakes staggered across the stage. But though Harriet made mistakes, she did not make them twice.

The girls, without exception, were helpful. They themselves had only just learned to work in unison, but they counted for her, pushed her, pulled her and retrieved her from inhospitable corners of the stage. Even Olga Narukov – a spitfire from the borders of Afghanistan who thought nothing of felling a dancer who displeased her with a kick like a mule's – kept her temper with Harriet, for the newcomer's grit and humility were curiously disarming.

'Follow the girl in front!' Grisha yelled at Harriet when her musicality threatened to lead her astray. '*Just follow the girl in front!*'

The girl in front, when the *corps* was arranged by height, was the French girl Marie-Claude, and there could be no one more worthy of being followed.

The creation of brown-eyed blondes has long been regarded as one of God's better ideas. Marie-Claude's eyes were huge and velvety, her lashes like scimitars, her upturned mouth voluptuously curved. To

48

this largesse had been added waist-length golden, curling hair which, had she chosen to sit on a rock brushing it, must have sent every sailor within miles plunging to his doom.

Marie-Claude, however, did not so choose. She was entirely faithful to her fiancé, a young chef who worked in an hotel in Montpellier, and though occasionally willing (if the price was right) to emerge from a seashell at the Trocadero or sit on a swing in some night-club clad only in her hair, she did so strictly to earn money for the restaurant which she and Vincent, as soon as they had saved enough, were proposing to open in the hills above Nice.

It was Marie-Claude and the Swedish girl, Kirstin, who found space for Harriet in the tiny room they shared in a hostel in Gray's Inn Road. It was already crammed full with their two truckle-beds, but the good-natured warden put a mattress on the floor for Harriet. The confusion and clutter were indescribable but to Harriet – used to the solitude and icy hygiene of her bedroom in Scroope Terrace – everything was a delight.

From her new room-mates Harriet learned a great deal about the Company. That the Russian girls were on summer leave from their dancing academies in Kiev and Odessa and would return to their native land in the autumn. That Simonova detested Maximov, who had once dropped her in the *grand pas de deux* at the end of *Sleeping Beauty*. That Masha Repin, the brilliant young Pole, was reputed to be sticking pins into a wax model of Simonova so that she could take over *Giselle* . . .

Neither of the girls was ambitious: of 'the dance' they asked only that it give them a living, and the fabled city of Manaus might have been Newcastle or Turin: it was somewhere they could work and be paid.

'Though there is a great deal of money to be made out there,' pointed out the practical Marie-Claude. 'Vincent's cousin works as a chef to an important man in Rio and he sends back enormous sums to Montpellier.'

Kirstin had been put to dancing by her father – a ballet master who worked in Scandinavia and London – and Marie-Claude by her half-English mother, an opera dancer who had been undulating between two camels in an open-air production of *Aïda* when a young farmer from the Languedoc decided to remove and marry her. Though only two years older than Harriet, their attitude towards the English girl was that of two worldly and experienced aunts.

49

'It must be incredible, being so beautiful,' said Harriet now, overawed by the sight of Marie-Claude in her shift preparing for bed.

'Not at all,' said the French girl dismissively. 'Until I met Vincent it was extremely disagreeable. From the age of six I had to go everywhere with a hat-pin – a very long one from my Tante Berthe's Sunday hat. Even so, it wasn't always so simple. For example, when I was fifteen there was an old gentleman who used to wait for me outside school and offer to give a thousand francs to the Red Cross if I would let him see me brush my hair. Obviously, simply to jab a hat-pin into such an old gentleman would not have been correct. It is, after all, a very good cause – the Red Cross. But now I have Vincent and everything is—'. She broke off to look aghast at the voluminous flannel nightdress which Harriet was pulling over her head. ' 'arriette, what is that that you have there?' she enquired, her excellent English fracturing under the shock.

'It's all I have,' said Harriet ruefully. 'My Aunt Louisa chose it.'

Marie-Claude deliberated. 'Perhaps if you undid the top button . . . and pushed up the sleeves, *comme ça?*'

'But I'm only going to bed.'

Kirstin, who had been rubbing methylated spirit into her slender feet, pushed back her straight pale hair and exchanged a glance with Marie-Claude.

'Only?' said Marie-Claude, speaking for them both.

But long after the other two were asleep Harriet, the top button of her nightdress obediently undone, sat up on her mattress recalling the day. She had escaped but she was not yet safe; a knock at the door could mean a policeman, recapture and the misery of a life which, now she had tasted freedom, she felt she could not endure again. Yet presently she found her fingers involuntarily marking out the steps in the snowflake waltz they had gone through at the last rehearsal, using instinctively the curious shorthand – a kind of deaf-and-dumb language – that dancers employ . . . And waking at dawn, she rose and in the deserted dining-room of the hostel, among the stacked chairs, she practised.

She practised on the top of the Number 15 bus going to the theatre, marking the steps with the tips of her toes beneath the seat; she practised in the tea-shop to which the others dragged her, hanging on to the edge of the table until her doughnut came. She danced with her bruised and bleeding feet, with her fingers, inside her head . . . and on the third day Dubrov, encountering her as she walked backwards up

50

the iron stairs to the dressing-room in order to ease the aching muscles of her calves, smiled happily. He liked that; he liked it very much.

There was everything to learn: how to put on make-up, how to allow space at rehearsal between herself and the others which later the costumes would fill . . . How to anoint and darn and squeeze and thump the ballet shoes which seemed to be as often on the girls' hands as on their feet.

But it was class that made Harriet into a dancer. Class, that unfailing daily torture to which dancers come on every morning of their lives. Class in freezing rehearsal rooms, in foyers, on board ocean liners carrying them across the sea. Class with streaming colds, class after their lovers have jilted them, on days when women would give anything to be spared . . . Class for the *prima ballerina assoluta* as for the youngest member of the *corps*.

It was in class that Harriet saw what it cost Lubotsky, the ageing character dancer, to get his muscles to warm up – yet saw too the marvellous authority he still carried. It was in class that she saw Maximov – the darling of the gallery – sweating, exhausted, crying out with the pain of a wrenched muscle . . . saw the grace and spirituality emanating from little Olga Narukov who ten minutes earlier had pinched a boy from the *corps* so as to draw blood.

And if Harriet watched the others, there were those who watched her. For even in class there are those who dance the notes and those who dance the music and, 'A pity, yes, definitely a pity,' said Grisha with increasing emphasis when Dubrov enquired after his latest swan.

*

It was not until two days before they sailed that Harriet saw the *prima ballerina* of the Company, for Simonova had been attending class privately with an old Russian émigré in Pimlico. She arrived for her first rehearsal with the *corps* on a grey drizzly morning, sweeping on to the stage in a ragged practice tutu set off by purple leg-warmers with holes in them. Her cheek was swollen from the ministrations of her dentist, her complexion was sallow; a muffler of the kind that old gentlemen wear when running along tow-paths during boat-races concealed her throat. Beneath her widow's peak, with the centre parting that is the hallmark of the ballerina, her black eyes with their pouches of exhaustion, her high-bridged nose and thin mouth gave her the look of a distempered bird of prey.

51

To Harriet, all this was quite irrelevant. 'She is a true *artiste*,' Madame Lavarre had said and Harriet's eyes shone with veneration.

Simonova raked the assembled girls and her eyes fell on Harriet. 'Who is that?' she demanded in her guttural and alarming voice.

Dubrov, who knew that she knew perfectly well who it was, introduced Harriet who curtseyed deeply. For a moment they gazed at each other – the ardent, worshipping girl and the weary, autocratic woman. Then, 'There is nothing in the least unusual about her ears,' pronounced Simonova in Russian, to the mystification of those who spoke the language.

She went over to the piano, unwound her muffler, handed her medallion of St Demetrius to the accompanist – and raised her eyebrows at Grisha.

'Act One, *Giselle*,' he confirmed. 'From the entry of the hunting party . . .'

Everyone had expected Simonova simply to mark her steps. This was a routine rehearsal to give the *corps* their positions in relation to hers; she would rehearse seriously with Maximov later.

But she did not. Simonova, on that grey and drizzly morning in a draughty tumbledown London theatre, danced. She danced fully, absolutely – danced as if she were back on the stage of the Maryinsky and the Tsar was in his blue and golden box. No, better than that – she danced as if she were alone in the world and had only this gift to pour into the heartbreaking emptiness.

And in the theatre for the first time there was real excitement; the mottled hands of grumpy old Irina Petrovna coaxed from the tinny piano some approximation to the delicious score, and Dubrov – who alone knew why she had done it – remembered not only that he loved this ageing, difficult woman, but *why* . . .

By midnight on Thursday the last of the props had been packed up and piled into the carts to go to Euston Station. The following morning, the sleepy girls followed the principals on to the train and late that afternoon, Harriet walked with unforgettable excitement up the gangway of the RMS *Cardinal* with her slim dark funnel and snow-white decks.

'Come, let's find our cabins,' said Marie-Claude.

But Harriet could not tear herself away from the movement and bustle of the docks, from the tangle of cranes and masts, the cries of men loading the freight and hung, huge-eyed and entranced, over the side. Here, now swinging high over the deck and dropping into the hold, was the wicker skip that she had sat on the night before so that the stage-hands could fasten the straps . . . and here the tarpaulin they had tied round the Act Two flats for *Fille*.

It was fortunate that she did not observe another, impressively strapped wicker basket waiting on the quay – a basket which had been unloaded earlier and contained three dozen silk shirts bound for Truscott and Musgrave in Piccadilly. For of gentlemen who sent back their shirts to Britain to be laundered, Harriet did not and could not approve.

A man with a megaphone came by, instructing visitors to leave the ship; a single hoot from the slender funnel announced their imminent departure.

It was only when she saw the ever-widening strip of grey and dirty water between herself and the shore that Harriet realised she had done it. She was safe.

CHAPTER FOUR

A SOFT breeze rustled the palm trees in front of the Palace of Justice; the flock of parakeets which had roosted on the equestrian statue of Pedro II flew noisily towards the river – and day broke across the Golden City. The cathedral bell tolled for mass; the first tram clanked out of the depot. Maids in coloured bandannas emerged from the great houses in the Avenida Eduardo Ribero, bound for the arcaded fish-market. A procession of tiny orphans in black overalls crossed a cobbled square. One by one the shutters went up on the shops with their exotic, crazily-priced wares from Europe: milliners and jewellers; delicatessens and patisseries . . .

Down by the docks the men arrived and began to load the balls of black rubber which were piled on the quayside. The fast-dying breeze sent a gentle oriental music through the rigging of the luxurious yachts crowded along the floating landing-stage; from the crazily-patched and painted dug-outs of the Indians on the harbour's fringe came the smell of hot cooking-oil and coffee. A uniformed official unlocked the ornate gates of the yellow customs house and on RMS *Cardinal*, at rest after her five-week voyage from Liverpool, sailors were scrubbing the already immaculate white decks.

But though this day began like all others, it was no ordinary day. Tonight the Opera House which presided over Manaus like a great benevolent dowager would blaze with light. Tonight carriages and automobiles would sweep across the dizzying mosaic square in front of the theatre and disgorge brilliantly dressed women and bemedalled men beneath the floodlit pink and white façade. Tonight there would be receptions and dinners; every café would be full to overflowing; every hotel room had been secured months ago. For tonight the Dubrov Ballet Company was opening in *Swan Lake*, and for the

54

homesick Europeans and the culture-hungry Brazilians there would be moonlit glades and Tchaikovsky's immortal music and Simonova's celebrated interpretation of Odette.

In the turreted stucco villa which she had christened 'The Retreat', young Mrs Bennett surveyed the blue silk gown which she had laid out on the bed, the matching shoes. The blue was right with her eyes, but should she wear the pearls or the sapphires? The sapphires would seem to be the obvious choice, but Mrs Lehmann's sapphires were so much bigger and better and the Lehmanns had the box next to theirs. 'The pearls, I think, Concepcion,' she said to her maid, a *cabacla* – half-Indian, half-Portuguese – with caring eyes. And her husband Jock, coming to kiss her good-bye, smiled with relief for today at least he would not come home to find her weeping over Peter's photograph or staring with red-rimmed eyes at a letter with its childish scrawl. Of course the boy was homesick, of course seven was young to be sent so far away. But what could one do? A British boy had to go to a decent school – and anyway, you couldn't bring up a child in this climate.

Still, today at least Lilian would be occupied. He himself did not care for ballet, but as he climbed into his carriage and was conveyed to his office on the quayside, Jock Bennett blessed the Dubrov Ballet Company from the bottom of his heart.

Unlike Jock Bennett, the six-foot-tall and massively bearded Count Sternov was a passionate balletomane and since dawn had roamed through the long, low house – which he had had built in imitation of his parents' *dacha* on the Volga – in a state of exaltation.

'I shall never forget her first *Giselle* – never,' he said to the Countess. 'The year before she left Russia. That unsupported *adage* in the last act!'

'That was the time they found Dalguruky in the back of the box making love to the governess, do you remember?'

The Countess was in her dressing-gown. She seldom dressed before the afternoon, the heat did not suit her and her *cris des nerfs* were famous, but today she was happy. Today it would end as it had so often ended in St Petersburg, discussing the finer points of a *cabriole* in a lighted theatre . . . and the next day was the party for the cast at Follina, that fantastic riverside *palazzo* where everything that mattered out here took place. And there will be girls, thought the Count happily – young, lovely *Russian* girls . . .

The girls were uppermost in the mind of Colonel de Silva, the

Prefect of Police, glancing at the clock in his office to see if it was time to go home and change. His scrawny domineering wife could stop him talking to them, stop him sending them flowers; she could drag him back to his carriage with her hand dug into his arm the second the curtain went down, but she couldn't stop him *seeing* them – their legs, their thighs, their throats – thought the grateful Colonel, rescinding the death warrant of a bandit who had turned out to be a distant relative. Opera was better for bosoms and hips, but in ballet one *saw* more.

By the afternoon a veritable armada of small craft had begun to converge on the city. From the far shore of the River Negro, some ten miles across, came Dr Zugheimer and his wife, sitting erect in the bows of the *Louisa*, already in their evening clothes. The bespectacled Herr Doktor, a paternalistic employer who had put his *seringueiros* into uniform, thirsted for *Lohengrin* or *Parsifal*, but no one missed an opening night at the Teatro Amazonas and the blue eyes of his plump wife – who spent her lonely mornings struggling to turn the pulpy mangoes and guavas of the tropics into the firm and bread-crumbed *Knödel* of her native land, shone with excitement. Opera, ballet or farce . . . what did it matter? Tonight there would be gossip, companionship, laughter.

A launch chartered by the Amazonian Timber Company at Boa Vista disgorged twenty of their employees, who made their way into the town carrying their evening clothes under their arms. The mission boat belonging to the Silesian Brothers at Santa Maria brought Father Joseph and Father Anselm, who knew that all art was for the glory of God and had made sure of excellent seats in the stalls.

The cafés were now filling up. A party of lady schoolteachers from a select seminary in Santarém, offered the choice of sleeping in the street or in Madam Anita's brothel, sensibly chose the brothel. The captain of the *Oriana* escorted two massive, middle-aged Baltic princesses, (on a round trip from Lisbon) down the gangway and into the car sent by the Mayor.

And now the lights were going up. Lights beneath the frieze of gods and goddesses on the Opera House façade; lights in the tall street-lamps lining the square. Lights in the blue and green *art nouveau* foyer; in the candelabra between the Carrera marble columns of the upstairs promenade . . . Lights limning the tiers of white and golden boxes; pouring down from the great eight-pointed chandelier on de Angeli's frescoed ceiling with its swirling muses of Poetry, Music and Art . . .

Light, now, sparkling and dancing on the tiaras of the women as they entered; on the diamond and sapphire choker of Mrs John P. Lehmann, on Colonel de Silva's Brazilian Star . . .

The seats were filling up; row upon row of bejewelled bosoms, of bemedalled chests. The stout Baltic princesses entered the canopied box reserved for the President and stood, dowdy and gracious, bestowing kind waves. In the orchestra pit, the musicians were ready.

But the performance could not begin yet; all the citizens of Manaus were aware of that. For the box next to that of the President was still empty – the box that belonged to Mr Verney, the chairman of the Opera House trustees. Until Rom Verney came from Follina the curtain would stay lowered – and knowing this, the audience settled down to wait.

*

Verney woke early, as he always did, on the morning of the gala; he stretched in the great *jaruna* wood bed and pushed aside the cloud of white mosquito netting to go to the French windows and look out on his garden.

There was no garden like it in all of Amazonia. Only the gardens of the Moghul emperors – of Akbar and his heirs – had the same vision, the same panache. Only those despots – like this wealthiest of all the rubber barons – had the tenacity and labour to make real their dreams.

On the terrace below him, orchids and hibiscus and the dizzying scarlet flame-flowers which the humming birds loved to visit rioted in flamboyant exuberance from their urns, but elsewhere he had maintained a savage discipline on the fast-growing plants. In the avenue of jacarandas, shiveringly blue, which stretched to the distant river, each tree grew distinct and unimpeded. Beneath the catalpas in his arboretum he had planted only the white, star-petalled clerodendron, so that the trees seemed to grow from a drift of scented snow.

By the aviary which his Indians, somewhat to his dismay, had built for him when he was absent on a journey, Manuelo was already sweeping the paths. Two other Indians worked by the pool with its golden water-lilies, scraping derris root into the water against mosquitoes. Old Iquita, Manuelo's mother-in-law, wearing a frilled petticoat left behind by an opera singer whose favours he had enjoyed, and a boa of anaconda skins, was poking her forked stick into a flower bed, busy with her self-appointed task of keeping his garden free from

57

snakes. From the patch of forest behind the house, deliberately left untouched, where his Indians built their village, came the faint, disembodied sound of Dame Nellie Melba singing the 'Bell Song' from *Lakmé*. However many records he bought them, this remained their favourite.

He showered, slipped on a khaki shirt and trousers and made his way downstairs – a most un-English-looking Englishman, lithe and dark-skinned, his black hair (though he was not yet thirty) exotically streaked with silver – to be waylaid as he crossed the terrace by the first of the many animals to whom he offered the hospitality of his home: a coatimundi with a great bushy tail who jumped off a chair and demanded to be stroked.

Moving on down the steps, Verney made his way between banks of glossy-leaved gardenias, through a trellised arcade of jasmine and passion flowers, towards the orchard where he grew mangoes and plantains and avocados to feed his workers. He missed nothing – a new patch of fungus, an infinitesimal split in the stem of a pineapple, a procession of ants endeavouring to set up a colony in his coffee bushes – all were instantly observed and silently assessed. And the little nose bear trotted along behind him, for this morning inspection of the estate was something which the coati regarded as very much his affair.

As he came to the bridge over one of the many *igarapes* that flowed through his land, an aged blue and yellow macaw flopped from an acacia branch on to his shoulder and screamed at the coati in jealous rage. The river was close by now, with his boats: the schooner *Amethyst*, which he used to convey guests to and from Manaus; the *Daisy May*, a converted gun-boat he had stripped almost to the hull to carry his botanical specimens . . . And the first boat he had ever owned, the little *Firefly*, rakish and indestructible, beside the dug-outs of his Indians.

It was in the *Firefly* on a morning such as this that he had found Follina.

He had been beating his way up the mazed waterways of the Negro during his second year on the Amazon when he found, between two floating islands, the hidden entrance to a river. A light, clear river down which he travelled for perhaps a mile, entranced by the skimming kingfishers, the otters playing round his boat – and pulling into a sand-bank, he tied up to a cassia entirely covered in rich gold blossoms.

At first there was just the feeling that the jungle here was less dark, less pressing than elsewhere. Then, wandering along the edge of a sand-bar, he had come across a ruined jetty and in growing excitement found as he edged along it a clearing on which the sun shone as benignly as if it were England – and in the clearing, half-ruined but with its walls still standing, a house. Only not a house, really: a small, Italianate, pink-washed *palazzo* with a colonnaded terrace running its length; the remnants of carved pillars and stone statues still lying where they had fallen.

It had taken Verney nearly a year to trace anyone who could authorise a sale, but at last he found the descendants of Antonio Rinaldi, the visionary or madman who had come to Brazil at the beginning of the previous century, struck gold in Ouro Preto and come north to the Amazon to build – six thousand miles from Italy – the *palazzo* of his native village, Follina.

Rinaldi had planted the avenue of jacarandas, the grove of hardwood trees. Verney – excavating, replanting, clearing – had achieved in eight years what in a temperate climate would have taken him eighty.

Before ever he came to Brazil, Verney had read the great Cervantes' description of the New World and what it stood for to those settlers who came there first from Europe. '*The refuge of all the poor devils of Spain, the sanctuary of the bankrupt, the safeguard of murderers, the promised land for ladies of easy virtue . . . a lure and disillusionment for the many – and an incomparable remedy for the few.*'

Verney had been one of the few. Fleeing his homeland, heartsick and savage, he had indeed found this country an 'incomparable remedy'. He had succeeded beyond his childish dreams; neither the heat nor the danger from disease nor the enmity of those whose policies he opposed troubled him, and the jungle which others feared or loathed had showered him with benisons. Yet now, passing the creeper-clad huts which housed his generators and ice-machine, he put up a hand to pull down the heavy yellow pod of a *cacao* tree – and in an instant everything before him vanished and he was back in the orchard at Stavely. It was late October, the frost had turned the long grass into silvered spears and he was reaching out for one last apple hanging on the bare bough: an Orange Pippin with its flushed and lightly-wrinkled skin.

Once they came, these images of England, it was best to let them have their way . . . to let himself walk through the beech copse where the pheasants strutted on the russet leaves . . . to ride out between Stavely's April hedges or climb, wind-buffeted, up the steep turf path to the Barrows while the black dog played God among the scuttling rabbits.

And soon it was over – this sudden burst of longing, not for England's customs and manners, but for the physical look of her countryside – and he was aware again of the heat on his back, the whirr of the cicadas and the coati peering at him expectantly from a clump of osiers.

'Yes, you're quite right; it's time for breakfast,' said Rom, and turning away from the river he made his way back to the house.

*

He had been christened Romain Paul Verney Brandon, but the Frenchified Christian name had been too much for the locals. He was known always as Rom – and for the first nineteen years of his life the woods and fields of Stavely were his heritage and his delight.

He was the son of General Brandon by the General's late second marriage to the beautiful foreign singer, Toussia Kandinsky: a most unnecessary marriage, the County thought it, having planned for the General – who was already well into middle age – a decorous widowerhood. He was, after all, not alone – there was his five-year-old son, young Henry Alexander, a sensible child who would make Stavely an excellent heir.

But the General, a distinguished soldier who had shown enormous personal courage during the bitter Afghanistan Wars and risked his life even more spectacularly during his leaves while pursuing rare plants in the cracks and crevices of the Karakorum mountains, failed to oblige them.

Eighteen months after the death of his wife, he went to a flower show in London and afterwards allowed a musical acquaintance to take him to a concert where a half-French, half-Russian singer was giving a recital of *Lieder*. The General did not care greatly for the *Lieder*, but for the woman who sang them he conceived a romantic passion which ended only with her death.

Toussia Kandinsky was in her thirties – a mature, warm woman with sad dark eyes, an extraordinarily beautiful mouth and one feature which made her face spectacular: hair which since the age of twenty had been as white as snow.

They married – the cosmopolitan woman with a tragic past (her father had died in a Tsarist jail) and the seemingly conventional British soldier, and he took her back to Stavely, where the County did their best with a woman who did not hunt but could be seen speaking to the horses tenderly in French, who used the Music Room for music and filled the Gallery with paintings by those mad and immoral Impressionists.

Gossip about the new Mrs Brandon inevitably abounded, but even the most virulent of her detractors had to admit that she was exceptionally good to her stepson. She spent hours with young Henry Alexander, read to him, played with him, took him about with her and celebrated his seventh birthhday with a party that was talked about for years. When her own son was born the following year, both she and the General redoubled their attentions to Stavely's heir. The day after Rom's birth, there appeared in the stables a white pony for Henry that a prince of the blood would have been proud to own.

No, it was Rom himself who did the damage, who ate into poor Henry's soul. A dark-skinned, quicksilver chilld with high cheekbones and the flared nostrils that are supposed to denote genius or temper (and generally both), he had inherited also the thick, ink-black hair which had been his mother's in her girlhood and her passionate mouth. Had it not been for the General's wide grey eyes looking out of the child's intense, exotic face, the County would have been inclined to wonder.

For it was not only Rom's appearance that was dramatic. The child, brought down by his nurse to the drawing-room at teatime, would throw his arms round his parents – round both of them – and speak to them of love. 'I love you as much as the sun and the moon and the stars,' the three-year-old Rom said to his mother in the presence of Mrs Farquharson who had come about the Red Cross Fête; and Henry, a decent, well-brought-up British boy, had to stand by and endure the shame.

Again and again, Henry's despised half-brother revealed his 'foreignness'. Rom chattered in French as easily as in English; he asked – he actually *asked* – to play the violin, and though Henry knew that forestry was respectable and that his father's plant-hunting trips were nothing to hide, to see Rom helping the gardeners to plant *flowers* was almost more than he could bear.

And then, just when Henry had consoled himself by utterly despising the outlandish half-brother who seemed to have no idea how to conduct himself, Rom would confound him by some spectacular act of courage, climbing fearlessly to the top of a tree so slender that even under Rom's light weight it bent and swayed as if it must break. It was Rom, not Henry (though he too was present) who jumped into the river by the mill-race to try to rescue a little village girl who had played too near the water's edge – and even then Rom couldn't behave like other children, for when he would have been a hero he lay down in front of the church door refusing to go inside because 'God shouldn't have let Dorcas drown'. It was Rom who found the black dog, snarling and wild, with his leg in a trap and who risked rabies and heaven-knows-what to free him – and soon Henry, dutifully walking his hound puppies, had the mortification of hearing Rom's wonder dog – with his intelligence and fidelity – spoken of wherever he went. It was Rom – not Henry, the eldest son, the heir – who smelled burning one wild night in October and led the white Arab – Henry's own horse, rearing and terrified – to safety.

No wonder Henry hated his younger brother, but there was nothing anyone could do. Mrs Brandon's efforts to shower her stepson with attentions began to border on the ludicrous; the General never betrayed by one flicker of his wise grey eyes that his younger son held his heart. Rom himself, at the beginning, looked up to Henry and longed for his companionship. It was useless. The jealousy that enslaved Henry was the stuff of myth and legend, and it grew stronger every year.

Then, when Rom was almost eleven, fate stepped in on Henry's side. Mrs Brandon fell ill; leukaemia was diagnosed and six months later she was dead.

'Hadn't you better pull yourself together?' said Henry (recalled from his last term at Eton for the funeral) to Rom, sobbing wildly in his mother's empty room – and stepped back hastily, for he thought that Rom was about to spring at him and take him by the throat.

Instead Rom vanished with his dog, managing to go to ground in the Suffolk countryside as though it was indeed the Amazon in whose imagined jungles he had so often played.

When he came back he was different – quieter, less 'excessive'. He had learned to consume his own smoke, but for the rest of his life he responded to loss not with grief but with a fierce and inward anger.

It was now that Henry was able to express a little of his hatred. The General, unable to bear Stavely without his wife, left for the Himalayas on an extended botanical expedition and Henry the heir – now home from school for good – began to issue orders that were obeyed. Rom's dog was forbidden the house; his unsuitable friends – children of the village whose games he had led – were banished. Most of the servants were loyal to the younger child and Nannie, now retired and living in the Lodge, had never been able to conceal her love for the 'little foreigner', but there were others – notably Grunthorpe the first footman, whom Rom had surprised in the gun-room stealing boxes of cartridges to sell in the local town – who were only too glad to ingratiate themselves with the heir.

Henry's triumph, however, was short-lived. The General returned; Rom was restored to his rightful place and presently he followed his brother to Eton, where he was safe from Henry's tricks.

And then, in the year when Rom became eighteen, Isobel Hope and her widowed mother came to live in the village next to Stavely.

Isobel's connections were aristocratic – her mother was the youngest daughter of the Earl of Lexbury; her father, who had died in the hunting field, had belonged to an ancient West Country family – but she was poor. As a small child Isobel had seen the great Lexbury estate go under the hammer, and her handsome father had lived on his Army pay and promises. Even before she met Henry, this lovely girl had decided that Stavely's heir would make her a suitable husband.

She met him first at a ball in a neighbouring house, but standing beside Henry on the grand staircase, relaxed and at ease, was his younger brother . . . and that was that.

The love that blazed between Rom and Isobel was violent, passionate and total. They met to ride at dawn, Isobel eluding all attempts at chaperonage, and were together again by noon to play tennis, wander through the gardens or chase each other through the maze. To watch them together was almost to gasp at their happiness; no one who saw them that summer ever quite forgot them. 'A striking couple', 'a handsome pair', 'meant for each other' – none of the phrases that people used came anywhere near the image of those two: the slender girl with her shower of dark red hair, her deep blue eyes; the incorrigibly graceful, brilliant boy.

Rom had won a scholarship to Oxford, but he persuaded his father to let him stay at Stavely. He had inherited the General's passion for trees and together they planned plantations, discussed rare hard-woods, spoke of a sawmill to supply the cabinet trade . . .

When Rom was nineteen he and Isobel became engaged. It was now that the General sent for them and told them of the will he

63

proposed to make. Stavely was not entailed, but there was no question of disinheriting his eldest son. Henry would have Stavely Hall, its gardens and orchards, the Home Park . . . To Rom he would leave the two outlying farms – Millpond and The Grebe – the North Plantation and Paradise Farm itself.

Rom was overjoyed, for he had an intense and imaginative passion for land, and Isobel, though she still yearned for Stavely itself, was satisfied, for Paradise was a perfect Palladian house, pillared and porticoed, built by an earlier and wealthy Mrs Brandon who had not cared for her daughter-in-law. Unless poor Henry married an outstanding woman – and this was not likely – Isobel knew she could soon make Paradise the social centre of the estate.

Three months later the General died of a heart attack, sitting in a chair with a bundle of Toussia's letters in his hand. When the funeral was over they looked for the will he said he had made, but it was nowhere to be found. Curiously the solicitor he had called in had gone abroad, and his clerk knew nothing of a later document. It was thus that the old will was declared valid – the will made before Rom was born – in which every stick and stone on the estate was left to Henry.

Why did Rom do nothing to save himself, people asked later? Why didn't he insist on an enquiry or bring pressure to bear on his brother to make an equitable division?

It was pride of course, the fierce pride of the gifted and strong who will take nothing from anyone; perhaps also the knowledge that if Henry had practised any kind of fraud the mills of God would grind him more surely than Rom could hope to do. But there was something else, something that Henry saw with a puzzled fury – a kind of exaltation, a glittering excitement at being stripped thus to the bone. To begin again somewhere else, to pit himself against the world, to make a fortune and a place for Isobel that owed nothing to privilege and class was a challenge to which Rom's passionate nature rose with a kind of joy.

'We'll start again somewhere quite different – somewhere in the New World. I shall build you a house fifteen times as grand as Stavely, you'll see!'

'Oh, Rom – in that wretched Amazon of yours!'

'No.' But he smiled, for one cannot entirely choose one's obsessions and since his ninth birthday his had been that vast, wild place of mazed rivers and impenetrable jungle. 'There's a fortune to be made there, but you would hate the climate. In North America – California, perhaps. Or Canada – wherever you please!'

He stretched out his hands to her, for he no more doubted her than he doubted his own right arm, but she shook her head. Isobel had seen her mother humbled when the great Lexbury estate was broken up. She was afraid – and she wanted Stavely.

Thus it was Isobel who succeeded where Henry had failed; it was she who broke Rom. A month after the General's death, she withdrew from her engagement. That night Rom found her in the Orangery with Henry and knew what she would do.

The next day he was gone and nobody at Stavely ever heard from him again.

*

Crossing the courtyard behind the house with the coati at his heels, Rom's way was barred by Lorenzo, his butler and general factotum, beaming with pleasure and surrounded by a cluster of indoor servants who had left their preparations for tomorrow's party for the ballet company in order to share their master's impending joy.

'It has come, *Coronel*!' said Lorenzo, throwing out an annunciatory arm. 'Roderigo has sent word from São Gabriel and Furo has gone to fetch it in the truck.'

There was no need for Rom to ask *what* had come. Follina was connected by a rough road, passable by motor in the dry season, to Manaus where he had his main office and warehouse. Another, much shorter track led to the tiny village of São Gabriel on the Negro where he had built a floating jetty, storehouses and a rubber smoking shed; it was there, rather than at his private landing stage, that goods for Follina were unloaded.

But though Rom could pioneer a dozen new enterprises, could import grand pianos from Germany, American motor cars, carpets from Isfahan, nothing excited his men so much as the arrival of the washing basket from Truscott and Musgrove in Piccadilly containing his freshly-laundered shirts.

To add to the stories of ludicrous and extravagant behaviour among the rubber barons had not been his intention. Mrs Lehmann who washed her carriage horses in champagne, or young Wetherby who walked a jaguar with a diamond collar through the streets, had Rom's utmost contempt. Yet unwittingly he had created a legend which outclassed them all. The travels of his laundry to and from London's most exclusive valeting service were spoken of in Rio and

65

Liverpool, in Paris and Madrid.

Rom ran Follina entirely with a native staff. He found that his Indians could be taught to do anything except perhaps to count; certainly they washed and ironed entirely to his satisfaction. His shirts travelled to England to be laundered because of a promise he had made to a generous and lovely woman and it was her memory, now, that softened his face.

Had it not been for Madeleine de la Tour, Rom's midnight flight from Stavely might have ended very differently. Arriving penniless in London, half-crazed with rage and pain, he had gone to the house of the only relative he knew his mother to possess: a distant cousin; Jacques de la Tour, who had a number of business interests and who Rom hoped might give him work.

Jacques was away on an extended tour of the East, but his wife Madeleine took Rom in. She took him in in all senses: into her house, her mind, her heart and – with marvellous flair and intelligence – into her bed. She soothed the appalling hurt that Isobel had dealt him; she civilised him and left him with a sense of gratitude that had never faded. In the end, sensing his need to start on his adventure, she insisted on lending him money for his fare to Brazil.

'Only don't turn into a savage, Romain,' she had said, standing at Euston brave as a grenadier – and much more beautiful – to see him go. 'Be particularly careful of your shirts – the starch must be just so. No thumping them on flat stones, promise?'

'I promise.'

Then the train went and she cried a little in the ladies' room and went on to the Summer Exhibition at Burlington House in a splendid herbaceous border of a hat because she was as gallant as she was good and knew that English ladies must not make a fuss.

Rom never repaid the money that she lent him. He waited two years and then went down to the Minas Gerais, that strange mineral-rich region of Brazil famous for its ornate and treasure-stocked churches, to seek out a hunchbacked craftsman who wrought precious stones into jewellery for the processional Madonnas. And a few months later a messenger arrived in Grosvenor Place and delivered a package which Madeleine opened to find – wrapped round a laundry receipt from Truscott and Musgrave – a necklace. A diamond necklace, each stone set in an intricately wrought halo of platinum, which her sensible husband – after a gasp of incredulity – fastened without too many questions around her lovely throat.

It was in an immaculate dress shirt from his laundry basket that Rom, delayed by a blocked feed-pipe on the *Amethyst*, entered his box in the Teatro Amazonas and saw – without undue excitement – the curtain rise on Act One of Tchaikovsky's ballet *Swan Lake*.

*

'I'm going to be sick,' said Harriet.

'You cannot be going to be sick again, 'arriette,' said Marie-Claude, exasperated, turning from the long mirror where the girls sat in their tutus whitening their arms, putting on false eyelashes, applying Cupid's bows to their mouths.

'I can—' said Harriet, and fled.

Act One had been called, but Act One is no business of the swans and the girls still had half an hour to complete their toilettes. It was a half-hour which Harriet did not expect to live through.

'For heaven's sake, there are *eighteen* swans in this production. Also two big swans. Also those idiot cygnets with their *pas de quatre*,' said Kirstin when Harriet returned, green and shivering. 'You don't *matter*! Why don't you tell yourself that?'

'I know I don't matter,' said Harriet – and indeed no one could have lived for eighteen years in Scroope Terrace and not known that. 'If I get it right, I don't matter. But if I get it *wrong* . . . all those people who trusted me . . . Monsieur Dubrov and everyone . . . making the company look silly.'

'You won't *get* it wrong. I'm in front of you most of the time and when it isn't me, it's Olga,' said Marie-Claude, piling up her golden hair and jabbing pins through the circlet of feathers in a way which would have driven the wardrobe mistress into fits. '*Merde*,' she said softly – and indeed the head-dresses had not travelled well. She turned and dabbed a spot of red into each corner of Harriet's eyes. 'There is no need to whiten yourself. You look like a ghost.'

'I must say, Harriet, such fear is *excessive*' said Kirstin. 'What would your Roman emperor say?'

But for once the thought of the great Marcus Aurelius did little for Harriet. The famous Stoic had experienced most of the troubles of mankind, but it was unlikely that he had ever made his debut before a thousand people as an enchanted swan.

If Dubrov's newest swan was nervous to the point of prostration, his *ballerina assoluta* was hardly in a state of calm.

'Why didn't you put it on the posters, that this was my farewell

67

appearance?' She yelled at Dubrov. 'I asked you to do it – and you promised. A simple thing like that and you can't do it!'

She was already dressed in her glittering white tutu. Beneath the shining little crown her gaunt face, trapped and desperate, was that of an old woman.

'I will announce it after the performance, *dousha*.'

He did not waste breath telling her to relax, to be quiet. There was nothing to be done about her terror; she went on stage each time as if she was going to her death. All he could do was to be there, pray that the hundred instructions he had given to his underlings would be carried out and let her rage at him.

'That cow Legnani! The first thing I shall do when I am retired is to go to Milan and slap her face!'

He sighed. Legnani, one of the world's great ballerinas, had been the first to introduce the thirty-two *fouettés* which make Act Three of *Swan Lake* so fiendishly difficult to dance, and Simonova's vendetta against her was unending.

She stopped pacing, came over, clutched him with feverish arms. 'But this is the last tour, isn't it, Sashka? Soon it will be over for good? Soon now we shall go and live in Cremorra and grow—'

But at that moment – fortunately for Dubrov, who was in no state to discuss the cultivation of vegetables – her final call came.

For Simonova, fine and experienced dancer that she was, the terror ended the moment that she went on stage. Alas, the same could not be said for Harriet.

*

Rom was not a balletomane. From his mother he had inherited a passion for the human voice and though he had refused all the other dignities that people tried to thrust on him, he had accepted the chairmanship of the Opera House trustees. To Rom fell the task of cajoling reluctant *prima donnas* from Europe; of arranging the entertainment for the cast. It was he who had taken six actors from a Spanish company to Follina to be nursed when they were stricken with yellow fever. But it was opera that held his heart and as the curtain went up on Prince Siegfried's birthday revels, the plight of this young man – Maximov in silver tights and straining cod-piece – left him relatively unmoved.

Act One is something of a prologue. The Prince is bidden by his parents to marry, but feels disinclined. Pretty girls come up to dance with him and he supports their *arabesques* with the resigned look of a conscientious meat porter steadying a side of beef. His mother gives him a cross-bow . . . the eerie music of the swan motif is heard and the Prince decides to go hunting. The curtain falls.

The second act is different. A moonlit glade . . . romantic trees . . . a lake . . . And presently, Simonova gliding on – fluttering her arms, still freeing herself from the water. A fine dancer – Rom had heard her spoken of on a visit to Paris and she deserved her praise. The Prince appears and sees her . . . he is amazed. She tells him in absurd but effective mime that she is an enchanted princess, doomed to take the shape of a swan for ever unless a prince will truly love her. *I* will love you, signals Maximov; I will . . . They go off together . . .

And now to muffled 'Ohs' and 'Ahs' from the audience, there entered the swans. In his box the Prefect of Police, de Silva, leaned forward avidly, to be jerked back by the iron hand of his wife. The Mayor, squeezed like a small black currant between the bun-like figures of the Baltic princesses, smiled happily.

And Rom picked up his high-precision Zeiss opera glasses and fixed them on the stage.

As a youth, Rom had never doubted that he would be faithful to Isobel. The whole strange concept of a Christian marriage with its oaths, its unreasonable expectation that one man and one woman can find in each other all that the human heart desires, had found an echo in his ardent and romantic soul. When Isobel betrayed him, he put away these thoughts – and the kindness of Madeleine de la Tour had been for him a bridge to another and equally ancient tradition: that of woman as an amused and amusing source of pleasure. Of women, since he had come to the Amazon, Rom asked that they should be beautiful, willing – and know the score. And perfectly fulfilling these demands were the girls of the theatre who touched down here – bringing their experience, their flair and talent for the game of dalliance. Gabriella d'Aosta, a singer in the chorus of *La Traviata*, with her black curls and great boudoir eyes . . . Little Millie Trant from Milwaukee, who had played the part of the maid in a mindless American farce – a delicious girl who had extracted more jewellery from him than he had ever bestowed on a human female and been worth every carat . . . And the russet-haired, barefoot dancer, the poor man's Isadora Duncan, whose high-mindedness had ended so delightfully after dark.

So now, though with considerably less excitement than in his former days, Rom raked his opera glasses down the line of swans.

In every chorus line there is one beauty and there now, fourth from the left and dancing with competent precision, she was. A blonde, surprising in a troupe of Russian girls, with big velvety eyes, a lovely mouth and perfectly rounded limbs. But as Rom followed her along the line of swans – nice girls, perfectly in step, doing rather fetching *emboîtés* – something peculiar happened. His extremely expensive opera glasses seemed to take on a life of their own, moving again and again to the left of the lovely creature he was pursuing in order to home in on the serious, entirely ordinary face of the girl beside her: a brown-haired, grave-eyed girl, the third from the left.

Only why? She danced with grace and musicality, but that was certainly not what had drawn him. Rather there seemed to emanate from her some extreme emotion: one that drew from him an instinctive feeling of protection and concern.

The swans had come to rest upstage, facing the audience, leaning their heads on their arms. The head of the serious brown-haired girl leaned very tenderly – she *cared* about the fate of her Queen – but Rom, watching her, saw now a faint but unmistakable trembling of her chin. She was frightened, very frightened indeed, and in an unexpected burst of empathy he saw what she was seeing – the infinite yawning gap of the auditorium with its blurred rows of potential executioners.

Her debut, then? Unlikely – Russian ballet girls were always put on the stage early . . . yet he felt it must be so. He tried to imagine her receiving a sudden summons in some dark, snowbound apartment in St Petersburg or bidding her family goodbye in a wooden house in Kiev, but none of the images fitted nor did a glance at the programme help. She might be Tatiana Volkoffsky, or Lydia Pigorsky or Natasha Alexandrovna – and she might not.

The idiot huntsmen appeared and threatened to shoot the swans and it was with considerable relief that Rom saw Simonova return and stand protectively in front of them, banishing the huntsmen with a great sweep of her arms. The third swan from the left, with her troubled eyes, had quite enough to put up with without getting shot.

Though he dutifully continued to study the blonde in the waltz that followed, Rom found himself returning rather more often than he intended to the girl beside her, checking up on her progress as might a good shepherd with a slightly wounded lamb. She was doing well; he could feel her confidence growing. She had, it occurred to him, rather a lovely throat.

But now the stage cleared, the slow, sweet strains of the solo violin rose from the orchestra – and there began the great *pas de deux* of love and plighted troth that for many people *is Swan Lake.*

Simonova had willed herself into youth. As Maximov – no meat porter now, but a manly and noble Prince – raised her from the ground, she pirouetted slowly beneath his arm . . . leaned against him in *arabesque penchée* . . . *developpé* forward to throw herself back with total trust against his chest. He lifted her high above his head, put her down again to revolve slowly *en pointe*, her free foot fluttering in little *battements.* When he held her it was by the wrists, leaving her hands free for their poignant, wing-like draping.

Thunderous applause greeted the end of the *adage* and the swans returned. To Rom it seemed that his little brown-haired swan was feeling distinctly better and he might have felt free once more to pursue 'the beauty' had he not seen at that moment a new and real danger that threatened her. A single feather had come loose from the circlet round her head and, still held at its base, trembled disconcertingly over one of her eyes.

The unfairness of this shocked Rom. She had begun to conquer her fear; she was dancing beautifully – and now this! Following her as she hopped and circled about the stage, he saw how manfully she attempted to avert disaster. Again and again her lower lip came out as she tried to blow away the offending feather, but without success.

The music was increasing in speed; the evil sorcerer, Rothbart, was making himself felt and Siegfried was hurtling about between the swans, seeking his Queen . . . He found her and now as dawn broke, they danced their farewell while the swans stood sadly by, their arms crossed over their breasts.

Not much longer to go, Rom said to her silently. *Hang on.* But as she stood there, a gust of air from the passing soloists completed the fell deed; the feather dislodged itself, fluttered upwards, descended again . . . and settled on her small and serious nose.

At which point, most understandably, she sneezed.

*

Rom might allow himself to enjoy his box alone during the performance, detesting the whispers and chatter that accompanied so much theatre-going, but in the interval he did his social duty and, making his way to the refreshment lounge, was soon the centre of a

71

group of friends – being stared at through lorgnettes by ladies who thrived on gossip about his affairs. Mrs Lehmann, permanently chagrined since he had made it clear that her obese and insufferable daughter was not destined to become mistress of Follina, nevertheless came up to tell him that he had done well to bring the Dubrov Company to Manaus. The Curtis twins, their hair up for the first time, edged closer to the exotic Mr Verney with whom, since he had procured lemonade for them at the Consulate fête, they were officially in love and were reproved by their tight-lipped Mama.

'I should have thought you would know better than to make eyes at a man who all but murdered a fellow countryman!'

'He didn't *murder* Mr Carruthers,' said Mary. 'He just threw him in the river.'

'Mr Carruthers had been ill-treating his Indians horribly,' said Alice. 'He tied them to ant-heaps and—'

'That's quite enough,' hissed Mrs Curtis, dragging her daughters past the group surrounding Verney. No doubt they would all be going on to the party at Follina on the following day, breaking the Sabbath. An orgy it would be, with every kind of carry-on. She herself would not dream of setting foot in the place, even if he should once deign to invite her! Everyone knew about his morals: opera singers and actresses! Even now he had probably picked out some girl on the stage who would stay behind when the others left and turn up next morning in the *Amethyst* with bags under her eyes and a pocket full of jewels. Disgusting, it was – absolutely disgusting!

'What did you think of the little blonde . . . you know, the fourth from the end?' asked de Silva, speaking hurriedly for his wife would return at any moment from the ladies' cloakroom.

'Charming,' said Rom, smiling at his friend. 'Though I think we should reserve judgement until tomorrow.'

'Yes,' de Silva sighed. What must it be like to know that any girl you wanted could be had for the asking? What was it about Rom? Other men were almost as wealthy, though few matched him for sheer nerve. Was it that corsair look of his, or the stories of his physical endurance – those mad journeys alone in the *Firefly*? Or just that he didn't really care one way or another?

Count Sternov arrived, bear-like and entranced, and the conversation changed to Russian.

'She is incomparable, Simonova!' said the Count. 'Incomparable! Sofka thinks her interpretation is finer than Kchessinskaya's, don't you, *coucoushka?*'

The Countess, splendid in a brocade kaftan and lopsided tiara, nodded. 'Kchessinskaya is more girlish, more frightened – but Simonova has the grandeur, the pathos . . . and *boshti moy*, those extended *arabesques!*'

'Ah, but will she manage the *fouettés?* She is no longer young.'

'She will manage them,' declared the Countess.

Young Mrs Bennett, in her blue silk gown, passed them and smiled shyly at Mr Verney. He was far too grand and important to speak to her, of course; Jock was only an accountant in the timber exporting firm of which Verney was director. But to her surprise, Verney not only bowed but came forward to address her, for he had remembered the shy little boy with the blond curls who had been everywhere with his mother.

'I was wondering if you and your husband would like to come to the party I'm giving at Follina tomorrow? It will be rather noisy, I expect, but you would be very welcome.'

'Oh!' Her big blue eyes, so like Peter's, lit up with pleasure. 'Thank you *very* much! I'll go and tell my husband.'

A party at Follina – an invitation for which the Lehmanns and the Roderiguez and that stuffy Mrs Curtis would have given their eyes! She hurried away, and for a few hours the small ghost which haunted her, waking and sleeping, was laid to rest.

But Nemesis now awaited Verney as he stood relaxed and at ease with his glass of champagne. The Mayor arrived and informed him that the Baltic princesses had requested he be presented to them.

'Ah, a summons!' Rom put down his glass, but as he prepared to follow the Mayor he turned and asked casually, 'Did anyone notice the little girl in the *corps* that sneezed? Third from the left as they came on?'

De Silva shook his head; so did the Count and Countess and the other men standing by.

'I didn't hear anyone sneeze,' said Sternov. 'I don't see how one could with all that row.'

'Odd,' said Rom.

Very odd, he thought, following the Mayor to the President's box. For it seemed to him that that small sneeze was what Act Two had rather been about.

Act Three is entirely swan-less. Prince Siegfried's parents give a great ball to which the princesses of many lands are invited, in the hope that one of them will catch his eye. The hope is vain. They dance for him, but the Prince says no to all of them. Then the evil Rothbart brings in his daughter, whom he has enchanted so as to resemble Odette. Dazzled by her virtuosity (the thirty-two *fouettés*!) and believing her to be Odette, the Prince promises to marry her and it is at this moment – and a very poignant moment it is – that the 'real' Odette appears at the window, a despairing shape fluttering in anguish to show the Prince that she has been betrayed.

It is in the last act that the swans reappear and they do so rising rather effectively from a bed of mist. At least, they do if the dry ice works, but dry ice on the Amazon is apt to be capricious. Thus some swans rose out of the mist; others, notably the swan that had sneezed, seemed likely to remain permanently immersed in it. Yet when the stage cleared and her serious face and graceful arms emerged, it appeared to Rom that she was very much improved in spirits. The little pucker between her eyes had gone and the rest of her feathers seemed to be secure. And considerably relieved, he lowered his glasses and prepared to watch Simonova dance her farewell *pas de deux* of forgiveness and reconciliation with Maximov before vanishing – this time for ever – into the lake.

The curtain fell on an ovation. Simonova was recalled again and again. Bouquets were showered on her: the bouquet ordered by the Opera House trustees, the bouquet of Count Sternov, of the Mayor . . . A large water-lily thrown by an admirer hit her in the chest like a cannon-ball and she did not flinch. The gallery yelled for Maximov . . .

'A triumph, *ma chère*,' said Dubrov, waiting in the wings with her wrap.

'Not bad, eh?' she agreed. 'Fifteen curtain calls! I was thinking, Sashka – let's announce my retirement at the *end* of the tour, what do you think? Right now it might be rather a disappointment for them.'

Swans do not take curtain calls. Harriet, back in the dressing-room, smiled like a Botticelli angel and said wonderingly, 'I'm alive. I'm still alive!' And then, 'Do you think anybody heard me sneeze?'

'Nobody heard you sneeze,' said Marie-Claude, who knew a great deal but not quite everything. 'And now please hurry, because tomorrow there is to be a very splendid party and I want some sleep.'

CHAPTER FIVE

FOR TEN days after Harriet's departure, Aunt Louisa and the Professor went about their business unconcerned over her whereabouts. It was naturally assumed that she was having a pleasant time with Mrs Fairfield and meeting the right people and Edward, though he missed her, had discovered a flea with a totally unexpected bristle on the third tergite and was much occupied in working out the implications of this breakthrough.

This peaceful state of affairs was shattered on the last day of April, when a concerned and friendly note arrived for Aunt Louisa from Mrs Fairfield. She and Betsy had been so sorry, she wrote, that Harriet had had to postpone her visit, but if the Professor's cousin was now recovered and they were returned from Harrogate, it would give them great pleasure if Harriet could come up for Betsy's dance. It was quite a small affair, nothing grand, but Betsy would be so very pleased to see her friend . . .

Aunt Louisa, reading the letter which came by the afternoon post, did not scream or faint. She controlled herself with masterly skill, but she went to 'the instrument' and telephoned the lodge of St Phillip's to ask the porter to find Professor Morton and request him to come home – something she had never done before in her life. After that, and perhaps unwisely, she telephoned her friend Mrs Hermione Belper at Trumpington Villa.

The Professor – arriving in an extremely unpleasant mood, for he had been interrupted while giving what he regarded as one of his most brilliant lectures – found Louisa's icy hand being chafed by the Tea Circle's president while other ladies offered sal volatile, tea and commiseration in voices from which they found it impossible to remove an undercurrent of glee.

'What has happened, Louisa?' he enquired sternly – and the ladies, responding to his manhood, withdrew into a corner.

Louisa held out Mrs Fairfield's note and the Professor paled. 'I don't understand this. Can Harriet have deliberately deceived us – or has she been abducted?'

'She has deliberately deceived us, Bernard! I have spoken to Mrs Fairfield on "the instrument" and the note they received with all that tarradiddle about Harrogate was definitely in Harriet's writing. Betsy knows it well.'

'Have you informed the police?'

'No, Bernard, please, not the police. The scandal . . . Surely there has to be some way of hushing it up? We must think. I suppose someone could have forced her to write that letter, but I don't feel it was that – she has been so strange lately. Oh, Bernard, I know! I'm sure I know!' Louisa sat up suddenly and the smelling-salts clattered to the floor. 'She has run away to that ballet company! She must have done. Do you remember how weirdly she spoke at that dinner-party? About it being the thing she had wanted all her life? That dreadful Russian who came to Madame Lavarre's . . .'

'Try not to be ridiculous, Louisa! My daughter would never disobey my specific orders.' But his daughter clearly had done so and cracking his pale knuckles, he said, 'I agree we must hush this up if we can. My position in the University if it got about . . . Of course, there *may* be a perfectly simple explanation . . .'

'The white slave traffic,' said Miss Transom, rendered authoritarian by the blessed absence of her mother.

'I've always thought the girl was no better than she should be,' hissed Millicent Braithwaite in a stage-whisper. She had not forgiven Harriet for making them look foolish at Stavely. For hours they had blundered about in that maze and then found her with a little red-haired boy and both of them laughing their heads off.

'We must go to see Madame Lavarre at once,' said the Professor. 'She will know the whereabouts of that Russian scoundrel.'

'If it is not too late!'

'Now remember,' said the Professor sternly, pointing his finger at the ladies, 'no word of this must get about. Not one single word!'

'Of course not, Professor,' said Mrs Belper soothingly. 'You can rely on us.' And so Herculean were the efforts of the ladies to restrain themselves that it was a good twenty-four hours before the milkman, whom Louisa had not tipped in twenty years, was in a position to

76

inform the man who kept the paper shop in Petty Cury that stuffy Professor Morton's daughter had run away to become a belly-dancer in a 'house of ill-fame' in Buenos Aires – and serve the old so-and-so right!

Madame Lavarre – when Professor and Miss Morton were announced – smiled the happy, relaxed smile of a well-fed cougar. She had had a note from Dubrov and knew that the Mortons were too late.

'No, I know nothing about Harriet, I am afraid,' she said. 'Since you have said that she may not come to my classes any more, I have not seen her.'

'We have reason to think that she may have tried to join the ballet company of that Russian who came to see you – the man who was going up the Amazon. You will oblige me by giving me his name.'

'Certainly.' Madame smiled and puffed a cloud of Balkan Sobranie into the Professor's face. 'His name is Dubrov. Sasha Dubrov. We are very old friends. In St Petersburg we have often been skating together on the Neva and also riding horses, although of course I could not do very much sport because at the Imperial Ballet School they did not permit it in case of injury to the legs.'

'His address, please,' fumed the Professor. 'You will instantly give me his address!'

'But certainly: 33 Mikhailovskaya. It is a beautiful apartment – the bathroom is particularly fine and in five minutes one can reach the Winter Palace and also the statue of Peter the Great, though I regard this as not absolutely the best work of Etienne Falconet; there is something a little bit exaggerated in the proportions and—'

'His address in London is what I want, Madame. Don't trifle with me!'

'I regret, Professor, that I do not know—'

'The woman's lying!' shrieked Aunt Louisa – at which point Madame summoned her servant and the Mortons were shown the door.

'Oh, heavens, Bernard, what shall we do?' Louisa was so distraught that she omitted to pick up from the pavement a pocket comb with only one tooth missing which, after a good scrubbing, would have done for the spare room.

But back at Scroope Terrace the valient Hermione Belper waved a newspaper she had just fetched from her home.

'There!' she said triumphantly. 'I thought I'd seen something about a ballet company going up the Amazon. They're at the Century

Theatre, in Bloomsbury.'

The Professor took it from her hand.

'We must leave for London immediately,' he announced. 'This newspaper is five days old and anything might have happened since then.' His decisiveness sent a flutter of approval through the ladies. 'If we hurry, we can catch the five-fifty-four.'

'But Bernard, that could mean a night in a hotel. The expense!' cried Louisa.

'Damn the expense!' said the Professor, and if anyone had doubted that he loved his daughter they could doubt no longer. 'If this escapade should reach the ears of the Master, with the Senate elections coming up . . .'

'Or Edward,' said Louisa faintly. 'If Edward came to hear of it . . .'

And an hour later the Mortons were on the train.

*

Stage-doorkeepers in general are not renowned for their loving kindness or the enthusiasm with which they greet unauthorised visitors, but even among that well-known band of misanthropes 'old Bill' at the Century stood out for the particularly poor view he took of human nature. Even before he had lost an eye in the relief of Khartoum in '85, his nature had hardly been sanguine, and now – with the aid of a scruffy and paranoid mongrel called Griff, who bit first and asked questions afterwards – he ensured that those who worked in his theatre were seldom unnecessarily disturbed.

'What d'yer want?' was his greeting to the Mortons as he stuck out his grizzled head from the window of his cubby-hole.

'We have come to see Mr Dubrov,' announced the Professor. 'The matter is extremely urgent.'

'Well, he ain't here. No one's here at this time of night.'

It seemed unlikely that he was lying; as the Mortons had walked round it, the Century Theatre had been silent and dark.

'We have come to make enquiries about a girl who may have joined the Company,' began Louisa, 'as a dancer.'

'Shut up!'

Bill was addressing his dog, but without rancour, for in growling even more hideously than usual and baring his yellow teeth, Griff was only confirming Bill's own view – that as far as people in general went, this toffee-nosed couple were bottom of the heap.

'She is an English girl,' persisted Louisa. 'There cannot be many

English girls in such a company.'

'Not any,' said Bill laconically. 'All Russian. All got Russian names. Got to have. No one'll stand for English names, not in ballet.'

'But there must have been a girl who spoke English? You must have heard the girls speak?'

'Me?' said Bill, 'Why should *I* hear them speak? I haven't got time to stand around chattering. Got me work to do, I have.'

Bowing to the inevitable, the Professor felt in his pocket and extracted a half-crown which he laid on the counter. 'Wasn't there just one girl who spoke to you? Said good morning, perhaps?'

Bill moved the coin slowly across the counter, but did not yet pocket it. Taking a tip could tie you . . .

'Aye,' he said. 'Come to think of it, there was one – a real smasher. Great goo-goo eyes, blonde hair and curves.' He sketched the delectable Marie-Claude in the air with deliberate crudity.

Louisa shuddered. 'That is *not* the girl we are looking for.'

'Now look here, my man; I am the girl's father and this is her aunt. If you know anything about her and conceal the fact, we shall have not the slightest hesitation in reporting you to the police.'

Bill lifted his eye-patch to scratch his forehead. Then slowly he slipped the half-crown into his pocket. It was doubtful if the old gaffer could do much, but there was never any point in getting mixed up with the police.

'The girl we want is plain,' said Louisa firmly. 'With straight brown hair and brown eyes. A *plain* girl.'

'Aye, there was a girl like that. Little thin thing. But she wasn't plain.' Bill remembered her well – had done so from the start. She had brought a large mutton bone for Griff all the way from the hostel where she was staying and talked proper sense to the dog. Griff had let her put the bone right into the bowl for him and that was rare enough. She was the one who stayed behind too, on the last night, helping the stage-hands get the stuff packed. 'Nothing plain about her,' he said, inexplicably furious with the pair. 'Had the sweetest smile you've ever seen.'

'Where is she, man? Hurry! Where is the company staying?'

Over Bill's face there now spread a look of unalloyed pleasure. Even his eye-patch seemed to lighten.

'On the Atlantic Ocean, sir,' he said. 'They've been gone the best part of a week,' . . . and shut the hatch.

*

79

'There must be something we can do,' said Louisa, 'without making it public that she has gone.'

The Mortons had not slept well and now sat at breakfast in their dining-room, removing with bony fingers the tops of their slightly sulphurous boiled eggs.

The Professor did not answer. While the possibility had existed that Harriet was in danger his rage had been modified by anxiety. Now sheer choler made it difficult for him to speak.

'You don't think . . . I mean, if she is so desperately keen to be a dancer, should one . . . simply wash one's hands of her?' asked Louisa.

The Professor put down his napkin. 'Are you suggesting that I permit my daughter – *my* daughter – deliberately to flout my wishes? Do you want me to be the laughing-stock of the University? Harriet is under age; she will be brought back and she will be punished.'

'Yes, dear. Of course. You are perfectly right. Only how?'

There was a pause, then the Professor gave a bark of inspiration.

'Edward!' he pronounced. 'Edward must show himself in his true colours.'

Identical furrows appeared on the long pale foreheads of the Mortons as they considered the true colours of Edward Finch-Dutton.

'You mean—'

'I mean,' said the Professor, 'that he must go in pursuit of Harriet and bring her back. He is young. I myself,' he lied, 'would have welcomed such an opportunity at his age.'

'But Bernard, surely that could not be considered respectable? If he were to return with Harriet, everyone would think . . . The gossip would be unendurable. She would be ruined.'

'She is ruined already,' said the Professor savagely. 'In my eyes she has put herself beyond the pale. But it shouldn't be impossible to think of something.'

'Mrs Fairfield would be willing to say that Harriet has been with them all the time in London – I am sure of it; she hinted as much on the instrument. So that if we met the ship and brought her back to Cambridge, everyone would simply think we had been fetching her from her friend,' said Louisa, mercifully unaware of the rumours even now flying round the city.

'And Edward would only need to say he had been on an entomological expedition,' put in the Professor. 'Those natural

80

scientists think nothing of wasting months in pointless field trips. But there is not a moment to lose – she already has nearly a week's start and who knows where that scoundrel might take her next – Rio de Janeiro, even New York . . . We have no evidence that he means to bring her back to England. Edward must leave at once.'

'Let us go to him,' said Louisa.

This was not a suggestion she would normally have made, and as they passed down long laboratory corridors and into rooms where Edward might have been – but wasn't – she was continually affronted by sights which she would prefer to have been spared. Young men in running shorts pedalled on stationary bicycles while pointers inscribed the furious zig-zag of their heartbeats on smoked drums . . . An appallingly identifiable yellow liquid bubbled fiendishly through a system of flasks, filter funnels and rubber tubing . . . In a glass-fronted altitude chamber, a bearded research assistant was slowly turning blue.

Term was over, but Edward was in the teaching lab sorting out demonstration slides. However, one glimpse of the Mortons advancing with set faces caused the colour to drain from his face.

'Harriet!' he said. 'She is ill? She has had an accident?'

The Professor looked round the lab to make sure that it was empty before saying, 'It might be better if she had.'

Five minutes later Edward, still holding the slide of a liver fluke he had been putting away when disaster struck, leaned against Henderson's parsnip tank, a broken man. Harriet had done this thing! Harriet whom he worshipped, whom he had selected from all the girls he knew for her gentleness and docility . . . Harriet had run away, had defied her father and was even now perhaps kicking up her legs in some hot theatre while greasy dagos watched her and licked their lips.

'I don't know what to say . . .' He put down the slide on the bench and stood shaking his head. 'It's a blow . . . the Mater . . .' Stunned and wretched, Edward saw years of careful planning brought suddenly to nought. The proposal at the May Ball; a visit to Goring-on-Thames to introduce Harriet to his mother . . . the little house in Madingley or Grantchester. 'She has put herself beyond the reach of a decent man.'

'No, Edward,' said Louisa, 'it may not be too late. She has been headstrong and foolish, but you may still be able to save here. Not to forgive her, perhaps – we do not ask that of you – but to restore her to safety and the parental home. We think,' she continued, coming down to earth, 'that we could hush things up so that no one need know of her flight.'

Edward was silent, still, shaking his long head sadly from side to side. Images of Harriet floated through his mind: the demure brown head; the clear and docile brow; the small ears peeping – rather wistfully, he had always thought – through her hair. Harriet's soft voice, her slow smile . . .

'How?' he said at last. 'How could it be hushed up?'

The Professor fixed him with a steely look. 'We want you to go after her, Edward. To bring her back. If you do this, we can avoid a scandal.' He explained about the Fairfields, while Edward stared at him dumbfounded.

'You want *me* to go to Manaus? But that's impossible! It's quite impossible. No one could ask it of me.'

'We would not expect you to marry her any longer, Edward,' said Louisa, laying her skeletal hand on his arm. 'Nor even to forgive her. Only to save her from her folly . . . and to save her family.'

'To show yourself a man,' stated the Professor.

'No.' Edward was resolute. Yet as he stood there, images of Harriet continued to jostle each other in his brain. The way she had laughed when that little baby had set off in its nappies across the sacrosanct Fellows' Lawn at King's. The way she had pulled down a branch of white lilac behind St Benet's Church and let the raindrops run down her face. And now perhaps she was ill with some jungle fever . . . or abandoned. 'Edward,' she would say when she saw him. 'Oh, Edward, you have come!'

'And in any case,' he said, 'I have my work.'

But that was a mistake. Images of Harriet were replaced by others more lurid, more feverish and, to a professional entomologist, reekingly desirable. The Brazilian rhinoceros beetle which stretched the length of a man's hand . . . the Morpho butterfly, like an iridescent blue dinner-plate, beating its way through the leaf canopy . . . fireflies by whose light it was possible to read. To say nothing of the wholly virgin territory of the Amazonian flea . . .

Implacable, with their characteristic look of having just stepped down from a cut-price sarcophagus, the Mortons stood before him.

'I would never be able to get leave,' said Edward.

That, however, was not necessarily true. He only had two practicals in the summer term; Henderson would do those for him and the head of his department was a great believer in field work – in getting what he called 'nose to nose with the insect'.

The images came faster. The Goliath beetle, six inches from mouth to sternum . . . the '88' butterfly, a brilliant airborne hieroglyphic for which private collectors would give their ears . . . Harriet lying on a pillow, her hair spread out; her limp body acquiescent as he carried her to safety up the gangplank of the ship . . . And *Peripatus* – ah, *Peripatus*! Edward's blue eyes grew soft as he thought of this seemingly insignificant creature, half-worm, half-insect, the world's oldest living fossil, crawling – as it had crawled since the dawn of time – through the unchanging debris of the rain-forest floor.

Torn beyond endurance, he gazed into the tank where Henderson's lone parsnip continued to respire silently in the cause of science. 'Look at my fate,' the captive vegetable seemed to be saying. 'Free yourself. Show yourself a hero. Be a man.' Making a final stand, Edward turned back to the Professor. 'And there is the fare,' said Edward, 'I cannot possibly afford the fare.'

A grimace, a convulsion of the thin lips, a kind of spasm – and then the Merlin Professor looked straight at Edward and said, '*I* will pay the fare.'

CHAPTER SIX

'I LOOK like a twig,' said Harriet a little sadly, gazing into the fly-blown mirror of the room she shared with her friends in the Hotel Metropole.

Marie-Claude and Kirstin did not attempt to deny it.

'I would like to know what exactly she is *like*, this Aunt Louisa of yours,' said Marie-Claude. 'How can someone actually enter into a shop and *buy* such a dress?'

It was the day after the opening night of *Swan Lake* and the girls were preparing for the party at Follina.

'Brown suits Harriet,' said Kirstin kindly.

'Oh, yes. Brown velvet in the winter with frogging, perhaps,' agreed Marie-Claude. 'But brown *foulard* . . . and the sleeves.' She laid a bunch of artificial flowers against Harriet's throat and shook her head. 'Better not to draw attention . . .'

She herself was dressed like a dancer – that is to say, like the image of a dancer that the world delights in: a three-quarter-length white dress, satin slippers, a wreath of rosebuds in the loose and curling golden hair.

'I'll stand at the back and hold my glass; no one will notice me,' said Harriet, whose ideas of party-going were conditioned by the dread occasions with which the Master of St Philip's celebrated events of academic importance.

'You will do nothing of the kind, 'arriette,' said Marie-Claude, slipping Vincent's engagement ring firmly on to her finger. 'This man is not only an Englishman but the most important—'

'An *Englishman*? The chairman of the Opera House trustees? Goodness!' Harriet was amazed. 'I'd imagined a kind old Brazilian with a paunch and a huge waxed moustache.'

'Whether he has a moustache or not, I cannot say,' said Marie-Claude, a little offended. 'Vincent's moustache is very big and personally I do not find a man attractive without moustaches. But Mr Verney is spoken of as formidably intelligent and since you are the daughter of a professor—'

'Mr Verney?' said Harriet, and there was something in her voice which made both girls look at her hard. 'Is that what he is called? Are you *sure?*'

'Certainly I am sure,' said Marie-Claude, exasperated by the unworldliness of her friend. Harriet had pestered everyone ceaselessly for the names of the flowers, the birds, even the insects they had encountered ever since they left England, yet she had not even troubled to find out the name of the most influential man in Manaus.

But Harriet was lost in remembrance, her hairbrush dangling from her hand.

'I'm Henry St John Verney Brandon,' Henry had said to her, turning his small face upwards, trusting her with that all-important thing: his name. And another image . . . the unpleasant Mr Grunthorne with his liver-spotted pate and rapacious hands, droning on beside the Van Dyck portrait of Henrietta Verney who had brought her beauty and her fortune to the house of Brandon.

It didn't have to mean anything – the name was not uncommon. Yet if Henry's 'secret boy' was some distant connection of the family brought up for some reason at Stavely . . . ? If against all odds she had found him and could plead Henry's case, what happiness that would be!

No, I'm being absurd, thought Harriet; it's merely coincidence. But she found herself suddenly looking forward to the evening ahead and – relinquishing the hairbrush to Marie-Claude – submitted with docility to having two side plaits swept on to the crown of her head and wearing the rest loose down her back to reveal what both the other girls regarded as tolerable: her ears.

Though she knew her host was rich, the first sight of the *Amethyst* waiting at the docks in the afternoon sunshine to take the cast to Follina, took her aback – not on account of the schooner's size, but because of her beauty. She was surprised too to find that a second boat was waiting to convey to the party not only the members of the orchestra but also the technical staff, who were so often forgotten.

'Very nice,' said Simonova condescendingly, walking up the gangway in trailing orange chiffon and accepting as her due the

85

attentions of Verney's staff, for had she not spent many summers on the Black Sea in a similar yacht owned by the Grand Duke Michael? She exclaimed ecstatically at the beauty of the river scene and firmly went below, followed by the other principals and most of the *corps*, to recline in the luxurious cabins with their bowls of fruit, boxes of chocolates and magazines.

'You of course will stay on deck and completely dissarrange your toilette while we travel?' suggested Marie-Claude and Harriet, grinning at her friend, admitted that this was so. So she hung over the rails, watching the changing patterns of the islands which lay like jagged ribbons across the smooth, leaf-stained water, until they turned from the dark Negro into her tributary, the Maura.

'Oh,' she exclaimed, 'it is so *light!*' And the boatman standing near her with a rope coiled ready in his hand nodded and smiled, understanding not her words but her tone.

The sails were furled now. Under engine, the *Amethyst* came in quietly beside the jetty – and Harriet, drawing in breath, saw what Rom had seen only in his mind's eye the day he first glimpsed Follina: a low pink-washed, colonnaded house at the end of an avenue of blossoming blue trees – and a garden whose scents and sense of sanctuary reached out like a benison to those who came.

'The place has style,' admitted Marie-Claude, emerging immaculate and ravishing from below. 'But I hope we are not expected to walk to the house.'

They were not. Three cars and a number of carriages waited to take them the half-mile to Verney's front door. Simonova, Maximov and Dubrov swept into the first of these; Kaufmann, the choleric conductor of the orchestra, got into the second; the others followed.

'I shall walk,' said Harriet.

'In this heat?' Even the easy-going Kirstin was shocked.

'Do you wish to arrive entirely dissolved in perspiration?' reproved Marie-Claude.

'Please . . . I must,' said Harriet, and they shrugged and climbed into one of the carriages and left her.

*

Rom surveyed his guests with an experienced air and was satisfied. Simonova, reclining on a couch on the terrace, was surrounded by admirers; the dancers and musicians wandered happily between the tables, helping themselves to iced fruit juice or champagne. Standing beside the statue of Aphrodite flanking the stone steps, Marie-Claude was regaling a group of dazed gentlemen with an account of the restaurant she was proposing to start with Vincent in the foothills above Nice. That this entrancing girl was bespoke and visibly virtuous had given Rom a pang of relief, a reaction he had not sought to explain or understand, preferring simply to enjoy the sight of de Silva, Harry Parker (who ran the Sports Club) and a host of others drinking thirstily at these forbidden waters.

During this hour before sundown, the house and the terrace were one. The lilting music from the Viennese trio he had installed in the salon wafted out through the French windows, the jasmine and wisteria climbing his walls laid their heavy, scented branches almost into the rooms themselves. The moment darkness fell he would relinquish his garden to the moths and night birds, close the windows and lead his guests to a dinner as formally served and elaborate as any banquet of state. But this present time was for wandering at will, for letting Follina work its spell, and he intervened only with the lightest of hands – introducing shy Mrs Bennett to the glamorous Maximov; removing the misanthropic conductor, Kaufmann, to the library with its collection of operatic scores.

Yet though no one could have guessed it Rom, as he wandered among his guests, was fighting down disappointment. He had been absolutely certain that he would recognise the swan who had sneezed so poignantly at the end of Act Two; it seemed to him that the serious little face with its troubled brown eyes was entirely distinctive, but he had been mistaken. A casual question to Dubrov when the girls arrived elicited the information that all members of the *corps* had come. 'No one could miss such an honour,' Dubrov had assured him, adding that he himself had personally counted heads as the girls came aboard the *Amethyst*. Therefore she must be in the group of Russians with their dark homesick faces, for she was not with Marie-Claude nor the pale-haired Swedish girl receiving, with evident indifference, the compliments of the Mayor. Well, people looked different without their makeup, he reflected, and shrugging off the matter as of no importance, paused by Simonova's couch to add his homage to her circle of admirers.

'Never!' the ballerina was declaring, throwing out her long, thin hands. 'Never, never, will I return to Russia! If they came to me crawling in the snow on their hands and knees all the way from Petersburg, I would not come!'

87

She fanned herself with the ends of her chiffon scarf, and looked at her host from under kohl-tipped lashes. What a man! If only she had not been committed to her art – and of course to Dubrov, though that was more easily arranged . . . *One must go where there is fire*, Fokine had once said to her and this devastating man with his deep grey eyes and that look of Tamburlaine the Great was certainly fire. But it was impossible: a night with such a man and one could hardly manage three *fouettés*, let alone thirty-two . . .

'Ah, Madame, what a loss for my country,' sighed Count Sternov.

'It is a loss,' agreed the ballerina complacently. 'But it is one for which they must take the blame. And in any case soon I am going to retire.' She waited for the groans, the horrified denials . . . and when they came, proceeded. 'Dubrov and I are going to live in the country in absolute simplicity with goats and grow vegetables. I have a great longing,' she said, spreading tapering fingers which had never touched anything rougher than Maximov's silvered tights, 'to get my hands into the earth.'

'You must allow me to show you over the kitchen gardens,' said Verney, concealing the smile that had flickered at the corners of his mouth.

'Yes. Later,' said Simonova. The plants she had seen on the way up to the house had seemed to her excessive, altogether too much *there* and looking in some cases as though they might contain insects, which were not in her scheme of things. And she leaned back more comfortably and allowed a servant to refill her glass with champagne.

But Marie-Claude now detached herself from the besotted gentlemen surrounding her and said something to Dubrov, who turned to his host.

'Marie-Claude is a little concerned about our newest member of the *corps*. Apparently she decided to walk up from the jetty, but that was quite a time ago and she isn't here yet.'

'She is English,' explained Marie-Claude, turning her incredible eyes on Rom and repressing a sigh. If things had been different . . . even without moustaches . . . But they were not and resolutely she continued, 'And it is impossible to keep her inside. You know how it is: the fresh air, *et tout ça*. And naturally one would not wish her to be eaten by a boa constrictor.'

'English!' said Rom, amazed. 'You have an English dancer?' No wonder he had been unable to visualise her in St Petersburg or Kiev.

Dubrov nodded. 'She only joined us just before we left, without any stage experience; she's done very well. Last night was her debut.'

'Don't worry,' said Rom. 'I'm sure she's perfectly all right. But I shall send someone to fetch her.'

This, however, he did not do. Briefing Lorenzo and his assistants, he slipped silently away and made his way down the steps.

She was not on the main avenue, not on any of the terraces, not in the arboretum, not by the pond . . .

He continued to search, not anxious but a little puzzled, Then from behind the patch of native forest he heard the great Caruso's voice.

'Your tiny hand is frozen . . . is frozen . . . is frozen . . .' sang the incomparable tenor, for the record – the first he had ever bought his Indians – was badly cracked.

Che gelida manina . . . a record valued even above the 'Bell Song' from *Lakmé*, but seldom played now owing to its fragile state. They had a visitor, then, and one they wanted to honour. With an eagerness which surprised him, Rom made his way between the trees.

The village was bathed in the last rays of the afternoon sun. Hammocks were strung between the dappled trees; a monkey scratched himself on a thatched roof . . . a small armadillo they had tamed rooted in a patch of canna lillies.

In the circle around the horn of the gramophone sat the women with their children, together with the few men too old to be busy in the plantations or helping at the house. Someone knowing them less well would have assumed that this was just the usual evening concert, but Rom – seeing the fruit set out on painted plates and the cassia juice in gourds on the low carved stool – knew they were welcoming a valued guest.

Only what guest? And where?

At first he could see no one unusual. Then, searching the listening faces, he saw a girl he had at first taken to be one of the tribe, for she wore a dress such as the missionaries forced on their converts and she was holding a baby, cupping a hand round its head – Manuelo's three-day-old baby which they were taking to Father Antonio at dawn to be baptised.

Then they saw him; someone took off the needle from the record and as they came towards him, chattering in welcome, she lifted her head and looked directly at him . . . and over her face there spread a sudden shock of surprise, almost of recognition, as though he was someone she knew from another life.

'You must be the last of the company's swans?' he said, coming

89

forward. 'I'm Romain Verney, your host.'

'Yes,' she replied, getting to her feet. 'I'm Harriet Morton.' The voice was low; scholarly. Old Iquita took the baby from her and he saw how hard it was for her to part with its soft warmth; how she drew her fingertips across the round dark head until the last possible moment, just as Simonova had drawn her fingertips down the arm of her lover before she *bourréed* backwards into the lake. 'God must be very brave,' she said, 'making babies with fontanelles like that. What if their souls should escape before they've joined? What then?'

'Oh, God is brave all right,' said Rom lightly. 'You see Him all the time, chancing His arm.' But he was startled, for she had smiled as she spoke and everything he had thought about her gravity and seriousness was suddenly set at nought. There was nothing wistful or tentative about that smile. It came slowly, but ended in a total crunching up of her features as though a winged cherub had just flown by and whispered a marvellously funny joke into her ear.

They made their farewells and he began to lead her back.

'They've been so *kind* to me,' she said, still not quite in the real world after her hour in the garden and the conviction which had burst from her as he stepped from the trees that this *was* Henry's 'secret boy'. 'Look what they gave me!' She took out of her pocket a small carving of a margay and held it out to him.

'They like to give presents.' But Rom was surprised, for the carving was one of old José's, their best craftsman; it was a lovely thing. 'How did you make yourself understood?' he asked curiously.

'I think if you want to, you can always understand people, don't you? And the ones who had grown up in the mission could follow a little Latin.'

'Ah, yes; Latin,' he murmured. 'A usual accomplishment in ballet dancers?'

'My father taught me,' she said briefly and a shadow passed over her face. But the next moment she was entranced again: 'Oh, that tree! That *colour* . . . and the way the flowers grow right on the trunk like that!'

'Yes, that's *Aspidosperma silenium* – pollinated by opossums, believe it or not!'

She liked that, wrinkling her nose. 'It's lovely that you know the names. I kept asking and asking, but nobody did.'

'Is it important that you know the names of things?'

'Yes. I feel . . . discourteous if I don't know. As though I've failed them somehow. Is that stupid?'

'No, I understand. But it's the devil naming things out here. There are literally hundreds of species of trees and only a handful have been classified. I was like a child in a sweet-shop when I first came out, not knowing where to begin.' He described briefly his discovery of Follina and her eyes grew wide at the wonder of it.

They had reached the edge of the arboretum and a great urn in which there grew a magical orchid – delicate, yet abundant with an overpowering scent.

'That's the Queen's Orchid. The *caracara*, the Indians call it. Some people find it a bit overwhelming.'

'Oh no, not against those dark bushes; they cool it.' She was running her fingers softly along the edge of the petals, tracing lightly the intricate shape of the stamens. He had never seen in a European such a physical response to things that grew. 'And over there, in the pool? That *blue*? That's not a water hyacinth, is it? They grow in drifts?'

'No – it's a kind of lobelia. An incredible colour, isn't it? The water gardens are a perpetual headache; you have to keep the water running all the time, otherwise the mosquitos breed, and that's the devil. I've installed a kind of cataract there . . .'

He explained, led her here and there. She was utterly enthralled and both of them had completely forgotten the time.

'I thought it would be all dark,' she said wonderingly. 'A dark forest and rows and rows of rubber trees.'

'There are rubber trees – thousands of them, mostly wild. I've made plantations too, but this garden is my folly.' And as she stood waiting for him to continue, he said, 'I fight a battle like some idiot crusader against the Amazon disease – the disease of all South America, if it comes to that. I call it the Eldorado illness.'

She turned to him, her eyes alert. 'The belief that there is a promised land?'

'Yes. Partly. Everyone here searches . . . the Indians, the Portuguese settlers, the people who came later. For gold, for coffee, for the green stones that the Amazon women gave their lovers . . . for groves of cinnamon trees – and now for rubber. They search and they find because the country is so abundant. But then someone comes along from some other country who is not content just to search. Someone who *plants* coffee or hardwoods, who mines gold systematically instead of picking the nuggets off the ground. And then the searchers are bankrupt, the villages become derelict and the people starve. It will be the same with rubber; you'll see. I've diversified; I run a gold mine at Serra Deloso, I export bauxite and manganese, I've organised a timber business. I shall be all right, but if the price of rubber really drops – and it is dropping as they bring it in from the East – then God knows how many of my friends I shall be able to save. Not enough.'

'It's always been so, hasn't it?' she said quietly. 'All through history. Solon trying to warn Croesus . . . don't lean back on your riches, he said, but no one listened. People don't.'

You do, Rom wanted to say. You listen as I have never known anyone listen. And he remembered how as a small boy at Stavely walking along the gravel paths absently scuffing the stones, he would suddenly – for no reason that he knew of – bend down to pick up one pebble, just one, and keep it in his pocket. He had never found it hard to share his toys, but no one had been allowed to touch such a pebble; it became his treasure and his talisman.

It had been like that, he now admitted, when he ran his opera glasses down the line of swans. 'This one,' a voice had said inside him. 'This one is for me.'

As they passed a clump of bamboo they heard a rustling and Rom stopped and gave a low whistle. The rustling ceased, began again . . . An inquisitive snout appeared, a pair of bright eyes . . . then the coati's gleaming chestnut body and stripy tail.

'He's offended,' said Rom. 'I give orders to have him kept out of the house when I have guests. You watch him deciding whether or not he will speak to us.'

The performance which followed would have done credit to a venerable Rotarian whom nobody had invited to make an after-dinner speech. The coati moved forward, thought better of it, sat up on his haunches and pretended to investigate a non-existent nut with busy forepaws . . . Once more he approached, once more he sat down – and at last, but with evident condescension, came to rub himself against Rom's legs.

'How tame he is!'

'Most things can be tamed if you take the time,' he said, sending the little creature off again with a pat on its rump. 'I found him when he was a few days old. Come, if you like animals I'll show you one more thing and then we really must get back.'

But as she followed him Harriet, in her mind, had left this magical garden and was back at Stavely while Henry told her what the family's disagreeable butler had said about the 'secret boy': 'Grunthorpe didn't like him . . . he said he was a changeling . . . because he could talk to animals, Grunthorpe said . . .'

She was sure, really – and had been from the moment she saw him step out from the trees. A straight line ran from the boy who had built a tree-house in the Wellingtonia and owned a dog who was his shadow, to this man, but oh, for proof!

They had reached the *igarape* and he led her on to the bridge which crossed it.

'I've told you how important it is to keep the water moving. Well, here is one of the methods I use.' He leaned over and slapped the surface of the water with his hand. 'Agatha!' he called. 'Come here. I've brought you a visitor!'

Harriet looked down into the water. At first she could make out nothing. Then slowly from under a patch of weed there appeared a mass of mottled grey and white whiskers, a snout . . . A soft blowing and snuffling noise followed; the almond-shaped nostrils twitched and opened . . . Then the head lifted and Harriet found herself looking into a pair of round, liquid, unutterably soulful eyes.

'Oh, what is it? What *is* it?' Harriet, who had taught herself never to touch anyone for fear of rebuff, had taken this stranger's arm. 'I've never seen anything like it. It's not a seal?'

'It's a manatee,' said Verney softly. 'A kind of sea cow. The sailors say that this is the basis for the stories of mermaids. Have you ever seen a more human face? More human than most humans, I always think.'

Harriet could not take her eyes from the trusting beast which was now looking at her unperturbed, a bunch of water hyacinths dangling like a dotty bouquet from her mouth. 'They're sacred to some of the Indian tribes,' said Rom, 'and anyone who tries to poach them on my land is in trouble. They keep the channels running clear, you see, by eating the water-weed.'

'A manatee!' said Harriet raptly. 'I've seen a manatee!' She turned away to trace the pattern of the creeper which had laid its stippled leaves along the hand-rail of the bridge, but not before he had seen the glint of tears on her lashes.

'What is it?' he asked gently.' 'Is anything the matter?'

She gave a small shake of the head. 'It's just that everything is so beautiful . . . so *right* . . . And it was here all the time, this rightness . . .

93

While I was in Scroope Terrace in that cold dark house. If only I'd known how to come out – if only I'd known that a place like this existed.'

'You know now,' said Verney lightly. 'And I have to tell you that there is absolutely nothing right about Agatha's husband; he's an entirely different kettle of fish – a nasty servile beast perpetually on the lookout for gratuities. In fact, I doubt if he'll come at all since I haven't brought any biscuits. No . . . wait; I've maligned him. Here he is!'

The animal which now surfacced did indeed look quite different from the gentle domestic-looking creature still staring lovingly out of the water. The male manatee's eyes seemed incorrigibly greedy; the short snorts he gave had a vaguely petulant air and the round head which imparted to Agatha such a benign and soothing look was covered, in his case, by large liver-coloured spots.

And as Rom had intended, Harriet laughed and said, 'I see what you mean.'

Furious at the lack of largesse, the male manatee nudged his wife a couple of times, gave a snort of disgust . . . and sank.

'Does he have a name?' asked Harriet.

'I call him Grunthorpe,' said Rom – and led her back to the house.

*

The party was in full swing. Sitting at damask-covered tables decked with exquisite silver, the guests ate roast tapir more delicate than pork, forest grouse wrapped in plantain leaves, a fricassee of turtle meat served in the upturned shell . . . Only where wine was concerned did Verney turn to Europe, serving a Chateauneuf du Pape which had Dubrov and Count Sternov exchanging a glance of solemnity and awe.

So now I know, thought Harriet, sitting with the girls of the *corps* at a long table. I have proof. He is Henry's 'boy' and that means I must speak to him, even though I don't know why he left Stavely or what scandal or grief may be hidden in his past. I must tell him how bad things are there and I must plead for Henry even if I am rebuffed and snubbed, because that was what I promised I would do.

She looked at the top table where Verney was sitting, saying something to Simonova which made her throw back her head and laugh, and a stab of pity ran through her for the red-haired child who had turned to her with such trust. 'If you find him, Harriet, ask him to

94

come back,' Henry had said, but this man would never return to England. She had never seen anyone who belonged to a place so utterly as he did here.

She accepted a second helping of an unknown but delicious fish. Beside her, the indomitable Olga was crunching to smithereens a leg of roasted guinea-fowl. Tatiana, who spoke no word of English, was bent over her plate

Only when? thought Harriet, thus left free to pursue her thoughts. *When* do I speak to him? After tonight I won't see him again, not ever, she thought – wondering why the exotic fish she was consuming seemed, after all, not to be in the least delicious. Verney might go to the other performances at the Opera House, but he would hardly trouble to seek out a humble member of the *corps*.

The entrée was cleared; bowls of pomegranates, paw-paws and pineapples were set out. Sorbets arrived in tall glasses and a concoction of meringue and passion fruit . . . The wine changed to the lightest of Muscadels . . .

But Harriet's appetite had suddenly deserted her, for the result of her deliberations had become inescapable. If she wanted to plead for the child who had so inexplicably wound himself round her heart, there was only one way to do it – alone. And only one time – tonight.

*

As a host Verney might appear relaxed to the point of being casual, but the ingredients which made up his famous parties – the food, the wine, the lights, the music – were most precisely calculated. So after the formality of the dinner he loosed his guests into the flower-filled enfilade of rooms which ran along the terrace and replaced the Viennese trio which had played earlier by a group of Brazilian musicians, knowing that guests too shy to waltz or polka in the presence of these professionals would soon be caught by the syncopated rhythm of Los Olvideros. And soon Maximov was dancing with young Mrs Bennett, the sharp-faced Harry Parker beat all other contestants for the hand of Marie-Claude and Simonova herself had led the enraptured Count on to the floor.

But a man who knows exactly when to welcome and feed and amuse his guests, knows also when to send them back. At midnight his servants came with jugs of steaming coffee, and with a flourish the curtains were drawn aside – to reveal a shining avenue of light from lamps strung between the jacaranda trees and at its end the *Amethyst* glowing with welcome, waiting to take them home.

*

'That went off very well, Lorenzo,' said Rom. 'You can clear up in the morning. I'm going to bed.'

But he lingered for a while, enjoying the silent house; relishing that moment of well-being which attacks even the most hospitable of men when their guests have gone. He opened a French window to let in the coati. The night was clear – the Milky Way spectacularly bright and Pegasus, up-ended and undignified to someone from another hemisphere, pointing to the north and what had once been home.

He was just about to make his way upstairs when he caught a movement in the doorway leading to the adjoining room. He turned – and a girl stepped forward into the light.

'Oh God!' said Rom under his breath. 'You!' and the dark face was suddenly creased with weariness.

'Mr Verney, I am very sorry to trouble you, but could I talk to you, please?'

He had looked away, missing the fear in her eyes and the way she laced her fingers to stop them trembling.

This girl, then, like all the others . . . this girl who in the garden had held out such different promise. The oldest ruse, the stalest trick of them all. Staying behind because something had been 'forgotten', because the boat had been 'missed'.

From the same doorway, after the other guests had gone, had stepped Marina in her bare feet, her blouse pulled off one shoulder, tossing her russet hair . . . And Dolores, the Spanish girl from the troupe he had nursed, whimsically wrapped in one of his Persian rugs because someone had told her that Cleopatra had been brought to Caesar wrapped in a carpet. Millie Trant too, who had used the same formula as Harriet: 'Let's you and I have a little talk, Mr Verney.' But Millie had been honest – there was no mistaking her intentions from the start.

He could laugh now to think how careful he had been not to talk to Harriet again once they came in from the garden, determined not to make her conspicuous. Yet he had watched her unnoticed; seen how she drew out Mrs Bennett, asking quiet questions about the absent child. Later Dubrov had told him a little of her story. Well, was it surprising that a girl who had run away from a good academic home should turn out to be what, seemingly, she was?

96

'Very well,' he said, fighting down his weariness, his desire to humiliate her by turning on his heel and leaving her. 'If you wish it, we will . . . talk.'

He pulled the bell-rope and Lorenzo, sleepy and surprised, appeared. 'Take Miss Morton up to the Blue suite and send someone to see that she has what she requires,' he said in rapid Portuguese. And to Harriet, who had not understood him, 'I will join you in half an hour.'

*

She was very tired and this made her confused – this and not knowing the customs of the country, Harriet told herself. Once in Cambridge she had been to a fund-raising luncheon with her Aunt Louisa in a very grand house, and afterwards the hostess had swept up all the ladies and taken them upstairs to a very cold bathroom. Harriet had not needed to do any of the things the other ladies needed to do, but this had not helped her. One went there; it was what one did.

So perhaps in the Amazon – where it was true one became extremely sticky – it was customary to offer people to whom one was going to talk not only the chance to wash their hands and tidy their hair and so on . . . but actually . . . a bath.

At first she had hoped that the room to which she was taken was not a bathroom; it was so large and contained things which she had not thought *could* be present in a bathroom: an alabaster urn full of lilies, a marble statue on a plinth, a deep white carpet. Not to mention mirrors . . . so very many mirrors in their gilt frames.

But the bath, surrounded by mahogany and absolutely huge, was unmistakably . . . a bath. What is more, not one but two servants were standing beside it – one adjusting the water which gushed from the great brass taps, another pouring rose-coloured crystals from a cut-glass jar into the foam – and both at frequent intervals pausing to nod and smile encouragingly in her direction. For Lorenzo, discovering that his master's latest acquisition was the girl who had played with Andrelhino's crippled boy and made old José laugh almost until he dropped by showing him the dances she did on one toe in the Teatro Amazonas, had not sent up the usual impersonal Rio-trained chambermaid who waited on ladies in the Blue Suite. Instead, he had tipped out of their hammocks not only his wife but also his niece and told them to attend her.

And attend her they did! Lorenzo might be a sophisticated *cabaclo* who spoke Portuguese and English and had once worked in an hotel, but for a wife he had turned to the Xanti, that gentle primitive tribe renowned for their knowledge of plant lore and the pleasure they take in the daily rituals of life.

So now Maliki nodded and smiled and beckoned, setting her nose ornament a-jingle, and her welcoming gestures were echoed by her pig-tailed niece. It was awaiting her, this lovely thing, this bath – she might approach!

'No,' said Harriet loudly. 'I don't *want* a bath!'

They understood not her words, but her tone. A look of hurt, of despair passed over both faces. The aunt approached the niece; they conferred in low agitated voices . . . came to a conclusion . . . rallied. Maliki rushed to the bath taps, turned off the hot and ran the cold to full. Rauni replaced the stopper of the cut-glass jar, ran to fetch another, tipped out a handful of green crystals and held them under Harriet's nose.

'Yes,' said Harriet. 'Very nice. It smells lovely. Only I—'

But the change in her voice, the obvious pleasure she took in the scent of 'Forest Fern', wrought a transformation in her attendants. They smiled, they were transported with relief; they threw up their hands to show how silly they had been not to realise that she wanted the water cooler and did not care for the smell of frangipani. And before Harriet could gather herself together for another effort Maliki had come forward and pulled the loose sack-like dress over her head, while Rauni – bending tenderly to her feet – removed her stockings and shoes.

I suppose I should kick and scream and shout, thought Harriet. But she was very tired and the women – who had announced their names with ritual thumping of the chest – were very kind. And surely it could not be that the man who had been so much her friend in the garden might intend her any harm? Surely a vile seducer could not have pulled aside the thorny branches of an acacia to reveal for her a nest of fledgling flycatchers with golden breasts?

The water was lovely – cool, soft, up to her chin. In Scroope Terrace it had been bad manners even to be on the same floor as someone taking their weekly bath, but her attendants showed no signs of departure. On the contrary, this delightful experience was clearly one to be shared. Maliki picked up a loofah and rubbed her back. Rauni ran back and forth proffering a succession of brightly coloured soaps; then bent to massage the soles of Harriet's feet with pumice-

98

stone . . .

And presently Maliki gathered up Harriet's crumpled clothes and carried them carefully to the door which led to the corridor.

'No!' Harriet sat up suddenly. 'No! Not my clothes. *Leave them here!*'

But this time the women did not panic. They knew now how to soothe her, how to make everything right. Of course they would not leave her without clothes, they gestured, sketching reassuring garments in the air. How could she think it?

And they did not! Maliki, removing Harriet's brown foulard, returned almost immediately and together aunt and niece held up, with pardonable pride, what Harriet was to wear.

Everything in Verney's house was of the best and so was this negligée – a confection of creamy Venetian lace with scalloped sleeves, soft ruffles at the throat and hem and a row of tiny satin-covered buttons.

What now? thought Harriet ten minutes later as she stood dried, powdered and perfumed in front of the largest of the mirrors, looking at a girl she did not recognise. Her eyes were huge, smudged with apprehension and fatigue; Maliki had brushed her loose hair forward to lie in damp strands across the creamy lace covering her breasts.

'Oh, Marie-Claude, I have been such a *fool*,' said Harriet, bereft and very frightened and homesick – not for the home she had never had, but for the company of her new-found friends.

But there seemed to be no way now but forward. Leaning towards the mirror she undid, with fingers she could scarcely keep from trembling, the top button of the negligée where it rested against her throat.

'I am ready,' said Harriet.

*

If she had still hoped that she might be mistaken, that hope was instantly dashed as her gratified attendants pushed her forward through the double doors and closed them behind her. The room, panelled in blue damask and richly carpeted, was dominated by the largest bed that Harriet had ever seen – a four-poster billowing with snow-white netting and covered with an embroidered counterpane the corners of which were undoubtedly turned back. And now rising from an armchair by the window was her host, Rom Verney, wearing over his dress shirt and evening trousers a black silk dressing-gown tied loosely – extremely loosely – with a silken cord.

Strangely it was not the way he was dressed that made the trembling which assailed her almost uncontrollable. It was the disdain, the hard look in the grey eyes. Was it a trick played by the shaded lamps or did he suddenly hate her?

'I hope you enjoyed your bath?' The voice was cold, icily mocking.

'Yes, thank you.'

Was that part of what was to happen next – that he should detest her?

She managed to take a few more steps forward, to reach the bedpost to which she put out a hand. At the same time her bare feet under the frothy hem arranged themselves instinctively in the first position *dégagé*, as though she was about to begin a long and taxing exercise.

'I don't want to . . . make excuses,' she brought out. 'I understand that ignorance is no defence . . . and that one is punished just the same.' And not wishing to be rude even in this extremity of fear, she added, 'I mean, I know that there are consequences of being ignorant . . . and that one must not try to escape them.'

He had moved towards her and seen how she trembled, and a hope as intense as it was absurd leapt in his breast.

'I'm afraid I don't entirely follow you,' he said, but the mockery had left his voice and she was able to say:

'I mean you have only to look at Ancient Greece to see . . . that not knowing what you were doing didn't let you off. Oedipus didn't know that Jocasta was his mother when he married her, yet the punishment was terrible – gouging out his eyes. Not that this is as bad as that, I expect . . .' She made a small forlorn gesture towards the bed and her impending fate. 'And poor Actaeon – he didn't *mean* to spy on Diana bathing with her nymphs; he didn't even know she was there, he just wanted a drink – yet look what happened to him! Turned into a stag and torn to pieces by his own dogs!'

'Go on.' He had moved still closer, but the moment of her doom was seemingly not yet upon her and she took a gulp of air and went on:

'I only mean . . . that I'm not trying to . . . get out of anything. If what I did . . . staying behind to talk to you . . . telling Marie-Claude I was taking the other boat . . . thinking I could go back with Manuelo's wife when she takes the baby to be christened . . .' She broke off and tried again. 'Only I think you are going to be very disappointed *because I don't know what to do.*' Her voice was rising dangerously. She was very close to tears. 'For example, if you were Suleiman the Great it would be correct for me to creep from the foot of

100

the bed into your presence. Only I can't believe . . .'

'I would prefer you not to creep,' he said gently.

But the return of the kindness he had shown her in the garden made everything somehow worse, and it was with tears trembling on her lashes that she said desperately, 'I only mean that at Scroope Terrace there was never any opportunity for being . . . ruined and ravished . . . and so on. *And I don't know how to behave.*' She could hold back no longer now and the tears ran steadily down her cheeks. 'I didn't even know that you had to go to bed with the top button of your nightdress undone,' sobbed Harriet, 'not until Marie-Claude told me.'

Rom made no attempt to comfort her. Instead he turned abruptly away from her and walked over to the window in the grip of a fierce and unremitting joy. She is good, he thought exultantly. I was right to feel what I felt. She is innocent and virtuous and *good*!

He went over to her then and, taking out his handkerchief, very gently wiped away her tears. And then his fingers moved slowly down, brushing her throat, until they found their object: the buttons on her negligée.

And in that moment, when rape and ruin was upon her . . . was inevitable . . . Harriet's terror melted like snow in the sun and she knew with absolute certainty that no ruin was possible here; that what this man wished she would wish also, and would always wish – and she moved towards him with a little sigh and lifted her face with perfect trust to his.

Which made it difficult for Rom to do what he intended – more difficult than he would have believed. But he mastered himself, and smiled down at her and smoothed her rumpled hair. Then carefully, methodically, he did up the small round button at the top of her negligée and kissed her once briefly on the tip of her nose.

'Now,' he said, taking her hand as one would take the hand of a child, 'I'm going to send you home. Tomorrow I shall come into Manaus and we'll talk, but now you must go.'

'Must I?'

'Yes, my dear. At once.' And his voice suddenly rough, 'No breath of scandal shall touch you while I live.'

101

CHAPTER SEVEN

THE LETTER which Stavely's young bailiff had brought to Isobel Brandon's room on the day that the Trumpington Tea Circle ladies were touring the house came from Hathersage and Climpton, the London accountants who had looked after the Brandons' financial affairs for many years, and accompanied a detailed report the results of which were unequivocal. As the result of the present owner's extravagances and speculations, the estate was now encumbered to the point of no return. If bankruptcy and disgrace were to be avoided, Stavely must be sold and sold immediately.

This letter, which drew from Isobel the exclamation that Harriet overheard, was in fact only a copy of the original which reached Henry Brandon in the Toulouse lodgings to which he had retreated in order to avoid his creditors. After which, conventional to the last, he retired to his bedroom, took out his father's army revolver and blew out his brains.

It was thus as a widow of ten days' standing that Isobel Brandon sat in front of the mirror in her suite at the Hotel Astor in London, pinning up the rich red braids of her hair. Black suited her, thank heavens, for she would be in mourning for at least a year; the velvet jacket, bought in one of the few shops where her credit still held good, brought out the whiteness of her skin; she was one of those fortunate redheads untroubled by freckles.

But the sight of her reflection was the only thing of comfort in the bleak wilderness that her life had become, for it did not occur to her to find solace in the small, bespectacled child curled up in an arm-chair with his nose, as always, in a book. Henry, with his pale, pinched little face, his unmanly terrors, was not at all the kind of son she had hoped for – and suddenly exasperated by his concentration, his inability to

102

see what she was enduring, she said, 'Really, Henry, you don't seem to realise at all what is at stake. It's *your* heritage I'm trying to save. Do you want us to go and live in a sordid little hut somewhere?'

With a tremendous effort of will, Henry rose twenty thousand leagues from the bottom of the sea, abandoning brave Captain Nemo who had just sighted a frightful monster with bristling jaws, and considered her question.

'Yes,' he said, 'I'd like that. With a palm-leaf roof. The *ubussu* palm is best; it keeps the hut cool when the weather's hot and doesn't let in the rain at all. I'd go out every day and shoot animals for food. And I'd fish in the river. I'd look after you,' said Henry to his mother.

'Oh, God!'

The child's face fell. He'd got it wrong again; his mother didn't believe he could provide for her. Harriet would have believed it . . . Harriet, who had said that spectacles were an *advantage* . . .

For a while he waited, wondering if this was the moment to ask what 'sordid' meant – was it some kind of hut – but his mother's face had that closed look again, and with a small sigh Henry sank back and rejoined his companions on the ocean bed.

Why did that plain little son of hers have to inherit the General's wide grey eyes, thought Isobel – eyes that her husband had missed, but that had so curiously lightened Rom's vivid dark face. But here she veered away, as always, from the memory of that quicksilver, brilliant boy she had loved so idiotically. It was ten years since anyone had heard from Rom and he might as well be dead.

Had it been such a crime to marry sensibly, thought Isobel, jabbing pins into the fiery coils of her hair? To want Stavely? Land outlasted passion, everybody knew that. Henry, then, had seemed a wise choice. Dear God, to let the mind overrule the heart – was that something she should have paid for with such misery only to be left a pauper at the end?

Who could have foreseen that this prudent marriage would turn out to be the kind of nightmare it had done? That she, who had hardly been able to let Rom out of her sight, would be unable to endure the caresses of his half-brother. And who could have foreseen that Henry, faced with her disgust, would go to the dogs as thoroughly and conventionally as he had formerly played the country gentleman? Even before she had shut him out of her bedroom he had begun to drink, to gamble, and afterwards . . .

She lifted her hand to the bell in order to ring for the manicurist who usually did her nails but dropped it again, remembering the appraising glance of the maître d'hôtel as he had noted – even while he bent over her hand, murmuring condolences on her loss – that she had come without her maid or a nurse for the child. He knew, as did the rest of London, that the sands were running out for the Brandons. Not that she had actually been refused a room, but there were none of the attentions she was accustomed to when she came to the Astor: no bowls of fruit or baskets of roses . . . and in the dining-room she had been shown to an obscure table in the corner.

Oh, God, it was impossible, intolerable! There had to be some way out of the trap. And like one of those awful recurring dreams from which one thinks one has awoken, only to find it start again, she recalled the interview she had had with old Mr Hathersage the previous day in his fusty office behind St Paul's.

'I'm afraid there is absolutely no help for it, Mrs Brandon. You must know that if there was any other way my accountants would have found it. But the figures are inescapable. You must sell, Mrs Brandon; you must sell for what you can get, and you must do so quickly.'

She finished buffing her nails and rose. 'We're going shopping, Henry,' she said. 'Come here while I make you tidy.'

'Could I stay here and read?'

'No, you couldn't. We're going to the dentist afterwards.'

Henry nodded. Shopping *and* the dentist. A sombre prospect, but not more than he had learned to expect, and he stood patiently while Isobel tugged at his Norfolk jacket with unpractised hands and jammed his cap on his head. The impertinence of that nursemaid, simply walking out without warning just because she had not been paid for a few weeks!

Usually there was nothing Isobel liked better than to shop and her mourning provided an excellent excuse for several new outfits, but there were only a few places now where her credit still held good. To these – little glove shops and hatters in the discreet, quiet streets round St James's whose owners, accustomed to serving the Brandons, had not learned to defend themselves – she now repaired. If she knew that the exquisite black kid gloves, the jet-beaded reticule and velvet toque she purchased would not be paid for, she concealed any anxiety she might have felt with remarkable success.

It had been hard for Henry to abandon the *Nautilus* and Captain Nemo, but now he trotted obediently beside his mother studying with

104

scholarly attention the posters on the hoardings, the men digging a hole in the road, the passers-by.

'Why do they make "*Little* Liver Pills"?' Henry wanted to know. 'If they made them *big*, wouldn't people's livers get better more quickly?' And: 'If those men in the road dug and dug and dug, would they be the right way up when they got to Australia, or would they be upsidedown?'

'Oh, Henry, be quiet!' They had just passed Fortnum's, in the window of which there was an exquisite ink-dark chenille gown which would have suited her magnificently, but the last time she had tried to charge anything here there had been a most unpleasant scene.

Henry made a heroic effort, forbearing to ask what made the red colour in the glass dome in the chemist's window and not even suggesting that they stop to give a penny to a beggar on crutches and with a row of medals on his chest. But when two men walked right across the pavement in front of him carrying a big wicker basket into a shop, he found it impossible not to pluck at his mother's sleeve.

'Look!' he said. 'That's my name on the basket – one of my names. It's spelled the same too.'

Isobel looked up, following her son's pointing finger, and saw on the side of a basket, with its heavy leather straps, the letters R. P. VERNEY.

'Is something the matter?' Henry asked anxiously. He had hoped for once to interest his mother, but not to interest her as much as that. She had stopped dead on the pavement, her hand at her throat.

R.P.V.B. Romain Paul Verney Brandon. How often had she seen those initials entwined with her own! Not carved in the bark of trees – Rom allowed no one to despoil his beloved trees – but he had drawn them for her on the clear, fawn sand when they spent a day by the sea; sown them in cress seeds on a bed of earth while the old gardener scratched his head and muttered at the foolishness of the young. If Rom had wanted to forget Stavely – forget her and the Brandons – what more likely than that he had simply dropped his last name – too careless, too arrogant perhaps, to make a more fundamental change?

'Wait here,' she said to Henry. 'I won't be long. Don't move and don't speak to *anyone*.'

'Yes,' said Henry.

There was nothing to be afraid of, Henry told himself as his mother pushed open the door of the shop which was labelled 'Truscott and Musgrave': and had windows which were covered up so that one couldn't see inside.

He knew she wouldn't forget him; she wouldn't go out through another door and leave him on the pavement. But nevertheless he began to feel that awful churning in his stomach which meant that soon he was going to be very afraid indeed, which was ridiculous if he wanted to be an explorer. It was more than two years ago when she had told him to wait on a black leather chair in the bank at Harrods, and had gone to meet a friend and left by another door and forgotten him, and it hadn't *really* been so bad. When after an hour he had begun to cry – which was silly, but he *had* been younger then – an old lady had come, and then someone from the shop, and they had fetched a policeman and taken him back to the hotel. And his mother had been very upset and sorry and bought him some marzipan.

Only of course he would rather not be forgotten than have marzipan . . .

I'll count up to a hundred, thought Henry, and then another hundred and another and then she'll come. Sinclair of the Scouts, in the *Boy's Own* paper – he wouldn't have made a fuss because he had to stand and wait for his mother in the street . . . and anyway they were going to the dentist. She might forget him but she would not forget the *dentist* . . .

Inside the shop Isobel had made an entirely hypothetical enquiry about laundering the damask for Stavely, receiving from the grey-haired and serious Mr Truscott a courteous and considered reply, and taken down some notes. If Mr Truscott was surprised that a woman of quality should attend to these matters herself rather than send her housekeeper, he kept this to himself. Then, as she was putting on her gloves, she said almost casually, 'I noticed your men bringing in a basket just now and it seemed to me that I knew the name. Verney was a family name of my husband's and he had a distant cousin named Paul.'

'It might well be, Mrs Brandon. I have never met Mr Verney myself, but we have dealt with his linen for eight years now. An excellent customer, always very prompt with his payment.'

'He lives in London, then?'

'London? Oh dear me, no! Far from it.' Mr Truscott smiled, for the legend of Mr Verney's washing did much to brighten the monotony of life in the shop. He paused, enjoying himself, and said, 'He lives in Brazil. In Manaus, one thousand miles up the River Amazon.'

'The Amazon!' Isobel's heart began to pound, but the implications

106

of what she had just heard were too extraordinary. 'But he *cannot* send his washing home from the Amazon! He cannot!'

'Well, that's exactly what he does do, Madam. Beautiful linen, quite outstanding workmanship. Every three weeks when the liner docks at Manaus, his servants put a basket on the ship. Then at Liverpool they put it on the train and we send our cart to Euston and return the clean linen. Oh yes, it's quite an event when Mr Verney's linen basket comes!'

'But it must cost a fortune!'

'Well, not a fortune, Madam, but certainly a fair sum. However, I imagine Mr Verney would have no regard to that. All the gentlemen out there live like princes and he is one of the richest, they say. It's the rubber, you see.'

He launched into a description of the rubber trade to which Isobel listened absently, her mind racing.

'And Mrs Verney – does she send her washing home too?'

'I have not heard of there being a Mrs Verney, Madam. Certainly we don't get her linen. But of course, we are more of a gentlemen's service on the whole.'

Isobel thanked him and promised to let him know about the Stavely damask. Enquiries would have to be made, of course, but that should not be difficult; Bertie Freeman worked in the Consulate at Rio and a cable to him should elicit the necessary facts. But if it was Rom – and really she had no doubt of it – then all her troubles were over. If Rom lived and was rich, her future glittered as brightly as a star. Rom would save Stavely – she had never seen in anyone such a feeling for a piece of land – and he would save her! Even if there was a dreary wife somewhere, she would not be able to prevent it. And as she made her way out of the shop, Isobel's lips curved into the special smile which belonged to her time with that extraordinary and brilliant boy.

Henry was standing obediently where she had left him and when he saw her his face lit up in a way which tugged at her consciousness, absorbed as she was. There was something not unpleasing about Henry – something a little wistful. A man with Rom's protective instincts might well be moved by the plight of such a fatherless young child.

'Would you like to go on a journey, Henry?' she asked now. 'A long one?'

And Henry said, 'Yes.'

107

CHAPTER EIGHT

'THANK YOU,' said Harriet tenderly to the waiter, who was placing before her a fried egg swimming in grease and a mound of peppery beans. '*Obrigado. Gosto muito!*'

Breakfast at the Hotel Metropole was not normally a beautiful experience; the same food appeared at all meals, the sluggish fan scarcely stirred the fetid air, swollen black flies buzzed on the overcrowded flypapers. But the morning after the party at Follina the world, for Harriet, was bathed in an all-embracing golden light.

She had returned unnoticed the night before; both Kirstin and Marie-Claude had been fast asleep – her adventure was unknown to anyone but herself. And Mr Verney had said that today he would come to find her. She must not depend on it . . . but he had said it.

'It is not necessary to give thanks for such a breakfast,' said Marie-Claude, shuddering. But she herself was in a good mood for her encounter with Harry Parker, the secretary of the Sports Club, had turned out to be extremely fortunate. She had been offered, and at very little personal inconvenience, a chance to augment by an appreciable sum the savings she and Vincent were amassing for the purchase of the restaurant.

'In two weeks' time,' she said now, lowering her voice, for the rest of the company was sitting at tables close by, 'I am going to burst at the Sports Club! From a cake! For seven hundred and fifty milreis in cash.' And as Kirstin and Harriet looked at her with raised eyebrows, she added, 'Mr Parker invited me: it is a thing that is very much done in gentlemen's clubs when there is a special dinner of some kind. This one is for the Minister for Amazonia, who is coming from Rio to discuss the organisation of river transport or some such thing. The cake is wheeled in for dessert and – hoop la!' She put down her fork to

108

sketch in the air the deliciously titillating eruption which woud follow.

Harriet was impressed. 'From a real cake, Marie-Claude?'

'No, idiot! It's an enormous wooden affair – generally pink and decorated with candles. Sometimes they release white doves at the same time, though then of course there are problems with the feathers and the excretion and so on. Sometimes there are men with trumpets who accompany the cake and a chef who plunges in the knife . . . and of course always balloons and streamers and a great deal of champagne.'

'Will Vincent like it?' enquired Kirstin.

'It is precisely for Vincent that I am doing it,' flashed Marie-Claude. But a pensive look spread for a moment over her heart-shaped face, for it was true that she had not precisely explained to Vincent the means she employed to increase their joint savings. Vincent himself was strait-laced and his family – notably his cousin Pierre under whom Vincent had trained – was positively gothic. Still, what could one do? It was necessary to be practical. 'You won't mention it to anyone?' she pleaded. 'The dinner begins very late; after the curtain goes down. No one at the theatre need know.'

'Of course not,' Harriet was overawed. Thus, she was sure, had Messalina erupted in the last days of Imperial Rome. 'Only, Marie-Claude, when you come out of the cake won't the gentlemen become over-excited and – you know?'

'Over-excitement is something I do not permit,' said Marie-Claude, pushing away her egg with a *moue* of disgust. 'I made this absolutely clear to Mr Parker. I burst; I dance a little on the table; I sit for a moment in the lap of the Minister – and that is all.'

'What will you wear?' asked Kirstin.

'Not very much,' Marie-Claude admitted. 'Mr Parker insisted on this. But there is always my hair which covers most things, and I have a special garter with a large rosette in which my Tante Bertha's hat-pin can be concealed. Not that it will be necessary, I assure you. The whole affair is strictly a matter of art – a kind of *tableau vivant* – and anyway, the Minister is old.' She paused and fixed her enormous eyes on Harriet. 'There is, however, a problem,' she said, lowering her voice still further and glancing over her shoulder at the alcove where Dubrov and those of the principals who could face the Metropole dining-room at breakfast were sitting. 'I have to see Mr Parker at eleven-thirty this morning to make the arrangements.'

'But it's the costume rehearsal for *The Nutcracker*,' said Harriet.

'Exactly. So you, Harriet, must be for me a mouse,' said Marie-Claude.

'Oh, Marie-Claude, I couldn't,' said Harriet, aghast. 'I've never been a mouse; I don't know the steps or anything!'

'There are no steps,' said Marie-Claude contemptuously. 'One scampers and runs about and bites toy soldiers in the legs.' She poured herself another cup of coffee and contemplated with gloom the bizarre events on which Tchaikovsky had wasted some of his loveliest music. And indeed it is not easy to see why little Clara is so delighted to get a nutcracker for Christmas nor why, almost at once, there is a battle between toy soldiers and some hitherto unsuspected mice.

'I'll help you, Harriet,' offered Kirstin. A little taller than the others, she was doomed to be a soldier and smite the attacking rodents with a wooden sword. 'And in any case the rehearsal will be chaos; everyone will be in hysterics long before lunch.'

She spoke no less than the truth. *The Nutcracker* was the only ballet in which Simonova did not star, but in ceding the role of the Sugar Plum Fairy to Masha Repin, Simonova was by no means quitting the field. She was going to supervise rehearsals, she was going to put her experience at the service of the younger girl; she was going to *help*.

'*Please*, Harriet?' begged Marie-Claude, laying a pearl-tipped hand on Harriet's arm. 'I would ask Olga, but she was sick in the night and the other Russian girls are such prigs.'

Of such a request there could only be one outcome. Harriet might hate deceiving Monsieur Dubrov and be frightened of the consequences, but it was out of the question that she should refuse to help her friend. Thus two hours later, entirely enveloped (at a temperature of ninety-two degrees) in simulated fur, her face covered by a mask, she was on stage being a belligerent and really rather unpleasant mouse.

*

Rom came in the little *Firefly*, a sentimental gesture which almost doubled his travelling time, and tying up at his private jetty made his way along the quayside, acknowledging the salutations of his men who were trundling their black 'biscuits' of rubber towards the lighters. He passed quickly through his warehouses and entered the chaotic office – with its maps, samples of *cahuchu*, telegraph machine and stained coffee-cups – from which his manager attended the needs

110

of the Verney empire.

'All is well, *Coronel?*' asked Miguel, lifting his pince-nez and removing a pile of files from a chair for his employer. But the question was rhetorical. Miguel, rescued from schoolmastering, had served Verney since he first came to the Amazon and it was clear that this morning his master was very well indeed. Was this the moment, Miguel wondered, to put in a word for his nephew who was just out of school and looking for a job?

But Verney was in a hurry. 'I have an appointment,' he said. 'We'll just do the most urgent things. I want the Pittsburg contract and the projection of the hardwood requirements for Bernard Fils in Marseilles. The rest can wait.'

Miguel nodded and produced the documents in an instant from the apparent confusion of his desk. 'One of de Silva's clerks came in this morning with a copy of the Ombidos report. He said you wanted to see it before the visit of the Minister.'

'That's right.' Rom's face was momentarily sombre at the mention of Ombidos, that plague spot from which rumours of ill-treatment and butchery of the Indians continued to filter through. 'I'll take it home.'

Less than an hour later Verney left the office, crossed the narrow harbour-side road and climbed a steep flight of steps to enter, through a blue door in a high wall, the bougainvillea-covered *Casa Branca*.

It was the smallest of houses – a toy place high above the huddle of buildings that looked out over the river; a white box with blue shutters and a handkerchief of a terrace with a fig tree. An unlikely dwelling for a rubber baron, but it was the first home Rom had owned and he had kept it, finding it useful when he had to spend a night in the city. Carmen looked after the house; Pedro acted as chauffeur for the Cadillac he kept in a neighbouring mews. No women came to the *Casa Branca* but it was here under the fig tree in the little courtyard suspended over the harbour that he had decided to give Harriet lunch. She would like the view; she would like Pedro and Carmen – and he did not want her exposed to the stares and nudges of the other diners in fashionable restaurants.

'A light meal, Carmen,' he said. 'An avocado mousse, some fish . . . And the Frascati to drink.'

'Will you want the motor, *Senhor?*'

'No.'

He went upstairs to shower and fifteen minutes later was letting

111

himself into the Teatro Amazonas by a side door.

Dubrov, watching out front, turned and half rose as Rom slipped into a seat beside him.

'You should have told us you were coming,' he said, pushing a hand through his dishevelled hair. 'Simonova would have wished to welcome you herself.' (She would have *wished* to . . . but he had left the ballerina in her dressing-room, screaming with rage at Masha Repin's refusal to be coached.)

'I've come to take Harriet out to lunch,' said Rom in a low voice, fascinated by the antics on the stage. 'If that's convenient? When do you expect a break?'

'It shouldn't be long now. There have been a few . . . difficulties.' So Mr Verney was interested in Harriet? Flattering; very flattering. 'It will do her good to get out,' said the impresario. 'She works so hard.'

'She certainly seems to be dancing with great aplomb. It must be very hot under those pelts.'

Dubrov smiled tolerantly. Mr Verney was a man of formidable intelligence, but no connoisseur of the ballet. 'Harriet is not dancing at the moment. Later you will see her; she is a snowflake.'

'Really? I could have sworn she was that one on the right, just coming out from behind the Christmas tree. With the tattered ear.'

Dubrov shook a decisive head. 'That's Marie-Claude. It's a crime to put a girl like that into a mask, but there!'

Somewhat to Dubrov's surprise, Simonova greeted the news of Harriet's luncheon engagement with satisfaction.

'It will annoy Masha,' she said simply. 'Did you notice the sheep's eyes she made at Verney yesterday?'

Dubrov nodded. Masha Repin had certainly made efforts to attract Verney's attention, but so had virtually every other woman who was there. Still, anything that distracted Simonova from Masha Repin's arrogance, her inability to take the advice which she, Simonova, had taken so gladly, so willingly from Kchessinskaya, from Legat – from absolutely everyone who was kind enough to help her – was all to the good.

It was not only Simonova who watched Harriet go with a feeling of pleasure at her good fortune. Lobotsky, the character dancer, patted her shoulder; the ASM wished her luck; even Maximov deigned to smile at her. Only Kirstin was disquieted. Harriet looked nice – even the absent Marie-Claude could not have complained about her blue

112

skirt and white blouse – but to expose to the gods a face of such unalloyed expectation and happiness seemed to the gentle Swede to be little short of madness.

Rom was right. Harriet liked the *Casa Branca*.

'Oh, the view!' she said. 'They always say something beautiful is breath*taking*, but it ought to be breath*giving*, oughtn't it?'

They had lunch in the shade of the fig tree and beneath them the life of the river unfolded for their delight. Rom had wined and dined innumerable women, flicking his fingers at servile waiters, but now he found himself watching over Harriet as if she was a child in his keeping, concerned lest even the smallest of bones should scratch her delicate throat; buttering her roll.

'Tell me, were you a mouse just now?' he asked. 'A mouse with a tattered ear?'

She looked up, flushing. 'Yes, I was.'

Rom nodded. 'I thought you were. Dubrov swore it was Marie-Claude, but I knew it was you.'

She put down her fork. 'How? I was completely covered with a mask. How could you know?'

'I *knew*,' said Rom. He let the words stand deliberately ringed in silence . . . but not for long. She must remain untroubled by anything for which she was not yet ready. 'Were you covering up for Marie-Claude?'

Harriet nodded. 'But please don't mention it to Monsieur Dubrov. She had to go away on business – for Vincent and the restaurant.'

'Ah, yes . . . the famous Vincent. Have you met him?'

'No, but I have seen his photograph. A *lot* of photographs!'

'And?' said Rom. 'Is he a match for your ravishing friend?'

'Well, it's strange. I mean, it's absolutely clear that she adores him. And of course he does have a very large moustache, which is important to her – all his family are famous for their moustaches – and photographs don't tell you very much about people, do they? I think it must be his personality.'

'A strong man, then?'

'Very *practical* and Marie-Claude likes that. She gets very annoyed with people like Romeo. He should have got a chicken feather, she thinks, and laid it on Juliet's lips to see if she was breathing, not rushed about and killed himself.'

'Vincent is a chicken-feather man, then?'

'Very much so, I understand.' Harriet hesitated. 'I can see Marie-

113

Claude's point. When I read about love in Cambridge – and I used to read a lot because my Aunt Louisa let me do my homework in the public library to save the gas – I got very discouraged. It seemed to me that as soon as you loved anyone very much, you were inevitably doomed. You know . . . Heloise and Abelard, Tristan and Isolde . . . To love in moderation was all right, but when it became excessive . . . total . . . you were punished. And yet it must be right, surely, to give everything? To hold nothing back? That must be what one wants to do?'

'Yes, one wants to do just that. And I assure you that there are plenty of people who have loved truly and found their Avalon or their Hesperides and set up house there and tended their crops and lit their fires. Only who cares for them? Who writes about the valley with no earthquake, the river that is not in flood?'

He smiled at her, the grey eyes serene and comforting, and led her on to talk not of her home which he knew would give her pain, but of Cambridge itself, that incomparable city. And if he had doubted his feelings, those doubts would have been banished by the greed with which he longed to share her childhood and her memories.

Carmen brought coffee and a bowl of fruit which Rom studied attentively before picking a golden-pink pomegranate which he placed not on Harriet's plate, but into her obediently cupped hands. 'Are you willing to take the risk?' he asked. 'They're dangerous things, pomegranates.'

She caught the allusion instantly, as he had known she would.

'Oh yes,' she said. 'It would be no punishment to have to remain here in this place. Or to return. Not for five months or fifty.'

She was silent, thinking of Persephone who had eaten her pomegranate in Hades, carried there by cruel Pluto, king of the underworld. Had she minded going back into darkness, compelled to return for as many months as she had eaten seeds, while the world in her absence turned to winter? Or had Pluto looked a little like the man who faced her? Dark-visaged; sardonic; a few silver threads in the ink-black hair. In which case she must have wished she had eaten *more* seeds . . . And smiling, Harriet picked up the silver fruit knife.

But Rom now had decided that it was time for her to speak, for he had not forgotten that this was a meal with a purpose and, sensing that she might find it difficult to begin, he prompted her.

'Tell me now, Harriet. Tell me why you stayed behind after the party. What was it you wanted to speak to me about?'

114

She put down the knife again, her face suddenly sombre. Increasingly it seemed impertinent to mention his past life. He must have contacts in every country in the world and certainly in England. If he had wanted to keep in touch with the place that had been his home, nothing could have been easier. And to give herself strength she summoned up again the image of the red-haired child in the maze, bewildered by the disaster that had struck his house.

'It was Stavely,' said Harriet in a low voice. 'It was Stavely that I wanted to talk about.'

'Stavely!'

The effect was extraordinary. The comradeship, the warmth that had been between them vanished in an instant. The dark, exotic face became blank, shuttered. But it was too late now to withdraw.

'Forgive me – but you did live there, didn't you, as a child?'

'Yes. I lived there for the first nineteen years of my life.'

She nodded. 'I knew. Even before you named the manatee. When you stepped out of the trees, I knew.'

He could make no sense of this and sat tracing the pattern of the tablecloth with one finger. From Stavely, where Henry and Isobel presumably dwelt in connubial bliss, there could come nothing that one way or another could fail to cause him pain.

'I don't know if you've heard,' said Harriet, forcing herself to go on, 'but things are very bad there.'

'No, I had not. In what way?'

'Well, the house is . . . unkempt . . . ill-cared-for; there are hardly any servants except horrible Mr Grunthorpe. And the garden – oh, the garden is heartbreaking. Such lovely plants and everything overgrown and neglected.'

He pushed away his chair and rose, the simple gesture taking on an extraordinary sense of violence, and moved across to where the fig tree leaned its branches over the terrace wall.

'He had no right,' she heard him murmur. 'Not the garden . . .' and for a moment he leaned his head against the smooth grey bark as if in unutterable weariness.

'There was no need for that,' he said, coming back to stand behind his chair. 'My father left enough.'

'Your father?'

'My father was General Brandon. I am his son by his second marriage.' He made an impatient gesture. 'I don't wish to go into that; I simply want to know why you have come to tell me all this.

115

Why *you*, Harriet?'

'Because of Henry.'

She was looking down, her head bent over the table, and missed the whitening of his knuckles as he grasped the chair-back, the shock that passed over his face.

Henry! As clearly as if he stood before him, Rom saw the smug pale face of his hated step-brother. Henry who had cheated him, betrayed him . . . who had stood smirking down at Isobel in the Orangery on that last day . . .

'Yes, it was because of Henry,' said Harriet. 'I met him there when I went on a visit and I liked him so much. I loved him, I think.' Her voice was ineffably tender; she made the gesture that women make when they express a sensuous surrender, cupping her hands round her own throat. 'I wanted to help him.'

Rom did not speak. His face as he struggled with the blow she had dealt him was that of a Tartar chieftain, foreign and cruel.

'Henry thought you might be here.' Her voice was still dreamy with remembrance. 'Because of the book you left behind with Nannie. Because you were always talking about the Amazon. He said, if I found you, would I ask you to come back. He thought you would be able to make everything all right again at Stavely. It was because of him, really, that I came,' finished Harriet. 'He made me brave.'

Only now did she look up. 'What is it?' she faltered. 'What have I done?'

Rom was in control again. She had spoken for scarcely two minutes, yet in that time he had torn from his heart every feeling she had aroused; every hope that loneliness was ended. Only his anger remained – the anger with which, since his mother's death, Rom had responded to loss.

'Let me get this clear, Harriet. When you stayed behind last night, it was to tell me what you have told me now? It was to plead for Henry Brandon?'

'Yes.' Separated by fear from the common-sense which might have saved them both, stupid with bewilderment, she could only repeat, 'I wanted to help him, is that so terrible? *What have I done?*'

'Nothing,' he said. 'You have done nothing. On the contrary, you have fulfilled your mission excellently. And now please go back and tell your protégé that I will see him in hell before I raise a finger to save Stavely. Just tell him that.' He stood for a moment looking down at the fruit on the table with the ghost of a smile. 'How wise you were

116

not to open it,' he said, picking up the pomegranate. 'Not a single seed eaten. No reason ever to return.'

He balanced the golden orb for a moment on his hand – then threw it with all his strength in a high arc over the wall. 'Pedro will take you back in the car,' he said – and without a goodbye, without a handshake, was gone.

*

Two days later the redoubtable Olga fell ill. Since their arrival Dubrov had relentlessly patrolled the Metropole dining-room, forbidding anyone to drink unboiled water on pain of instant dismissal; he had handed out quinine, had himself checked the mosquito netting in the girls' bedrooms and confiscated all fruit bought from barrows in the street. Even so, several members of the company had complained of stomach pains and with three days of the first week's run of *Swan Lake* still to go, Olga was definitely too ill to dance.

'Seventeen swans again,' said Grisha gloomily.

But more serious than the inconvenience of rearranging the choreography for the *corps* was the need to rehearse a new 'Odette-at-the window'. For Olga had been the girl who, dressed as the Swan Queen in her white tutu and glittering crown, flutters at the window in such anguish to show the Prince that he has been tricked – that the girl he has just promised to marry is not the real Odette, but an usurper.

It is a short scene, scarcely three minutes in all – yet it is rare for anyone to leave the theatre without recalling the image of that beseeching, moonlit figure, exiled from happiness and love.

'Kira is the nearest to you in size,' said Dubrov to Simonova as she lay on the yellow silk couch of her dressing-room, fanning herself with a moulting ostrich fan.

'Impossible! I will not be represented by a girl with square thighs.'

Dubrov sighed. 'Lydia then. She is a little taller than you, but the colouring's right.'

There was a pause while Simonova pulled up her kimono and studied her left knee. Then, 'Give it to Harriet,' said the ballerina.

'Harriet?' Dubrov looked up, surprised, from the knee he had automatically begun to massage. 'I hadn't thought of giving her anything extra – she is so new. But you're right, she is the same height as you and the same build.'

'She will know what to do,' said Simonova. 'A little too well,

117

perhaps.'

'Yes.'

Harriet had returned from her luncheon date with a blind, lost look that had made Dubrov want to shake the handsome and generous Mr Verney. Since then, saying nothing to anyone, she had worked if anything harder than before. It should have been a relief to be free of the child's enthusiasms; Dubrov had suffered as much as anyone from Harriet's determination to befriend the loathsome vultures that sat on the verandah of the hotel, holding out their black wings to dry after the rain, or the glad cries with which she announced the presence of a green and crimson frog who had taken refuge in the showers. But to see her become once more the quiet resigned girl she had been in Cambridge was hard.

'What happened?' Marie-Claude had demanded of Kirstin, returning to find Harriet white and silent, practising at the *barre*. And reproaching herself: 'I should have stayed to see to her toilette.'

'Oh, Marie-Claude, everything isn't clothes. I saw how he looked at her when she came out of the stage-door. It was a misunderstanding, a quarrel – it must have been.'

Her summons to Dubrov's office filled Harriet with alarm. Had he discovered after all that she had stood in for Marie-Claude?

'You are to be the swan at the window instead of Olga,' announced Dubrov, adding firmly, 'It is an extremely small part and naturally there will be no increase in privileges. Or in pay.'

'Oh!' Her thin face lit up. Whatever happened there was still work. 'But why me – surely one of the others . . . ?'

'It was Madame Simonova's suggestion. Grisha will show you the movements after lunch. Then we shall rehearse once with the lights before the performance. You go on tonight, of course.'

'Tonight! I can't . . .' she began to say, and stopped. For she could, as a matter of fact. This she *could* do.

Simonova herself attended the rehearsal, as did Dubrov and a surprising number of the cast. Harriet learned the steps quickly and indeed there was little enough to do except stand on her *pointes* and flutter her piteous arms. Nor was it possible for her to miss her cue for it was the swan motif itself, with its haunting oboes, that heralded her brief entrance. In half an hour it was clear that Harriet would manage, and indeed there was no girl in the *corps* who could not have managed this unexacting task.

All the same, those who watched her were in their different ways

118

displeased.

'Poor child! It is a mistake to be like that,' said Simonova, flopping down on the bed when she was back in her room at the Metropole. 'Of course, it is good for one's dancing afterwards.' She took off her shoes and dropped them on the floor. 'What was the name of that hussar, do you remember? In the Rodenzky regiment? The year I met you.'

'Count Zugarovitch,' said Dubrov, coming to sit beside her on the bed. The young blue-eyed hussar had been killed in a duel soon afterwards and he could afford to be magnanimous.

'Yes. It is because of him that I am unsurpassed in *Giselle*,' said Simonova with her usual modesty. 'Still, it is awful, this love.' She laid her head with unaccustomed tenderness against his shoulder – a gesture which, though it was intended for the dead hussar, Dubrov proceeded to turn to good account.

Marie-Claude, accosting Harriet as she changed in the chorus dressing-room, was simply angry.

'There is no need for you to act like that; it is only a rehearsal and the whole scene will be played behind gauzes and there is no extra pay.'

'Like what?' asked Harriet, bewildered.

'As though you were really suffering. As though you were really outside and lost and frightened and looking in on happiness from which you were excluded *et tout ça*. It is not *necessary*,' raged Marie-Claude.

'You are certainly a good actress, Harriet,' said Kirstin. 'You seemed absolutely anguished.'

'Did I?' Harriet was surprised. 'It's just that I know . . . what it is like. I know how it is to be at a window . . . outside . . . and to look in on a lighted room and not be able to make anybody hear.'

'How can you know? You have not experienced it.'

Harriet hung Odette's glittering crown on a peg above the mirror and reached for her comb. 'Perhaps I am going to one day,' she said. 'There is a man in England who says that time is curved and that we can sometimes see . . .'

But Marie-Claude was entirely uninterested in metaphysical theories about time. 'It is only necessary to do the steps,' she snapped.

And after all Marie-Claude was right, for when Harriet came on that night she was just a distant, half-lit figure vanishing in an instant – and the only man who might have known that it was Harriet and not Olga who trembled and beckoned at the window was a hundred miles away.

119

CHAPTER NINE

'EAT, *Coronel*,' begged Furo, pushing the tin plate towards his master.

The brightly patterned fish, salted and grilled on a driftwood fire, smelled delicious but Rom shook his head. He sat leaning against the twisted trunk of a mango, letting the fine sand of the *praia* on which they had made camp run through his fingers. Nearby the *Daisy May* floated quietly at anchor. A cormorant turned a yellow-ringed and disbelieving eye on the intruders and flapped off across the river. In the still water, the colours of the sunset changed from flame to primrose and a last glimmer of unearthly green.

Rom, usually aware of every stirring leaf, noticed nothing; he was lost in the horror of what he had just seen.

He had meant simply to spend a few days on the river, wanting to shake off the memory of that ill-fated lunch with Harriet. Taking only the silent and devoted Furo – loading the boat with the usual gifts of fish-hooks and beads and medical supplies – he had travelled up the Negro, bound for an island where tree orchids grew in incredible profusion and the snowy egrets made their nests.

Then something – he had no idea what it was – made him turn up the Ombidos river. There had long been rumours of gross ill-treatment of the Indians by the men who ran the Ombidos Rubber Company, and the report de Silva had sent down had made disquieting reading, but Rom had seen too many do-gooders and journalists make capital out of the rubber barons' wicked treatment of the natives to be seriously disturbed. Moreover the company was entirely Brazilian-owned. Rom might fight exploitation ruthlessly where it was inflicted by Europeans, but he did not meddle in the affairs of his hosts.

Yet at the end of the second day, the *Daisy May* was chugging at a steady seven knots up the Ombidos. Perhaps it was hindsight, but it seemed to Rom a frightful place; the 'green hell' so beloved of the fiction writers come hideously to life. Oppressive, dark, ominously silent: only the mosquitos, incessant and insatiable even in the hissing rain, seemed to be alive on that Stygian stretch of water.

That night they had tied up in a creek, concealed by overhanging trees. The next morning Rom put on a battered sombrero, slung a rifle over his shoulder and, with his pockets full of trinkets, disappeared along a jungle track in the direction of the village. With his two-day stubble, his shirt stained by grease from the *Daisy May*'s engine, he passed easily enough for a poor-white trader come to cheat the natives out of basket-work or cured skins for a handful of beads.

He was away for twenty-four hours. Since then he had spoken only to give Furo orders which would take them away fast, and faster, from that accursed place. Even now, fifty miles down-river in as halcyon a spot as anyone could hope for, he sat like a man in a trance and in that steaming jungle, looked cold.

'It was very bad, then?' enquired Furo at last.

Rom stirred and turned.

'Yes.'

He took the bottle of brandy that Furo had pushed towards him and tilted it to his mouth, but nothing could blot out what he had seen at Ombidos. He had believed that he knew of all the cruelties which men had inflicted on the Indians in their insane greed for rubber . . . Workers flayed into insensibility with tapir-hide whips for bringing in less *cahuchu* than their master craved; hirelings with Winchesters dragging into slavery every able-bodied man in a village . . . He himself had been offered – by a drunken overseer on the Madeira – one of the man's native concubines, a girl just nine years old . . .

But he had seen nothing. Until he had been to Ombidos, he had not known what cruelty was. And with the men who had done . . . those things . . . he had smiled and joked. He had not killed one of them; had not throttled with his bare hands a single one of the torturers, because he had to return and bear witness.

'Is it true that messages have gone to the Minister in Rio to tell of the bad things at Ombidos?' asked Furo, staring trustingly at his master.

'Yes, it is true. To Antonio Alvarez, the Minister for Amazonia.'

'And he is coming to Manaus. So he will go to Ombidos and see for himself? He will make it right?'

121

Rom shook his head. 'He will come, Furo. He will dine at the Sports Club and go to Madame Anita's brothel with the Mayor and attend some meetings at the Town Hall in his tight suit and pointed shoes. But he will not go to Ombidos.'

Antonio Alvarez, a man approaching sixty . . . A gourmet who travelled with a French chef; a dandy who kept a retinue of hairdressers, valets and masseurs in his mansion in Rio . . . Nothing on God's earth, thought Rom, would get Alvarez to that hell-hole. It was said that once he had been different – an idealist and a patriot – but that had been decades ago. Some personal tragedy was supposed to have turned him into the man he now was, the man Rom knew: wily, powerful, idle . . .

Yet it was only Alvarez and the government he served that could clean up the cess-pit that was the Ombidos Rubber Company. The company had no foreign shareholders: impossible to evoke, as Casement had done on the Putumayo the conscience of Great Britain or the United States.

'Shall I sling the hammocks now, *Coronel*?'

Rom nodded. Yet long after his servant slept, he still sat and watched beside the moonlit river.

'But he shall go,' he said aloud. 'He *shall* go to Ombidos.'

*

The first week's run of *Swan Lake* ended as it began with fifteen curtain calls for Simonova, though the last of these needed a little assistance from Dubrov who seized the winch-handle from the stage hand who had been turning it and had been about to pack up and go home. The following week was to open with *La Fille Mal Gardée*, a relatively undemanding ballet in which the ballerina is merely required to be enchanting, innocent and tender, qualities which Simonova believed herself to possess in abundance. With the dreaded *Nutcracker* in which Masha Repin was to star still a week away, and Olga signalling her recovery by biting the thermometer in half and demanding *borscht*, the Company settled down to their well-earned Sunday rest.

At least . . . most of the Company. In the bedroom which Harriet shared with Kirstin and Marie-Claude, a rehearsal was in progress.

Marie-Claude's star was rising high. Her meeting with Mr Parker had been wholly successful. He had given her a substantial sum for her costume and expenses, and promised that her sizeable fee would be waiting for her, in cash, on the evening of her appearance. With her usual efficiency, Marie-Claude had left instructions about the music with which she was to be accompanied, the topography of the cake, the arrangement of the concealed footstool which would enable her to leap effortlessly on to the banqueting table. She had even agreed to a brief run-through on the actual morning of the dinner – but to polish up the finer points of her routine she preferred the privacy of the Hotel Metropole.

'I *wish* my Aunt Louisa could see you,' said Harriet, grinning at her friend.

Marie-Claude was in costume: a pair of black fish-net stockings, an inch-wide band of black froth which apparently constituted knickers and two minuscule black and crimson rosettes which adhered by some mysterious process to her breasts. They had put their three chairs together in a circle to constitute a 'cake'; the beds, pushed into the shape of a horseshoe, stood in for the banqueting tables and in the middle of the centre one, an upright bolster impersonated the Minister for Amazonia.

'Harriet, you must do the music,' instructed Marie-Claude. 'It's the Offenbach first. Then when I'm on the table, it's the slow bit from *The Odalisque* – I've marked it there . . . Then back to the Offenbach for my exit.'

Harriet nodded. Since her lunch with Verney she had waited patiently for the ache left by his rejection to fade. It had not done so, but now, as she had set herself to work, so she set herself to help her friend. And trained to sight-read in the Bach choir at Cambridge, she launched into a very respectable rendering of *La Belle Hélène*.

In the bottom of the 'cake' crouched Marie-Claude, wrapped in the golden mantle of her hair. Then – at precisely the point where the music soared to a crescendo of expectancy – she burst!

It was a splendid spectacle: sudden, dramatic, timed to a split-second. Even Kirstin, busy sewing a miniature scabbard for Tante Bertha's hat-pin, gasped and Harriet was so overcome that she lost her place in the score. One moment there had been nothing and the next second there was Marie-Claude, her dimpled arms extended, her lightly rouged palms turned upwards and her smile held with undiminished vigour until even the most distantly placed of the diners must have feasted on its rich promise.

When she was certain that the gentlemen had looked their fill, Marie-Claude caught hold of the iron ring which the Metropole kindly supplied for those guests who travelled with their own hammocks and, swinging her legs high over the chair, jumped down on to the floor.

'In the proper cake there will be a little wooden ledge,' she explained and, indicating to Harriet a quickening of the tempo, began to dance.

The sight was unforgettable. In Cambridge the plump and brassy Lily at Madame Lavarre's had occasionally given the girls a glimpse of what she did in her class for 'stage'; and it had seemed saucy and titillating in the extreme but Lily, as Harriet now realised, was an infant. It was fortunate that Marie-Claude was familiar with the music to which she danced for Harriet, gazing wide-eyed at her friend, was providing only the sketchiest of accompaniments.

Her ravishing smile unimpaired by her exertions, her hips apparently hinged only most lightly to her torso, Marie-Claude performed movements that Harriet had scarcely known existed. She smoothed down her own waist, she lifted her legs so high that it seemed as if the froth of lace must be torn most hideously asunder . . . She did incredible things with her hair – now covering her face with it; now tossing it away so that it whipped out behind her; now, as the music grew softer, winding strands of it round her wrists. She bent forward to let her crossed hands dabble in the dimples of her knees, then backward so that the solitary brilliant in her navel shone straight into the 'eyes' of the bolster that was Antonio Alvarez.

'Ça va?' she enquired as Harriet, hoarse and overcome, limped to the end of the passage. 'That was about seven minutes, I think?'

'Six and a half,' said Kirstin, looking at the ormolu clock they had borrowed from the hotel lounge.

'I understand now about Salome,' said Harriet. 'Why they gave her John the Baptist's head, I mean. I used to think it was too much: a whole head just for a dance.'

Marie-Claude was not at all pleased with the compliment. 'She was a gloomy lady. They are altogether an exceedingly depressive people, the old Hebrews, and veils are not at all fashionable. But I use some of the same effects when I get on the table. One has to be more *legato* on tables – especially out here, I suppose, with so many insects eating into the wood.'

Marie-Claude's routine on the table, performed to a sugary but voluptuous tune from a French musical, was certainly less exuberant but its effect, as her smile became sleepier, her velvet eyes more specific in their promise, was staggering.

124

'Then just for a moment, if he is not too drunk, I come and sit on the knees of the Minister,' said Marie-Claude, sliding down to bestow a cursory hug on the bolster. 'But before he can do anything, there is a fanfare on the trumpets and – bang – the lights go out! I have arranged a signal for this with Mr Parker – it is when I raise my right arm so it can happen earlier if there is any unpleasantness. And when they can see again, I am back in the cake blowing kisses and being wheeled away!'

They rehearsed several times and would have gone on longer had it not been for a mineral prospector from Iquitos who had been trying to have a siesta in the room beneath them and who came up to complain.

'We'll try it again tomorrow, but I think it will be all right, *hein?*' enquired Marie-Claude.

Her friends reassured her. Harriet, however, was forced to express a reservation.

'Only I'm afraid, Marie-Claude, that the gentlemen *will* get over-excited, whether you permit it or not. I don't see how they can fail to!'

'Ah, well,' said Marie-Claude philosophically, 'it is for the restaurant,' – and removed her garters.

*

Rom disliked the Manaus Sports Club and visited it as rarely as possible. Built at the beginning of the rubber boom, it was a colonial-style mansion on the edge of the town which combined all the things he had disliked most in Europe: snobbery, reactionary politics and a leering 'Oh, la la' attitude to women who were excluded from virtually all its functions. The heavy red plush furniture was disastrous for the tropics; the food was indifferent. There were even two old gentlemen straight out of a *Punch* cartoon who sat in the bar reading aloud the obituary columns from the five-week-old *Times*.

The day after his return from Ombidos, however, Rom drove his Cadillac up the drive to discuss with Harry Parker the dinner for Alvarez in two days' time. He had never hoped to avoid the occasion; Alvarez, a connoisseur of food and women, was also a connoisseur of plants and had visited Follina. The Minister had particularly asked for his presence and Rom had no intention of snubbing him. He had hoped, however, to be involved as little as possible. Now he had changed his mind.

'Verney!' said Harry Parker, coming out to greet him. 'I heard you'd been away and I don't mind telling you I was terrified in case

125

you didn't make it for Saturday! The thing is, we have agreed that someone ought to make a speech in the Minister's honour, just a short one before the toasts. It must be in Portuguese, of course, and everyone suggested you.'

'Yes, all right. I'll do it.'

'I say, that's terribly decent of you,' said Parker, surprised and greatly relieved. 'Everyone's coming! De Silva, the Mayor, Count Sternov . . . I'm putting you on the right of Alvarez with the Mayor opposite. I'll show you the seating plan.'

They walked together past the tennis courts, the swimming-pool, the new one-storey wooden building which Parker had had built in the grounds to provide acommodation for visitors defeated by the Golden City's inexplicably ghastly hotels. Rom cared little for Parker's views, but he had to admit that the young man – brought out from England to run the club on 'British' lines – was doing a good job.

'Actually there's been a bit of a fuss,' said Parker. 'We've just heard that Alvarez travels everywhere with his own chef – got a delicate stomach or something. Some high-up French fellow . . . He intends to bring him here to supervise his own dishes for the banquet. You can imagine how my kitchen staff's taken it! I hope there won't be any bloodshed.'

He led Rom through into his office and showed him the plans.

'That seems all right,' said Rom. 'I shall want to speak to Alvarez privately before the dinner. Tell him I want to brush up on his new honours before my speech. Can you clear the smoking-room and give us drinks in there?'

'Of course. No trouble. I can't tell you how grateful I am that you're helping us out. You know the fellow, don't you?'

'Yes, he's been out to Follina once. He is a keen gardener.'

'I've laid on a bit of . . . you know . . . afterwards,' said Parker, and over his sharp-featured face there spread a middle-aged leer. 'A surprise. The old man likes women, I gather?'

'Yes.'

But if Parker had hoped to be asked more about the 'surprise' he was destined to be disappointed. Odd fellow, Verney, the secretary thought. A devil with the women, they said, and certainly that singer two years ago had been the most staggering female he had ever seen. Yet when men stayed behind to tell a certain kind of story or compare notes of their conquests, Verney always seemed to melt away.

'Come and have a drink, anyway, before you go,' he suggested.

In the bar Carstairs and Phillips were where they always were: one on either side of an overstuffed sofa, beneath a portrait of King Edward VII at Sandringham despatching grouse. Carstairs' bald pink pate was bent over the slightly yellowed pages of the five-week-old *Times* and he was reading out the current crop of deaths to the wheezing Phillips, who sat with one hand cupped round his whiskery ear.

'Arbuthnot's gone!' he yelled across to his friend. 'Remember him? Andy Arbuthnot. Seventy-three, he was. Pity when they go young like that.'

Phillips shook his wispy head 'Don't remember him. What about Barchester? Peregrine Barchester. Been waiting for him to go these ten years. Always had a dicky heart.'

Carstairs peered at the paper with his bloodshot eyes. 'No. No Barchester here. Berkely . . . Bellers . . . Birt-Chesterfield! That must be the widow – the old man went years ago. Yes, that's right – Mabel Birt-Chesterfield. Ninety-eight, she was.'

'She'll cut up nicely – oh, very nicely.' Phillips' head bobbed sagely on its withered stalk.

'Well, I should hope so; they've waited long enough. Always in straits, the Birt-Chesterfields. Someone here's going to be cremated: Borkmann.'

'Don't hold with that. Womanish business, cremation. Still, I daresay he'll be foreign.'

'There's a very young fellow here. Brandon. Henry Brandon. Never heard of him. Only thirty-eight.'

'Hunting accident, I suppose?'

'Can't be. Died in Toulouse. Henry Brandon of Stavely Hall, Suffolk. They don't hunt in Toulouse, do they?'

'There was a General Brandon in the Indian Army. My brother knew him. Might be his son I suppose.'

'Excuse me, but might I look at your paper for a moment?'

A look of incredulity and outrage spread over the old gentleman's face. He would have been less shocked if the man had come into his bathroom and asked to look at his wife. As a matter of fact it would have been easier to hand over Florence while she lived. And it wasn't as though the man was an outsider. He was a well-thought-of chap: Verney, a member of the Club.

'It's *The Times*, you know,' he said, thinking that Verney had not understood. 'It's just come off the boat.'

'I know. I won't be a moment. You mentioned a name I thought I knew.'

'Ah.' Well, if the fellow had suffered a bereavement that wasn't quite so bad. He handed over the paper, pointing with his rheumatic finger at the obituary column.

There was silence while Rom looked at the entry.

BRANDON: On May the 3rd, suddenly, at Toulouse, Henry Alexander St John, of Stavely Hall, Suffolk, Aged 38. Funeral private. No flowers by request.

'Friend of yours?' enquired Carstairs presently.

'No,' said Rom and handed back the paper.

*

La Fille Mal Gardée is a light and charming ballet without the depths of *Swan Lake* or *Giselle*. It ends happily: the village girl, Lise, gets her handsome young farmer; the rich and foolish suitor departs in confusion. There are dances with ribbons, harvest frolics and of course the chickens with their *échappés*.

But there is, in the last act, an extraordinarily moving passage of mime which has become a classic. It occurs when the heroine, shut into her house by her strict mother, lives in imagination – and to the tenderest of melodies – the future that she hopes for with her love.

It was this passage which Simonova was rehearsing while Harriet – who should have been elsewhere – stood in the wings, unable to tear herself away. Almost a week had passed since Verney had stormed away from her at the *Casa Branca* and the ache of his rejection never quite seemed to go away, but now she forgot herself utterly as she watched . . . and saw the gaunt, eagle-faced woman turn into a tremulous young girl . . . saw her put on with reverence her wedding-dress . . . saw her pick up her first-born and rock it in her arms . . . count out the other children she would have – and chide them, as they grew, for disobedience.

There were no props and only ancient Irina Petrovna with her cigarette playing the upright piano. Simonova was in a tattered practice dress and hideous bandeau, but it was all there: the glory of married love and its marvellous and celebratory ordinariness.

'So! What are you doing here? There is no rehearsal for the *corps*!'

The ballerina, sweeping off, had encountered Harriet.

'I'm sorry, Madame . . . only I had to watch,' said Harriet, rising from her curtsey. 'You were . . .' She shook a wondering head. 'I shall

128

never forget it. Never! It seemed so simple . . . there isn't even really any dancing.'

'Oh yes, there is dancing,' said Simonova. 'Make no mistake! Every finger dances.' She looked for a moment at Harriet's rapt face. 'It is one of the glories of our tradition, that mime. When Karsavina does it, it is impossible not to weep.'

'Nobody can to it better than you!'

Harriet's husky-voiced adulation made the ballerina smile. 'Kchessinskaya taught it to me. Perhaps one day I shall teach it to you, who knows?' She patted Harriet on the cheek, swept up her accompanist and was gone – but her words sang in Harriet's head. It meant nothing of course, it was only nonsense; she would never dance Lise. But if just once in my life I could do that mime, thought Harriet – and still in a dream, she moved out on to the empty silent stage.

Thus Rom, coming to find her, stood in the wings and watched as she had watched Simonova. He had put out of his mind this girl who had been Henry's creature: he would do nothing now except gently break to her the news he had brought, and leave her. Yet for a moment it seemed to him that the men who had dragged marble from Italy and porphyry from Portugal, who had ransacked the jungle for its rarest woods and paid their millions to build this opulent and fantastical theatre, had done so in order that a young girl with loose brown hair should move across its stage, drawing her future from its empty air.

Harriet was humming, trying to remember . . . After Simonova had stretched out her hand in church for her lover's ring – had she knelt to pray? No, surely she must have looked up, lifted her face for the bridal kiss. Yes, of course she had. She had pushed back her veil, turned, lifted her head . . .

So Harriet turned, lifted her head . . . and saw Verney standing in the shadows.

'I must speak to you, Harriet.' His words were curt, his face guarded again. The insane desire to step forward into her dream had passed. 'We can go to the trustees' room; there will be no one there.'

He led her through a baize door, along a corridor . . . up a flight of steps to a richly panelled room dominated by a vast, satinwood table.

'Sit down.'

She sat obediently, looking very small in one of the twelve carved and high-backed chairs, like a studious pupil facing a board of examiners.

'What I have to say will upset and sadden you,' he began and she

129

made a movement of acquiescence. Anything he said while he still looked so angry and bitter would do just that. 'But I felt you should know while you were out here and had a chance to . . . forget a little. Henry is dead, Harriet. Henry Brandon. He died a week after you left England.'

Her reaction was worse than anything he could have imagined. The colour drained from her face and she shrank back in the tall chair. She was completely stricken.

'No . . . Oh, no, he *can't* be! God couldn't . . .'

She had really loved him then, that pale deceitful slug of a man, thought Rom, noting with detached surprise the degree of his own wretchedness.

'I'm afraid it's true, Harriet. I cabled for confirmation.'

'He was perfectly all right when I saw him . . . he was in the maze . . . he was reading your book,' she said wildly. 'He admired you so much.' Her mouth began to tremble and she bit her lip with a desperate effort at control. 'How did he die?' she managed to say. 'What happened?'

He had decided to tell her only if she asked. 'He shot himself.'

Her head jerked up. '*Shot* himself? But that's impossible! How can a little child shoot himself? Did they let him play in the gun-room? Surely even that horrible Mr Grunthorpe wouldn't have let—'

'Wait!' Rom took a steadying breath. At the same time everything suddenly grew lighter – the room, the lowering sky outside. 'Harriet, I am talking of Henry Brandon, the owner of Stavely – Isobel's husband. A man of thirty-eight.'

'A man? Oh, I suppose that's his father. I never met him. My Henry will be eight in June.' Her face as she took in what Rom had said became transfigured. 'It's all right, then? My Henry is all right?'

'Yes, I'm sure he is. We'll cable anyway, but there's not the slightest reason to assume otherwise.' He had been standing, needing to be distanced from her grief. Now he pulled out a chair in order to sit beside her. 'I didn't know there was a child,' he said slowly. 'I took good care to know nothing about what went on at Stavely.' He stared for a while at the swirling clouds outside, massing for the afternoon downpour. Then: 'When you talked of meeting Henry . . . of loving him . . . it was of my brother that I thought you spoke. Of the man who has just died.'

She looked up, amazed. 'But I never even met him! And if I had, I wouldn't plead for a grown man who had deserted his family. It would be none of my business . . . well, it isn't anyway, I suppose. But if you had seen Henry – my Henry – he's lost all his milk teeth and he worries about wearing spectacles and he had this image of you. I think the idea of you somehow kept him going.'

She fell silent, realising how uncannily accurate the child's description of Rom had been. Rom *could* save Stavely; he could save anything or anyone he chose.

'Yes, I see. I'm afraid it's a case of Romeo and the chicken feather,' he said ruefully. 'I should have thought – it was obvious really – but I was too angry. I have no reason to be fond of my half-brother.' There was a pause. Then, 'Did you see Isobel Brandon?'

'I saw her for a moment through a doorway. She seemed very distressed. And very beautiful.'

'Yes, I can imagine she would still be beautiful.' He looked about for something to help him through what was to come, found Harriet's hand and appropriated it, feeling it to be his due. 'I think it's time I told you about my youth at Stavely. I was once engaged to Isobel, you see.'

He began to speak then, and in the hour that followed he held back nothing.

Harriet learned of his childhood, his veneration for his father, the desolation he had felt at his mother's death. Of his brother he could not speak even now without hatred, but the passage of time made it possible for him to be fair to Isobel. He emphasised her youth, the agony she had experienced when her grandfather was ruined.

'I saw only her betrayal,' he said. 'Now I see that she must have suffered. I expected too much from someone so young.'

'No.' Harriet's denial was scarcely audible, but he caught it and smiled, unfolding her fingers to make a fan which he spread out on the satinwood table.

'I was penniless, futureless; she wanted to be safe.'

He went on then to tell Harriet of the kindness of Madeleine de la Tour, of his early adventures on the river. But there remained with Harriet the image of a woman, beautiful and high-born, whom he had passionately loved – a woman who belonged to his own world – and a place for which he still craved. And she saw that in calling up help for Isobel's child, she had also invoked help for Isobel whose first – and surely last – love he had been.

131

Chapter Ten

'I'M SORRY,' said Henry in a small, croaking voice. It hurt him to speak, his head throbbed and though the nuns had closed the shutters of the long windows of the sanatorium, a ray of light entering through a crack pierced his eyes as if it were a dagger. 'I'm awfully sorry I'm ill,' said Henry to his mother.

'Don't be silly, Henry,' said Isobel, sitting beside his bed. 'It's not your fault.'

But she found it hard to conceal her impatience. It was there behind her words, in her quick, restless movements so different from the gentle movements of the nuns in their white habits. Feverish as he was, Henry knew them all: Sister Concepcion, round and soft and soothing; Sister Annunciata, beautiful and stately with hands that seemed cool even in the dreadful heat; tall, bony Sister Margharita with her pebble glasses, who could make the pillow stop wrinkling and the medicine slip down his aching throat.

Oh, why did I bring the child, thought Isobel for the hundredth time. It was unbearable being trapped here in Belem, with a thousand miles still to travel down the Amazon. Henry had been good on the Atlantic crossing, it had to be admitted, making friends with the Portuguese crew in spite of the language barrier and not troubling her much – which was as well, for the only other British passenger, a rather ludicrous entomologist, had not been at all helpful about amusing the child. Dr Finch-Dutton had been pleased enough to introduce himself as an erstwhile visitor to Stavely, but when it came to answering Henry's questions or making himself useful, that was another matter. But as they approached the coast of Brazil, Henry had become evidently and unconcealably ill.

The doctor of the *Vasco da Gama*, only too aware of the lethal fevers which raged in that part of the world, had greeted with unconcealed relief the appearance, the day before they were due to dock at Belem, of the tell-tale white spots inside Henry's mouth.

'Measles, Madame, without a doubt,' he said in excellent English. 'You must be extremely relieved . . .'

'Yes, indeed. Now we can travel on down to Manaus. I have friends there who can make him comfortable.'

'Travel on!' The doctor was shocked. 'Certainly not! There is no question of subjecting the child to the river journey in this heat. He needs careful nursing – and I have my other passengers to think of.'

'It is probably the other passengers he caught it from,' flashed Isobel. 'Those dirty people in the steerage.'

But the doctor was adamant. 'I hope there will be no complications, but damage to the eyes or the chest cannot be entirely ruled out. We shall ask the nuns of the Sacred Heart to take him in. They are excellent nurses and will not, I think, refuse the child.'

And the nuns, seeing Henry with streaming eyes and a temperature of 104°, had not refused.

'I'm absolutely all right.' Henry's painful croak came once more from the high white bed. 'You don't have to stay.'

'I shall stay until Sister Concepcion comes back,' said Isobel. But she took her watch surreptitiously from her pocket and looked at it. There was really nothing to do for Henry – all the proper nursing was done by the nuns – and it made these vigils very long.

How dreadfully unattractive he looked, poor scrap. His rash was at its blotchiest; his hair, darkened by sweat, clung to his scalp. The nuns had removed his glasses and the grey eyes were swollen and streaming. Would Rom be put off by such a charge? After all, Henry was the child of a man he had every reason to detest. She had rehearsed so often her appearance before Rom – helpless, a little penitent, holding her defenceless child by the hand.

But not a child who looked as Henry looked now.

Oh, God, the frustration of being baulked when she was so close to her goal! Should she have sent a message to Rom by Doctor Finch-Dutton, who had travelled on with scant concern – it seemed to her – for the fate of his stranded countrywoman? No . . . Her instinct to surprise Rom was sound, she was sure. Warned of her appearance he might refuse to see her; she had not forgotten his face that last day at Stavely. To keep the reason for her journey secret from everyone, even the child, had been wise, she was certain.

133

Henry moved his aching head on the pillow. His mother's impatience came across to him as tangibly as if she was pacing the floor or biting her nails. Yesterday, knowing how badly he had failed her, he had tried to get out of bed and find some of that white stuff which the nuns put on his rash to make it itch less. He had thought that if he covered his face with it properly, they might think he was better and let him travel on – and then his mother would be happy again. It was a silly thing to think, but measles made you muddled . . . and anyway it hadn't worked, because before he could get to the cupboard the room had begun to spin round and Sister Concepcion had come and scolded him and carried him back to bed.

Only I must get better *quicker*, thought Henry. It was awful, letting down his mother when she had taken him on a proper adventure. The ship had been lovely; everyone had been so kind. They had seen dolphins and flying fish and the captain had let him go on the bridge. And then, just when the best bit was about to begin – the journey down the Amazon – God had sent him the measles.

But it wasn't only that he had spoiled the journey. Though she had said nothing, Henry knew why his mother was so impatient – she wanted to get on quickly and find the 'secret boy'. He had known from the start that they were going to look for him. It had been his name on the washing basket and he *was* on the Amazon, as Henry had known. Suddenly his mother hadn't minded speaking about him – she had wanted to – and the stories she told him were better even than old Nannie's.

All the while as they prepared for the journey, his mother had been in a good mood, talking and laughing and looking so beautiful in her black dresses. Even when they came and put up boards to say that Stavely was for sale, she hadn't seemed to mind. 'We're just going on a holiday,' she had kept on saying, but Henry knew better.

And now he had spoiled everything. Now it was like it had been before when he could do nothing right.

A spasm of coughing seized him, painful and dry.

'Henry, you mustn't cough in people's faces. Where is your handkerchief?'

Where indeed? He groped under the hot sheet, eventually found a crumpled handkerchief and covered his mouth. It was odd how everything could hurt at once: his head, his chest, his throat, even the backs of his legs . . .

Would it help if he told his mother that it was all right? That the 'secret boy' was probably found already and knew how much they needed him? Harriet had promised she would try to find him and he trusted Harriet as he trusted no one in the world. So far he had said nothing, since he was not supposed to know the reason for their journey, but surely anything was better than to have her so worried.

He cleared his throat. 'It'll be all right,' he said, 'because of Harriet. Harriet will have found him.'

'Found who?'

'The "secret boy".' Aware that his idol was now grown-up and had a name, Henry still clung to the old usage.

'Harriet?' His mother's sharp voice made Henry close his eyes 'Who is Harriet?'

'She was in the maze.' Henry was very tired now. 'With the "tea ladies". Only she wasn't a tea lady; she was a girl.'

'And what has she to do with all this?'

Henry moistened his cracked lips. 'She said she was going to the Amazon . . . And I said would she find him and tell him . . . about Stavely. And she said she would.'

'What sort of a girl? Grown-up?'

'Yes.' Under his eyelids Henry saw Harriet as she had been in the maze, looking down at him so tenderly. He could see her white blouse and her blue skirt with the bands round the hem and her crunchy, friendly smile. 'She was lovely,' Henry said now. 'She was really beautiful.'

Fury gripped Isobel. She remembered now catching a glimpse of one young girl among the dreadful spinsters and overdressed matrons who had tramped through Stavely. She had stood for a moment, watching from the corridor. Not pretty, of course; perfectly plain and ordinary, but young – eighteen, perhaps.

Oh, God, that wretched child, what had he done now? Henry had not known Rom's name at the time and could hardly have told her much, but a determined girl asking for an Englishman of Rom's wealth and status could find him easily enough and worm her way into his house. If she found Rom closeted with some prissy English girl, what then?

'You had absolutely no right to do that, Henry,' said Isobel. 'Blabbing about our affairs to a stranger. I'm ashamed of you.'

A tear forced its way between Henry's lids and ran down his cheek. He would always get it wrong – *always*. Well, at least with the measles one's eyes were always streaming. No one could *prove* that one was crying, thought Henry, and turned his face to the wall.

CHAPTER ELEVEN

TRUE TO his word Rom cabled once more to MacPherson, his representative in London, for news of the occupants of Stavely. He received a reassuring reply. Mrs Brandon and her son were believed to be in good health and travelling abroad. However, MacPherson added another piece of information over which Rom pondered in silence, standing with his back to his cluttered office and looking out over the riverside. Then he wrote out one more cable. Considering that it contained the blueprint for his future life it was surprisingly short – scarcely a dozen words – but Rom did not employ agents who needed pettifogging instructions in order to carry out their work.

After which he set himself to the amusement of the Dubrov Ballet Company.

Though it was customary for the chairman of the Opera House trustees to entertain visiting companies once at Follina, it was not customary for him to organise excursions to the Tumura Falls, the 'wedding of the waters' and islands on which scarlet ibis nested in their hundreds. No one, from Simonova herself to the most bovine of the Russian girls, was deceived as to the reason for these outings to which everyone except Masha Repin and her clique came – no one except (as Verney had intended) Harriet herself. Her humility made it impossible for her to conceive that she could seriously interest a man such as himself, and Rom was content to have it so. Not to use his power over her, not to hurry or hustle her, young as she was, was his main concern and it took all his strength, for with every hour he spent in her company he grew more certain that in this unobtrusive and scholarly girl he had found his solace and delight.

The day before Alvarez was due in Manaus, Rom organised an outing on a lake in the forest whose waters were entirely covered by the giant leaves and peony-like flowers of the Victoria Regina water-lily; a still, mysterious place beneath overhanging trees.

'Magnificent!' declared Simonova as she sat in the first and most luxurious of the carriages Rom had hired, but she did not feel it necessary to descend. The knowledge that soon she would be leading a purely rural life, the mistress of goats, kohlrabi and Brussels sprouts, made it unnecessary for her to risk the long grass by the water's edge, and with a commanding gesture she kept Dubrov and Grisha by her side.

'I wish that someone would stand on a leaf!' announced Maximov. His magnificent physique outlined by a cream shantung tropical suit, he had loaded the good-natured Kirstin with a tripod and various boxes and was directing his camera at a leaf the size of a table with an upturned edge.

There was a certain lack of response. Olga curled her lip and muttered an oath in Pushtu, the rest of the Russians backed away – and Marie-Claude looked incredulously at the *premier danseur*. She was in an excellent mood. The *Vasco da Gama*, docking that morning, had brought a most exciting letter from Vincent. He had found the perfect place for the restaurant: an old *auberge* in the foothills of the Alpes Maritimes whose proprietor wished to retire at the end of the year. Quite a small sum as a deposit, Vincent had written, would give them the option to buy, and this sum he hoped to have in a couple of months if he was lucky with the tips. The knowledge that he would have it after her eruption on Saturday whether or not he was lucky with the tips had made Marie-Claude extraordinarily happy – but not so happy that she was prepared to risk her filmy white dress by standing on a leaf.

Harriet waited to see if anyone else would come forward. Then 'Shall I?' she said. 'I could try . . .'

She picked up her skirt and stepped carefully on to the leaf nearest her, then on to a larger one. She was scarcely heavier than a child and the leaf held. To a spatter of clapping from Lobotsky and the girls, she raised her arms and took the classical *attitude* of the Winged Mercury, smiling shyly at Maximov as he stooped to his viewfinder. And Rom, standing beside Simonova's carriage, put a question he had refrained from asking, as though the answer might cause him pain.

'Has she a future as a dancer?' he asked. 'A serious future?'

Dubrov and Simonova exchanged glances, but it was Grisha who spoke.

'When she came we thought it was too late. She was too much an amateur. We still think it, but we don't think it as much as we did.'

'We remember Taglioni, you see,' added Dubrov.

'I am afraid I don't know much about her,' confessed Rom. 'She was a great Italian dancer, but that's all I know.'

'Her father sent her to Paris to study,' explained Simonova, 'while he prepared a great debut for her in Vienna. But when she returned he found that she was entirely unprepared. Weak. Hopeless!'

'Everyone said cancel the debut,' put in Dubrov. 'But he didn't. He was obstinate. He worked with her and worked with her and worked with her.'

'Three sessions a day with no food, no water . . . In the morning, exercises for the legs and feet. At midday, aplomb . . . At night, the jumps. Again and again. She cried, she collapsed, she fainted,' said Simonova gleefully. '*Often* she fainted.'

'But at her debut she was ready,' finished Grisha. 'And more than ready.' He glanced over at Harriet, still posing on her leaf. 'She was eighteen years old.'

'I see,' said Rom. Do I have to do that for her, he thought? No, damn it, I won't have her fainting. Yet he felt a kind of chill – almost a premonition of something that could touch his happiness.

'It would not happen now, I think,' said Simonova. And then: '*Chort!*' she cried, 'she is sinking!'

Kirstin had given a little cry and run forward to take the camera from Maximov, who was closest to Harriet, so that he could pull her to safety, but the *premier danseur* had no intention of risking his new suit and clung firmly to his apparatus. It was Rom, some twenty yards away, who seemed in an instant to be by Harriet's side. 'Jump!' he said and she jumped, laughing and unperturbed, into his arms.

'You have spoiled your dress,' scolded Marie-Claude, for Harriet was wet almost to her knees.

'Aunt Louisa's dresses cannot be spoilt,' said Harriet. 'That's their one advantage.'

'There might have been pirhanas,' scolded Lobotsky.

'Might there?' Harriet asked Rom.

'Unlikely.' But it was not that unlikely; the water was stagnant and deep. She was almost too fearless, he thought, too much at ease in this place.

They picnicked in style and drove back relaxed and comfortable for the evening's performance of *Fille*. Rom, who had dutifully accompanied Simonova on the outward journey, was travelling with Harriet and her friends and much enjoying the unquenchable Marie-Claude's stories of her future as a restaurant proprietress seated behind a big black till.

Their carriage was in the lead as they drove through the outskirts of the city, crossed the Avenida Eduardo Ribeiro – and turned into the square on which stood the Hotel Metropole.

'Oh, stop! Stop! Please stop!' It was Harriet's voice, but scarcely recognisable. She had slumped forward on her seat, covering her face with her hands, and now she sank down on to the floor almost beside herself with fear.

'What is it? What is it, my dear?' Rom was amazed. Could this be the girl who had danced on the lily leaves?

'That man over there . . . Don't let him see me! Oh, can't we turn back, please . . . *please* . . .'

Rom looked out of the carriage window. A heat-flushed man in a topee and crumpled linen suit was sitting in a cab on the other side of the road. Around him was piled his luggage: a tin trunk, a number of nets and canvas bags, a holdall. His expression was disconsolate, not to say peevish, as he gazed over the head of the flea-bitten horse whose twitchy ears pierced a sombrero with a hibiscus flower on the brim and he was engaged in an altercation with the driver who, by frequent shrugs and wavings of the arms, indicated that he understood nothing of what was being said and cared even less.

In this apparition Rom recognised a familiar sight: a man recently landed from a liner, defeated by the Golden City's inexplicable lack of hotels, wondering where he was going to lay his head – but nothing to explain Harriet's terror.

'It's Edward,' she said, fighting down a sob. 'He's come to take me back – my father will have sent him.'

'Is he a relation?'

'No. They wanted me to marry him, I think, but I never would have. But it means they know I'm here – my father may be with him too. Oh God, it can't be over yet, it can't!'

'That's enough, Harriet.' Rom's voice was deliberately harsh. 'He seems to be alone and you are far from friendless – he can hardly carry you off by force.'

'We'll help you! We'll hide you!' declared Marie-Claude.

Rom ignored this noble sentiment as he had ignored Harriet's terror.

'Let me just get this clear, Harriet. Were you engaged to him?'

'No!'

'And he has no legal hold over you?'

'No, but—'

'All right, that will do.' He leaned forward and gave some instructions to the driver. 'The carriage will turn round and take you to the back of the hotel. Meanwhile,' said Rom, opening the carriage door, 'I think I will go and introduce myself to your friend.'

*

Edward had suffered since he had agreed to go in search of Harriet. It had been rotten luck finding that there was no British boat for a fortnight, so that he'd had to cross the Channel and trust himself to foreigners. Then on the voyage there had been the unscrupulous behaviour of Isobel Brandon to contend with; Edward had not seen Mrs Brandon on the recent visit to Stavely, but he had no difficulty in identifying the beautiful red-haired widow listed among the passengers – though why she should seek solace in her bereavement by travelling to the Amazon was hard to understand.

But his friendly gesture in introducing himself and reminding her of his mother's acquaintance with the General had caused Mrs Brandon to unloose on him – in a totally unbridled manner – her small son. 'Go and ask Dr Finch-Dutton,' Edward heard her say a dozen times a day – and presently Henry would appear to ask the kind of questions with which children and philosophers trouble their betters. Why do spiders have eight legs and insects six, Henry wanted to know. Do flying fish have souls? Why is there a green streak in the sky just before the sun goes down . . . on and on and on.

Which did not mean that Edward was pleased to see him carried off the boat at Belem. There was no real harm in the child and the relief of travelling on alone had been vitiated by the appalling heat as soon as they left the fresh Atlantic breezes. And now in Manaus, where he had hoped for a cool bath and a chance to muster his forces, his troubles seemed only to have begun.

'Good afternoon.' Rom had reached Edward's side and stood looking up at the cab with amused friendliness. 'Can I help at all? Are you in trouble?'

'Oh, I say! Yes! That's jolly decent of you. Didn't expect to see a fellow countryman here,' said Edward. 'My name's Finch-Dutton – Dr Edward Finch-Dutton, from Cambridge. The truth is, I'm in a bit of a fix. I've just come off the *Vasco da Gama* and spent the whole afternoon driving round trying to find somewhere to stay. I tried the Hotel Metropole, but it's booked to the roof – so is the Europa, not that I'd put a dog there. And then that scoundrel' – he glared at the driver, busy spitting melon seeds into the road – 'drove me to a place he *said* was a hotel – ' But there Edward broke off, unable to speak of what had happened after he had asked for a room at Madame Anita's. 'And now he proposes to dump me and my luggage and charge me a perfectly ludicrous sum which I have not the slightest intention of paying.'

Rom turned and fired off half-a-dozen rapid sentences at the cabby, who became servile and explanatory. The Englishman had not understood: he had tried to tell him that the hotels were always full when a company was performing at the theatre but the man would not listen. He himself had done his best, but he now wished to receive his fare and attend the festivities for his niece's confirmation at which he was already overdue.

'Your niece's festivities – which interest me little – will, however, have to wait,' said Rom pleasantly. 'And if you don't want to lose your licence, you will stop spitting into the road.' He turned back to Edward. 'Perhaps I can help. My name's Verney, by the way. I'm on my way to the Sports Club to pick up a message; it's quite a decent place, run by an Englishman – Harry Parker. They sometimes accommodate travellers for a few days – members of expeditions and so on. I can't promise anything, but I daresay he might fit you in.'

'I used to know a Harry Parker at my prep school,' said Edward. 'He kept a weasel in his tuck-box. Don't suppose it's the same chap.' But he brightened visibly at the thought of someone in this steam-bath of a city who might conceivably have been at Fallowfield preparatory school on the bracing and healthy Sussex Downs.

'You're a zoologist, I see,' said Rom, giving the driver his orders and climbing over Edward's collecting gear and large tin trunk – for Edward was not a person who travelled light or thought that field work excused one from appearing decently dressed for dinner.

'Well, yes. Entomology's my field, actually. The *Aphaniptera* in particular. Fleas,' explained Edward. 'I'm a Fellow of St Philip's.'

'So you'll be staying a while?'

'Yes . . . Well, not too long, I hope. I mean . . .' He looked at the man who had come to his rescue. Handsome; a bit foreign-looking but obviously a thoroughgoing gentleman by his voice and his clothes,

142

and the cab-driver had become positively servile in his presence. So Edward, who had manfully kept his secret on the long journey, now said, 'I don't mind telling you that I'm also here for another reason – not just collecting. I'm looking for a girl who has run away from home. A dreadful business. Her father's the Merlin Professor of Classics, and I . . . well, before this happened I was interested in the girl myself. Not now of course,' he added hastily. 'We think she's with the ballet company which is playing here at the Opera House. As soon as I'm settled and have got rid of my stuff, I intend to start making enquiries.'

'What is her name?'

Edward hesitated, but his rescuer's face as he looked out at the street·showed only the most polite and casual interest.

'Harriet Morton. This is strictly between you and me, of course.'

'Well, she may be here,' said Rom lazily. 'But as I understand it, all the girls are Russian. However, perhaps I may be able to help you. I happen to be the chairman of the Opera House trustees and the director might let me have information he would not disclose to a casual enquirer. The girls are very strictly guarded, you see.'

'I say, that's terribly decent of you! It's for her own good, but she *must* be brought back and the whole thing hushed-up if possible.'

Rom turned his head. 'Hushed-up?' he said, surprised. 'One would rather imagine it to be a cause for boasting, to have a daughter accepted by such a distinguished company.'

Before Edward could digest this unexpected remark, they had reached the club. The Harry Parker who welcomed them was not the one who had kept a weasel in his tuck-box and Edward had not really expected such a stroke of fortune, but all was not lost for it turned out that the Featherstonehaugh for whom Parker had fagged at Stowe had mentioned being related to a Finch-Dutton of Goring-on-Thames who had stroked for Cambridge in the year in which they sank.

'My father,' said Edward with quiet pride.

Rom's patronage would have secured for Edward one of the rooms in the annexe in any case, but these revelations made it certain that in Harry Parker he had found a lifelong friend.

'Well, I shall leave you to settle in,' said Rom, 'and see what I can find out for you. The great thing is not to hang round the stage-door or go to the theatre by yourself. Monsieur Dubrov is apt to set the police on stage-door johnnies!'

143

And waving away Edward's thanks, he climbed back into the cab – whose driver had disclaimed all interest in his niece's confirmation – and was driven back to the theatre.

'Well,' said Dubrov, 'what's the position?' News of Harriet's pursuer had spread through the cast like wildfire.

'He's certainly after Harriet and has been instructed to bring her home. As you may have gathered, he once intended to become her fiancé. However, he himself has no legal power and he is also an oaf. If we can keep him quiet, I see no reason why Harriet shouldn't finish her tour in peace . . . and then we shall see.'

Dubrov looked at him curiously. 'Might I ask why you are taking so much trouble over Harriet's career as a dancer when . . .'

He left the sentence unfinished, but Rom did not pretend to misunderstand him.

'I want her to have a choice. She's eighteen, Dubrov, and I don't want her to come to me because there's nowhere else for her to go. However, I'm sure we can manage – only if her father gives orders to have her repatriated could there be trouble, and I cannot see why he should do that. Above all, he seems anxious to avoid a scandal and if he starts involving the law he can hardly do that. As a matter of fact, I have an idea which might serve. If Madame Simonova would co-operate . . . ?'

He outlined his plan to Dubrov, who burst out laughing. 'Well, nothing can be lost by trying it. Will you speak to Harriet? She is very upset.'

'Yes, I will speak to Harriet.'

She came already dressed for her part in *Fille*, wearing a white dirndl with a laced bodice, a blue apron and a blue kerchief round her neck.

'You look charming. That blue is a perfect foil for your eyes.'

She tried to smile, but her face was wretchedly anxious.

'Is he . . . does he know I'm here?'

'Not yet, but he will do very soon because I am about to tell him!'

'Oh no! Oh please, please, no!' She put a hand entreatingly on his arm. 'I know it can't go on for ever . . . being happy . . . but just a little longer!'

'Harriet, you cannot hide night and day for as long as he chooses to pursue you. He seems to be a very persistent and obstinate young man. I think it would be much better if, so to speak, we turned the tables on him.'

'How? I don't understand. How could we do that?'

'Leave it to me. And have courage, my silly little swan. You're so intrepid, paddling about among the pirhanas, yet you let an oaf like that frighten you.'

'It's not just him; it's my father. I'm under age, you see, and if he chose—'

'But he won't choose; we'll see to that. You will go back to England at the appointed time and with your head held high – if that is what you wish. You might even get your father's blessing on your career as a dancer.'

'No . . . never! You don't know what he's like.' She tried to smile. 'I must go. Will you be watching? No, of course, you saw the *première*.'

'All the same, I'll be there, holding my breath while you thread the ribbons like everybody else.' He lifted a corner of the kerchief. 'You should wear blue,' he said. And, breaking his rule, 'You *shall* wear blue,' he said – and left her.

Edward was in the bar drinking with Harry Parker and a few of the regulars, when a servant came with a message to say that Mr Verney would be pleased if Dr Finch-Dutton would join him in his box at the theatre at eight o'clock.

'I say,' said Harry Parker, 'that's a real honour. Verney nearly always watches alone.'

'Yes, but I didn't bring my tails,' said Edward, fingering his black tie anxiously.

'If you're with Verney you could go in plus-fours,' said Harry Parker. 'There's nothing you can't carry off when you're with him.'

Edward had seen the Opera House during his fruitless search for a hotel, but the sheer opulence of the foyer and the clothes and jewels of the patrons here in this place amazed him.

'Ah, there you are!' Rom detached himself from a group of friends and came forward. 'Look, we only have a few moments. Better come up to my box, where we can talk quietly.' And as they went, he continued, 'Your girl *is* here. She's known as Natasha Alexandrovna, but there is no doubt she is the girl you're looking for; I've checked with Dubrov. Only you must be very careful: your coming here could make things extremely awkward for her.'

'For *her*?' said Edward, dumbfounded, and stumbled on a marble step.

'Naturally, for her. One hint that she is being pursued by a man and her position in the Company might be seriously jeopardised.

145

Followers are strictly forbidden and Madame Simonova is an absolute stickler.'

'But I'm not pursuing her! I'm trying to save her!' cried Edward.

'Better not put it like that to the Company. Or to anyone in the audience. I'm afraid Professor Morton is under a misapprehension regarding—' He broke off. 'Ah, here come the Sternovs!' and he led Edward towards his friends. 'Allow me to introduce Dr Finch-Dutton, just out from England. Count and Countess Sternov and the Countess Sophie.'

By the time they were seated in Verney's box, Edward's head was spinning. The Countess had taken him aside to confide that her sixteen-year-old daughter was ballet-mad and quite heartbroken because an inequality of the toes prevented her from being accepted by the Dubrov Company. A young Englishwoman, Mrs Bennett, had congratulated him on being allowed to see these dedicated and unapproachable dancers perform. Was it possible that the Professor really *was* mistaken about the status of ballet girls in polite society, thought Edward, unaware that Rom's friends would have done a great deal more for him than utter a few white lies.

But now the conductor entered, the house lights dimmed and all thoughts vanished from Edward's mind except one. After the long, exhausting journey, the sorrow and wrath she had caused him, he was going to see Harriet again.

Or was he?

The curtain went up on a farmyard and a ballet of chickens of whom Harriet was not one . . . A funny lady who was really a man came and chided her daughter for dancing with a handsome farmer . . . It was all rather jolly and the tunes were nice.

And now a lot of village girls came on and danced with the heroine. Pretty girls in white dresses, each with a different coloured apron and scarf around her throat.

'Well, what do you think of your friend?' whispered Rom. 'They are very pleased with her work in the Company.'

Edward frowned with concentration. Harriet must be on stage then – and indeed there were so many village maidens that one of them was bound really to be her. He leaned forward, peering intently at the twisting, shifting patterns made by the girls with their twirling skirts. There was a thin girl with brown hair at the end on the right, but there was another one at the front and a third just vanishing behind a hay-cart.

146

'It *is* a bit difficult to pick her out, actually. I'm not used to dancing,' he said helplessly.

Rom shot him a look of contempt and handed him the opera glasses. But the glasses only made things worse. One got a head here and an arm there and then they were gone. Edward tracked now this girl, now that, before handing back the glasses with a disconsolate shake of the head.

'She's the one with the dark red kerchief,' said Rom maliciously.

'Oh, yes. Yes, of course! I see now,' said Edward gratefully.

And for the rest of the evening, Rom had the satisfaction of seeing the moron who had professed an interest in Harriet devoutly pursuing Olga Narukov across the stage.

*

As Rom had expected, he experienced no difficulty in setting up the luncheon which was to put Edward in his place once and for all. In every ballerina there smoulders the conviction that she is also a great actress; Rom's plan had only to be outlined and Simonova was already planning her costume and instructing her underlings, and by the time he returned to the theatre at noon with a case of Chateauneuf du Pape as a thank-offering, the transformation from glamorous ballerina to fierce duenna was already complete.

'The girls know what they have to do,' she said, 'and everything is ready. My clothes are good, you think?'

'Indeed I do.' Simonova wore black to the throat; a black hat with a veil shielded her face and a jet-handled parasol lay on the chair. He bent for a moment over her hand. 'I am truly grateful, Madame. Not everyone would go to such trouble for a girl in the *corps*.'

Simonova shrugged. 'She is a good child . . . though she does *not* have Natasha's ears,' she murmured mysteriously, and swept out into the corridor where she could be heard yelling instructions at the girls.

Rom had called at the Club earlier to brief Edward. 'It's a great honour you understand, this invitation? In fact, I know of no one else who has been allowed to lunch with Madame and the girls.' And he went on to caution Edward to be extremely careful in his use of language and not to mention that he was staying at the Sports Club, which would certainly be considered flighty.

'I myself,' said Rom with perfect accuracy, 'never mention my connection with the Club to any lady of my acquaintance.'

At a quarter to one, therefore, Edward – in his new light-weight suit

– made his way towards the theatre. He had imagined his first meeting with Harriet a hundred times. He had visualised her abandoned in a hovel, backstage in a scandalously short skirt, or driving with a rich protector in a carriage. But he had not imagined her crossing the Opera Square in crocodile with twenty other girls, wearing a straw hat and long-sleeved foulard dress, in the wake of a formidable woman in black and a portly gentleman in a frock-coat.

Edward approached, raised his hat.

'Ah. You are Dr Dunch-Fitton,' stated Simonova. The procession came to a halt while she raked him with her charcoal eyes. 'Mr Verney has asked that you may join us at luncheon, but it is out of the question that my girls can be seen walking through the town accompanied by a man. You may meet us at the Restaurant Guida in ten minutes. In the private room, naturally.'

And leaving the flabbergasted Edward standing, the row of girls with their parasols held aloft passed with downcast eyes across the square.

In the restaurant, Verney's instructions had been obeyed to the letter. A private room, totally screened from the rest of the patrons, had been prepared; white cloths and virginal white flowers decorated the tables; a portrait of Carmen expiring at the feet of her matador had been replaced by a Madonna and Child.

The girls filed in under Simonova's eye. Edward, arriving confused and perspiring, was permitted to sit on her left with Harriet on his right. Marie-Claude and Kirstin sat opposite; the Russian girls stretched away on either side.

The first course arrived: platters of hot prawns in a steaming aromatic sauce. Edward, who was hungry, leaned forward.

'We will say Grace,' said Simonova.

Everybody rose. There followed nearly ten minutes of an old Russian thanksgiving prayer during which Lydia, giggling into her handkerchief at the ballerina's unusual embellishments to the sombre and simple words, was kicked into silence by Olga. Then they all sat down and Edward glanced hopefully at the prawns.

'And now you, Harriet.'

So everyone rose again and Harriet folded her hands. '*Oculi omnium in te respiciunt, Domine*,' she began – and thus it was that the first words Edward heard the abandoned girl pronounce were those which preceded every meal at High Table in St Philip's.

Harriet had been badly frightened at the thought of this encounter,

148

but the incredible way the Company had rallied to her support – and above all, Rom's quick pressure on her hand as they set off – had given her the courage to play her part and when they were all seated at last she turned to Edward and said composedly, 'I trust you found my father well?'

'No, Harriet, I did not. I found him deeply distressed by your conduct. How could you run away like that?'

'Run away?' Simonova's lynx-like ears caught the phrase and she fixed her hooded eyes on Edward. 'Natasha Alexandrovna did not run away. She was called!'

'All of us were called,' said Kirstin. Her gentle sad face and soft blue eyes were making an excellent impression on Edward. 'Many of us struggled, but God was too strong.'

'It is a vocation,' pronouced Simonova. 'Nuns and dancers, we are sisters. We give up everything: friends, family, love . . .' Her eyes slid sideways to Dubrov. 'Particularly love!'

Edward, temporarily nonplussed, tried again. 'Yes, but dash it—'

Simonova raised a peremptory hand. 'Please, Dr Funch-Dutton – no language before my girls! I am like the Abbess of a sisterhood. Tatiana!' she suddenly called sharply down the table. 'Where are your elbows?'

'Yes, but . . . I mean, poor Professor Morton,' stammered Edward. 'The anxiety . . . and naturally I myself felt—'

'Yes, yes, you feel; it is understandable. When Teresa of Avila left her home there must have been many who suffered. Yes, there are always tears when a pure young soul offers herself to higher things: the Dance, the Church – it is all one. Consider St Francis of Assisi –'

But here Dubrov pressed her foot in warning, remembering – as she would presently – that the gentle saint had signalled his conversion by removing all his clothes and setting off naked for the hills.

The entrée was brought. Fresh mineral water was poured into the glasses.

'You like being here, then?' asked Edward, turning once more to Harriet and noting with a pang that even after all she had done, her ears still peeped out from between the soft strands of her hair just as they had done in King's College Chapel.

'I like it in one sense,' said Harriet carefully. 'It is such a privilege to be under Madame's tutelage. But naturally I miss the freedom of Cambridge.' She glanced sideways under her lashes to see if she had gone too far, but Edward's face was devoid of incredulity.

149

'The freedom?'

'Well, in Cambridge my Aunt Louisa sometimes allowed me to walk alone on the Backs and I was occasionally permitted to go to tea with my friends. Here nothing like that is possible. We are chaperoned and watched night and day. But I feel I must accept these restrictions, knowing they are for my own good.'

'But Harriet . . . I mean, you are coming back, aren't you?' said Edward, his long face falling. Aware that the situation was out of hand, that his intention to carry her back – covered in shame and contrition – had somehow misfired, he fumbled for words. 'I thought . . . I mean, I was going to take you to the May Ball and all that.'

At this point Marie-Claude, who had been unusually silent, intervened. Harriet could be relied upon not to lose her nerve while the young man was pompous and self-important, but if he turned pathetic anything might happen.

Pushing her golden curls firmly behind her ears, Marie-Claude addressed Edward. She addressed him exclusively and she addressed him in French, rightly concluding that a man expensively educated at a British public school would understand about as much of what she said as a backward two-year-old, and the effect on Edward was considerable. Though aware that people born abroad could sometimes speak their native language, to hear this beautiful girl pour forth sentence after sonorous, unhesitating sentence when he himself had suffered such torments over his French exercises, filled him with awe. Moreover, such words as he did understand – *bois*, for example, and *campagne* – seemed to indicate that her discourse concerned the beauties of nature, than which no topic could be more suitable. And indeed he was quite right, for it was of the outside amenities of the *auberge* above Nice that Marie-Claude spoke: of the grove of pine trees where Vincent intended to put tables in the summer and the freshness of the country produce he would use to prepare his famous dishes.

The meal ended, as it had begun, with Grace and then Edward was dismissed by Simonova.

'Now, Dr Dinch-Futton, tomorrow is a special day of quiet for the girls while we prepare for *The Nutcracker*. Tchaikovsky is for us a sacred composer and there can be no frivolity. But as Mr Verney has assured us of your good character, you may see Harriet for half an hour between four-thirty and five – in the presence of a chaperone, of course.'

And before Edward could think of anything suitable to say, gloves had been donned, parasols unfurled and two-by-two the girls set off across the square.

*

His luncheon with the Company left Edward deeply confused. He went to the post office to send a cable to the Mortons and tried at least five different variations before settling for: HARRIET SAFE FURTHER NEWS FOLLOWS. This at least would set their minds at rest and give him time to think. For of course Harriet must be returned to her father's house – only it was not easy to see how.

'Do you think I ought to put the whole thing to the British Consul?' Edward had asked Verney. But it seemed the Consul was on leave in São Paulo and Verney advised most strongly against Edward taking the matter into his own hands. 'Quite honestly, if you tried to force her to return with you they would think you were abducting her for your own purposes and you might well find yourself cooling your heels in the local gaol. Now you are here, why don't you concentrate on your work? In any case, there's no sailing for another week. I would be very happy to help with transport and in any other way I can.'

This was advice Edward was inclined to take. He had replenished his collection of fleas most effectively on the boat – there had been fleas on the crew, fleas on the passengers, fleas on the captain's fox terrier . . . But he had glimpsed, here in Manaus, insects as fabulous as any he had dreamed of in Cambridge.

The annexe of the Sports Club, in which Edward slept, was a low wooden building edging on to the forest. On the morning after his luncheon with Harriet, he took his nets, his collecting bottles and his tins – and entered his heritage.

He had expected the morphos, the nymphalids, the humming-bird hawk moths – but their sheer size, their musculature, the power it needed to kill them, intoxicated him. In an hour, on the track leading from the back of the Club, he collected enough specimens to line the walls of his little research room at Cambridge and for the first time in his life he felt a catch of butterflies as weight. The heat was staggering and he was not only the hunter but the hunted as sand-flies, tabanids and piums feasted on his crimsoning skin. But Edward hardly noticed the discomfort. That butterfly with the red wing-eye – he had never seen that described anywhere . . . And to fill his cup of happiness to overflowing, there on a cluster of sloth droppings was what he could see, even with the naked eye, as an entirely new species of flea.

151

His meeting with Harriet next day only confirmed what he had learned at luncheon: that she was as closely guarded as a religious postulant. Harriet had been polite and friendly, but it was clear that nothing less than brute force would get her to leave the Company and at the moment he could see no justification for applying it, nor any likelihood of success should he attempt it.

This being so, Edward felt free to accept the invitation from two German naturalists, who had arrived at the Club annexe on the previous night, to join them in an expedition to a valley above the Tamura Falls. Even without a sighting of that fabulous missing link, the 'insect-worm' *Peripatus*, he felt confident of adding to his collection in a way which would gratify the head of his department and make the whole journey worth-while.

'So you see,' said Rom, reporting to Harriet on the morning of Alvarez' arrival, 'everything is going splendidly. With luck he'll be away until Tuesday at least and you can concentrate on supporting Madame Simonova through her ordeal!' For the dreaded *première* of *Nutcracker*, with all that it implied, was almost upon them.

Harriet smiled. 'Yes . . . I suppose it's wrong to hope that Masha Repin doesn't have too much of a success, but I can't help hoping it just the same.' She looked up at him, her eyes warm with gratitude. 'You have been so kind. I still can't believe that it can come right . . . that they will just let me dance. But at least you have shown me how not to be frightened.'

'There's a lot more to show you still,' said Rom lightly. 'I shall be tied up with business for the next two days.' Even to Harriet, he could not speak of Ombidos and his determination to make Alvarez see what went on there. 'But after that I intend to take you out in the *Firefly*. Just you, this time. If you will come?'

'I will come,' said Harriet.

CHAPTER TWELVE

THE DINNER for Antonio Alvarez was the grandest and most elaborate the Club had ever prepared. Harry Parker was everywhere, supervising the decorations, the arrangement of the vast silver epergne of knights in armour, the seating of the musicians. The arrival of Alvarez' chef – with the pomp attending the appearance of a field marshal at manoeuvres – had been less of a disaster than expected. Monsieur Pierre, whose moustaches were the most impressive ever seen on the Amazon, had brought a case of gleaming instruments and taken possession of the kitchens; but his personality was such that within a few minutes the staff, who had been hostile and resentful, were scudding about at his bidding, and it was clear that the menu would be as impressive as his reputation.

But the undoubted triumph, the *chef-d'oeuvre* of the evening – Parker was sure of it – would be the eruption from her cake of the prettiest girl to arrive in the New World for a decade . . . He himself had personally supervised the construction of this cake: a massive three-tiered plywood gateau painted a mouth-watering pink and decorated with ribbons, mock icing-sugar hearts and cupids – the whole delectable concoction resting on a trolley whose mechanism was concealed by a sea of subsidiary confectionary lapping at its base.

Now, looking round the Club's banqueting room with its mirrors, gilt lamps and red-damasked walls, Parker could not help feeling that he was upholding a fine and worthwhile tradition. Not at Maxim's, not at the Café de Paris could they offer anything better than Marie-Claude, clad in her hair, erupting to the music of *La Belle Hélène*.

In the smoking room, Parker's satisfaction was far from being shared by Rom. He had been drinking with Alvarez for nearly an hour and the Minister continued to be charming, urbane and impeccable.

Immaculately dressed, his hair and moustache pomaded to perfection, his feet in their narrow, hand-made shoes resting on a brocaded footstool, Alvarez showed interest in Rom's horticultural innovations, gossiped about his fellow politicians, was informative about the state of Brazilian drama – and again and again led the conversation away from Ombidos.

'If you could go there yourself, sir – just for a day. That damnable company *must* be disbanded and the people brought to book!'

'My dear Verney, if I personally investigated every rumour of that sort on the river, I would be quite unable to attend to my work.'

'Ombidos is like nowhere else. I assure you that the report seriously understates what is going on up there.'

'Well, well, we shall see.' Alvarez selected a cigar, a matter which appeared to absorb his entire attention. 'I'll have a second look at the report in the morning and then we can have another talk. Now tell me, is it true that Calgeras is selling his interests in the Minas Gerais? It seems an odd move just now in view of what's happening to rubber, but de Silva swore it was true . . .'

Half an hour before the dinner was due to begin, a message was brought to Parker to say that young Wetherby was down with a bad attack of malaria and would be unable to attend.

'Damn! That means we're down to thirty-five – I hate odd numbers,' he said to his assistant. 'I suppose it would be best just to remove his place – he was right down at the bottom of one of the side tables anyway.' He stood for a moment, frowning. Then: 'No, wait a moment!'

He hurried out to the annexe where Edward was lying on his bed disconsolate and bored. The expedition he had accompanied had run into trouble and although a price had been agreed with the porters, an altercation had developed at the end of the first day and the men had decamped, leaving the scientists no choice but to return.

'Listen, Finch-Dutton,' said Parker now. 'There is a vacant place at the banquet – one of the guests is ill and can't make it. Why don't you come along? I can lend you some tails. You would be a good long way from the action and between a couple of Brazilians, so there's no need to say much. Just clap and cheer in the right place. You'd be doing me a good turn, actually – an empty space looks bad at a do like this.'

'I say, that's very decent of you,' said Edward. 'I was just going to go to town and look for a bite to eat . . .' and greatly cheered, he rolled off his bed and followed Harry Parker to his room.

Meanwhile in the Teatro Amazonas, where the curtain had gone down on *Fille*, Marie-Claude had grown pensive removing her make-up.

' 'arriette, I think it would be kind if you came with me, to the Club? I think it would be better if I came with a friend, so that the gentlemen don't get any ideas.'

Harriet was surprised, for Marie-Claude had always seemed so unconcerned about anything the gentlemen might get up to. 'Don't you have your Tante Bertha's hat-pin?'

'Yes, I do. I have it. And while I am performing there can be no question of . . . anything. But—' She broke off. ' 'ariette, please come?' For to tell the truth, she had not actually erupted in quite that way since her engagement and somehow it was not as it had been before. 'You see, I do this for Vincent . . . for the restaurant . . . but of course one knows that Vincent himself would not necessarily approve. He comes from a very strict family. And you being the daughter of a professor . . . that always lends a certain something.'

'Of course I'll come, Marie-Claude. I can take a book and wait until you've finished.' She smiled. 'Monsieur Dubrov has a copy of *The Maxims of de Rochefoucauld* in his office. If I carry that, then everyone can *see* I'm the daughter of a professor. Shall I put my hair in a bun?'

'Thank you, 'arriette.' Marie-Claude's ravishing smile was a little more wistful than usual and though Harriet was wearing one of Aunt Louisa's least fortunate purchases – a sludge-green dress spotted in purple – she forbore for once to criticise.

And ten minutes later they were in the cab which Harry Parker had sent, bound for the Sports Club.

*

'Everything is ready!' said Parker, coming forward to meet them.

'This is my friend, Miss Morton,' explained Marie-Claude. 'Her father is a professor.'

Harry Parker, recognising the girl that Verney had brought from the garden at Follina, cordially shook her hand. 'Good, good! They're just on the last course – you're in excellent time. Everything is laid out for you. The cake looks splendid, I must say!'

'And the money?' asked Marie-Claude sharply.

'The money is waiting for you as promised,' said the Club secretary a little stiffly.

155

They passed through the service door and into the kitchen quarters. From the banqueting room they heard the noise of laughter, of raised voices, to which Marie-Claude listened with a professional air. 'Drunk, but not too drunk,' she said, turning to Parker. 'In fact, exactly right! Where do I change?'

'In the little room along the corridor. We can wheel you straight in from there. There will be four men in livery and Monsieur Pierre, the Minister's chef, will accompany you and pretend to plunge in his knife just before you come out. It should give a really good effect. He's a great tall fellow with an amazing moustache and in his white hat—' He broke off, for Marie-Claude had given a little cry and clutched Harriet's arm. 'Good heavens, there's no danger of his hurting you,' he said reassuringly. 'He's a very good amateur conjuror – used to have everyone in stitches back in Montpellier, we understand. He showed us how to bunch the sparklers so that they looked like Catherine wheels; in fact he's been most helpful altogether.'

They were walking down the corridor and, passing an open door, caught a glimpse of an enormously tall, hatchet-faced man haranguing an underling.

'Here we are,' said Harry Parker, throwing open another door to reveal the trolley with the waiting cake in all its splendour. 'We've put a screen there, and a mirror – and there is a wash-basin behind those curtains. No one will disturb you. Shall I fetch another chair for you, Miss Morton?'

'There is no need, thank you.'

'Well, that's fine, then. About fifteen minutes?' he said to Marie-Claude.

Harriet glanced at her friend. Surely she couldn't be suffering from stage-fright? She had gone quite white and totally silent.

'I'm sure that will be fine,' Harriet said and, aware that Mr Parker was waiting for something, added, 'The cake looks absolutely beautiful.'

'Yes, I think it's a success,' said the secretary with quiet pride. 'I'll leave you alone, then. Just knock on the door when you're ready.' And he went, throwing a puzzled glance at Marie-Claude. How pale she was! The artist's temperament, no doubt. But what a stunner!

Marie-Claude had vanished behind the screen.

' 'ariette, please come!' The voice was unrecognisable as that of the self-assured and cheerful French girl.

Harriet peered round the screen. Marie-Claude had made no

attempt to change, but stood looking down at the envelope containing her fee which she held in a trembling hand. 'I can't do it, 'ariette! I can't perform. It's impossible!'

'But, Marie-Claude, why? What's the matter? They're just a few old men having dinner; they won't harm you.'

'Certainly they won't harm me!' For a moment, Marie-Claude showed some of her former spirit. Then her face crumpled. 'That man in the kitchen – the chef who is to cut the cake – he's Vincent's cousin! He's the head of the whole family and very, very strict. He was not at all in favour of Vincent becoming engaged to me because I am a dancer, but Vincent persuaded him that ballet was respectable. If he sees me it will be the end of everything. He will write and tell Vincent—' And Marie-Claude, the practical and invincible Marie-Claude, broke into piteous tears.

'Then you must say you can't do it,' said Harriet decisively. 'Say you have been taken ill and then we can go out quietly before Monsieur Pierre sees you.'

'It's too late, I'm trapped here,' sobbed Marie-Claude. 'If he even knew I intended to do it . . . You have no idea what he's like. He is a man who makes three genuflections before he cooks a *profiterole*. And I have taken Mr Parker's money!'

She looked down at the notes in her hand – almost the exact sum needed to make up the deposit for the *auberge* – and fresh tears welled up in her eyes.

'You must leave the money and go out quickly the way we came,' said Harriet. 'I'll stay and explain to Mr Parker. I'm sure he won't give you away.'

From the banqueting room came the sound of clapping, followed by cheers. The speeches were finished. Soon now, very soon . . .

'They are waiting.' The disgrace of letting down her public, built into Marie-Claude since she was six years old, added to her anguish and her tears came faster.

'Marie-Claude, if I could do it for you, I would,' said Harriet, 'but—'

Marie-Claude lifted her head. She picked up the envelope containing the money which she had just put down. 'Oh, 'arriette, if you *could*! You are an excellent dancer, better than me, and the light will be very dim. That will keep everyone happy and while Pierre is in there, I could escape.' She looked at Harriet standing there in her Aunt Louisa's dreadful dress – and then at the fishnet stockings, the

157

garters, the little rosettes to cover the breasts which she had brought. 'No,' she said, 'you are right.' She put down the money once more and gave a heroic sniff. 'Come then; let us go! Perhaps it will not be as bad as I think.'

Harriet did not move. She was re-living two moments in her life which resembled this: the moment when she had been called into Mrs Fenwick's study to be told that her father was taking her away from school; and the moment when she had brought home a stray puppy and Aunt Louisa had pushed it down the front steps to let it run, frightened and unheeding, into the traffic. This moment, with the feeling of being caught in a nightmare from which she could not wake, was the third.

At the same time, she was thinking. The gentlemen had to be kept quiet. Harry Parker had to be placated so that he would keep Marie-Claude's secret. Marie-Claude had to make her escape.

'Get behind the screen, Marie-Claude. Stay there until the cake has gone – then go quickly while everyone is in the banqueting room. If you're caught, tell Monsieur Pierre that you came to protect me – to plead with me not to do it – but that I wouldn't listen.' She gave a crooked smile. 'Say that I was too depraved . . .'

'You're going to do it, then?' Marie-Claude stared at her friend. 'You're going to do what I do?'

Eagerly she picked up the stockings, the garters, ready to help Harriet dress.

'No, I can't do what you do. But I can do . . . something.'

'Are you ready?' Harry Parker's voice came from outside the door.

'Just a minute,' called Harriet. 'My friend is nearly ready.'

She took off her dress . . . her shoes . . . her stockings. Aunt Louisa's meanness had had its effect even on Harriet's underclothes. Her broderie anglaise petticoat was much too short – it came only to her calves – and she wore a narrow bust bodice of the same white material laced at the front.

'Like that you are going?' said Marie-Claude incredulously. And seeing Harriet's face, 'No, I cannot let you do it!'

'*Laissez-moi*, Marie-Claude,' said Harriet wearily – and climbed into the cake.

*

The table had been cleared, the port brought. Blue smoke from the men's cigars wreathed the chandeliers.

'Gentlemen!' said Harry Parker, stepping forward with a self-satisfied smile. 'The dessert!'

There was a blast of trumpets, the huge double doors were thrown open and there appeared, pushed in by four men in crimson livery, an enormous and sumptuously decorated cake.

'Oh, God,' thought Rom, sitting beside Alvarez at the centre table. 'Not that old bromide!'

He had made the required speech with the expected eulogies and jokes, had set himself to amuse and entertain the Minister; but beneath the veneer of good manners he was savage with frustration and contempt. This idle, venal man would do nothing to help his countrymen; he would not set foot outside Manaus with its comforts and the flattery that was showered on him there.

And now this tired music-hall rubbish . . .

Edward, sitting at the foot of one of the side tables, had already drunk a great deal more than usual. Now, aware that something was about to happen that did not happen after dinner at St Philip's, he leaned forward eagerly with an excited flush on his long face – and Rom, noticing him for the first time, threw him a scornful glance.

A tall chef in a white hat entered, followed by two assistants carrying a silver platter with a long-handled knife. On the dais, the six-piece orchestra broke into the music from *La Belle Hélène*.

And out of the cake there burst a girl!

Except that 'burst' was not quite the word . . . It was the slight air of puzzlement, the cessation of voices which might otherwise have been expected to go on talking through an event of this kind, which made Rom turn from Alvarez and look over the silver epergne which concealed him to see what was going on.

And certainly the figure which had emerged from the sea of tissue justified the mystification of the diners. Dressed like their little sisters bound for the bath, her arms folded in incorrigible modesty across her chest, the girl's dark eyes were wide with fear and from her limbs there came a faint but uncontrollable trembling.

A man in a blond toupee broke into laughter. The leader of the orchestra raised his eyebrows at Parker, whose ferrety face as he recognised the Professor's daughter twitched with despair. Disaster clearly was upon them.

Then, from behind the silver epergne, there came the sound of clapping. Enthusiastic, thoroughly supportive clapping, evincing pleasure at the spectacle to come. Verney's lead was always followed

159

and Alvarez, who had clamped his monocle to his eye at first sight of the girl, had already joined in. Now the others followed suit; there were good-humoured cheers, fists thumped the table.

It was all that was needed. Harriet's terror receded. She could make out no faces in the blue-wreathed, overheated room, but she sensed that the applause was kindly and now she climbed on to the rim of the cake, leapt lightly down on to the floor – and began to dance.

She danced naturally and with a perfect innocence, making no attempt whatever to match the gestures of Marie-Claude, but to the men watching her she purveyed an extraordinary sense of happiness, of fun. It was the delight of a young girl allowed to stay up for a party that Harriet shared with her audience – the excitement, the wonder of being awake in this glittering grown-up world – and the leader of the orchestra, getting her measure, quietened his players so that the showy, exuberant music revealed its charm and tenderness.

'*Who is she?*'

Alvarez' aside to Rom had none of the languor that had character-ised his utterances hitherto. The dissipated, puffy face looked younger, almost vunerable, as he followed the girl's movements with his eyes.

'One of the dancers from the Dubrov ballet.' Rom's own expres-sion, as he watched and waited, gave nothing away – yet he was amazed by her performance. Though he had seen in the first instant that Harriet was pursuing some appallingly difficult task which she had set herself, it had taken all his control not to seize her by force and carry her from the room. But now, as she danced, he found himself – along with all the other sated, experienced men – following her movements with a forgotten thirst for innocence, for those dreams of a selfless life and a noble love that are the gift of youth. Without one step that could not be seen in any dancing class, without one 'revealing' gesture, Harriet held her watchers spellbound, fastened by an invisible thread to her soft limbs, her tender eyes and loosened hair.

Only a few bars now to the end of the Offenbach and she moved closer, looking beneath the folds of the damask for the footstool. It was difficult, the next bit . . . Marie-Claude had practised it a great many times; there was only a small space between the diners, but she had to do it – she mustn't be afraid.

And now she had done it! Jumped in a graceful, soaring leap on to the table!

160

They had not expected that. There was a hiss of surprise, and glares of disapproval at the drunken Englishman on a side table who cried out and might have disturbed the concentration of the little dancer as she stood, pensive and relieved, testing the damask with her bare toe.

'It is necessary to be more *legato* on tables,' Marie-Claude had said. Moreover the table was narrow, the pink blurs that were the gentlemen's faces disconcertingly close. Harriet let the first, languorous bars of *The Odalisque* go by before she knew what to do. Then she smiled . . . stretched her arms slowly above here head . . . began, most musically, to yawn . . . and to cover the yawn with splayed and slender fingers.

And for the men who by now would have been horrified had she as much as lifted her petticoat by a few inches, Harriet danced the irresistible, slow and delicious onset of sleep as it overcame the excited, now overtired girl she had been down there on the floor. She let her head droop forward . . . brought up her folded hands to make a cushion for her cheek. She rallied to perform a few quick pirouettes, as if she could not yet bear to let the bright day go . . . and faltered, overcome once more by weariness.

Silently counting the bars that were bringing her nearer deliverance, Harriet moved down towards the centre of the table, for she knew that it was in front of the Minister that she must come to rest in her final pose. As she came past the man in the blond toupee, confused by her nearness, put out a hand as if to grab her ankle – and recoiled, blanching, as Alvarez spat out three words of insult in Portuguese.

She was there! The Minister's high-backed chair was opposite, his medals gleamed beneath the chandelier – and as the music moved into its dying fall, she prepared to sink slowly, driftingly, romantically on to the cloth in front of him.

Except that the epergne was in the way!

A frown mark like a circumflex appeared for a moment between Harriet's brows. Then a man's hand – strong, tanned and shapely – came round the base of the massive silver object and with extraordinary strength pushed it away.

Now all was well; there was room – and as she sank down she turned her head to smile her thanks.

The men had been behind her all the way, but there was nothing they liked better, nor recalled more often afterwards, than the sudden, anguished squeak – half-mouse, half-fledgling – that escaped her when she saw the face of her benefactor.

161

Then she threw up her arms and at this signal the lights went out. When they came on again, the girl and the cake had gone.

*

The departure of the guests left Harry Parker bewildered but gratified. The eruption from the cake of the dark-haired professor's daughter had apparently given great pleasure – and this despite the fact that as far as he could see she had done nothing of the kind that was normally reckoned to gratify gentlemen after such a dinner. There was no doubt, however, that the praise had been sincere and Alvarez, before he left in Verney's car, had congratulated him with real emotion on the entertainment he had provided. Harriet herself had stayed only long enough to explain to him, in the anteroom, the reason for the substitution and to beg him to keep Marie-Claude's secret and this Parker was perfectly willing to do. Monsieur Pierre was returning to Rio the next morning; the chef had seen no sign of Marie-Claude, who had successfully made her escape, and Parker would not have dreamed of upsetting the most beautiful girl who was ever likely to come his way.

But out in the grounds of the Club, poor Edward stumbled through the foliage in a state of total despair. Inexperienced, prurient and drunk, he alone had entirely missed the point of Harriet's performance. He had just been through the most shattering experience of his life, he told himself. Harriet – sweet, good, obedient Harriet, brought up by Professor Morton to be everything a young girl should be – had burst from a cake . . . had danced on a table in her underclothes!

Had she always been wanton? Edward asked himself as he leaned his aching head against the trunk of a tree, uncaring of the ants, the termites, the poisonous spiders it might harbour. Was it just this damnable climate or had it gone on all the time? Had she crept out at night in Cambridge to come out of cakes in Trinity . . . out of seashells in Sidney Sussex . . . out of cornucopias in St Cat's?

A gigantic moth flew into a lantern; it was new to science, but he let it pass. *Peripatus* itself could have lumbered across his feet and he would not have bent to pick it up.

He had meant to marry this girl whose ankles had been gaped at by three dozen gentlemen at dinner . . . He had meant to commit his life to her in Great St Mary's and approach her reverently in a honeymoon hotel in Bognor Regis . . . He had meant to introduce her

162

to the Mater!

What fools they had made of him in that ballet company – of Verney too, or was he in on the act? Probably they all erupted, even that skinny ballerina – from pies, from ice-cream cones . . . thought Edward dizzily.

After a while the events of the evening took their toll and he was violently sick. Then, tottering to the annexe, he lay down on his bed. Tomorrow he would cable the Mortons and tell them to what depravity Harriet had sunk. They must give him powers to have her restrained until she could be taken to the boat and returned to England. But would they want her back? Would a girl like that be acceptable in Scroope Terrace, soiling and corrupting the whole city? Would he himself be willing to accompany her?

Such little breasts she had . . . but very much there . . . thought Edward, drifting into sleep – and woke sweating to rise from his bed and take a cold shower: the first of many that he was to take as he contemplated the descent from cake to gutter of the girl he had once loved.

Chapter Thirteen

THE MINISTER for Amazonia had sent for Rom.

It was the morning after the banquet. Rom had spent the night at the *Casa Branca* and had not slept well. The presence of Edward Finch-Dutton at the dinner had been as unexpected as it was unfortunate, and the flushed face and drunken mutterings of Harriet's erstwhile suitor as he staggered from the room made it clear that all his own efforts to reconcile Harriet's family to her activities must now be set at naught.

But Harriet's affairs must wait. He had come to do battle with Alvarez and arriving, punctual to the minute, at the Palace of Justice, he was shown into the room set aside for the Minister.

'Come in, Verney.'

Alvarez, immaculately dressed as always, was sitting at a vast desk shuffling a pile of papers, but he rose and shook Rom's hand.

'I wanted to see you about the Ombidos report,' he said. 'I've read it again.'

'Yes.' Rom braced himself for a repetition of the excuses of the previous day.

'And I have decided to go!'

Surprise and relief chased the shadows from Rom's face.

'You will go yourself?' he repeated incredulously. 'To Ombidos? Oh, but that's splendid! You are the only person who can put things right up there.'

'It means delaying my return to Rio and I am sending home my domestic staff. I want you to take me as far as Santa Maria in the *Amethyst*; I shall let it be known that we're off on a fishing trip. Can you spare a few days?'

'Of course.'

'De Silva can meet me there in a government launch with a suitable escort. We'll go by night and take them by surprise. Nominally it will be merely a courtesy visit, but if half of what you say is true, then the rest will follow.'

'Would you like me to come all the way to Ombidos? I can bring a dozen of my own men and follow you.'

Alvarez smiled at the eagerness in Rom's voice, but shook his head.

'I know how you feel, but this is a job for my own countrymen. You have already made quite enough of a reputation as a rescuer of the oppressed. Now it is my turn for some of the glory!'

Rom was not fooled. Alvarez faced a dangerous journey and the hostility of his fellow politicians in Rio, for there were powerful men making money from Ombidos.

'Could I ask you what made you change your mind about going?'

'Yes, you could ask. And I will tell you.' Alvarez sat down again behind the massive desk and motioned Rom to a chair. 'It was that girl last night – the girl in the cake.'

'*What!*' Rom leaned forward, unable to believe his ears.

'Yes, the girl in the cake,' repeated Alvarez. 'You can thank her that I'm risking my neck up that hellish river.' He felt in his pocket, brought out a wallet and extracted a faded sepia photograph which he handed to Rom. 'Do you see the resemblance?'

The picture showed a young girl in a wedding-dress holding a bouquet of lilies. The portrait was conventional enough, but transcending the stiff pose, the studio props, was the expression on the thin face – a look both brave and eager, as though she could hardly wait for the adventure of her life to begin.

'Yes,' said Rom quietly. 'The eyes, particularly.' And then: 'Your wife?'

Alvarez nodded. 'Her name was Lucia. It was an arranged marriage; she came to me direct from her convent . . . there was some family connection. But straight away . . . on the first night . . . I realised that I had found what half the world is looking for.' He took back the picture, letting it rest in the palm of his hand. 'She was no more beautiful than that girl last night was beautiful, but she was so intelligent that she could think herself into beauty. Intelligence . . . they don't talk about it much, the poets, but when a woman is intelligent and passionate and *good* . . .'

Rom had taken a silver propelling pencil from the desk and was turning it over and over in his hands. 'Go on, sir, if you will.'

'I was very young in those days, and very idealistic. I thought Brazil would become the moral leader of the New World. There were a few of us who formed the Green Horizons Party – you may have heard of it. We planned to educate the Indians, build the finest schools and hospitals in the world . . . oh, all the usual dreams. They thought of me as a leader, but my fervour – even my ideas, many of them – came from my wife.'

'I knew they had great hopes of you.'

'Great hopes,' repeated Alvarez. 'We were going to get rid of yellow fever, set up irrigation schemes in Ceará . . . I was put in charge of a population survey in Pernambuco and Lucia went with me on most of my journeys. She insisted and I let her – selfish swine that I was – because I so hated us to be apart.'

'What happened?'

Alvarez took out a monogrammed silk handkerchief and wiped his brow.

'Cholera. It was in one of those villages in the survey. She knew, but she wouldn't stay behind. God, what an illness . . . well, I have no need to tell you, you must have seen enough of it. She literally wasted away . . . just her eyes . . .' He broke off, shook his head. 'After that I didn't care and when they deposed Dom Pedro I just drifted with the scum. I must have had a hundred women since and they have meant nothing.' He shrugged. 'I thought I had forgotten; after all, it was more than thirty years ago. And then last night there was this girl with just that look Lucia had.'

'She would have wanted you to go to Ombidos?' asked Rom. 'Your wife?'

'Yes.' Alvarez carefully put back the photograph in his wallet. 'And you know, I thought the other one would have wanted it too – the girl last night who danced on the table. Absurd, isn't it!' He looked sharply at Rom from under his oiled eyebrows and leaned forward to retrieve the propelling pencil from which Rom had just broken the lead. 'Now, how soon can you have the *Amethyst* ready? I'd like to leave today.'

*

The first cable which Edward sent, announcing that Harriet had been found and was well, strangely produced less apparent pleasure than the second which brought to Louisa's eye – and to the eye of Hermione Belper, as she virtually snatched it from Louisa's hand – a

166

glimmer of something which could not really have been satisfaction but looked remarkably like it.

Mrs Belper had come from Trumpington Villa to inform her friend that Stavely Hall, which had been put on the market a month ago, was sold and to an unknown buyer. She had brought the piece in the *East Anglian Times* which related this event and featured a view of Stavely's south front. But the interesting speculations this item of news aroused were quite set aside when the maid arrived with the cable which poor Edward had despatched the night after the dinner in the Club.

HARRIET SUNK TO UNSPEAKABLE DEPRAVITY STOP MUST REQUEST AUTHORISATION FOR HER DETENTION AND IMMEDIATE REPATRIATION STOP PLEASE CABLE PREFECT OF POLICE MANAUS STOP EDWARD.

'Oh, heavens!' said Louisa, putting her hand to her chest. 'Yet it is only what we expected.'

'What all of us must have expected from the start, dear Louisa, even if we didn't like to say so.'

'What will Bernard say? Oh, how the poor man has been plagued by that girl. The bad blood there must have been in her mother!'

'She was a dreadfully flighty little thing; I remember her well. Always mooning over the piano.'

'What do you suppose he means by "unspeakable depravity", Hermione?' said Louisa, grasping her friend's arm. 'Could there be some scandal that . . . that one simply cannot hush up? Something . . . medical?'

The Professor's key in the lock put an end to this line of speculation. He entered the drawing-room and, without preamble, Louisa put the cable into his hand.

He read it once, read it again. 'This tells me nothing that I did not already know,' said the Professor heavily. 'It was perfectly obvious that the first cable was just moonshine. No girl would defy her father and throw in her lot with those scoundrels unless she was thoroughly sick in her soul. And her body.' His voice shook with anger. 'Harriet had everything here: a good home, upright companions, financial security. It was you' – he rounded on Louisa – 'who told me to give her a guinea. Without that, she could not have done it.'

Louisa bowed her head. 'Yes, Bernard. I admit it. I let my generosity overcome me – but see how I have been punished!'

The Professor took out his watch. 'Too late to go up to London now;

167

I shall take the first train in the morning. This is a matter for the Foreign Office. Cedric Fitzackerly will know what to do; he's a Junior Secretary now.'

'That was the student you actually approved of, wasn't it?' said Louisa. 'The one that didn't argue or fall asleep in tutorials?'

She had not expressed it exactly as the Professor would have wished, but substantially she was correct. Unlike the idle, womanising undergraduates it was his misfortune to teach, Fitzackerly had been attentive and polite, thanking the Professor at the end of every lecture and devoting his final-year dissertation to the Professor's own views on the odes of Bacchylides, so that when the young man came to him for references it had been a pleasure to write something that would make those fellows in Whitehall sit up.

'I shall go and telegraph Fitzackerly now and tell him to expect me. It's too late to hush things up – matters have gone too far. Edward must be given every assistance by the authorities out there. Better even that Harriet should be locked up until the boat sails rather than —' But here for a moment he was unable to continue. 'We must not forget our debt to Edward. To travel back with a girl such as she has become involves a considerable sacrifice. If, that is, he means to bring her back himself.'

'He has wasted a great many words on that cable,' said Louisa. 'There was no need to put MUST – it would have made quite good sense without it. Or PLEASE. To put PLEASE on a cable is quite unnecessary. No one expects it.'

But for once the Professor, usually sympathetic to Louisa's passion for frugality, was impatient. 'This is hardly the moment to think of such trivialities, Louisa. We had best give our minds to thinking of how Harriet can be punished when she returns.'

'Do you mean to have her back here, then, Bernard? Would it not be better if she was sent to some kind of institution where they deal with . . . girls of that sort?'

'When she has been returned, we shall decide what to do,' said the Professor.

He then left for the post office and Hermione Belper also prepared to take her departure. A discussion of who had bought Stavely and what would happen to the Brandons would clearly have to wait for another day and, determined to be the first to spread the news of Harriet's degradation through the city, she too hurried away.

*

'*Merde*,' said Marie-Claude, giving the traditional first-night greeting but without much hope that the expected good luck would follow. The *première* of *Nutcracker* was upon them and backstage the atmosphere was tense. Masha Repin was not popular. Her ambition was so violent, it had not yet acquired the cloak of good manners and while Maximov might dislike Simonova, he felt secure with her as he did not with the Polish girl. The tension filtered through even to the *corps*. Lydia, finding her head-dress too tight, burst into tears. A limping boy rubbing his calves showed that Olga, too, was not immune to the general stress – and the temperature stood at 101 degrees.

Harriet, reaching for her snowflake costume, was forestalled by Marie-Claude who held it out, ready to help her slip it on.

'Marie-Claude, you mustn't! I can manage, honestly.'

During the two days since the banquet, Marie-Claude's gratitude had been a heavy cross to bear. She insisted on tidying Harriet's locker, fetched coffee for her during rehearsal breaks and commandeered her dancing shoes in order to shellac the linings and darn the toes.

'But you *have* to take half the money,' she had cried when Harriet returned from the Sports Club. 'You ought to have all of it, you know that.'

Harriet's refusal had been steadfast. 'I don't want it; it's for the restaurant.' And as Marie-Claude continued to look at her beseechingly: 'I must have somewhere really special to sweep into with my admirers when I am a *prima ballerina assoluta*, you must see that!'

Her little joke had fallen flat; neither Kirstin nor Marie-Claude had smiled. Harriet's work was becoming very good; she was beginning to be talked about.

Out front, Simonova sat very straight in Verney's crimson-lined box on the *bel étage*. He had left his key for them before he went upriver and now Dubrov – letting things go hang backstage – was beside her and lending silent support. She was looking splendid and formidable in a jade green silk dress and turban and the ear-rings he had bought her after her first *Giselle*. Only her hands, clenching and unclenching on her lap, showed the ordeal this occasion was for her.

The curtain rose to sighs of appreciation from the audience. Stifling in evening clothes, living in a land without seasons, they were enchanted by the great Christmas tree, its spire reaching almost to the proscenium arch. The children arrived at councillor Stahlbaum's party; little Clara – played by Tatiana, the prettiest of the Russian

169

girls – received her nutcracker. No tension, so far – Masha Repin as the Sugar Plum Fairy did not appear until the second act.

The transformation scene next. The ornaments dropped from the tree, the councillor's drawing-room vanished . . . and the snow began to fall. Snow and snow and still more snow, turning the tree into a miracle of white . . . They loved that, the Brazilians, many of whom had never seen this strange substance, and applause ran through the house.

The snowflake fairies entered and Simonova leaned forward intently to look at the *corps*.

'She grows strong,' she whispered. 'Grisha is right.'

There was no need for Dubrov to ask of whom she spoke. A strange friendship had grown up between the ageing ballerina and the newest, youngest member of the *corps*. Harriet never put herself forward, but she could not conceal her avid interest for everything that touched Simonova's life. To pass on memories and experiences to the young is a great longing – if the young will listen. Harriet listened.

Act Two now, and Simonova's hands were gripping the edge of the box like talons. The Kingdom of the Sweets – and there was Masha with her dreaded youth, her smile, her blonde hair and little crown, sitting on her throne . . . descending . . . looking very beautiful . . . executing her little dance *en pointe* . . .

Excuting it damnably well and getting a roar of applause from the audience, who were very much taken by this ballet which demanded so little of them and produced such a festive atmosphere. And she was pretty, this Sugar Plum Fairy, in her pale pink tutu covered in delicate, sugar-plum lace, her crown of stars. Here was a heroine much to the Brazilian taste.

The ensemble nonsense which followed gave Simonova a chance to compose herself. Spanish dances, Arabian dances, dances for marzipan shepherdesses . . . The 'Valse des Fleurs' next, the most loved of all Tchaikovsky's waltzes, and it was Dubrov's turn to notice how well Harriet was dancing. Whatever happened to her off-stage seemed to send her further into her work.

But now came the moment of high drama when the Prince leads out the Sugar Plum Fairy for possibly the most sensational and difficult duet in all Tchaikovsky's works: the *grand pas de deux* to music that is the apotheosis of ballet.

Oh, God, thought Dubrov; she's a bitch, but she can dance – those arabesques, those sweeping *attitudes* . . . the speed, the dazzle! And

170

Maximov was partnering her well, unselfishly. He too was on his mettle against the usurper, youth.

Her solo now – and how the audience loved it: the tinkling bells, the sugary music, the pretty ballerina untouched by agony or time.

Maximov was back, lifting her . . . She soared, smiled. Smiled too much for Dubrov's taste, but not for the audience.

And Simonova sat beside him with that unnatural, contained stillness, very upright, watching, watching . . . for mistakes, for human frailty.

There were no mistakes, no frailty.

It was only as the dancers came together for the final tableau that Dubrov perceived his danger.

Stumbling from the box, running down the corridor, choked by his collar, he heard the clapping begin – the stamping, the cries of '*bravo!*' and '*bis!*' That would be one curtain call already . . . two, three . . . Oh, God damn the fools who could not distinguish between a technically competent dancer and the flawed, true artist Simonova was!

He had reached the heavy door that led backstage and now pushed against it.

It did not open.

All doors between the auditorium and the stage had to be open by law in case of fire, but this door would not move. Someone had locked it.

Cursing, perspiring, the portly little man ran back again, up the stairs to the next floor . . . And still the applause came undiminished, and the roars.

The upstairs door was open, but there was a twisting iron staircase to negotiate before he reached the level of the stage.

A group of people were standing in the wings, among them Harriet with a towel over her shoulder, and her face creased with anxiety as she watched the curtain rise once more.

'How many?' panted Dubrov.

'Eighteen,' said Harriet miserably. 'Grisha tried to stop them, but they wouldn't listen.'

She motioned to the stage-hand still turning the winch-handle to let Masha – as loaded with flowers as a hearse – curtsey ecstatically to her audience.

'That's the nineteenth now,' said Harriet.

Nineteen . . . Four more than Simonova. Dubrov shook his weary

171

head. No good intervening now; the damage was done. And still the curtain rose and fell . . . Twenty . . . twenty-one . . . twenty-two . . . Until at last it was over and with a triumphant smile, Masha Repin swept away.

Dubrov had expected Simonova to rage and stamp and make a scene, but it was worse than that. She came backstage to congratulate her rival; she insisted that they drink champagne.

'She is good, Sashka,' said Simonova quietly when they were back at the Metropole. 'She is young and she is good, and the public loved her.'

'Idiots!' raged Dubrov. 'She's a balletic clothes-horse, all tricks and glitter.'

'No. She is inexperienced, but the feeling will come.'

Dubrov was silent, wondering if the door had been locked on purpose and waiting – praying – for the abuse, the tantrums, the talk of retirement and Cremorra with which he knew so well how to deal.

But she was quiet, almost docile, and remained so for the rest of *Nutcracker*'s initial run, and knowing her as he did, he was afraid that something had been damaged inside her in a way that he could not soothe or talk away.

And he was right for three days later, at the *première* of *Giselle*, Simonova hurt her back.

It was an inexplicable injury. The Act One *pas de deux* in which it occurred was as familiar to her as breathing and Maximov, as everyone agreed, was blameless. Yet as he came up behind her to lift her, turn her and set her down in *arabesque* her body sagged, she gave a despairing cry – and fell, to lie prone and unmoving on the floor.

The orchestra stuttered into silence; the audience hissed their consternation and as Maximov bent over the ballerina in anguish and Dubrov ran in from the wings, the curtain came down on a great dancer – and a great career.

*

An hour later, Simonova lay very white and very still in her bed at the Metropole.

'Well, Sashka, it's over,' she whispered to the man who had loved her for twenty years. 'But it was good while it lasted, wasn't it?'

There had been three doctors in the audience and though their diagnoses had differed, there was one thing on which they had all agreed, and in the injured woman's presence – that she would never dance again.

'It was very good, *doushenka*. It was the best,' he said, and sat holding her hand until she fell into a chloral-induced sleep.

But Dubrov did not sleep. Instead, he surveyed the future. There was no question now of going on to Caracas or Lima. As soon as she was well enough to travel, she must be taken back to Europe – to Leblanc in Paris, the most famous orthopaedic surgeon in the world. If it really was a haemorrhage into the spinal canal, as one of the doctors had suggested, there was probably little that could be done, but she must have every chance. Which left the rest of their time in Manaus . . . He couldn't run *Nutcracker* for a whole fortnight, nor could he afford to shut the theatre and lose all the takings. So Masha Repin must have *Giselle* . . .

In the small hours, in the still stifling heat, Simonova woke in pain and her mind turned to the past – to Russia and the snow.

'Do you remember those drives from the theatre in your sledge?' she whispered. 'Sitting all wrapped up in my sables, squashing the poor violets on my muff?'

'Yes, I remember. The frost made your eyelashes longer. You were so vain about that.'

'And the street-lamps making that lilac mist . . . There is nowhere else in the world where they do that – only in Petersburg.'

'We could go back,' he said with sudden hope. 'I still have the apartment.'

Ill as she was, she fought him. 'No! Not after the way they treated me at the Maryinsky. Never!'

It will be Cremorra, then, thought Dubrov; there is no escape – and half in jest, mocking his own misery, he moved over to a pile of books on the bureau and pulled out a brightly coloured volume which he had hoped never actually to read.

'Yes!' said Simonova eagerly. 'Read it aloud to me. I can't sleep anyway, and I must learn. I must prepare myself. At first of course I'll only be able to watch from the verandah, but when my back is better, ah, you'll see! We'll be so happy!'

The book was in English, as books on vegetable gardening are apt to be, and as the humid oppressive night wore on Dubrov read to her about the fan training of espalier plums, about the successive trench sowing of broad beans and the preparation of decayed vegetable matter to make a mulch.

'What is it, this mulch?' came Simonova's hoarse voice from the

173

bed.

Dubrov consulted the book. 'It is something to put on the roots to stop them drying out. There is also a verb: to mulch . . .'

He looked up. Simonova, who had not cried out once when they lifted her battered body on to the stretcher, who had not shed one tear when the doctors pronounced their implacable verdict, was weeping.

'I do not want to mulch!' cried the ballerina – and burst into uncontrollable sobs.

*

Cedric Fitzackerly, anxious to get rid of the tiresome old Professor for whom he no longer had the slightest use, duly sent a cable to Manaus requesting that Edward Finch-Dutton be given every assistance in securing the return of Harriet Morton, a fugitive and a minor, to her native land.

The telegram carrying an awesome Foreign Office signature duly arrived on the desk of the Prefect of Police, where young Captain Carlos put it into the 'In' tray and hoped it would go away.

To have been left in charge of the police station was an honour, but it was one which put the Captain – scarcely out of his teens – under considerable strain. De Silva had taken three-quarters of the city's military police along with him on his mission; they had been gone nearly a week, no one knew where, and young Carlos (whose title of Captain was a courtesy one borrowed for the occasion) lived in dread of an occurrence with which he would find it impossible to deal.

'Here he comes again,' said Sergeant Barra – a huge muscular *cabaclo* with a broken nose – looking up from the children's comic he had been laboriously trying to read.

Captain Carlos put down the mirror in which he had been studying the progress of his incipient moustache and sighed.

'I suppose we'd better let him in.'

Edward Finch-Dutton, still clutching his butterfly net, was admitted as he had been yesterday and the day before and the day before that. Though his Portuguese had not reached even the phrase-book stage which would enable him to complain that there was a fly in his soup, he had – by endless repetition of Harriet's name, the word 'England' and what he believed to be Morse code noises – managed to make the Captain understand that he was enquiring whether a cable had arrived for him from his native land.

'*Nao*,' said Carlos, shaking his head as he had done on all the previous days. '*Nada*. Nothing. No.'

This had always been enough to send the Englishman away with a disconsolate air, but today it failed. Edward, still suffering from the shock of Harriet's depravity, and from a touch of fever as he tottered from the Sports Club into the jungle on collecting forays and back again, suddenly lost control. There was no one to whom he could turn; Verney was still away, the consul was in São Paulo and he had not dared to mention his connection with Harriet to Harry Parker. Now his frustration boiled over and he began to shout and bang his fist on the table.

'I don't believe you. You're lying! It must have come! Have a look, damn you – go through those papers there and look!'

He pointed at the pile of documents in the tray. Reluctantly the Captain pulled it towards him and shuffled a few of the envelopes.

'Go on! Go right through the lot. Let me see for myself.'

Half-way down the pile Nemesis overtook poor Captain Carlos.

'There! That one in the yellow envelope. Read it!'

The Captain picked up the cable and stared at it. 'Eenglish,' he said gloomily.

'Then give it to me,' said Edward, reaching across the desk.

This the Captain was naturally reluctant to do. At the same time it was clear that this irritating foreigner would now have to be dealt with, and even before de Silva's return. He compromised.

'Get Leo up from the cells,' he said to the Sergeant.

Leo, when he appeared clanking his bunch of keys, turned out to be the gaoler, a retired Negro boxer who had once worked for Pinkerton's detective agency in New York, spoke English and could even read.

'It's the real thing, all right,' he said to Captain Carlos when he had perused the contents of the cable. 'The British Foreign Office sent it, no mistake. They want the girl back in England and they want you to help this gentleman get her there.' And he nodded without irony at Edward before depositing a gob of tobacco spittle at his feet.

'You see!' said Edward triumphantly. 'I told you.' He turned to Leo. 'Now listen carefully. Tell them I want at least two men, strong ones. I want them outside the theatre on Friday evening just before the performance ends, and I want a closed cab waiting too. They're to seize the girl as she comes off stage – without hurting her, mind you – bundle her into the cab and take her down to the docks. The *Gregory* sails at dawn – there will be a cabin waiting for her. She must be

175

locked in – I have spoken to the stewardess, but she will want to see your authorisation – and I'll let her out myself when we're safely down-river. Got it?'

He leaned back, extremely pleased with himself. The plan, masterful and simple, had occurred to him as soon as the *Gregory* arrived – a white oasis of British calm and hygiene in the turmoil of the docks – and two cabins for the return journey had unexpectedly become available.

Leo spoke to the Captain, who nodded. It might have been worse – he had been afraid he would be expected to hold the girl in his gaol. And at least the Englishman was going with her. Not to see Edward Finch-Dutton's long, equine face ever again had become the Captain's most passionate desire.

He turned to Leo. 'Ask him how we're to know which girl to grab?'

'I shall of course come with you to identify her,' said Edward. 'Naturally . . .'

CHAPTER FOURTEEN

THE DISASTER that Simonova's accident represented struck the Company afresh on Friday as they rehearsed with Masha Repin for the evening performance of *Giselle*. The Polish girl, having plotted and schemed for just this chance, was nervous and hysterical, abused the conductor for his *tempi*, complained of Maximov's lifts and threw her costume at the wardrobe mistress. Simonova's rages had been no less violent, but in a curious way they concerned – in the end – the performance as a whole. Masha's panic was for herself.

For Harriet, Simonova's injury had been a personal blow. As long as she lived she would never forget the moment when the proud, arched body crumpled and fell – and if she hated any human beings it was those doctors who, uncaring of the injured woman's presence, had pronounced their horrendous verdict.

The tragedy had entirely put out of her mind her own danger. She had not seen Edward at the banquet and if she thought of him at all, it was to assume that he was still away on his collecting trip. Of Rom she did think, and incessantly. He had said he would be absent for two days, but had been away for almost a week and the city was rife with rumours of some cloak-and-dagger affair up-river in which he was said to be involved. Knowing what she would feel if anything happened to him made it impossible for her to remain in ignorance of her emotions, and she could only be glad of the incessant rehearsals which filled the day.

Not so Marie-Claude.

'Oh God, those *dreary* Wilis,' she complained, jamming a myrtle wreath on her golden curls.

'They're not dreary, Marie-Claude. They're sort of vengeful and icy and implacable, but they're not dreary,' said Harriet.

But Marie-Claude, who had danced her first Wili at the age of sixteen, had scant patience with those spectres of betrayed maidenhood who endeavour to dance to death any gentlemen foolish enough to cross their path – and two hours before the start of the evening performance, she announced her intention of going to look at the shops.

Neither of her friends went with her. Kirstin had joined the group of girls comforting Maximov – who needed to be told some twenty times an hour that he was not to blame for Simonova's accident – and Harriet had decided to hurry back to the Metropole to see if the new doctor expected that afternoon held out any more hope.

The city was golden in the late afternoon sun. People sat in cafés on the mosaic pavements; children splashed in the fountains. Marie-Claude walked with pleasure, enjoying the full delights of window-shopping as experienced by those untroubled by any intention to buy.

Rejecting a pink and white striped silk suit, approving a blue organdie, she wandered along the Rua Quintana, crossed a busy square and paused by a kiosk at the edge of a small park overlooking the harbour were she bought a bottle of lemonade.

She was just selecting a bench on which to sit and drink it when she saw, coming down the steps of the porticoed police station, the gangling figure of Dr Finch-Dutton. He was carrying a small wooden box and apparently dressed for travelling.

So he wasn't away in the jungle as Harriet had thought. Strange . . . why had he made no contact? And what did he want with the police?

Repressing the natural instinct of flight so common in people acquainted with the Englishman, Marie-Claude studied him. He had entered the park by the other gate, sat down in a chair by the bandstand and now proceeded to take out of the wooden box something at which he stared with great intensity.

'*Bon jour, Monsieur.*'

Edward looked up, blushed, jumped to his feet. He had avoided all truck with the ballet company – complete surprise was the essence of his plan to snatch Harriet away – and he no longer felt capable of trusting anyone. But the sight of Marie-Claude, her face gilded by the rays of the westering sun, entirely overset him. Whoever had been responsible for Harriet's eruption, it could hardly be this enchanting girl with her staggering facility in oral French. And lifting his hat, he held out the glass specimen bottle he had been studying and said simply, 'Look!'

Marie-Claude looked, gave a small shriek and retreated. Inside the bottle lay a large, dead reddish-brown worm with a great many baggy legs and two stumpy antennae.

'It's *Peripatus!*' said Edward raptly, staring for the hundredth time at this miracle which he had been vouchsafed. 'I found it this morning. You can't imagine what this will mean to the head of my department. It's absolutely crucial, you see – the missing link between the Arthropods and the Annelids.'

He launched into an account of the creature's significance, while Marie-Claude's jaw tightened in an effort not to yawn.

But there was no stopping Edward, who saw himself as a man sanctified and set apart. For he had not meant to go into the forest again; he had been packed and ready, made his farewells at the Club when, with half an hour to wait before the cab was due, he had decided to go bug-hunting just once more.

And there on a damp patch of leaf-mould beneath a clump of kapok trees, he had found it!

Edward's joy had at first been purely entomological. But no man can feel a rapture as intense as his without undergoing a general change in outlook. As he prepared *Peripatus* for the long journey home, Edward had seen himself as a man who had failed in magnanimity. Harriet, it was true, had to be apprehended; she had to be taken to the *Gregory* by force – there was no way out of that – but he had intended to have as little to do with her on the journey as possible. She would be aired and exercised like the prisoner she effectively was until he restored her to her father, and that was all.

But as he drowned the wriggling creature in alcohol, Edward had realised the pettiness of such thoughts. Once the ship was safely away and there was no question of Harriet making scenes or asking to be taken back, he would make it his business to help her . . . to *heal* her. He would go into her cabin . . . her dark, quiet cabin . . . he would let her weep; he would even put his arm round her and stroke her hair. There was no question of marriage now, of course, but there were . . . other relationships, thought Edward, seeing afresh his duty to this luckless and fallen girl.

'That it should happen like this,' he said now, holding up the bottle to the light. 'On my last day!'

'Your last day?' said Marie-Claude sharply, putting down her lemonade.

'My last day . . . in the jungle, I meant,' said Edward, mopping his

179

brow with his free hand. This wretched fever was making him stupid. It was most important not to reveal his movements to anyone. And anxious to confirm that Captain Carlos had done his work properly, he said, 'You are dancing in *Giselle* tonight, aren't you? All of you? Harriet, too?'

'Yes.' Marie-Claude sighed. 'We are Wilis in three-quarter-length tutus and veils with much mist.'

'Veils!' said Edward, horrified.

'Only at first. We're the souls of deceased girls who have been betrayed by men. It is extremely tedious.'

'Not a very long ballet, I believe?' asked Edward casually. 'Curtain comes down about ten-thirty, I understand?'

'That's right.' Marie-Claude's suspicions were now definitely aroused. 'Do you expect to be there?'

'No . . . no. Too much work to do, I'm afraid.' He looked down at the bottle once more and as always when he gazed at the wondrous worm, exaltation overcame caution. 'You were always Harriet's friend, I know,' he said. 'So I want you to understand that in spite of all she has done—'

'Done?' put in Marie-Claude quickly. 'What has she done?'

Edward, confirmed in his assessment of Marie-Claude's virtue, said hoarsely, 'I don't want to talk about it . . . it was in the Sports Club . . . last week . . .'

Marie-Claude's heart sank. He had been at the banquet then, this priggish oaf, compared with whom Monsieur Pierre was a dangerous libertine.

'But you will not be angry with Harriet?' she prompted and moved closer, in spite of the loathsome creature in its bottle, to look entreatingly into his face.

Edward swayed slightly, overcome by the scent of her hair and the sweetness of her breath.

'No. I *was* angry, I admit it; but not now. And I want you to know that I shall let no harm befall her. She will be safe with me.'

'With you?' enquired Marie-Claude, who had not missed Edward's involuntary glance at the *Gregory* riding at anchor in the harbour below. 'But you are leaving soon, I think? And Harriet is staying with the Company. So how will she be safe with you?'

Too late, Edward saw his mistake. 'I spoke in general terms. When she is back in Cambridge I shall visit her, that's all I mean. I shall not cut her dead.'

And afraid of giving himself away further, he replaced *Peripatus* in its mahogany travelling case and took his leave, walking away – a little unsteady with fever – across the park.

Left alone, Marie-Claude came close to panic. What she had heard could only have one explanation: Edward, shocked by Harriet's performance at the Club, had decided to take her back to England by force. If he was acting alone the attempt would be futile, but if he had the support of the police . . .

Oh, God, thought Marie-Claude, blaming herself; what shall I do? She could warn Harriet not to dance tonight, to shut herself in her room – but what was to stop them following her there? She could speak to Dubrov, but he had scarcely left Simonova's side since the accident. And it was only an hour until curtain-up . . .

Below her, she could see the ant-like passengers already making their way up the gangway of the *Gregory*. The ship left at dawn, everyone knew that. Then she started forward, staring intently across the water. Still under sail, lovely as a dream, the *Amethyst* was coming into harbour.

Picking up her skirts, Marie-Claude began to run.

*

Rom stood on deck, his eyes narrowed against the rays of the setting sun. He wore a stained khaki shirt, a gun-belt; a strip of linen covered a bullet graze on his hand. There had been no time to attend to his own affairs, for he brought the men who had been wounded at Ombidos to the hospital. Yet his eyes as he looked at the gilded city were peaceful. It was done. Alvarez and de Silva were still collecting evidence, taking statements – but the Ombidos Rubber Company was no more.

He himself had not stayed behind on the *Amethyst* while the others went to Ombidos. It had never been his intention to do so. From his own encounter with the men who ran that hell-hole, he knew that they would not stay to argue with anyone who surprised them at their sport; they would try to shoot their way out and take to the jungle. Rom's own business was with one man who must not escape. He had not done so and Rom's thoughts now were of a long, cool bath, a meal and then Follina . . . and sleep.

The sails were lowered. The *Amethyst* came in quietly on her engine. One by one the stretchers were carried down the gangway to the ambulances waiting on the quay.

181

'Jesu Maria! I didn't realise I was dead already,' said the last of the casualties – a handsome and cheeky lieutenant with a flesh wound in his leg. 'I suppose it's no good asking an angel to give us a kiss?'

Rom turned his head. Panting, agitated, her eyes huge with entreaty, Marie-Claude came running up to him.

'Please, Monsieur . . . I must speak to you. Oh, quickly, *please* . . .'

*

Act One was safely over. Masha had done well enough as Giselle, the village girl in love with the nobly-born Albrecht who is secretly betrothed to a princess. She had discovered his treachery, gone mad, killed herself. Only Count Sternov and a handful of connoisseurs had missed the pathos and depth which Simonova had brought to the role.

In the *bel étage*, Verney's box was empty.

And now Act Two – the last act. Not swans this time, nor snowflakes but Wilis, all eighteen of them, entering the moonlit grove in the wake of their Queen . . . Welcoming Giselle as she rises from her grave . . . Telling her that she too is a Wili now and must be revenged on any man she meets.

Albrecht, bereft in black velvet, appears with lilies. The Wilis surround him. He must be danced to death. No, begs Giselle . . . not Albrecht! Save him!

It was at this point that Captain Carlos reached the stage-door, showed his police pass and was admitted. With him were the hulking Sergeant Barra detailed to perform the actual snatch and Leo, the negro gaoler, to act as assistant and interpreter.

And following behind them Edward Finch-Dutton, feeling like Judas. He had only to point out Harriet, himself remaining out of sight. Compassionate as he knew himself to be, afraid that a struggling, terrified Harriet might weaken his resolve, he had arranged for Carlos and his men to push her into the cab and take her down to the ship without him. It was they who would see that she was locked in her cabin where the stewardess, aware that the law was taking its course, had agreed to administer a mild sedative. By the time he came to open Harriet's door the next day, it would be as a saviour rather than an assassin that she would regard him.

All the same, his heart was pounding as he followed the policemen, in their ill-fitting uniforms, into the wings.

At once the sound, the heat, hit him. The girls were in a V-formation, those on his side comfortably close. This was not like it had been in Verney's box, just seeing a row of faceless girls. He could make out the individual dancers quite well. Well, fairly well . . .

'Which one?' whispered Leo. 'The Captain wants to know which one's the girl?'

Edward narrowed his eyes, frowning. The Wilis were getting into rather a state, dashing about a lot, and in the centre Giselle and her Albrecht were dancing a pretty ferocious *pas de deux*. Then his brow cleared. There were several lightly-built, brown-eyed girls, but here now was Harriet, conveniently close to their side of the stage.

'That one,' he said, pointing. 'Fourth from the end.'

Leo scratched his head. 'You're sure? They all look alike to me.'

Edward nodded. Any kind of hesitation at this stage would be fatal. 'She's the thin one with dark hair.'

'Jesus, that darn stuff gets up my nose,' complained Leo. 'Do they have to have so much blooming mist?'

There was certainly a lot of mist. From swirling round the dancers' legs it had risen to envelop them to the waist. Now it was rolling out towards the footlights and the conductor had begun to cough. Still it crept across the stage, while old Fernando chuckled with glee and poured another bucket of hot water on the crystals in his tray. He had recognised the chairman of the Opera House trustees instantly, even with the stubble on his chin and the old clothes he wore, and the instructions Verney had given him had made the old man extraordinarily happy. Even without the bank-note Verney had slipped into his pocket and the quick promise of recompense afterwards, Fernando would have gone on making mist. They never let him go on long enough with anything: not the thunder sheet, nor the coconut for the horses' hooves . . . and now to be *ordered* to go on making mist and mist and still more mist . . . !

A Wili, whipping into a *chaîné* turn, cannoned into her neighbour and cried out as she received a slap across the face. Mist or no mist, one did not cannon into Olga Narukov. Maximov, groping for Masha's arm, grabbed the extended leg of the Wilis' Queen who crashed to the ground. Upstage yet another Wili lay, felled by the tombstone on Giselle's grave.

The mist had reached the front of the stalls and a lady in a tiara rose and hurried away, a handkerchief across her mouth. There were exclamations, titters.

'Just keep your head, Doctor,' said Leo. 'She'll be coming off this way if she's the one you said. No need to panic.'

183

'I'm not panicking,' said Edward as he peered with watering eyes into the gloom.

Masha Repin came off after her solo, letting off a volley of oaths in Polish. This was Simonova's doing, all of it – a plot to ruin her triumph – but she would not be beaten, the curtain was to *stay up* – and hearing her cue, she shot on stage again in search of Maximov.

Two stage-hands came and dragged away Fernando who was laughing like a maniac, but it was too late for he had tipped out another bucket full of water and the mist rolled on unimpeded. The act was drawing to a close; soon now the clocks would chime for daybreak and the Wilis melt away into the forest . . .

'Now!' Leo whispered. 'The Captain says they'll do it now, while she's on her own. That *is* her over there by that rock?'

'Oh, yes, that's definitely her.' Edward spoke with authority, for the pose was one he knew well – the dark head bent, one foot resting against the opposite leg.

'Hell!' Sergeant Barra swore under his breath. One minute the girl had been there, standing by the jutting plywood rock. The next minute she had vanished.

'We've lost her,' said Leo. 'She must be with that bunch just coming this way. Look out for her as they come through those trees.'

Edward searched frantically among the milling girls just dancing off. Perspiring, confused, rubbing their eyes, they halted in the wings. One was bending over an injured comrade, another was groping for her lost wreath . . . That wasn't Harriet . . . nor that one . . .

Then someone opened a door, there came a gust of air dispersing the clouds of mist . . . and with an upsurge of relief, Edward found himself looking straight at Harriet.

'There!' he hissed. 'Over there, quickly! Standing with her foot on the chair.' Harriet's familiar face, narrow and grave, her contemplative pose as she tied her shoe, nearly unnerved him. 'Don't hurt her,' he begged – and turned away as Judas himself had done while Sergeant Barra, his cloak at the ready, moved purposefully forward.

And after all it was over very quickly. She struggled, but her cries were lost in the noise and confusion and no one saw her bundled out by the two ruthless men. Hurrying after them, Edward caught only a glimpse of a pinioned white figure being pushed into the cab – and then the driver whipped up his horses and the deed was done.

*

'Where are you taking me?' asked Harriet. She sat leaning back against the seat of the car, still in her white tutu, the wreath of myrtle leaves tumbled in her lap. The terror and agitation one might have expected from a girl snatched off the stage by an attacker who had put a hand over her mouth and pulled her backwards into the shadows, was absent. Though her expression in the darkness was not clearly visible, she appeared rather to emanate a kind of dreamy peace.

'To Follina, of course,' said Rom, frowning at yet another patch of water through which it was necessary to nurse the great black car. 'I must say that you seem to have behaved rather strangely. Why no struggles? Why no screams?'

'I knew it was you. As soon as you put your hand over my mouth, I knew.'

'In the dark, from the back, you knew?'

'Yes,' said Harriet.

He had negotiated the swamp. The road to Follina, impassable in the wet season, was not the best of roads even now, but he had wanted to get Harriet away as quickly as possible. Heaven knew what Edward would do once he discovered his mistake.

'I don't mind being kidnapped,' said Harriet. 'Don't think that. Only I wondered why? I mean, I would have come anyway.'

'I was . . . constrained by circumstances. Edward had arranged a rather less agreeable form of kidnapping. You were supposed to have been snatched by a most unattractive policeman and bundled onto the boat. In fact you should even now be a captive on the *Gregory*, preparing to steam out into the river.'

'Oh!' The news should have terrified her, but it was difficult to be frightened of anything when she was sitting close to Rom. 'I thought we had convinced him that I was leading a blameless life?'

'We had, till you burst out of that damnable cake. He was at the banquet and you can imagine the kind of conclusions he would come to.'

'I didn't see him.' She looked sideways at Rom's shadowy profile. 'I'm sorry about the cake. I did have a reason, only I—'

'I know the reason; Marie-Claude told me. It's because of her that I was able to get you away. She met Edward in the park and guessed what he was up to. I meant to go to the police first and call them off, but then I decided it would be cruel to keep Edward here any longer: the climate really doesn't suit him!'

'Yes, but when he finds out that the police haven't got hold of anyone—'

'Ah, but they have! I don't exactly know who, but I can guess. Edward finds it a little difficult, you see, to tell one dancer from another – and of course the mist didn't help. It was inevitable that once I had grabbed you from behind the rock he would think some other girl was you. But don't worry – it's only a week to Belem – whoever she is, she can be brought back and compensated before the Atlantic crossing starts. I have an office there and I shall see to that. Don't worry, Harriet.'

'I'm worrying a *bit* about that,' admitted Harriet. 'And about poor Monsieur Dubrov being two Wilis short. But mostly I was worrying about your hand. If someone hurt it on purpose, I could kill him perhaps?'

He briefly turned his head. 'It's already done, my dear. And it's only a scratch.'

Oh, God, thought Rom, this is going to hell. I will not touch her until I can cut the legal tangle and ask her to marry me. She shall have sanctuary at Follina and nothing else – but she should not say such things to me.

'Marie-Claude told me about Madame Simonova's injury,' he said, determined not to be personal. 'It's serious, I understand?'

'Very serious. The doctors don't seem to know what it is. They're trying everything – electrical pads, injections of bee venom . . . one old doctor even suggested leeches – but nothing seems to help.'

'The Metropole must be an awful place in which to be ill. I'll offer Dubrov the *Casa Branca* until they leave – if she is strong enough to be moved. Carmen and Pedro will look after her.'

There was still one other thing, which Rom told her as they drove down the hazardous jungle track. That he had decided to return to Stavely – and in doing so would make himself responsible for Henry as she had asked.

'I think I would have done so anyway, once my brother was dead. The place meant everything to my father. He was one of the best men who ever lived and I don't think I could bear to think of it going to rack and ruin. God knows I love Follina, but the Amazon is no place to bring up children.'

'No. I don't think Henry is exactly delicate, but—'

Rom smiled, for it was not Henry that he had had in mind. But he would say no more to Harriet now. When MacPherson confirmed that the purchase of Stavely was completed he would speak to her of

186

the future, but not now – not to a tired child just plucked from danger.

So he is going back to Stavely now that Isobel is free, thought Harriet. It was what I expected and I am glad. I *must* be glad. It was because of Henry that I came here and was allowed to know Rom and I must not – I *must not* – make a fuss when it happens, because it's what I want. It *has* to be what I want. Only, let me not waste one minute of the time that I am allowed with him. That's all I ask, God – that you give me the courage not to waste one minute, not one second of that time . . .

An hour later they drove up the sweep of gravel to Follina. Late as they were, light streamed from a window; Lorenzo came running down the steps and other servants, their dark eyes bright with relief at their master's safe return, clustered round them.

I have only been here once before in my life, Harriet told herself. It is not my home. But the sense of homecoming, the lovely familiarity of everything she saw was overwhelming. The coati coming to rub itself against her legs, Lorenzo's gold-toothed smile . . . Maliki and Rauni, her bath attendants, who had tumbled out of their hammocks at the sound of her voice and now bobbed their welcome, fingering admiringly the skirts of her white tarlatan – so much prettier than the brown dress they remembered.

Though Rom had been absent for a week his rooms were filled with flowers, the furniture gleamed with beeswax, the chandeliers blazed . . .

'You must be starving. I've asked Lorenzo to serve supper in half an hour – I must clean myself up; I'm not fit to join you like this. Only listen to me carefully, Harriet.' Rom was very tired and his frown as he groped for the right words was formidable. 'The only way you can be safe now, for a while at least, is here at Follina. My estate is guarded and no harm can befall you here. If Edward gives up and goes back to England, then it will be different – and once de Silva returns from Ombidos there will be no nonsense from the police. The laws on extradition and repatriation are far more complex than poor Carlos realises. But for the moment, it would be disastrous for you to leave here.'

'Yes. I see that.'

'However, in view of what happened the last time you were here . . . I want to assure you that what I offer you is sanctuary pure and simple. You are very young and—' He broke off, too weary to make a speech about her youth. People, in any case, were apt to know how old

187

they were. 'I expect nothing from you, Harriet. I'm arranging for you to have the guest-rooms on the other side of the house – they are completely self-contained and private. The last person to sleep there,' – his mouth twisted in a wry grin – 'was the Bishop of St Oswald. So you see!'

'Thank you. You are extremely kind.'

Rom looked at her sharply as she stood before him in her favourite listening pose: her hands folded, her feet in the third position. It occurred to him that neither in her face nor her voice was there the relief and gratitude that he expected – that indeed he felt, to be his due.

He went away to take a shower then and Harriet was led by the Rio-trained chambermaid to the rooms which had been occupied by the bishop, where she washed her face and hands and combed her hair. She could see how suitable the accommodation had been for the eminent cleric: the rooms were panelled in dark wood, books lined the wall, there was a high and unmistakably single bed. Nothing less like the Blue Suite, with its exotic bathroom and voluptuously-curtained bed, could be imagined.

Lorenzo had set a meal in the salon, at a table by the window. In order not to embarrass Harriet, Rom had dressed informally in a white open-necked shirt and dark trousers. Showered and shaved, his hand lightly bandaged, he had shaken off his fatigue and felt tuned-up and expectant, a change that he regretted. There was nothing that he must expect.

'I'm afraid I couldn't put on anything different,' said Harriet apologetically. 'I suppose I must do something about getting hold of my clothes.'

He smiled. 'There's nothing more becoming than what you're wearing. Most of the clothes women buy are aimed at achieving just that effect – ethereal . . . a bit mysterious . . . and exceedingly romantic.'

No, that was a mistake. He must not be personal; he must pay her no compliments and quite certainly he must not stretch out a hand to where her winged and devastating collarbone curved round the hollow in her throat. A 'neutral topic', that was what was required. Her work, then . . .

'They're a strange lot, those Wilis,' said Rom. 'Why are they so determined to dance all those poor men to death?'

'Well, they're the spirits of girls who died before their wedding day

188

– because they were deserted by their fiancés, I think, though one is never told exactly.'

'But Albrecht seemed to be all right? Maximov was still going strong when I pulled you from the rock, as far as I could see.'

'That's because Giselle saves him by dancing in his stead. She goes on and on, throwing herself in front of him, until the dawn comes and the Wilis have to leave.'

'Why, though? Surely he betrayed her, didn't he, in Act One?'

Harriet lifted her head from her plate, surprised. 'She loved him. *Him*. Not what he did. So of course she would try to save him.'

The topic was not turning out to be as neutral as he had hoped. He began, in response to her shy questions, to tell her a little about Ombidos now that the horror was past, and of Alvarez' courage once he had decided to go.

And another 'neutral topic' ran into the ground as he recalled the Minister's voice when he spoke of Lucia, who had had Harriet's eyes . . . and who must have looked at Alvarez as Harriet was looking now, her lifted face full of trust and happiness.

Only why, thought Rom a little irritably, for he felt that Harriet somehow was not really *helping*. Why does she look like that? She must be aware of my reputation . . . of what everyone would think.

'It's late,' he said abruptly. 'You must be tired – don't let me keep you up.'

'Could we go onto the terrace first,' she begged. 'Just for a moment?'

He nodded, pulled out her chair and led her out through the French window.

Another mistake. The scent of jasmine overwhelmed them with its sweetness and the moths hung drunkenly over the tobacco flowers. There was a moon.

'It's a proper *in such a night as this* night, isn't it?' she said.

'Yes.'

Shakespeare's words, over-familiar, endlessly quoted but indestructible, unfolded their silver skeins in both their minds.

In such a night stood Dido with a willow in her hand upon the wild sea banks, and waft her love to come again to Carthage . . . In such a night Medea gathered the enchanted herbs that did renew old Aeson . . .

In such a night . . .

And Rom, staring out at the moonlit strip of river, was pierced by a deep and unconquerable sense of loss, of waste. If all went as he

189

hoped, he would marry her; they would be together and it would be good. But this particular night as they stood on the terrace, both released from danger, bathed in the scent of jasmine, this would never come again.

And roughly he said, 'Come! We must go in.'

She followed him in silence. Back in the salon, he asked, 'Did you find everything you wanted in your rooms?'

'Yes, thank you. It was all very comfortable.'

'I'll say good-night, then.'

She did not go immediately, but stood with bent head looking down at a bowl of lilies. Then, 'It seems very difficult to be ruined in this house,' said Harriet petulantly.

He was certain that he had misheard her. *'What?'*

She did not repeat her sentence, merely looked up once in order to scrutinise his face. Then she nodded, for she had found what she sought, and walked over to the bell-rope and pulled it.

The bell rang loudly as it had rung on that other night which, incredibly, was less than four weeks ago.

'Coronel?' Lorenzo, still shrugging on his jacket, turned to his master.

'It was I who rang.' The authority in her voice surprised Rom and augured well for the future he had planned. 'I have decided to sleep in the Blue Suite – please see that it is prepared. And be so kind as to ask Maliki and Rainu to come to me. I wish,' said Harriet, 'to take a bath.'

CHAPTER FIFTEEN

'I AM ruined,' said Harriet, waking in the great white-netted bed. The word seemed to her so beautiful that she spoke it again to herself, very softly: 'Ruined. I am a fallen woman.'

She turned her head on the pillow. Rom's dark head was half-buried in the sheet, one arm thrown out in sleep. The problem now was what to do with so much happiness; how to contain it and not let it spill out and disturb him. Happiness like this could almost certainly disturb people and Rom must not be woken by her. Not ever woken . . .

I have put myself beyond the reach of decent women, thought Harriet, trying out different variations of her fall and smiling at the ceiling.

A new world lay before her – a world at whose existence she had not even guessed. The mystics knew it, and perhaps God Himself and possibly Johann Sebastian Bach in places . . . but none of them had been ruined by Rom, so they could not know it as she knew it.

Moving very slowly, very carefully, she put one foot on the ground, looking at it speculatively because the foot, like the rest of her, had been ruined and felt totally beautiful and totally good, as though each separate toe had shared the extraordinary bliss of the previous night. The negligée that Maliki had wrapped around her after her bath was lying across a chair and she put it on, because she was not yet accustomed to being a loose woman and was not certain that she ought to walk around the room with nothing on. Moreover she was going on a pilgrimage, and pilgrimages were better conducted in negligées.

Because she had to remember this room. It was Rom's own room, to which he had carried her from the Blue Suite, and she had to remember every single thing in it so that years later she could come back here in her mind. Even on her deathbed she must be able to come back here and walk across the deep white carpet, knowing that behind her Rom still slept . . . Particularly on her deathbed. She had to remember this chair on which his clothes lay and the pattern made by his shirt against the gold brocaded silk . . . and she traced with one finger the *fleurs de lys* woven in Lyons two hundred years ago so that she, a ruined girl and the happiest person in the world, could delight in their intricacy.

She had to remember for always the shape of the carved handles on the chest of drawers and the glint of the carriage clock, its hands at ten to six. She had to remember the books lying on the low table – three books with leather bindings and beside them a small bronze dragon and Rom's fountain pen. She had to remember the Persian rug spread on the carpet and that was going to be difficult: she must work and work at remembering that, for the squares and diamonds of cinnamon and amethyst and pearl were unbelievably complex.

She must remember how it felt to walk barefoot to the window and lift the curtain a little . . . The mosquito netting had trapped a moth, which must not die because nothing was allowed to die on the morning of her ruin, and which she freed and saw flutter up to the lamp. Which meant that she must study the lamp, too: five petals of rosy glass held by a silver chain . . .

'Who gave you permission to leave my side?'

She spun round. Rom was leaning on one arm, looking at her. He was awake, alive – he had not perished in the night!

'I was getting to know the room,' she said.

'So I saw. But you happen to be further away than I care for.'

'Then I will come back.' She came to him and hung her head, for what she saw in his eyes was too much even for a woman as officially depraved as she now was.

'I thought perhaps I should get dressed?' she suggested.

'No, I'm not very keen on that,' said Rom in conversational tones.

'Actually it's difficult, because I only have my Wili costume. But I can't go out into the garden without my clothes.'

'Ah . . . But you aren't going into the garden.'

'Am I not?' She considered this. Then her face crunched into the urchin smile which had so surprised him when he first saw her with Manuelo's baby under the trees. 'Well, I will come back – only I would like to creep from the foot of the bed into your presence, like the

192

odalisques did with Suleiman the Great.'

'Over my dead body will you creep!'

'But if I *wanted* to?'

He pulled her down so that she lay against his shoulder. 'It's bad for people to get what they want – it deprives them of their dreams. I'll explain it to you. Later . . .'

Harriet lifted her head. 'How many times a day can one be ruined?' she asked – not in any way displeased, just interested.

'We shall have to find out.' And his mouth suddenly twisted: 'Oh, God, I have ruined you, too, you gallant girl, but I swear—'

She had begun obediently to put up a hand to the buttons of her negligée, was beginning to undo the one at the top.

'How *dare* you?' he said roughly, pulling her fingers away. 'Leave it alone! That button is *mine*!'

*

In the days that followed, Harriet became somewhat beautiful. Her skin glowed, her hair – Rom swore it – grew thicker and heavier almost by the hour and like most lovers he both rejoiced in what improved her and swore that he wanted nothing about her to change.

He had sent word to the Company that she was safe and Marie-Claude, the sensible girl, had packed Harriet's clothes and taken them to Verney's office for Miguel to send to Follina. However, this helped Harriet little for Rom promptly gave orders to have them burned.

'Nothing personal, you understand. Just a difference of opinion between me and your Aunt Louisa. Later we'll buy some more. The blue skirt and the white blouse are all right – and your petticoat; you can keep that.' He grinned down at her. 'Who knows, after all, when you may get the urge to dance on tables!'

But clothes were not really Harriet's problem, for the white cloud bed with its mosquito netting – from which she occasionally still rescued the moths that became trapped in its folds – had become her world. She saw it now as a white-sailed ship on which she voyaged with Rom to Monserrat or Venusburg.

'I think God has made a mistake about love,' she said to him, lying with her head in the hollow of his arm. 'If one can find it – all this ecstasy, and seeing the world in a grain of sand like this . . . then one isn't going to struggle to be properly religious and good.'

'If you knew how rare it was, Harriet,' he said, smoothing back her hair. 'What we have here. God wasn't chancing His arm much, I assure you. Not many people are deflected from the pursuit of the good by a requited passion. I have chased it all my adult life – and I found it the day you came.'

'It's because they haven't got you that they don't find it. But then why should *I* be given this chance? Why me?'

She could make no sense of this. Wickedness had led to ecstasy. Only temporary ecstasy, of course – she would lose him and she knew how. But already she had had so much more than she was entitled to.

'Only I'm not completely happy all the time,' she pointed out, 'because you won't let me creep from the foot of the bed into your presence. So perhaps God will let me—'

'Oh, Harriet, let Him be. He's not after you, poor God! You're His suffering creature now bathed in love. Come here and I'll show you.'

When Rom was working in his study or at the loading bay at São Gabriel, Harriet had baths. Maliki and Rainu presided over these hour-long rituals from which Harriet emerged smelling now of frangipani, now of hibiscus or increasingly – as her helpers became aware of her passion for the scents and unguents of their country – of essences they themselves had compounded from plants which she had not even known existed. Even so, she could never defeat Rom who, after burying his face in her hair only for a moment, would announce firmly, 'Cedar-wood' or 'Cattelya' or 'Moon Lily', before unwinding the snowy towel in which she was wrapped in order to make certain that he had guessed correctly.

When she was not having baths, Harriet ate pomegranates.

It is difficult to speak well of this fruit. Once opened, it disgorges enormous quantities of slimy reddish pips which laboriously have to be consumed because there is little else. Just how many seeds there are in a pomegranate, is hard to discover – more, certainly, than can be counted with ease.

Harriet, however, ate them: seed by seed, forcing them down . . . at breakfast . . . at lunch, enduring the insipid taste, the stickiness . . . for the legend of Persephone was alway with her – Persephone, who had been forced to remain in Hades for as many months as she had eaten pomegranate seeds. Not expecting the impossible, Harriet had altered the time-scale: one pomegranate seed, which had kept Persephone with her dark-visaged lover for a month, was to give her one day with Rom.

'That's five hundred and twenty-three, I think,' she told him triumphantly. 'Five hundred and twenty-three whole days with you sometime in my life—' and went off to wash her hands.

After a while she took the only sensible course and, watched by her cheerful attendants, she ate her pomegranates in the bath.

*

When Harriet had been at Follina for a week, Rom went into Manaus where he called first at the police station. He had no fears for Harriet's safety. Not only had he doubled the guard on his gates, but he had indicated to his Indians that Harriet was not to be unattended in his absence, and as he drove away, a glimpse of Manuelo's one-eyed uncle, old José with his machete, and Maliki and Rainu with their weaving – all converging on Harriet as she sat reading on the terrace – made it clear that any kidnapper trying to snatch her would have his work cut out.

But the news young Captain Carlos gave him when he enquired about the troublesome English girl was entirely reassuring. Yes, they had taken the girl on to the *Gregory* and locked her into her cabin. Dr Finch-Dutton had gone on board an hour later – since when neither the girl nor the doctor had been seen.

'But what a girl!' said Captain Carlos, shaking his head. 'No wonder the English are like they are if that is how their women carry on.' Then, looking anxiously at the influential Mr Verney – known to be Colonel de Silva's closest friend – he asked, 'I did right? The Colonel will be pleased?'

'You did quite right, Carlos,' said Rom and left the Captain a happy man.

His next call was at his quayside office, where he gave instructions to Miguel to cable Belem and order the overseer to send a man to meet the *Gregory*, escort the girl travelling with Dr Finch-Dutton to a hotel and return her to Manaus on the next boat.

'He is to see she has everything she wants for the return journey – no expense spared.' Then, grinning as if at some private joke, 'No . . . better tell him to send *two* men!'

After which he made his way to the Hotel Metropole.

He found the members of the Company depressed and listless, for Simonova's accident had affected everyone. Masha Repin, convinced that the world was against her, shut herself into her room between performances; Maximov still needed to be reassured constantly that he was not to blame for the ballerina's injury; and attendances were

195

falling. It was not of fame and triumph that the tired dancers thought now, but with increased longing of Europe and home.

But Marie-Claude, when Rom found her reading a novel in the lounge, was rapidly transported into a state of bliss by the request Rom made of her.

'Ah *yes*, Monsieur, I will be *delighted* to do that! I know her size exactly and you will not be disappointed.'

'Good girl,' said Rom, placing a wad of bank-notes into her hand. 'I would like one of the dresses to be blue – the colour of that kerchief she wore in *Fille*.'

Marie-Claude nodded, 'I will do my best. Madame Pauline has some new stock from Paris: I'll go there first.'

'And I would like you to buy a dress for yourself, to compensate you for your trouble. Something not *too* suitable for a restaurant proprietress!'

Marie-Claude shook her head. 'No, Monsieur, that is not necessary. Harriet is my friend and I love shopping. I want nothing for myself.'

'Nevertheless, you will please me very much if you accept. And you will not be so cruel as to deprive Vincent of the pleasure of seeing you beautifully dressed,' said Rom – and went upstairs to knock on the door of Simonova's room.

Entering, he found himself in an atmosphere of gothic gloom and hopelessness. The shutters were three-quarters closed; bouquets of heavy-headed flowers sent by well-wishers wilted in vases; a macabre arrangement of electric batteries and spinal pads lay on a table and the sickly smell of chloroform pervaded the air.

Rom had brought some French novels, a basket of fruit, a single spray of the Queen's Orchid which Harriet had picked dew-fresh at dawn, but as he moved over to the bed he saw that the ballerina was beyond reading or any of the consolations of the sick-room. Even to lift her emaciated hand to kiss it would be to jolt the frail exhausted body.

But Simonova, pain-racked and despairing though she was, could still respond to the presence of a handsome man.

'So! You have taken the only girl who might have made a serious dancer. I hope you are ashamed of yourself!'

He smiled, shook his head. 'No, Madame; I am not ashamed.'

'Well, you are right,' she said, relapsing into apathy. 'See how it ends.'

196

Rom turned to Dubrov, who was keeping watch as always in his chair. 'I came to offer you the *Casa Branca*, but I imagine it would be difficult for Madame to be moved?'

'Impossible,' came Simonova's weak voice from the bed. 'I cannot even turn over by myself. To be carried to the boat will be bad enough.'

'And the doctors have no suggestions?'

Dubrov shrugged. 'One says it's a haemorrhage into the spinal column, another that it's a compression of the intervertebral space . . . Yesterday a young German came from the hospital and said she had torn the lumbar nerves . . . We are only anxious now to reach Leblanc in Paris; we think perhaps he can operate.'

Rom frowned. Without a diagnosis, a back operation on a woman as exhausted as this seemed a recipe for disaster. But he hid his disquiet and for a quarter of an hour set himself to amuse and please Simonova – talking of her triumphs, flirting with her, until a little colour came back into the hollow cheeks.

'Bring the child to say goodbye to me,' she said, as he made his farewells.

Outside in the corridor, Rom spoke to Dubrov. 'It seems strange to me that the doctors can't find the cause of her injury. Many of them are fools, but not all. Dr Stolz from the hospital has an excellent reputation. You were there when Madame was injured. Can you tell me exactly how it happened?'

Dubrov described the accident, but Rom's puzzlement only increased.

'There is something there that I don't understand,' he said. 'Something that doesn't fit   Meanwhile, let me know in what way I can be of service to you. I'm well aware that in depriving you of two Wilis I have a debt to pay.'

Dubrov shook his head. 'It's of no importance now. We are only filling in time. But perhaps if you could have a word with the people in the shipping office? We're trying to alter some of our bookings so as to go back on the *Lafayette* on the fourteenth – it's a question of getting Madame straight to Cherbourg – and they are not being too co-operative.'

'I'll certainly do that. The Captain of the *Lafayette* is a good friend of mine – there shouldn't be any trouble. And you ought to have Olga back by the end of next week.' He raised enquiring eyebrows at Dubrov. 'It was Olga Narukov, wasn't it, that Edward took?'

'Yes,' said Dubrov, 'it was Olga,' and for the first time since Simonova's accident he laughed.

Rom had taken his hat from the stand and was about to leave when Dubrov said, 'And Harriet? I have a ticket for her on the boat.' He was silent, thinking of the girl he had picked out at Madame Lavarre's and wanted against all odds, seeing from the start the dedication, the intelligence. 'She stays with you?'

'Yes,' said Rom. 'What I have, I hold. I'm through with scruples.'

*

At Follina, Harriet's ruin continued. Her happiness spread in ripples through the house, the gardens, the village . . . Returning after a morning's work, Rom would hear bursts of laughter from behind the trees and find her teaching old José how to do an *entrechat* or pretending to be a lone swan which had got out of step with the music. Manuelo's baby was said to have smiled his first undoubted smile at her; Manuelo's mother-in-law gave her a charm against rheumatism: a pleasing confection of batskins, jaguar claws and human teeth. Even Grunthorpe, the ill-tempered manatee, was unable to resist such evident radiance and occasionally condescended to surface at her behest.

For Rom, since he had snatched Harriet from the stage, there had been no moment of hesitation, no second when he did not know his mind and heart. She was everything to him – beloved companion, intellectual equal and passionate mistress – one of the world's naturals for that mysterious act which human beings use to break down the barriers of the self. Nor could he doubt her love. Love streamed from her – it was in every word she spoke, every breath she drew. Yet he could not get her to speak of the future. This girl whom he had discovered throwing scraps to a wicked-looking caiman in the creek grew visibly terrified when he spoke of the time when they would leave Follina.

Three days after he had been to Manaus, the expected confirmation arrived from MacPherson in London. The technicalities were now completed and Stavely was his. A letter to Professor Morton, asking permission to marry his daughter, lay ready on Rom's desk.

That morning he took her out in the *Firefly*. He was teaching her to handle the little boat; she was quick to learn and never happier than when she was on the river helping him to feed logs into the temperamental fire-box, wrinkling her nose at the lovely smell of

198

woodsmoke and steam or handling the tiller with that grave concentration that was her hallmark.

It was a magical day, free of the sullen rain-clouds that so often mustered by noon; the clear, calm water mirrored the peaceful sky.

'The Maura must be the most beautiful river in the world,' said Harriet blissfully. She was wearing the old blue skirt and white blouse she had saved from the holocaust, not trusting her new clothes to *Firefly*'s whims. There was a smut on her cheek, but Rom had decided against removing it; it was a becoming smut, dear to his heart. 'Oh, look – isn't that your otter?'

He nodded. 'That's the male. They've been in that bank since I came – a most faithful pair. In a moment you'll see a clump of palms on the left leaning over the water – there's usually a sun bittern there . . . Yes, look, he's just flying up now. Incredible, isn't it, the orange and gold . . .'

'You know it all,' said Harriet wonderingly. 'You *give* people this river.'

Rom shook his head, turning to adjust the throttle. Not people, he could have said: just you.

He came over to sit beside her, putting his hand over hers on the tiller, not because she needed help but because he wanted to be where she was.

'Harriet, I know you love Follina and being here and God knows I do too. I'll do everything I can to hang on to the place – but it is time to think of the next step. If I am to put Stavely on its feet, I can't delay too long.'

Feeling her grow tense, he laid an arm across her shoulders. The bullet graze from Ombidos was almost healed and even in her panic she smiled at that. 'If it's any consolation to you, I think the good times are almost over out here. My own fortune is safe – I have seen this coming for some time and shifted my interests to Europe – but there's going to be real hardship and little enough one can do to help.'

He was silent, seeing goats grazing in the parks of the Golden City, the Opera House closed, the 'black gold' that was rubber lying unclaimed on the docks because the world could buy it at half the price from the new plantations in the East.

'Yes. I know, Rom. I understand that you . . . that one has to go back. And I promise I won't make a fuss when it happens – how could I, when it was I who begged you to save Stavely? Henry needs you, he really does, and Stavely's beautiful – there's nowhere more beautiful

199

in the world. And . . . Mrs Brandon will be so grateful to have your help in bringing up Henry.'

Rom smiled down at her, his face alight with tenderness. It touched him very much, this incessant concern for the child. 'You think I would be a good example to him, do you?'

'Yes. I do think that, as a matter of fact.' She had seen his eyes grow soft at the mention of Isobel's name and it became necessary to take a few deep and steadying breaths. 'I think that a child who had your example before him would grow up to be—' But she could not go on. It was overwhelming her – this image of the woman he had so passionately loved welcoming him as saviour of her home – and the tears she was powerless to check spilled over, making a channel through the smudges on her cheek.

'My darling . . . oh, my love.' He wiped her face, took the tiller from her and gathered her to him with his free arm. 'What is it, Harriet? What are you frightened of? Tell me, my heart, for I swear that whatever it is—'

'Nothing . . . honestly, Rom, nothing. I have everything anyone could want. I am probably the happiest person in the world. Only please, *please*, could we not talk about . . . what comes next? Could we just live each day fully and properly, savouring every second like in *Marcus Aurelius*?' And again, 'I *promise* not to make a fuss when the time comes to leave. I *promise*.'

He left it then. 'Of course,' he said cheerfully, giving her the tiller once more. 'There is not the slightest need to think about it now. Steer for the far side of that little island – there's a wonderful spot there for our picnic. That was a turtle which just plopped into the water. Maybe we'll find some eggs and have an orgy . . .'

But that night, long after she was sleeping in his arms, he lay awake puzzling out the reason for her fear. Did she feel herself incompetent to run Stavely? She must know that he would help her in every way, that she would have a first-class staff. Was it something to do with Isobel? She seemed to pronounce her name with difficulty. He had meant to offer Isobel Paradise Farm – there seemed no other way to keep an eye on Henry and that he should do so was clearly Harriet's dearest wish. Did she imagine that Isobel as an older woman would interfere in her affairs? Surely she must know that he would never permit that? Or was it her love for Follina that made the thought of leaving such a dread?

No, there was nothing there to account for Harriet's terror. It had

200

to be something far deeper than that. And as he lay wakeful in the dark, there came to him the image of Harriet balancing on her leaf by the lake with the Victoria Regina lilies – and the answer Simonova and the others had given to the question he had found it so hard to ask.

'When she came, we thought it was too late . . . But we don't think it as much as we did . . . We remember Taglioni, you see.'

And three days ago in Simonova's sick-room: 'You have taken the only girl who might have made a serious dancer.'

Did Harriet know how good she was? Was that it? That much as she loved him, she couldn't bear to give up dancing? Once at Stavely he had found his mother sitting at the piano, her hands on the silent keys and a blind, lost look on her face. God knows she had loved her husband if any woman had, but had she paid too great a price?

Now it was Rom's turn to be afraid. He looked down at Harriet and she seemed to sense his regard, for without opening her eyes she burrowed deep into his shoulder with a sleep-drugged sigh of utter contentment.

'No,' thought Rom, banishing his spectres. 'I don't believe it.'

The next day he left early to inspect a consignment of redwoods unloaded at São Gabriel. Returning earlier than expected, he let himself silently in his drawing-room.

From the horn of the gramophone came the sound of a Brahms impromptu. Harriet was standing with her back to him, her fingertips resting on the arms of a chair.

He had often seen her dance . . . for his delighted villagers, for Maliki and Rainu, creating a 'ballet of the bath' in which, suffocated with mirth, they brought her towels *en pointe* – and once, unforgettably, at night in his room after love when she had spun like a dervish, expressing her ecstasy in movement; for she was not a girl who suffered from the *tristesse* that is supposed to follow passion.

But now she was working. Relentlessly, steadily, Harriet practised her *pliés* . . . bending . . . rising . . . bending . . . while he watched her straight, slim back, the tendrils of soft hair lapping her neck. His territory – *his* – and now turned away from him in the iron discipline of class.

He stood for some time in the doorway, his face taut. It seemed to him that it would have been easier to see her absorbed in another man than to watch this impersonal dedication, this being lost to everything except the need to perfect each movement. Then he went out silently and made his way to his study.

Harriet had woken that morning chiding herself for letting her happiness make her soft. She must keep her muscles supple, her body in shape, for she must not be a burden to Rom. She must be able to find work as a dancer – if possible far away, for she did not think she could bear to be in Cambridge knowing he was so close. The others had gone without complaint, those girls he had brought to Follina and honoured with his love. She would not be less brave, less competent than they.

And so she worked, murmuring instructions to herself, and saw him neither come nor go, while in his study Rom stood looking down at the letter he had written to Professor Morton . . . and then tore it slowly into shreds.

CHAPTER SIXTEEN

'THAT WOMAN is not fit to have charge of a child,' said the plump and motherly Sister Concepcion. 'It's insufferable the way she paces up and down like a caged animal in front of him. Every time she is with him for an hour, his temperature goes up.'

She put down her cup and glared round the bare, white-walled refectory in which the nuns were taking a brief break. It was midday but the convent, built around a tree-shaded courtyard, had no truck with the noise and bustle of Belem harbour where the *Gregory* had just docked, down from Manaus, and was taking on cargo before setting off across the Atlantic.

'Poor little scrap!' Sister Margharita's eyes behind their pebble glasses were angry. A schoolteacher before she took the veil, Sister Margharita – who helped Sister Concepcion in the infirmary – spoke a little English and she had formed an excellent opinion of Henry. Not even at the highest point of his fever had the child failed in courtesy to those who nursed him. 'He needs at least a week convalescing quietly, and a fortnight would not be too much, but she was on again this morning, trying to tell me he was well enough to travel. I shall be glad when the *Bernadetto* goes out tonight. There isn't another sailing for a week, so maybe she'll settle down.'

'Not her,' said Sister Concepcion. 'She's possessed by some devil.'

'Or some man,' said Sister Annunciata. She had been a considerable beauty before she took the veil, but if this made her understand Mrs Brandon better than the others, she judged her no less harshly. Henry had been extremely ill. Bronchitis had set in just as his rash was fading and for a few days they had feared pneumonia, that dreaded aftermath of measles. While the child's life had been in danger Mrs Brandon had shown a proper concern, but now her restless impatience was once more in full flood. To see Henry's anxious eyes following his mother round the room, to see the touching way in which the weakened little boy tried to respond to her injunction to sit up properly and endeavour to put his feet on the ground, was to have feelings about the beautiful widow which, as handmaidens of the Lord, they had hoped to have put behind them.

'Anyway, she is out for the morning,' said Sister Concepcion. 'So the child will get some sleep.'

Isobel was, in fact, sitting on the pavement of an elegant harbour-side café eating an ice-cream. Fashionably dressed in black muslin, her hair swept up under a wide-brimmed hat, she attracted a good deal of attention, but she was as indifferent to the admiring glances of the passers-by as she had been to the friendly greetings of the women drinking lemonade at a neighbouring table, or the laughter of the children playing beside the boats. Only the black and scarlet funnel of the *Bernadetto*, just beginning to take on passengers for the journey to Manaus, pierced her absorption – taunting her with her incarceration in this wretched place. It was a slow boat, taking nine days for the voyage and stopping absolutely everywhere, but at least it would have got her there.

Ever since Henry had mentioned Harriet, Isobel's need to be on her way had become a kind of frenzy. She had told herself again and again that she was being absurd; Henry could not even have known Rom's name when he spoke to Harriet in the maze – yet she could not free herself of the image of a young girl crossing the main square of Manaus, walking up the imposing flight of steps to the mansion that must be Follina, being admitted by two powdered footmen . . . and then the door closing behind her. Closing . . . but not opening again to let her out. An absurd image, but one which gave Isobel no rest.

But little as Isobel was aware of her surroundings, she did notice a tall man in a crumpled linen suit who had come off the gangway of the *Gregory* and was now walking in a somewhat dazed manner in her direction. Surely – yes, it was the irritating Englishman who had travelled with her and was now, presumably, on his way home.

'Dr Finch-Dutton?'

Edward turned, stopped, lifted his hat. He seemed to be overcome with embarrassment, and this was not surprising for he presented an extraordinary sight. His fingers were criss-crossed with strips of sticking-plaster and another massive piece of plaster traversed his forehead. Two deep scratches ran from the top of his collar to his chin, and a piece was missing from the lobe of his right ear.

'Good heavens, Dr Finch-Dutton – what on earth has happened to you? Have you been in the jungle?'

'Yes, I suppose I have. In a sense. Yes, you could say that,' answered Edward heavily. 'Blood-poisoning cannot be entirely ruled out, the doctor says.'

'What kind of animal was it?' enquired Isobel, puzzled by the doctor's injuries. Too slight for a jaguar, the scratches had definitely been made by something with long, sharp claws.

'You may ask,' said Edward. 'Yes, Mrs Brandon, you may well ask.'

In response to her nod he took the chair beside her and Isobel, seeing that he was too distraught to place an order himself, asked for a *cafezinho*. 'I cannot tell you what I have been through,' Edward continued. 'You wouldn't believe it. Indeed, I find it impossible to believe it myself. But these injuries' – he held up his fingers, touched his bitten ear – 'were conferred on me by a human being. A human female. In short . . . a girl.'

'Impossible!'

'You might think so. But I assure you I speak the truth.'

'Good heavens!' Isobel, trying not to laugh, looked at him in mock concern. 'Would it help you to tell me about it?'

'Yes,' said Edward, nodding gratefully, 'I think it would. To tell the truth, I'm at my wits' end and I simply don't know what to do. I can't keep going up and down the Amazon like a yo-yo. I suppose I ought to take her back to Manaus, but I don't know if that's what she wants. A couple of men came from Verney's office just now to transfer her to the *Bernadetto* and she just kicked them in the shins and shut herself into her cabin. They—'

'*Verney?*' said Isobel, her heart pounding. 'Who is . . . this Verney?'

'A good point,' said Edward mournfully. 'I don't know. I thought he was a friend, but now I think perhaps he was double-crossing me all along. I fancied I caught a glimpse of him on the stage in all that mist . . . only then I decided I must have been mistaken, because the fellow hadn't shaved. Very well-turned-out fellow, Verney, you see. But now I wonder – maybe he snatched her. Got in first, so to speak?'

'Snatched who?'

'This girl I came to save. Decent girl, well-brought-up, only she went to pieces out here. Verney told me she was in good hands, but now I ask myself whether it wasn't he who made her come out of a

205

cake.'

'Out of a *cake?*'

'Yes, incredible, isn't it? So I thought I'd bring her back by force – for her own good, of course. It was what her father wanted. Only those idiots seized the wrong girl. Well, it was I who told them to, but I could have sworn it was her. She used to tie her shoes just like that . . . only of course, they all tie their shoes like that in the ballet – you can see it in those paintings by that French fellow, the way they bend over. And they all whiten their arms and scrape back their hair – it's the absolute devil trying to make out who is who.'

'So you got the wrong girl?'

'Yes. Only I didn't realise it until we were a good hundred miles down the river. The stewardess gave her a sleeping draught, she kicked up such a shindy. And of course she talked Russian all the time, but we thought she was just putting it on. And then at last I went down to open the cabin door . . .' He fell silent, remembering the moment of exaltation up there on the deck before he went below to forgive Harriet. 'And then she simply flew at me. She just went for me like a tigress – biting, scratching, kicking. There was no way I could defend myself. But that wasn't all – *my* injuries are nothing; it's what she did to—'

He swallowed. It seemed he could not yet say the creature's name without being overcome by emotion.

'To what?'

'*Peripatus*,' Edward brought out. 'I had it with me in a travelling case – you can't leave something as valuable as that lying about in a cabin. And she tore the box from my hand and threw it on the ground and then when the bottle rolled out she . . .' He fought for control once more. 'She *stepped* on it. Deliberately. Ground it into the floor with her heel. The specimen is totally destroyed.'

'What on earth is *Peripatus?*'

Edward told her. 'I can't tell you what a knock it is. I wouldn't have thought anyone could do that . . . deliberately.'

'Well, the creature was dead, wasn't it? So it didn't suffer?'

'*I* suffered,' said Edward. 'I don't think I shall ever get over it. There are things a chap never forgets. And now what am I to do with her? She doesn't speak a word of English and just kicks anyone who comes near her; she's raving mad. Of course she's had a bad time, I can see that. She keeps saying all these names – Yussop and Grigory and Alexi – over and over again, and passing her finger across her

206

neck, so I suppose she means they're her brothers and they will cut my throat. But if she comes from a large family, maybe she's homesick?'

Olga had got a splinter of glass into her foot through grinding the tube into the ground with her ballet shoes. She'd gone quite quiet while he took the splinter out of her heel – such a hard, muscular foot she had. All of her was hard and muscular, which was not what he had expected; well, not quite all of her . . . But then when he'd finished she'd started wrestling with him again. Verney's men had thought it a great joke when she wouldn't go with them, but what the devil was he to do?

'And what of the girl you came to save?' Isobel asked.

Edward shrugged wearily. 'What can I do? She's completely depraved. Mind you, there is no way Harriet could have done that to Peripatus. She may come out of cakes—'

'*Harriet*! Is that her name?'

Edward nodded. No good trying to shield Harriet now, things had gone well beyond that. 'Her name is Harriet Morton. Her father's a professor at my own college, St Philip's, and she used to be a thoroughly decent girl. At least, I thought she was. As a matter of fact, we were at Stavely only three months ago.'

'Tell me about her. *All* about her,' said Isobel, forcing herself to look appealingly into his eyes.

So Edward told her the story of his courtship and pursuit, the distress Harriet had caused to him and her father, and the part that Verney had played in the story while Isobel listened, here and there putting in a question, and storing away everything she heard, for knowledge was power and power she now needed desperately.

'And you think she's still in Manaus?'

'I'm sure she is. And I'll bet Verney's got hold of her. The more I think about it, the more certain I am that it was him I saw behind that rock. You mark my words, he wants her for himself!'

Isobel had risen, was putting on her gloves and unhooking her parasol from the back of the chair. 'Well, if I can find out anything more for you, I'll let you know. You say her father wants her back?'

'Yes . . . That is, I think so. Yes, I'm sure he does. But it's Olga I'm thinking about. The *Gregory* leaves again in a few hours and I simply don't know what to do. I suppose you can't advise me?'

'I'm afraid not, Dr Finch-Dutton,' said Isobel coldly. 'The matter is one that you must decide for yourself.' There was nothing more to be got from this fool and very little time now in which to act.

It was only as Isobel was bidding him goodbye that Edward thought to ask after Henry. 'How's the little chap? Getting on all right?'

'Henry is quite better, thank you,' said Isobel firmly and walked away quickly in the direction of the shipping office, leaving Edward to pay for her ice-cream.

An hour later, she was back in the convent.

'I have made up my mind,' she informed Sisters Concepcion and Margharita, who were giving Henry a blanket bath. 'We are travelling on to Manaus tonight. There's a spare cabin on the *Bernadetto* – a nice breezy one,' she lied. And as they stared at her incredulously she went on firmly, 'It will do him good to be in the fresh air; he can lie in a deck-chair and drink beef tea. We don't mollycoddle our children in England like you do out here. And Henry will *wish* to travel on, won't you, Henry?'

'Yes.' Henry's hoarse croak came with incredible gallantry from the bed. He did want to travel on; he longed, as a matter of fact, for alligators and boa constrictors. It was only the dark and his mother's anger that Henry feared. Only it was going to be a little bit difficult. Even sitting up seemed to make his head go round and round.

'It's an outrage!' stormed Sister Concepcion, returning to the refectory. 'The child hasn't even been out of bed! I shall call Dr Gonzales.'

But even Dr Gonzales, when he came, could not make Isobel change her mind. It was, she told herself, Henry's own heritage that she was trying to save; it was because of Henry and Stavely that she must find Rom at once and get rid of the hussy who had, after all, managed to make herself known to him. To be soft now, decided Isobel, turning away from the white face and dark-ringed eyes of her small son, would be to do Henry no service. Even now some dreadful school or institution might be making an offer for Stavely and those wretched trustees would accept anything to get their money.

So Henry was dressed, his things packed – and presently he sat on his bed waiting for the cab that was to take them to the harbour. His legs, thinner than ever, dangled from the high white bed and every so often he coughed – a racking, prolonged cough that shook his small frame – but he sat as straight as a ramrod and when his mother said, as she did from time to time, 'You feel better now, don't you, Henry?' he answered, 'Yes, thank you,' in as convincing a voice as he could manage. And sometimes he was rewarded by her smile.

208

The cab arrived. Sister Concepcion bustled in, her face creased with concern, and kissed Henry who clung to her in a way which Isobel thought excessive. Sister Annunciata picked up Henry's case.

'Thank you,' said Isobel to the nuns, holding out her hand. 'You have been very kind and I am grateful. When I get back to England, I will make a donation to your Order.'

Sister Margharita murmured a suitable acknowledgement, while Henry slipped off the side of the bed and stood up. This turned out to be more difficult than he had expected, but it was possible. And it had to be possible, too, to walk to the door. One simply put out one foot and then the other . . . I *can* do it, said Henry to himself. But he couldn't – not quite. Far more weakened by his illness than he realised, he swayed as the room spun round and would have fallen, but that Sister Concepcion caught him in her motherly arms and carried him out to the cab.

Isobel, walking ahead, had seen nothing.

Those who believe that nuns are gentle soft-voiced souls who speak ill of no one, would have been surprised could they have heard Sister Concepcion and her two helpers in the Convent of the Sacred Heart after the evening meal. But by that time Isobel and her son had steamed out of harbour and were once more en route for the Golden City.

Chapter Seventeen

'I must say I think they have it all wrong, the people who say that to part is to die a little. It seems to me,' said Harriet, 'that to part is to die really quite a lot. I mean, thirty-six hours without you . . .'

She stood on the terrace wearing the extraordinarily becoming blue dress that Marie-Claude had bought, waiting for Furo to bring round the black car in order to drive her to Manaus. For the Company was leaving the following day, due to embark on the *Lafayette* on Friday evening ready to sail at dawn, and she was going to say goodbye to Madame Simonova and spend a last night with her friends at the Metropole.

Rom stood beside her, troubled for no reason he could understand. *She holds my shadow*, he thought, quoting the phrase his Indians used to describe someone who had them in their power. Once it had seemed to him that this country was the 'incomparable remedy'. Now it was this quiet, unspectacular girl, whose loss would utterly diminish him.

But why should he lose her?

'Do you want me to go back with the Company?' Harriet had asked a few days earlier. 'Would that be . . . the right thing to do?'

'*Want* you to go back? Want you to? God, Harriet, do you have to ask me that?' Rom had replied. 'Do you want to go with them?'

'No, I don't. I would like to stay . . . if it is convenient.'

'*Convenient*? Sometimes I think you're a little mad. Perhaps you should come upstairs,' he had said furiously. 'I don't seem to be able to make you understand anything when you're on your feet.'

Since then she had abandoned herself to a degree of creative loving which exceeded anything he had ever imagined, her passionate physical response balanced by a respect for his work that gave him both rest and stimulus. But for her solitary practice sessions each morning at her makeshift *barre*, he would have sworn that she was utterly content.

'I wish I could have gone with you,' he said yet again. 'I hate you to go alone.'

He had intended to take Harriet to Manaus himself and make good his promise to Simonova to bring her to say goodbye, but Alvarez – his work at Ombidos completed – was calling at São Gabriel on his way home, and to Alvarez Rom owed a debt that must be paid. There was no question of Harriet being in danger. Edward had been seen standing on the deck of the *Gregory* as she steamed away from Belem, and it was most unlikely that a man who had made such an idiot of himself once would return to the attack. Moreover de Silva was back in Manaus and well able to control the antics of his men.

Why, then, this unease?

'You've given me too much money,' protested Harriet. 'Even if I buy presents for absolutely everybody, I can't spend it.'

'It is not for buying presents for absolutely everybody,' he said sternly. 'It's for you.'

She shook her head and reached for his hand, counting the knuckles carefully, checking them off one by one with her fingertips to make sure that everything was as it should be and that she would not forget – in the day and night she was to be away – the configuration of his little fingernail or the exact place where a vein to which she was particularly devoted changed its course.

'I got to one thousand and forty-three seeds last night,' she said. 'In the bath. So it's absolutely all right.'

'Of course it's all right,' he said roughly. 'All the passengers have to be on board by eight o'clock, so you'll be back in time for a splendid supper. I'm putting a bottle of Veuve Clicquot on ice – no doubt you will merely get hiccups again, but we must persevere.'

But now they were back, his Indians. He had shooed them away twice before, explaining that Harriet was only going to Manaus and would be back tomorrow, but here again were old José, Andrelinho with his crippled boy, Manuelo with his wife, his baby . . . and that old witch, Manuelo's mother-in-law, who now wore her boa of anaconda skins over Harriet's brown foulard . . .

The missionaries had taught them to wave – prolonged goodbyes were one of their accomplishments, but there were too many of them today and Maliki and Rainu were snivelling. And now Lorenzo, who was an educated man and should have known better, came forward

211

with a gift for Harriet which he placed in her hand – and which made Rom turn on him angrily with a few low words in his own dialect.

'Is there something wrong?' asked Harriet, troubled, looking up from the tiny, perfectly carved wooden canoe with paddles the size of splintered matchsticks and an intricate pattern of blue and scarlet painted across its bows. 'Should I not take it?'

Rom shook his head. 'It's all right.' But as Harriet thanked Lorenzo, his sense of wretchedness increased. The gift was one traditionally given to ensure safety for those travelling far away across water – and Harriet wasn't even going in the *Amethyst*, Lorenzo knew that perfectly well. What the devil had got into them all?

The car arrived. Furo got out and held open the door and Harriet turned to Rom. 'Could you be so kind as to remember that I love you absolutely?' she said quietly, almost matter-of-factly. 'Could you be so kind as to remember that?'

He bent down then to kiss not her mouth, but her fingers, holding them in a strangely formal gesture to his lips.

'Yes,' he said. 'I could remember that. Were I to forget it, Harriet, it would go very ill with me.'

Long after the car was out of sight and he had returned to the house, his Indians still stood on the steps, waving and waving and waving . . .

*

The theatre was dark and silent, the seats already shrouded. It would be a month before another company made its way to Manaus – a Cossack choir from Georgia.

Would they be the last? Harriet wondered, picking her way across the deserted stage. Was Rom right and would this marvellous and fantastical theatre be given over to the mice? Would bats hang from the chandeliers and moths devour the silken hangings? But if it was so – if Mrs Lehmann's carriage horses had drunk their last champagne and the grandly dressed audience would no longer sweep across the great mosaic square – it had still been a splendid and worthwhile dream to build a theatre here in this place . . . and one day, surely, it would open its doors again, music would stream from the pit and men, perhaps still unborn, would wait with bated breath for the gold glimmer of the footlights that meant curtain rise.

Down in the wardrobe she found a lone stage-hand who at first greeted her with respect, not recognising in the elegantly dressed girl the little dancer in her shabby clothes – and then as she smiled, he asked her to sit on the last of the skips so that he could close it, as he had asked her to do three months ago in the Century Theatre when the adventure began.

Then she went back to the stage-door where Furo was waiting and was driven to the Metropole where she went, first of all, to say good-bye to Simonova.

During the fortnight since Harriet had last seen her, Simonova's thinness had become spectacular: now she lay like a death's head on the single pillow. Dubrov for once was absent, supervising the loading of the scenery.

'So,' said the ballerina as Harriet approached and curtseyed. 'You are happy. One can see that.'

'Yes, Madame. Extremely happy. But I wish that you—'

'Oh, never mind, never mind,' said Simonova irritably. 'Let them clap Masha Repin. Myself, I will be thankful if I can even walk again.'

'But you will, you will! Professor Leblanc is the greatest specialist in the world.'

'Ach, specialists, what do they know? I believe nothing.' She turned her head restlessly on the pillow and pierced Harriet with her eyes. 'It will not last, this love of yours, you know that?'

'Yes, I know. At least, it will for me but not for him. He is going back to the place in England where he was born and there is a woman there who . . .' But this did not seem to be a sentence that one finished.

'Yes, yes. It is always so. Dancers, singers . . . we are for pleasure, but it is others who become the *châtelaines* of great estates. So you must see that you get some jewels and you must work and *work*. Remember what Grisha always tells you about your shoulders – the left one in particular.'

'Yes, Madame, I will. And I will never forget your Odette – or your Giselle – not if I live for a hundred years. Never, never will I forget them.'

'And my Lise?' came Simonova's sharp voice from the bed. 'My Lise in *Fille* – what was wrong with my Lise?'

'Your Lise too.' Harriet was close to tears. 'To have been in your company even for such a short time has been the greatest privilege in the world.'

'You are a good girl. Now I must rest for the journey, but first . . .' She seemed to be coming to some decision, a frown etching deep lines

213

into the worn forehead. 'Yes, I will do it. Go over there to that blue suitcase.'

Harriet stepped round the stretcher lying ready to convey Madame to the boat and found the case.

'Lift the lid. There is a pair of ballet shoes on top – my last pair. The pair I wore when I had my accident. Take them out and bring them here to me.'

Harriet did so and Simonova seized them in her bony hands, stroked the pink silk with one long finger as a mother traces the features of an infant in her arms. 'See,' she said tenderly, 'they are hardly worn; I fell so soon. They should go to a museum perhaps – the last shoes of Galina Simonova – but who goes to museums? Take them. They are for you.'

Harriet, unashamedly crying now, shook her head. 'No, Madame, I can't! There must be someone who . . . matters more.'

'Masha Repin, perhaps,' sneered the ballerina. 'Or that pretty friend of yours who thinks only of restaurants. Take them. Take them quickly. And now go!'

*

It was a very long time before the three friends slept that night. Marie-Claude had a great deal to tell them, for Vincent had secured his *auberge* and she was to be married in December. 'And it's because of you, 'arriette. You made it possible for Vincent to give the deposit and never, never will I forget what you have done.'

As they talked sleepily in their beds it seemed that Kirstin, too, might soon hang up her dancing shoes, for there was a young man in a village on the Baltic not far from the town were she had been born – a childhood friend who for a long time had been willing to be something more. His father owned a fleet of trawlers which Leif would inherit and he had never been to the ballet in his life, which to Kirstin was very much in his favour. 'I don't know,' she said now. 'It may not work out, but I think I will go back and see. It's such a pretty place – the red wooden houses, and the water . . .'

'So you see, it is you who must be a great dancer, 'arriette,' said Marie-Claude, 'so that we can bring our children to see you and tell them that with this divine *prima ballerina assoluta* we once shared a horrible room full of cockroaches in the city of Manaus.' She sighed, seeing Harriet's face. 'But of course it is this man you want for always – and no wonder,' she said, motioning to a froth of pale green muslin

214

on the chair: the dress she had bought at Verney's insistence when shopping for Harriet.

'Perhaps this earl's grand-daughter to whom he goes in England no longer loves him?' suggested Kirstin. 'Perhaps she has met someone else?'

'And then when he has recovered from his broken heart, he can put you into a villa in some suitable district with your own carriage. In Paris it would be somewhere near the Bois . . . or in St Cloud, perhaps, but in London I don't know . . .'

'St John's Wood, I think,' said Harriet, recalling the novels she had dipped into while doing her homework in the public library. 'Somewhere near the Regent's Park Canal. A Gothic villa with a wisteria in the garden.' Her eyes grew bright at the thought that she might after all have a future as a kept woman, awaiting Rom's visits twice a week in a violet tea-gown. No, that was greedy. Once a week. Once a *fortnight*, because the trains were dreadful from Stavely and the roads even worse. It was ridiculous of course. Isobel would not have met someone else – no one who had ever loved Rom could possibly stop – and a man married to a woman as beautiful as Isobel would scarcely trouble to travel to London to visit his mistress in St John's Wood. Moreover Rom, once he married, would be faithful, Harriet was sure of that. But the daydream had done her good and trying to work out how many days she would see him if he came every other week for, say, five years . . . wondering if that was what the pomegranate seeds had meant . . . she fell asleep.

In the morning there was an unexpected development. Grisha and some of the Russian girls, going down before breakfast to meet the *Bernadetto* as she docked, returned to say that Olga had not been aboard, nor had the crew any idea of her whereabouts.

'It is extremely strange,' said Grisha, returning to the Metropole dining-room where the rest of the company sat at breakfast. He turned to Harriet. 'Monsieur Verney sent some men to fetch her from the *Gregory*, I think?'

'Yes, he did,' said Harriet, and beamed at the ballet master because he had pronounced Rom's name. 'I'm sure of it.'

Grisha shrugged. 'I suppose she has decided to wait for us in Belem,' he said, and instructed Tatiana to pack Olga's things and see that they were put on board.

The rest of the day passed in a bustle of last-minute shopping, packing, promises and plans. Harriet bought farewell presents for her friends: a deceptively demure nightgown for Marie-Claude and a blouse for Kirstin. She also bought a record of 'The Last Rose of Summer' for the Indians and found for Rom, in a dusty shop full of maps and oleographs, a book with pictures of the tapestry of 'The Lady and the Unicorn' – a wonderful stroke of luck, for above the golden-haired virgin and her obedient beast were embroidered the words: *Mon seul désir* – and these were the words which Rom had whispered to her two nights ago as she lay in his arms.

By the time she returned with her purchases, the preparations for Simonova's removal were already under way. Two orderlies were coming from the hospital to lift her on to the stretcher and carry her to the ambulance; a nurse had just arrived and was sterilising her instruments in the kitchens prior to giving the ballerina the pain-killing injection which would enable her to endure the unavoidable jolting as they drove to the quay.

Under these circumstances Harriet would not have attempted to seek out Dubrov, to whom she had not yet said goodbye, but as she made her way across the hall she was waylaid by the harassed stage manager. 'If you're going past his door, could you give this to the boss? It's just arrived at the theatre, sent on by the London office, and looks as though it might be important,' he said, handing Harriet a letter with a Russian stamp and a massive and elaborate seal.

Dubrov was not in his own room, but Harriet's quiet knock brought him at once to Simonova's door.

'I came to bring this letter, Monsieur, it's just arrived. And to say goodbye – and thank you.'

He put up a hand to pat her cheek. 'There's no need to thank me. You have worked hard and could have been—' He paused, the blue eyes suddenly sharp, took the letter and quickly broke the seal. 'Wait!' he threw over his shoulder at Harriet, and carried the heavy embossed paper over to the window.

'Well, what is it?' came Simonova's fretful voice from the bed.

Dubrov, however, was unable to answer. It was necessary for him to mop his eyes with his handkerchief several times before he could trust his voice. Then: 'It is from St Petersburg,' he said. 'From the Maryinsky.' Another sniff, another dab at his watering eyes . . . 'From the director, the man who dismissed you.'

'And?'

'He asks . . . he invites you . . . to dance at a gala for the Romanov Tercentenary! To dance *Giselle* before the Tsar!' Dubrov abandoned

216

the effort to check his tears, which now ran unhampered down his cheeks. 'The honour! The incredible honour! Now, at the end of your career! We will keep it always, this letter. We will frame it in gold and hang it on the wall and when we sit in our armchairs in Cremorra—'

'*Armchairs? Cremorra?*' Simonova's voice pierced like a gimlet. 'What are you talking about? Give the letter to me!' And to Harriet, tactfully edging her way out of the door: 'You will remain!'

The letter which caused Dubrov to weep, overcome by pride and the tragedy of its timing, had an entirely different effect on Simonova.

'Let me see,' she murmured in a businesslike manner. 'March the fifteenth . . . Nine months. Ha! Only two other ballerinas are invited – that will teach Pavlova to desert her native land. Think of it – all Russia will be *en fête* for the Tercentenary! The Grand Duke Andrei asked for me specially – he remembered!'

'Ah, *dousha*, the honour! The distinction of having been asked!' Dubrov was still awash with emotion. 'We shall never forget that you were invited . . . that you could have—'

'What do you mean, *could* have?' Why are you always so pessimistic? Just because I have wrenched my back a little – I have done it a hundred times – and I have told you already that *I will not mulch*! Now let me see, we will go to Paris, yes, but not to that idiot specialist – to buy clothes! There will be a reception at the Winter Palace without a doubt and several balls. Then straight on to Petersburg to work with Gerdt. No performances, just work, work, work!'

'Galina, I beg of you, be reasonable.' Dubrov was aghast at this new turn of events. 'You are severely injured. The doctors—'

'The doctors? Do you think I care about the *doctors*?' This woman who had not lifted her head from the pillow since her fall had now propped herself up on her elbow and was – incredibly – sitting up! 'Send Grisha to me at once, and the masseuse. *Chort*! I'm as weak as a kitten and no wonder, lying here for two weeks. After Gerdt I shall work with Cecchetti on my *port de bras*, and if he's with Diaghilev he must leave him and come to me.' She had pushed back the sheet, put her long, pale legs to the ground. 'Ah, to see Masha Repin's face when she hears of this!'

'Your back!' cried Dubrov in desperation, rushing forward, for she was pulling herself up on the arms of the chair, was actually *standing*!

'We will no longer discuss my back,' said Simonova regally. Still needing the support of the chair she showed, however, no signs of

217

serious discomfort. 'For heaven's sake, stop fussing, Sasha, and take that stupid stretcher away. How the devil am I supposed to move with it lying there? Now listen, you must immediately send a cable to the Maryinsky to say we accept. And then come back here quickly, because I have had a new idea about the Mad Scene. You know where I *bourrée* forward and pretend to pick up the flower? Well, I think it would be better if—' She broke off, her charcoal eyes now focused on Harriet. 'Ha!' she said. 'Those shoes I gave you yesterday – there is a lot of wear in them still and they are perfectly broken in. Go and get them, please. At once!'

*

It had already been dark for some time when Harriet made her way quietly up the avenue of jacaranda trees towards the house.

Saying goodbye to her friends had been hard, but she was home and had been really brave living without Rom for nearly two whole days, but now needed to be brave no longer. For as she walked past the acacia with the flycatcher's nest which Rom had shown her on that first day, crossed the bridge over the *igarape*, she felt not only the intense joy of the coming reunion but for the first time some confidence in the future. Rom had been so certain that he did not want her to return with the Company, and there had been no further talk of Stavely. There were probably weeks still to be with him, even months – and perhaps the journey back to England. Surely one did not say, '*Mon seul désir*' in quite that way to a person one intended to part from soon.

What's more, she had saved at least two extra hours to be with him. Dubrov had insisted on getting the Company aboard early to avoid Simonova exciting herself any further and – coming off the ship after her farewells – Harriet found herself hailed by the Raimondo brothers aboard their rackety launch and offered a lift to São Gabriel. She knew the brothers, knew the speed of the *Santa Domingo*. It had taken her only a few minutes to scribble a note to Furo, due to meet her at the Casa Branca at eight, and despatch it by a seraphic-looking urchin. Then she had been aboard.

She was approaching the first of the terraces. Light streamed from the downstairs windows of the house and from one window which she had not seen lit up before. Moving quietly, but hurrying now – already in her imagination stretching out her hands to Rom – she began to climb the steps.

Something was standing by the balustrade: a small white shape half-hidden by a stone urn filled with tobacco flowers. Not one of Rom's tame creatures . . . A little wraith? A ghost?

Then the wraith gave a squeak of purest joy and ran down the steps into her arms.

'*Henry*! Oh, Henry – I don't *believe* it!'

'It's honestly me, though!'

They clung to each other, as overjoyed to be together as if they had been lifelong companions instead of having met once in an English garden.

'I *knew* you would come before I went to sleep; I just knew,' said Henry, his arms tightening around her neck. 'I wanted to see you so much!'

'And I you, Henry!' She had been right to love him; there was nothing else to do with this child. 'Only how did you get here? I had no *idea*—' They had moved a little, so that the light of the terrace lantern was on his face. 'Are you all right, Henry?' she asked, startled. 'You haven't been ill?'

'I had the measles, but I'm all right now. We came this morning and a nice man called Miguel brought us here in a little boat and I saw an alligator right close to, truly I did, and everything is absolutely marvellous, Harriet, and it's all because of you.'

'Why me, Henry?' She drank in his soapy smell, put a hand on his ruffled hair. Soon it would come, the next bit, but she had a few moments still to relish his presence and his happiness.

'Because you found him – the "secret boy" – you told him about us and that we needed him. He knew all about Stavely and it was because of you, he told me. And Harriet, he's *bought* it – bought Stavely, did you know?'

'No.'

'You can do that,' explained Henry. 'You can buy places without being there. You send a cable and it goes snaking out along a tube at the bottom of the sea – and then the bank gives people money and you buy their houses. He did it just as soon as you told him about us, and it's because of you that someone else didn't buy it first. I *told* Mummy you'd find him; I told her!'

'She's here then, your mother?' asked Harriet, noting her own idiocy. Where else would she be, the mother of such a child? The pain was beginning now – not unendurable yet . . . just mustering.

'Yes! And she's so happy! She hasn't been cross all day – well, only

219

when I asked Uncle Rom a lot of questions, but he said I had a refreshing mind.' Henry paused and beamed up at her. The discovery that he had a refreshing mind had set the seal on this joyous and successful day. 'He's so *nice*, isn't he – Uncle Rom? He's just right for a "secret boy", even though he's grown-up. I thought uncles might be ... well, you know, *uncles* ... but he isn't. He showed me the manatees and some poisoned arrows he got from an Indian and the coati took a nut from my hand.' His attention caught by something in her expression, he said anxiously, 'You do like him too, don't you, Harriet?'

'Yes, Henry. I like him very much.'

'Because he likes you a *lot*. He said we had a ... mutual friend and that was you. And, Harriet, he told me all the things he's going to do at Stavely. He's going to make a tree-house, only not in the Wellingtonia because it's too high; not that I'd be frightened, but it's not *convenient* for it to be so high. And he's going to get a huge dog – a wolfhound – and show me how to train him – and he's going to get rid of awful Mr Grunthorpe and let old Nannie come and live in the house again. He told me all that while Mummy was resting, and it's all because of you, Harriet – otherwise someone else might have bought Stavely first, but you found him and you made everything come right.'

'I'm glad, Henry.' The pain could definitely be said to be limbering up. She had imagined it often, but there seemed to be aspects that one could not in fact anticipate and the physical part was beginning to be a nuisance: the nausea, the trembling that assailed her limbs – and needing cover, she moved away a little so as to be out of the brightest rays of the lamp.

'Mummy said I could stay awake and tell you all about it as long as I didn't bother Uncle Rom.' Henry paused, remembering his mother's unaccustomed gentleness as she put him to bed. 'She said I could watch out for you and tell you *everything* because you've been so kind to us.' He moved closer to Harriet because there was still one anxiety that he needed to share with this best of friends. 'When she was saying good night, Mummy told me that she had to marry my father when she was young because he made such a dreadful fuss when she said she wouldn't, but now he's dead she can marry Uncle Rom. Only Harriet, when she marries him he'll be my stepfather, won't he? Like Mr Murdstone in *David Copperfield* and all those cruel step-people in fairy stories. And Mr Murdstone was nice to David

220

before he married his mother, but then he was *awful*. Only I don't see how Uncle Rom *could* be awful, do you?'

One last effort and then she could let go . . . crawl away, be sick, howl like Hecuba . . .

'Henry, if you don't mind my saying so you're being a little bit silly,' said Harriet, managing to make her voice matter-of-fact – almost reproving. 'Surely you have read the *Jungle Book*?'

'Yes. Yes, I have.' She made no attempt to prompt him, but waited quietly until understanding came. 'You mean Mowgli!' cried Henry. 'Mowgli had a stepfather!'

'Exactly.'

'Yes, he did, didn't he? An absolutely marvellous stepfather! A proper wolf!' Henry was radiant. 'Oh *yes* – and Uncle Rom's a bit like a wolf, isn't he – sort of brave and wild?' As he smiled up at her he noticed that the gaps in his teeth were almost filled; it was three months since they had met in the maze. 'Would you like to come and see Mummy?' he went on. 'She was in the sitting-room just now, hugging Uncle Rom and everything, but I expect they've stopped now.' He broke off, his russet head tilted in concern. 'Are you all right, Harriet? You're not getting the measles?'

'No, Henry. I'm . . . perfectly all right.'

'I'd better go back to bed then or Mummy will be cross.' He put up his arms and she kissed him for the last time. 'You're *sure* you're not getting the measles?' And as she nodded, 'I'll see you in the morning. You're my best friend in the whole world, Harriet.'

'And you are mine.'

At the top of the terrace he turned. 'Do you know what I'm sleeping in, Harriet? A *hammock*! Uncle Rom said I could – honestly!' said Henry and pattered away towards the house.

He had gone, but she wasn't sick and the trembling had stopped. Because of course it couldn't be true, what Henry had said – it couldn't be over so suddenly, so completely, without the journey back still to be with Rom. Henry wouldn't lie, but he must be mistaken. He was so intelligent that it was easy to forget that he was just a little child.

She went quietly up the last of the steps, made her way towards the windows of the salon. The curtains were open and light streamed out on to the terrace.

Inside, two figures, unaware of her . . . absorbed.

('I know what it's like . . . I know how it is to be at a window . . .

221

outside . . . and to look in on a lighted room and not be able to make anyone hear.'

'How do you know? You have not experienced it.'

'Perhaps I am going to one day. There is a man in England who says that time is curved . . .')

Rom stood with his back to her, the dark head bent, one arm resting on a bookcase. Isobel faced him, almost as tall as he, and for a moment it seemed to Harriet that she looked straight at her, but of course she could not have seen her in the darkness – that was absurd. She had loosened the beautiful red hair which flowed like a river over her black gown and as she leaned towards Rom, smiling, putting a hand on his arm, their sense of kinship came across to Harriet as clearly as if she had proclaimed, 'We belong, this man and I! We inhabit the same world!'

Then, perhaps responding to something Rom had said, she moved forward, stumbled a little . . . seemed as if she might fall – and as he moved quickly towards her, her arms went round him and her head came to rest against his shoulder. And as she stood thus in sanctuary, staring past the place where Harriet stood, her face was transfigured by pride and happiness and love.

'It is only necessary to do the steps,' Marie-Claude had said.

But there were no steps for this: no piteous undulations of the arms, no *bourrées* backwards. Just a slow turning to stone . . . a nothingness . . . a death.

Then she turned and walked away – moving, this lightest of dancers, like an old, old woman – and vanished into the dark.

*

'No! No! No!' yelled Grisha, whacking at Harriet's shins with his cane. 'You are a *durak* – an idiot! Why do you bend your knees like a carthorse? The line must be smooth, *smooth* . . .' He demonstrated, flicked his fingers at the old accompanist – and in the cleared Palm Lounge of the *Lafayette*, Harriet resumed her *assemblés*.

She had been working for two hours and before that there had been class and Grisha, formerly so kind, had bullied and shouted and despaired of her as he had done each day of their journey across the calm Atlantic. For Harriet was no longer just a girl in the *corps* – Simonova was taking her to Russia; she was to be a serious dancer and for a girl thus singled out there could be no mercy and no rest.

Nor did Harriet want rest. Every muscle ached, the perspiration ran down her back, but she dreaded the moment when Grisha would dismiss her. She would have liked to collapse with exhaustion, to weep like Taglioni and faint like Taglioni. To faint particularly, and thus find the oblivion that sleep did not bring as in her dreams she tore through bramble thickets, clawed at stone walls, searching in vain for Rom.

'Sixteen *grandes battements* – then twelve *ronds de jambe en l'air*,' said Grisha viciously as Simonova swept in to study the progress of her future pupil. It had been a brilliant idea to take Harriet along. For Cremorra no longer figured in Simonova's itinerary. A triumph at the Maryinsky and then a return to Paris to open a school and become, as she had been the world's greatest ballerina, its greatest teacher of the dance – this was what she now intended. And who was better suited to be a show pupil than this work-hungry English girl?

'You may go,' said Grisha. 'Return at two.' Even before Harriet had risen from her curtsey it had seized her again, the pain, tearing and clawing – and embarrassed by the unseemliness of an agony so unremitting, she stole off to her favourite hiding place between the life-boat and the railing of the deck.

At least she had caught the boat, she told herself for the hundredth time. Stumbling away from Follina, still numb with shock, she had found the Raimondo brothers fishing with flares in the bay off São Gabriel and given them the last of Rom's money to take her to the *Lafayette* before it sailed. Because of that she had this chance. Many people had nothing to do with grief like hers, whereas she could turn it into art. Dubrov had explained this when he had told her that they would take her to Russia. He had been quite confident about it all; the Russian girls had travelled on a group ticket and there had been no sign of Olga at Belem. No one would ask for names if the numbers were right – and aghast at Harriet's state, he had found for her the only consolation she could accept.

Only now, standing with her hands folded across her chest so that what was happening inside her could not escape and make people recoil from her, she wondered if it could be done. If this beast tearing at her entrails could be transformed into those moments of high art when Odette lets her fingertips run lightly down the Prince's arm before she vanishes for ever into the lake. How many years would have to pass? How many aeons?

'''ariette, you must *eat*!' scolded Marie-Claude, coming to find her as she always did and taking her down to the dining-room – and at two she was back with Grisha, welcoming the ache in her limbs, the soreness, which people who did not understand were stupid enough to confuse with pain.

So the ship steamed eastwards and Harriet worked and pledged herself to make it come at last: the day when, contained in the iron framework of a flawless technique, she could reveal to those who watched her the heartbreak and the glory of an immutable love.

Four weeks after they left Brazil, punctual to the hour, the *Lafayette* steamed into Cherbourg. Harriet had scarcely thought of Cambridge or her home and she walked unthinkingly off the ship with her friends, bound for the custom sheds and the train to Paris.

Waiting at the bottom of the gangway – black-clad, menacing, flanked by two gendarmes with truncheons – stood her father and her aunt.

CHAPTER EIGHTEEN

HARRIET HAD been locked in her attic for nearly a month. Her clothes had been removed; she was conveyed to and from the bathroom by Aunt Louisa or those of the Trumpington Tea Circle ladies who came to take over when Miss Morton had to go shopping or merely needed a break. A doctor had been to examine her – not the old family doctor who had once recommended dancing classes, but a new man suggested by Hermione Belper – and had confirmed the Mortons' worst fears. Pending further treatment of the unfortunate girl, Dr Smithson had given instructions for her to be kept in a darkened room and on a meatless diet to avoid over-stimulation – instructions which Louisa obeyed meticulously, feeding her niece mostly on semolina and rusks of oven-baked stale bread.

The purpose of this regime was reasonable enough: to break Harriet's will, to make her understand the enormity of what she had done, and to confess it.

'And then?' asked Louisa as the days passed and Harriet remained silent. 'What is to be done with her then?' She had enjoyed the drama of the original recapture and imprisonment, but the daily task of keeping Harriet guarded fell on her, and the whispers in the town – the suggestion that the Mortons had gone too far in inflicting punishment – were far from pleasant.

'We shall see,' Professor Morton had replied. Obsessed with the idea of a grovelling, weeping daughter begging for mercy, he could think no further than Harriet's utter subjugation.

In deciding how best to deal with Harriet, the Mortons were under the disadvantage of knowing nothing of her life in Manaus for Edward Finch-Dutton, on whom they had relied, seemed to have disappeared. It was not Harriet's former suitor who had informed them that she was arriving in Cherbourg, but an anonymous well-wisher who had been kind enough to cable St Philip's from Manaus.

And Harriet would say nothing. She was willing only to apologise for having caused them anxiety by running away, and for nothing else.

'I was happy there,' she had said at the beginning. 'I did nothing of which I am ashamed. It was the best part of my life and I would as soon apologise for breathing.'

And incredibly the weeks of confinement, the near-starvation, the appalling monotony – for they had taken away her books – had not weakened her resolution.

'The name of your seducer!' Professor Morton yelled at her on the rare occasions when he visited his daughter. 'Assuming there was only one!'

But she had shaken her head and as day followed wretched day she neither broke down nor admitted her wrong.

Harriet endured because she had been loved by Rom. This honour had been accorded her, this ultimate benison, and she must not let them break her because to do so would be to denigrate his love.

So she kept herself sane and she did it by remembering. Not a haphazard wallowing in past happiness, but a disciplined, orderly progression through the rooms of Follina, through its gardens . . . along the banks of the river. Waking hungry in her cold and dismal room Harriet, in her mind, rose from the cloud-netted bed where Rom still slept, felt the softness of the carpet beneath her feet . . . took three steps – exactly three – to the brocaded chair to trace the pattern of the golden *fleur de lys* . . . read the titles of the books on the low table: *The Collected Works of John Donne*; *The Stones of Venice*; *The Orchid Grower's Manual* . . . moved to the window to draw aside the curtains and name, with the same rigorous precision she had once accorded her work at the *barre*, the plants that grew on the terrace beneath.

While she could do this – while she could drift in the *Firefly* past the bank where the otters played and see the sun bittern fly into the light – they could not touch her, and knowing she had to keep well so as to garner these memories, to make them part of her for ever, she ate every morsel of the food she was given and kept her muscles active with exercises as she well knew how to do.

And so the days passed and nothing the Mortons could do deflected her, though her stricken eyes seemed to grow ever larger in her face. Then, during the fifth week of her incarceration, she woke as usual and in her mind walked as usual across Rom's room, drew aside the curtains, turned to cross the Persian rug so as to make her way back to the bed where he waited . . . and found that she could not remember the pattern of that rug. She had known it would be hard to remember, but she had studied it so carefully – so very carefully. Was it the outer border that was amethyst, with diamonds and zig-zags of bronze? Or was it the pearl-grey rim with its stylised flowers that came first? Desperate, she sat up in bed, her heart pounding. She had to remember, she *had* to! If she could forget one thing, she could forget it all – she could forget even Rom, and then there would be nothing left to live for in the world.

But the pattern would not be recalled. In her exhausted brain shapes and colours swam in an indistinguishable blur and whatever she did she could not reassemble them.

It was Hermione Belper who came that day to remove Harriet's luncheon tray, and when she came down again she had good news for Louisa who was returning from the shops.

'She is weeping uncontrollably, Louisa – and she has not touched her food. It seems her spirit is broken at last. How thankful you must be!'

And the Mortons were thankful. But if Harriet now lay listlessly on the pillow and showed none of her former defiance, she still did not speak of her time in Manaus and she was growing so thin that it was not easy to see how she could, as it were, be 'produced' again in public. Moreover they themselves were being subjected to an increasing amount of unpleasantness. It was easy enough to discount the smear campaign of a woman like Madame Lavarre, but when the Provost of St Anne's crossed the road rather than speak to the Professor, the Mortons were increasingly compelled to seek ways out of their dilemma.

It was at this point – just two weeks before the beginning of the Michaelmas term – that the Professor came home in a state of more than usual indignation.

'Do you know who I met today? Edward Finch-Dutton! He was creeping round the walls of the Fountain Courtyard and trying to avoid me, I'm sure.'

'Good heavens! But why has he not been in touch with us ?'

'I have no idea. Apparently he tried to bring Harriet back and it went wrong. He had a black eye and his nose was covered in sticking-plaster; I can only conclude that he has taken to the bottle. But I will tell you this, Louisa. I asked him what had made him send that second cable and he said it was because Harriet came out of a cake. In her underclothes.' And as Louisa stared at him, speechless with incredulity: 'That's what he said. *In her underclothes.* Then he mumbled some nonsense about her perhaps not having meant any harm and bolted. I tell you the fellow was drunk; he will have to resign his Fellowship, no doubt about that.'

But the news had given Louisa her cue. 'Bernard, don't you think we ought to face the fact that Harriet is seriously unbalanced? I have thought so all along, but this really decides the matter. Isn't it time we found a good institution where she can be helped? Homes for the mentally ill are extremely liberal these days: wholesome food, fresh air, basketwork . . . Dr Smithson knows of a specialist in London who has made a study of cases like hers. If Mr Fortescue certified that Harriet is not in her right mind, Smithson would second the diagnosis and her removal to somewhere suitable would follow automatically.' And as the Professor still seemed to hesitate, she concluded, 'I am thinking only of Harriet. She needs professional care and attention if she is to be healed. To refuse her that would be very selfish, would it not?'

This was a plea to which the Professor could scarcely be deaf. Dr Smithson accordingly was appealed to, and contacted his eminent colleague in Harley Street and it was arranged that Mr Fortescue would come down as soon as possible in order to examine Harriet.

After which, having got her way, Louisa was really quite kind to Harriet and sent up jam with her semolina and butter with her rusks, but for Harriet – slipping away into the shadows – these attentions came a little late.

*

Fate had played into Isobel's hands in a most remarkable way. The Raimondo brothers, who had taken Harriet back to Manaus to catch the *Lafayette*, took the absurdly large sum she had given them, collected two girls from Madame Anita's brothel and set off for their home town of Iquitos in Peru. The seraphic urchin to whom she had entrusted the note for Furo had been less seraphic than he appeared; he got into a fight in an alley on the way to the *Casa Branca*, lost the note and bolted for home. Thus Furo, waiting in increasing anxiety for Harriet, had not returned to Follina until the small hours and by the time Rom was back in the city to see what had become of her, the

Lafayette had sailed.

It was thus only Henry who remained as a witness of Harriet's return to Follina and it was he himself who had given Isobel her cue.

'Uncle Rom will be awfully sad too,' said Henry, blinking back his tears at the news that Harriet had decided to go and be a famous dancer, that she would not be coming back. 'He likes Harriet; he likes her very much.'

'Yes, he does,' said Isobel. 'So I'm afraid he will be extremely sad. What will make him particularly sad is that she said goodbye to you and not to him. It will hurt his feelings, don't you think? So perhaps, Henry, it would be really kind not to tell him? Just to keep it a secret? You're grown-up enough for secrets, aren't you?'

Henry was. Sinclair of the Scouts, in the *Boy's Own Paper*, was continually keeping secrets, some of them calculated to burn a hole in a lesser person's breast. Aware of the child's passionate desire to please her, Isobel was sure that he would keep his word – and if anything went wrong she could plead, naturally enough, an unwillingness to cause Rom pain. There had only remained the sending of the cable to Professor Morton – for it was not Isobel's intention to let Harriet reappear in Rom's life as a glamorous ballerina – and the deed was done. After which she settled down to her role as comforter.

'You must be happy for her, darling,' she said to Rom. 'I met Dr Finch-Dutton at Belem and he told me that it was all that Harriet had wanted all her life. Just to dance . . . always to dance.'

'We will not speak of Harriet,' was his only answer.

Yet he accepted without question Isobel's version of what had happened. Count Sternov, whose friendship it was impossible to doubt, had been at the Metropole just after Simonova's miraculous recovery and had heard her offer to take Harriet to Russia. Both he and the Metropole manager had seen the ballerina depart in triumph, walking to the hansom with her arm round the shoulder of the English girl, while Miguel himself had seen Harriet go aboard with the company.

So what had occurred was clearly what Rom had both feared and expected. Overcome by this sudden marvellous opportunity, Harriet had gone and perhaps wisely made the break cleanly without messages or farewells.

He made no further enquiries and, concealing from everyone the degree of his wretchedness and the hurt she had caused him by not trusting him enough to speak honestly of her ambitions, he pursued his plans: transferring his possessions, making provision for his Indians, issuing instructions to MacPherson concerning Stavely. He had set himself to restore his father's house and he would do so, but the burden of loss he rolled through his days – as Sisyphus rolled his stone – seemed only to grow heavier as the grey weeks passed.

Isobel, however, did not give up hope. It was of course absurd that she should live in Paradise Farm, even with the generous allowance Rom had proposed, while he ruled alone at the Hall. The suggestion was an insult. Her place was by Rom's side and as his wife, and now that the detestable girl was gone he would come to see this. So she changed her clothes five times a day, flirted, brushed against him 'by accident' and would have been surprised to learn how infrequently Rom even noticed that she was there.

Harriet had been gone for a month when, in the hour before sunset, Rom walked through the tall trees towards the Indian village, bound on business with old José. The light had slanted in just that way when he had first gone in search of Harriet and found her cradling Manuelo's baby. He had known then really, that he wanted no children which were not hers – and suddenly the sense of desolation so overwhelmed him that he stopped and put out a steadying hand to the trunk of a tree.

At which point there entered a *deus ex machina*.

It entered in an unexpected form: that of a lean, rangy and malodorous chicken. Exuding the *sangfroid* of those reared as household pets, enjoying its customary evening stroll from the village, the bird stopped, examined the unexpected figure blocking its path, gave a squawk of displeasure – and retreated . . .

Leaving behind a small mottled object . . . A single chicken feather, to which Rom stooped and which he held for a surprisingly long time in the palm of his hand.

Then he turned abruptly and made his way back towards the house.

Henry, conversing on the bridge with the manatees, was the first person to see him. Uncle Rom looked different – the way he had looked on the first day, not all grim and shut-in as he had appeared since then – and emboldened by the change in his hero, Henry beamed and said, 'Hello!'

'Hello, Henry!' Rom, ashamed now of the way he had been neglecting this endearing child, held out his hand. 'I was just on the way to find your mother. I'm going back to Europe tomorrow; I'll book a passage for you soon, on a fine steamer, but I have to leave at once.'

Henry nodded. 'You're going to find Harriet, aren't you?' he said with the quick insight of those who love.

'That's right,' said Rom, greatly surprised.

'I'm so glad!' The little face was transformed with relief. 'I've been awfully worried about her because I *knew* she shouldn't dance when she had the measles! I went to a dancing class once and it was horrible: you go round and round very fast in slippy shoes, and if you did that with the measles you'd fall down and get bronchitis and—'

'Wait a minute, Henry. When did you think Harriet had the measles? In the maze at Stavely?'

'No, when she came here to—'

He broke off, bit his lip, hung his head in misery. He had betrayed a secret and now would never grow up to be like Sinclair of the Scouts.

'When was that?' Rom had managed to speak calmly, almost casually, but the child shook his head and cast an involuntary glance of fear in the direction of the terrace where Isobel reclined.

They had reached a trellised arbour with a stone seat, to which Rom led the little boy. 'Henry, do you remember what it says on the mantelpiece in the Hall at Stavely? Carved into the wood?'

'Yes, I do remember. It says: TRUTH THEE SHALT DELIVER — IT IS NO DREDE. And "deliver" isn't like delivering milk, it's like making you feel better. Only keeping secrets is good too,' said Henry and sighed, caught on the horns of this ancient and troublesome dilemma.

'Yes, it is. It's very good.' Rom made no attempt to minimise the seriousness of the problem. 'Except when someone is in danger – or ill – and then keeping a secret is not as important as telling the truth.'

Henry deliberated in silence, made up his mind. 'You see, Mummy said it would hurt your feelings if you knew that Harriet had come back and not said goodbye to you. Only, I didn't realise she was going away because she had a basketful of presents all wrapped up in interesting paper. And she was so *nice* to me when I was afraid of you being my stepfather.' He paused, flushing, but his uncle's face was so utterly kind that Henry knew he would not be offended by anything he said and in a rush – blessed with the total recall of those who have uncluttered minds – Henry repeated his last talk with Harriet. 'She *said* she didn't have measles, but her eyes were streaming like anything when I kissed her good night and she was shivering – and the spots come later, you know.' His face grew pinched again. 'And

231

I'm *sure* she shouldn't dance if she feels like that. If she got that thing you get after bronchitis, she could *die*! And I don't want Harriet to die!'

'She won't die, Henry,' said Rom. 'I promise you!' And as Henry gazed up at his uncle he knew that he had been a little bit silly once again. Because when Uncle Rom looked like that – so powerful and triumphant – no one could possibly die. No one could do anything except live and be happy.

'I'm extremely grateful to you, Henry,' said Rom, getting to his feet. 'Indeed, I am utterly in your debt. And I don't think it's necessary for us to mention our conversation to your mother. Gentlemen often have private conversations of this sort among themselves. I'm leaving very early in the morning, but we shall meet in England and have some splendid times.' And shaking Henry's hand with gratifying formality, he strode away.

Left alone, Henry made his way back to the manatees. The carving on the mantelpiece had been quite right, he reflected. Truth *did* deliver you. He felt much better. He felt, in fact, absolutely fine!

*

Half an hour before Mr Fortescue was due from London, Aunt Louisa went upstairs to Harriet's room to put a clean towel on the wash-stand and to change Harriet's nightdress for a high-necked one of bleached calico. It was her own, but she did not grudge it to the errant girl, for the few but shamefully luxurious things which Harriet had brought from Manaus had all, of course, been confiscated and sold.

'Goodness, she *has* got thin!' said Mrs Belper, who had come to be with Louisa on this important day. Just returned from a week's visit to her sister, she was startled by the change in Harriet.

'She is thin because she doesn't eat!' snapped Louisa. 'I hope you don't think that we are starving her.'

Mr Fortescue was due at two-thirty and in deference to the occasion Louisa had ordered coffee and even a plate of digestive biscuits to be sent to the drawing-room.

'I wish Bernard could be here,' she said. 'But he never will miss giving a lecture.'

'Perhaps it is as well, Louisa; it might be a little painful. After all, if the diagnosis is what we expect, it will virtually be a statement that his daughter is—'

A shrill peal of the door-bell brought both ladies to their feet and

232

out into the hall.

Mr Fortescue was as well-dressed as they expected and the gleaming Rolls-Royce in which his chauffeur waited was evidence that this Harley Street specialist was in the top rank, but he was surprisingly young.

'I have come to see Harriet Morton,' he announced, handing his hat and gloves to the maid.

'Yes, indeed. We were expecting you,' said Louisa, all affability. 'It is good of you to come all the way from London. We have naturally been very much concerned – my poor brother has been distracted – but we really feel that an institution of some kind is the only answer. Though of course it is for you to say after you have examined her.'

Mr Fortescue did not appear to be a man of many words.

'Perhaps you will take me to her?' was all he said and Louisa, explaining the sad circumstances, her niece's inexplicable depravity and the course which on the advice of Dr Smithson they had been compelled to take, led him to the top of the stairs, where she took a key from the bunch at her belt.

'You keep her locked in?'

'Oh, yes, Mr Fortescue. Yes indeed! We would not be willing to take the responsibility of leaving a girl of that sort unguarded.'

She inserted the key in the lock – only to find that the specialist's lean brown hand had closed firmly over hers.

'Give me the key if you please. And be kind enough to wait for me downstairs. I always examine patients of this kind alone.'

'But surely that is not customary?' Louisa was distinctly flustered. 'Surely another person is always present when—'

'Are you telling me how to do my job, Miss Morton?' The voice was silkily polite but the glint in his eyes sent Louisa scuttling back downstairs.

He waited until she was out of sight and then turned the key.

The room was bare, cold, scrupulously clean. In the narrow bed Harriet lay on her back and did not turn her head.

Rom walked over to her.

He had imagined this meeting a thousand times: the happiness, the love that would flow between them, the joy with which they would laugh away their misunderstanding. Now there was none of that. A red mist covered his eyes; rage savaged him: he thirsted to kill – to take hold of the woman he had just seen and beat her head against the wall – to press his fingers slowly, voluptuously into the jugular vein of

233

the man who had done this to Harriet.

Harriet opened her eyes. For a moment she stared unfocused at the figure bent over her. Then over the face of this girl he had believed to value her career above his love there spread a look that he was never to forget as long as he lived.

Next came a desolate whimper of pain, a fractional movement of the head.

'No,' said Rom quietly, 'you're not dreaming. I'm here, Harriet! In the flesh – very much in the flesh.' Aware that she was on the edge of the abyss, that he must call her back very gently, he laid only the lightest of hands on her hair. 'You've led me the devil of a dance! I went to St Petersburg first! Simonova's in fine fettle, I may say.'

She could not speak yet. Only her eyes begged for the power to trust in this miracle.

'I must say that I find that a perfectly detestable nightdress,' said Rom cheerfully. 'Your Aunt Louisa can certainly pick them!'

It came then. Belief. He was real, he was here. She sat up and threw herself forward into his arms – and among the frenzied words of love and agony and longing Rom caught, surprisingly, the name of a well-known London suburb.

'You want to live in St John's Wood?' he asked, startled. Later it occurred to him that this salubrious district had probably saved Professor Morton's life, for the passion with which Harriet now pleaded to be set up as a kept lady so intrigued him that he forgot his murderous rage.

'It is an entrancing prospect, certainly,' he said. 'Especially the Gothic windows. However, I am not going to install you in a villa in St John's Wood. I am going to install you at Stavely where you will be my love, my companion and also – by tomorrow afternoon – my wife.'

'No.' Harriet had had her miracle. She needed no more and lifting her face a daring inch away from his, she informed him that he was going to marry Isobel.

'Harriet, do be quiet about Isobel. I never had the slightest intention of marrying her and if you had not been so obstinate and blind you would have seen that at once. I don't even like her any more – the way she treats Henry would put me off for a start. In fact, in the month I've spent with her I've grown quite sorry for my brother. Now listen, I must get hold of the necessary documents and go and find your father, but I'll be back—'

No. She was not able to be left. Her eyes grew wide with fear. 'If you

234

go, they'll find some way of separating us. They'll lock me in again and tell you I'm mad and—'

'All right then, we'll go together,' he said, cheerfully matter-of-fact. 'You can wait in the car. Get dressed and—'

'I can't. They've taken away my clothes.'

Rom gritted his teeth against a renewed attack of fury. 'Never mind.' He pulled a blanket off the bed, wrapped it round her, picked her up. 'Poor Harriet, I'm always abducting you in unsuitable clothes.'

'Good heavens, Mr Fortescue!' Louisa, with Mrs Belper hovering behind her, was waiting in the hall. 'Whatever does this mean?'

'It means that I am taking away your patient immediately,' said Rom. 'I have diagnosed pernicious anaemia, tuberculosis of the lung and an incipient brain tumour. It is possible that I can save her with instant treatment at my clinic, but there is not a moment to lose.'

'But that's impossible . . . I must consult my brother. This is not what we expected at all . . .' Louisa was entirely at a loss. 'And the fees at your clinic would be quite beyond us.'

Rom took a steadying breath. 'If you want a corpse on your hands, Miss Morton, and a court case, that is your affair. You have called me in; I have given my diagnosis. Now, please fetch the patient's birth certificate at once: it is required by the governors of my clinic as a condition of admission.'

'I told you she was too thin,' bleated Mrs Belper.

Totally flustered, Louisa made as if to go to the telephone, only to find the extraordinary surgeon standing in front of it while still holding Harriet in his arms.

'Her birth certificate,' he said implacably. 'At once.'

The Rolls had driven off and the ladies were trying without success to calm themselves in the drawing-room, when the doorbell rang again.

'Good afternoon,' said the obese, grey-haired gentleman standing on the step. 'You are expecting me, I know. My name is Fortescue . . .'

*

Professor Morton was lecturing, pacing the rostrum, his gown flapping, his voice managing to be both irascible and droning; while in the front row Blakewell, a fair-haired, good-looking young man destined for holy orders, wondered if boredom could kill and kicked

235

Hastings who had gone to sleep and was sliding from his chair.

'And this man who calls himself a scholar,' rasped the Professor, 'has the effrontery – the unbelievable effrontery – to suggest that the word *hoti* in line three of the fifth stanza should be translated as—'

The door burst open. An agitated College servant could be seen trying to restrain a man in an extraordinarily well-cut grey suit who pushed him aside without effort, closed the door in his face and proceeded to walk in a relaxed manner to the rostrum.

'Professor Morton?'

'I am Professor Morton, yes. But how dare you walk in here unannounced and interrupt my lecture. It's unheard of!'

'Well, it has been heard of now,' said the intruder calmly, and the students sat up with a look of expectancy on their faces. 'I came to inform you that I have removed your daughter firmly and finally from your house and to ask you to sign this document.' He laid a piece of paper with a red seal on the lectern. 'As you see, it is your permission for my marriage to Harriet.'

The Professor grew crimson; the Adam's apple worked in his scraggy throat. 'How *dare* you! How dare you come in here and wave pieces of paper at me! And how dare you kidnap my daughter!'

'I think the less said about that the better. I found Harriet half-starved and confined like a prisoner because she tried to have a life of her own. If you would like me to tell the students of the state in which I found her, I should be happy to do so.'

'How I treat my daughter is none of your business. Harriet is sick in her body and sick in her soul—' But he took an involuntary step backwards, aware of a sudden menace in the stranger's stance. 'Who are you anyway?' and rallying: 'I won't be blackmailed. Harriet is under age—'

'Professor Morton, it is only because you are Harriet's father that I have not actually throttled you. Anyone else who had treated her as you have done would not have lived to tell the tale. I choose to believe that you are misguided, pompous and opinionated rather than sadistic and cruel. But unless you sign this document without delay I will take you out into the courtyard, debag you and throw you into the fountain.'

The look of expectancy on the students' faces changed to one of deep and utter happiness.

'You wouldn't dare!' blustered the Professor.

'Try me,' said Rom. He looked down at the row of upturned faces.

'I can do it myself, but it would be easier if I had help. If anyone is willing to help me debag the Professor, would they put up their hand?'

There were fourteen students in the lecture room and thirteen hands shot up without an instant's hesitation. Then Ellenby, sole support of a widowed mother, shook off his moment of cowardice and also raised his hand.

'I think you should sign, you know,' said Rom pleasantly. 'After all, it's no tragedy to have your daughter installed as mistress of Stavely.'

'Eh? What?' The Professor peered at the document and registered the fact that Harriet's suitor was Romain Paul Verney Brandon of Stavely Hall, Suffolk. 'Good heavens!'

If the Professor had continued to defy him, had kept up his bluster, Rom might have felt a reluctant respect for the detestable man. But over Professor Morton's face there now spread a look of servile amazement and awe – and unscrewing his fountain pen, he signed his name.

He was, however, not destined to resume his lecture. Rom might have left the room, but he had shown the students a lovely and fulfilling vision; he had unleashed primeval forces which were not to be gainsaid.

Blakewell rose first and even when he became a bishop he was to speak with nostalgia of this moment of release. Hastings followed – then Moisewitch, whom the Professor had humiliated in front of the entire tutorial group, took off his spectacles and laid them carefully on the window-sill. No words were necessary as every student in the hall moved as one man towards the rostrum.

'His trousers first,' said Blakewell. 'Start with his trousers . . .'

*

Rom drew back the curtains and looked out on Stavely's moonlit avenue of beeches, the silver pools of light in the meadows of the park, drank in the sharp clean smell of the air with its first touch of frost. He was back home and with every reason to rejoice. To the place he had left as a penniless and rejected youth, he had returned as master – and he had brought his future bride.

Away to the left he could see the chimneys of Paradise Farm, but no light showed from the house. Isobel was back, having sulked all the way across the Atlantic, but she had decided to remain in London and spend some of the allowance Rom had bestowed on her. Her son was with her now, but a message from the housekeeper had informed Rom that he could expect Master Henry at the end of the week. Clearly it was not going to be difficult to keep an eye on his nephew!

He stayed for a while, still, by the window, but the dreams he had had for Stavely eluded him. It was probably just reaction from the constant exercise of will, the long journey and fruitless delay in Russia, that made him feel both restless and weary. What else could ail him, after all – and knowing that he would not sleep, he nevertheless turned from the window and began to prepare for bed.

He was interrupted by a knock at the door – quiet, but not noticeably timid – and Harriet, still in her Aunt Louisa's appalling nightgown, entered the room. At which point Rom became aware of what had ailed him . . . and ailed him no longer.

'I'm sorry to disturb you,' said Harriet, 'but I woke up and I wondered if I could make a request of you?'

She had folded her hands and now with a rush of expectancy he looked down at her feet which she proceeded to fold also.

'What request would that be, Harriet?' he asked, matching her own grave and measured tones.

'Well, you said we were going to be married tomorrow, didn't you? Because of the special licence?'

'Yes, I did say that. If you wish it, that is?' he teased.

How did she manage to look like that after the ordeal she had been through? Did she somehow consume and metabolise love; this extraordinary girl?

'I do rather wish it,' said Harriet. 'I wish it like someone who has been lying in a cold grave might wish for the day of resurrection. Or like an extremely hungry lion might wish for a Christian. And I mean to be immensely respectable and wear a mob-cap and have quarrels with you about the coal bill to show how independent I am. Only there is one thing I so very much want to do, still, and it isn't a very married thing. I know you don't approve of it and I do understand that, but it would make me so happy because you know how *interested* I have always been in Suleiman the Great.'

He looked at her and felt the tears spring to his eyes, because after all she had been through she had kept the gift of laughter, could offer him what he longed for with such gallantry and grace.

'You want to creep from the foot of the bed into the presence?' he asked with mock severity.

Harriet admitted that this was so. 'They weren't abject, the odalisques,' she explained. 'People have that wrong. They just worked very hard at love – it was all they had.'

But Rom, aware that the time for conversation was running out, was applying himself to the practical aspects of the problem.

'Under the counterpane or over it, do you wish to creep?' he enquired.

Harriet's face crumpled into its urchin grin, acknowledging a hit. Then she raised her arms as does a child who wishes to be gathered up and in two strides he was beside her.

'We will creep *together*,' announced Rom idiotically and carried her – this lightest and most beloved burden – to his bed.

EPILOGUE

'HURRY, GIRLS!' cried Hermione Belper. 'The bus will be here in a minute.'

The 'girls', however, were not easy to hurry. It was not as in the old days, when a word from their president had the ladies of the Trumpington Tea Circle jumping to attention. Now, ten years since they had last been to visit Stavely, the changing times had taken their toll. Bobbed hair, a penchant for rag-time and radical ideas of all sorts had spread through the ranks. Even Eugenia Crowley, one of Harriet's erstwhile chaperones, wore a skirt which cleared her ankles by a good nine inches.

But it was not the fact that the ladies no longer sprang to attention at her command which annoyed Mrs Belper; it was the condescending and superior behaviour of Louisa Morton, who had declined to accompany them.

'My dear, I regard Stavely as my second home,' she had said snootily. 'It is hardly necessary for *me* to go there in a charabanc.'

The remark was quite untrue, of course. Harriet was polite and friendly to her aunt, as she was to her father, but Romain Brandon – who mercifully had come through the war with only an arm wound and a string of medals – always seemed to be absent or unavailable when the Mortons visited. What *was* true was that Louisa was compelled to spend more and more time looking after her brother, for since that extraordinary episode when his entire class had thrown him in the fountain and gone virtually unpunished, the Professor had become something of a recluse and now took almost no part in the life of the University.

The bus arrived. Mrs Transom's daughter had died of Spanish influenza in the last year of the war, as had Mr Belper, the president's

240

undersized husband; but Mrs Transom (now in her ninety-eighth year) seemed to grow younger every day and was easily hauled aboard by her attendant.

'This will be no ordinary outing, Cynthia,' explained Mrs Belper to her god-daughter, who was paying her a visit. 'As I have told you, I have known Mrs Brandon since childhood. I understand we are to be shown round by a member of the family and that there is to be a sit-down tea!'

As they drove in between the tall gates, the ladies were amazed by the change in Stavely. The Hall had been a military hospital during the war but now, three years after the Armistice, all signs of the army's occupation were gone. Making their way to the front door, the visitors passed through one of creation's undoubted masterpieces: a lovingly tended English garden on a fine day in June.

And sure enough, a member of the family *was* waiting to show them round! Not Harriet Brandon, shortly expecting her third child, but a tall good-looking young man with russet hair – the owner's nephew, who had grown up at Stavely and was to inherit Paradise Farm and a substantial parcel of land as soon as he came of age.

'That's Henry Brandon, Cynthia!' hissed Mrs Belper, pushing her god-daughter forward and wishing that the girl's mother had had the sense to do something about her teeth. 'Stay close by his side and ask questions. Gentlemen always like to tell you things.'

Henry has shed his fears and his spectacles, and his good nature was proverbial. Nevertheless, his detestation of the 'Tea Ladies' who had made Harriet's childhood a misery was almost as great as his uncle's. If he had volunteered to show them Stavely, it was by way of a thank-offering – for on the previous day he had won his long-standing battle with the man who had been more than a father to him. Rom had fought harder than the old General, for Henry was an excellent scholar and to let him turn down three years at Oxford seemed madness; but in the end he had conceded defeat.

'Go back, then, if you must. God knows they'll welcome you with open arms at Follina. I don't think the good times will come again, but perhaps one doesn't want them to – the world's a different place now and something can be done still, I'm sure. Alvarez' report actually throws up some interesting angles where the minerals are concerned. And of course Harriet will expect you to have the Opera House open again for Natasha's debut!'

If his offer to show the ladies round had sprung from gratitude,

Henry found himself enjoying the tour, for he never wearied of pointing out the beauties of Stavely or ceased to take pleasure in the contrast of the cold, neglected house of his early childhood and the lovely cared-for place it had become.

'Goodness, who is that lady?' asked the buck-toothed Cynthia, who was obeying her god-mother's instructions to the letter. 'She looks most unusual!'

They had reached the picture gallery on the top floor and that part of the house reserved for recent portraits of the family and friends.

'That's Galina Simonova – the ballerina. It was painted in 1913 after her triumph at the Maryinsky. That diamond star she's wearing was given to her by the Tsar.'

The slight melancholy which attacked the ladies at the mention of the murdered Tsar was dispelled by the next picture – that of an imperious-looking, red-haired woman in a white gown, standing on the steps of a flag-bedecked mansion and flanked by a pair of elephants *en grande tenue*.

' "The Lady Isobel de Larne",' read Cynthia, giggling coyly. 'She has exactly the same colour hair as you, Mr Brandon. Is she a relative?'

'My mother,' admitted Henry, looking with amused affection at the flamboyant portrait of Isobel, now living in immense style with her diplomat husband in Udaipur.

In front of an enormous Sargent entitled 'The Brandon Family at Home', the ladies insisted on staying for a considerable time. Painted three years earlier in the last months of the war, it showed Rom Brandon still in his Colonel's uniform, his arm in a sling and on his face the exact look of boredom at this time-wasting procedure which was to be seen on the portrait of his father on the opposite wall. Beside him, very close to her husband, was Harriet, one slim hand resting on the fawn hair of her daughter, Natasha, in an effort to hold her down long enough to enable the painter to do his work. Henry himself stood beside Harriet and on a low stool – still boasting his baby ringlets and apparently strangling (with loving concentration) the white puppy in his lap – sat Paul Alexander, Stavely's heir whose birth Henry had greeted with unconcealed relief. For Henry had never wavered in his determination to return to the Amazon and but for Paul's birth would have felt obliged to repay his debt to Rom by learning to take over at Stavely.

The furthest part of the gallery had been set aside for photographs and Henry led the way towards these with alacrity, for he had become a keen photographer and many of the pictures were his own.

The ladies exclaimed at the christening pictures of Paul Alexander in the arms of his French godmother, of whom Henry had taken more photographs than were strictly necessary. There was a photo of Madame Simonova, upstaging a French duchess who was declaring open the Simonova *École de Dance*; a recent one of the eight-year-old Natasha as a butterfly at Madame Lavarre's end-of-term dancing display . . .

And one at which Cynthia stopped and said, 'Goodness! What on earth is that?'

'A goat,' said Henry. 'A very special one. It has won innumerable prizes.'

But the picture was not only of a goat. Hanging on to the animal was a man in *Lederhosen* with embroidered braces and a Loden hat. Also in the picture, but a little out of focus, was a peasant lady in a kerchief holding what appeared to be a basket full of enormous runner beans.

'Strange!' said Mrs Belper, peering at the photograph. 'The face looks familiar.' And then: 'Good gracious – it *is* him! It's the young man Louisa wanted for Harriet!'

Henry grinned at the picture which he himself had taken last summer and labelled *Dr and Mrs Finch-Dutton at Cremmora*, for the story of Edward and Olga was one of which the family never tired. The first months had been hard for poor Edward, concealing his young bride in lodgings at the edge of the town and trying to hide his injuries as he crept in and out of college. Nor had the war years been easy, for with Edward away in the Pay Corps Olga had gone to live with the Mater in Goring-on-Thames. Whether or not the experience had shortened the Mater's life was hard to say; at all events she had succumbed to a heart attack just after Edward's demobilisation, leaving him a considerable sum of money. Now, in the wooden house which Dubrov had thankfully sold them, the Finch-Duttons lived in harmony rearing prize goats, prize vegetables and children – and if anyone bit Edward these days, it was almost certainly a goat.

The tour was over. The ladies thanked Henry – and with half an hour to go until the sit-down tea in the dining-room, they followed their president out into the grounds. Exclaiming, praising, responding graciously to the salutations of the many gardeners, they walked through the topiary, down the Long Walk, passed the place in the sunken garden where, all those years ago, they had had their picnic.

Mrs Belper was well in the lead when, coming round a corner, she stopped suddenly and stiffened. A sighting! Undoubtedly a sighting!

Rom Brandon himself was coming out of the rhododendron copse which edged the lawn and with him was his wife. Unaware of Mrs Belper's presence, they walked together across the smooth grass – and even as she wondered whether or not to hail them they reached the pool of shade made by the crown of an ancient copper beech, turned towards each other – and kissed.

It was a quite extraordinary kiss. Even indoors at night, where such things sometimes happened, it would have been disconcerting – but here, out in the open air in the middle of a sunny afternoon, it was unutterably shocking. This man with his silvered hair and his honorary post as Financial Advisor to the Cabinet had gathered his wife to him as if in acute hunger, then and there, for her presence. And Harriet . . . What was one to say of a woman close to her thirtieth year, and obviously pregnant, who stood on tiptoe in order to put up her arms and pull down her husband's head?

Mrs Belper stared. For the briefest of moments she remembered the opening bars of a Mozart sonata which her mother had liked to play, and that she had once thought there were angels. Remembered too Mr Belper, who had brought her white violets when they were engaged, cupping them in an unexpected manner in his hands for her to smell, but was now dead.

Then she pulled herself together. The spectacle was a disgusting one, the sighting useless . . . and turning away, she retraced her steps and shooed the oncoming ladies firmly back to the house for tea.

244